Miss Julia Delivers the Goods

Miss Julia Delivers the Goods

ANN B. ROSS

**Doubleday Large Print
Home Library Edition**

VIKING

This Large Print Edition, prepared especially for Double-day Large Print Home Library, contains the complete, unabridged text of the original Publisher's Edition.

VIKING
Published by the Penguin Group
Penguin Group (USA) Inc., 375 Hudson Street,
New York, New York 10014, U.S.A.
Penguin Group (Canada), 90 Eglinton Avenue East,
Suite 700, Toronto, Ontario, Canada M4P 2Y3
(a division of Pearson Penguin Canada Inc.)
Penguin Books Ltd, 80 Strand, London WC2R 0RL,
England
Penguin Ireland, 25 St. Stephen's Green,
Dublin 2, Ireland
(a division of Penguin Books Ltd)
Penguin Books Australia Ltd, 250 Camberwell Road,
Camberwell, Victoria 3124, Australia
(a division of Pearson Australia Group Pty Ltd)
Penguin Books India Pvt Ltd, 11 Community Centre,
Panchsheel Park, New Delhi – 110 017, India
Penguin Group (NZ), 67 Apollo Drive, Rosedale,
North Shore 0632, New Zealand (a division of Pearson
New Zealand Ltd)
Penguin Books (South Africa) (Pty) Ltd, 24 Sturdee
Avenue, Rosebank, Johannesburg 2196, South Africa

Penguin Books Ltd, Registered Offices: 80 Strand,
London WC2R 0RL, England

First published in 2009 by Viking Penguin, a member
of Penguin Group (USA) Inc.

Copyright © Ann B. Ross, 2009

Publisher's Note
This is a work of fiction. Names, characters, places,
and incidents either are the product of the author's
imagination or are used fictitiously, and any
resemblance to actual persons, living or dead,
business establishments, events, or locales is
entirely coincidental.

ISBN 978-1-61523-034-1

Printed in the United States of America

This Large Print Book carries the Seal of Approval of N.A.V.H.

This one is for my John and his boys, Jack and Jake.

Several people were kind enough to answer questions relating to this story, and I'd like to thank them for putting up with me.

District Court Judge David Fox, Henderson County, North Carolina, patiently gave me valuable information even though I called him at home near dinner time; Deputy Register of Deeds Nancy Cochrane, Henderson County, North Carolina, was most generous with her time as she pointed out the details of the Records of Deeds; Obstetrician/ Gynecologists David Ellis, M.D., and John M. Ross, M.D., kept me on the right medical track, and Kathryn Wells gave me a pearl even though I accosted her on the sidewalk as we walked to a football game.

If I misunderstood anything relating to the many facts they each gave me, it is entirely my fault.

Miss Julia Delivers the Goods

Chapter 1

"Miss Julia?"

I turned from the rain-streaked window of my bedroom to see Hazel Marie's head poking through the half-opened door. "Come in, Hazel Marie. Are you feeling better?"

"A little, I guess," she said, edging into the room. "Are you busy?"

"Not at all. I could use some company."

"I don't want to bother you."

"You're not bothering me." I indicated the easy chair opposite mine by the double windows. "Come watch the rain with me. I thought we were having another dry summer, but just look at it come down."

Hazel Marie sat down and, like me, turned to look out at the soggy yard, dotted now with standing puddles of water. I'd not turned on any lights although the dim room could've used some, so we sat in companionable silence for several minutes. After a while, I frowned, recalling that she'd bypassed breakfast, saying that she wasn't hungry. Now here she was, doing something else unusual. It wasn't like her to sit any length of time without chattering away about something. She was normally full of wonder and awe and bubbling over about one thing or another. I liked that about her. You would think that after some years with me, she would've become used to a life without financial worries. You would've thought that she'd have begun taking her carefree days for granted. But she hadn't. Oh, she enjoyed herself immensely, don't get me wrong. But the most endearing thing about her was that she was so eternally grateful for her good fortune, even though it had come at the expense of my knowledge that she'd carried on with my first husband in such an inappropriate manner. But that carrying on had produced a child who covered a multitude of sins.

Lloyd was no kin of mine—try as I might I couldn't figure out any relation. There was no name for a husband's child by another woman, but that didn't stop a kinship between me and the boy that went beyond bloodlines. Lloyd was more like me than any child I could've had, but didn't. And his mother was like a ray of sunshine in my life—as long as I didn't dwell on what she'd done. And I didn't. I didn't because her sweet disposition and wide-eyed wonder at whatever came her way made me value her for herself alone without letting her unsavory past poison the present.

The only thing I could never figure out was why she'd been attracted to Wesley Lloyd Springer in the first place. He was certainly no bargain, although I may be prejudiced. In fact, though, I don't think she was ever specifically attracted to him. I think he found her when she was at a low point, which was where she'd been since birth, and took her up. He gave her a place to live, such as it was, and then she found herself with child and that was it for a good many years. She wasn't the first woman to find herself trapped with a man she neither liked nor loved for the sake of a child.

Her first taste of freedom, and mine, too, for that matter, came when Wesley Lloyd passed, and I was finally able to put aside my terrible anger and open my home and my heart to my husband's mistress and their little son.

All the while that these thoughts were running through my mind, she'd sat staring out the window, her elbow propped on the chair arm and her chin on her hand.

"Hazel Marie?" I said. "Is something on your mind?"

She sighed, looked down, and began to fold pleats in the cream-colored crepe trousers she wore. "I'm not sure," she mumbled.

"Well, I can see that you're worried about something. So tell me and let's try to fix it." Then a jolt of anxiety shot through me. "Is it Lloyd? Is something going on with him?"

"Oh, no. He's fine. He's almost finished with his summer reading list." She glanced up at me, then down again at the pleats she'd made. "You know how organized he is. He's really enjoying the tennis clinic, too."

"Then, Mr. Pickens? Is he worrying you?"

I could see how he would, since he was as stubborn as a mule when it came to settling down, which, considering the favors I assumed she granted him, he should've done some time ago. Of course, I didn't know for sure what went on between them, but I hadn't just fallen off a turnip truck.

"No." She shook her head, her eyes still downcast. "No, J.D.'s . . . all right, too. It's just, . . . oh, Miss Julia." She looked up again and I saw tears welling in her eyes.

I leaned toward her, concern in my voice. "Hazel Marie, what's the matter?"

"Oh, Miss Julia, I think . . . I think something bad's wrong with me."

Chapter 2

"You mean you're *sick*?" Alarmed, I leaned over and clasped her hand.

"I think I am. I'm afraid it's something . . . terrible." She nearly choked on the word.

"Wait. Wait, now." I had to take myself in hand in order to reassure her, but it was hard. I wanted to appear calm and rational in spite of the dire possibilities that were rushing into my head. "Tell me why you think that. What are your symptoms? Or is it just a general feeling?"

"I don't know what it is, but I'm just so tired I can hardly do anything. And I feel like crying all the time, just sudden-like. I mean, sometimes I feel real happy and then all at once, everything just falls apart."

"Mood swings," I said, nodding as if I knew what that meant. "What else?"

"Well, I don't have much of an appetite, and, anyway, everything I put in my mouth comes right back up. And I get so hot and sweaty sometimes that I have to change my clothes." She wiped her eyes and went on. "The worst thing, though, is that I just can't keep anything down and I feel so weak I can hardly move."

"How long has this been going on?"

"I've been feeling bad, you know, tired and sicky-feeling, for a good while, but the real throwing up just started last week. And now I think I'm running a fever."

"Why, Hazel Marie, I wish you'd told me. I knew you'd been looking a little peaked, but I had no idea you were having such a hard time." To tell the truth, I was upset with myself for not looking after her better. "I want you to stop worrying now, because we're going to get to the bottom of this."

"I'm so afraid," she said as she buried her face in her hands, "so afraid that I've got something bad and maybe already given it to Lloyd and to you and everybody else, and I didn't mean to. It's just gotten worse and worse, and I'm so sick to my stomach I can hardly stand it."

"Hazel Marie," I said, squatting down beside her chair to put my arm around her shoulders. I knew I might never get up again, but she needed comforting. "Hazel Marie, listen to me. I don't think you've given anything to anybody. Now, one more question, if you don't mind my asking. What about your, you know, your times of the month?"

She looked up with a tear-streaked face. "What about them?"

"I mean, how are they? Normal, erratic, or nonexistent?"

"They're, well, I never have been exactly regular, so it's hard to tell."

"Well, when was your last one?"

"I don't know. Sometime last month, I think. Maybe the month before."

"Then I'll tell you what I think," I said, leveraging myself up on the arm of her chair. "I think you have female trouble. And I know you'll hate to hear this, but it could just be the change of life." At her shocked look, I quickly went on. "I know you're a little young for it, but it hits some people early and, who knows, it could be strung out over ten years or more." Actually, Hazel Marie wasn't all that young, somewhere in her forties. She was always vague about exactly *where*, which made putting candles on her birthday cakes somewhat of a hit or miss proposition. She was like me when it came to age: It was nobody's business what the number of our years happened to be.

"Ten years!" she cried. "I'll go crazy before that. I'm feeling awful, Miss Julia. I couldn't stand it that long."

"Well, goodness knows, I'm no doctor, so I could be wrong. The thing to do, though, is to get you to a doctor and find out what's going on. When did you have your last checkup?"

"I don't know. Not in a long time, anyway. I never get sick and this, this is just doing me in."

"Well, we're going to do something about it. There's no reason for you to suffer like this, and I expect they've got medications now that they didn't have when I had the same malady. And listen, Hazel Marie, remember that every woman goes through it, and most of them survive. So you have to bear up, see a doctor, and do what he tells you. I'll call Dr. Hargrove right now and tell him he has to see you. If he thinks you need to go to a specialist, we'll get you one of those, too."

"Oh," she said, a stricken look on her face, "you think it's serious, don't you? Other people don't have to see a doctor when they go through the change. I mean, it's supposed to be normal."

"Yes, they do. They just don't tell anybody. Now you run upstairs and get ready. I'm calling Dr. Hargrove right now."

I helped her out of the chair and watched as she wove her way out the door. She was feeling miserable, that was plain to see, and scared half to death. And to tell the truth, I wasn't feeling much better. It was easy enough to pass off her complaints as the change of life—like she said, that was normal. But, even with my meager medical knowledge, I knew there were other things under the heading of female trouble that could cause the same symptoms but were far from normal. When something starts messing with hormones and the organs and glands that produce hormones, why, it could be a lot more serious than a normal, but rocky, time of life. And she was at just the right age—whatever that was—for her internal works to start acting up.

I wasn't about to suggest anything like that to her, but my internal works were boiling over with worry. Not the least of those worries concerned her temperature—I'd heard of menopause causing almost every symptom in the book, but never a fever.

I sat in the doctor's waiting room, trying to calm my nerves. I'd had to insist that his receptionist put Hazel Marie on the schedule, even though the woman had kept telling me that the schedule was full. "This is an emergency," I'd told her, "so surely allowances can be made." And, of course, she'd had something to say about an emergency that had lasted for days hardly qualifying as urgent. I would've reported her to Dr. Hargrove, except he wasn't there. Off somewhere in the middle of the ocean on a cruise, of all things, at the end of summer. So Hazel Marie was inside being seen by some new and unknown fill-in doctor, and who knew what his qualifications were.

After the receptionist gave in and allowed us to come, we'd ended up waiting a full half-hour before Hazel Marie was called into the examining room. I'd gotten up to go with her and was stopped cold by a bossy and unsympathetic nurse. So I was trying to calm myself down. First, for being overcome with worry and, second, for being shut out of whatever was going on behind those closed doors. And there wasn't a current magazine in the place.

"Mrs. Murdoch?"

I looked up to see that same nurse beckoning to me. "You can come back now."

I hurriedly gathered my pocketbook and followed her down the hall to a small examining room. Hazel Marie was sitting on the examining table, looking so pale and weak that I feared she might fall off.

"Hazel Marie, are you all right?"

She shook her head. "I feel terrible. I just threw up all over their floor, and they put me in here while they clean it up. I'm so embarrassed, but I couldn't help it."

"Don't worry about it. I expect they're used to it, and, if not, they should be after making people wait so long. Now, what did the doctor say?"

The door opened behind me and in walked the poorest excuse for a medical practitioner I'd ever seen. He was tall and lanky with a long face and slumping shoulders and, Lord help us, an earring and a ponytail. And, I suppose to counteract those feminine accoutrements, he had a sprig of whiskers right below his lower lip. From the looks of him, I expect that was all he could grow. I could perhaps have overlooked all that, but the man was wearing blue jeans and a T-shirt under a white coat. And on top of that, he had toe-revealing sandals on his feet, and, believe me, the revelation was not pretty. And, to cap it all off, he looked barely twenty years old. I couldn't help but wonder how he'd ever gotten into medical school, much less through it.

"How're we doing in here?" he asked, walking right up to Hazel Marie and staring down at her. "Feeling better now?"

She shook her head, and I got ready to intervene with a few questions of my own. He beat me to it.

Turning swiftly to me, he said, "I'm Dr. McKay, but call me Rick. I'm filling in for Dr. Hargrove for a couple of weeks. And you're Hazel Marie's friend?"

"Julia Springer Murdoch," I said, offering my hand but put off by his casual manner. I should say, *Rick*. This wasn't a social occasion by any stretch of the imagination. "And you're from?"

"Down around Wilmington."

"I meant, from what school?"

"Ah," he said with a slight smile, "Chapel Hill, and I'm with a group of *locum tenens*, which means . . ."

"I know what it means, and I don't mind telling you that I'm distressed about Dr. Hargrove being gone and not telling us he'd run in a substitute. I expect you'll do fine, though, if you follow his instructions. Now, what's wrong with Hazel Marie? I'm worried about her."

"Well, I am, too," he said with a frown, which did nothing to reassure me or her. "Hazel Marie, I'm not finding anything obvious, other than dehydration from the vomiting. And that's causing the fever, I think. But at this point, I can't rule out some kind of systemic infection. Have you been out of the country lately?"

"Just to San Francisco a couple of months ago," Hazel Marie said. "Oh, and I went to Mexico earlier this year, but I was real careful what I ate and drank."

Dr. McKay frowned. "Still, with all the gastrointestinal problems you're having, I don't want to overlook some sort of parasitic invasion. We'll admit you to the hospital and get some intravenous fluids started and do some blood work. And, while you're there, run a few other tests. We'll know something after that. Now, Hazel Marie, I want you to go right on over to the hospital and get settled. I'll order some medication for the vomiting and we'll get those tests started."

Parasitic invasion? I was stunned at the thought, immediately wondering if I should call Lillian and tell her to get out the Lysol and start wiping down the walls. I opened my mouth to ask if we were talking microscopic infestation or would we be able to see them but never got the chance. Dr. McKay patted Hazel Marie's thigh in an altogether too familiar a manner, whirled around, his long coat flapping, and sailed out of the room. Doctors never hang around very long in case they're asked something they don't know.

"The hospital?" Hazel Marie looked at me, fear etching her face. "I don't want to go to the hospital."

"It'll be all right," I said, trying to reassure her and myself in Dr. Hargrove's absence. "I'm sure he's just being on the safe side, checking everything out. Actually, Hazel Marie, I'm glad he's doing that. He's awfully young, you know, so he hasn't had time to get much experience. I'd rather he do too much than too little." Lord, I thought, how much would a shore-to-ship telephone call cost me?

❧❧

I drove Hazel Marie the three blocks to the hospital, wondering all the while if parasites could jump from one person to another. I didn't have time to worry too much about it, though, for I had to stop twice to let her lean out the door to throw up. If I hadn't already known how ill she was, the fact that she totally ignored what the rain was doing to her hair would've clued me in.

By the time we got there, it was all I could do to go through the rigamarole it took to get her in and out of the admitting office. They were so accustomed to filling out forms and filing insurance claims that they couldn't understand a cash deposit. Hazel Marie had insurance—Sam and Binkie had seen to that—but she didn't have her card with her, and you would've thought she'd come in naked the way everybody in that office carried on.

But before long, she was ensconced in a private room, which I'd had to insist on, undressed and redressed in a flower-strewn hospital gown. I warned her not to get out of bed or she'd be exposing more than she wanted to, but there was little fear of that. She didn't feel like doing anything but lying there and letting one nurse after another minister to her.

First, they connected intravenous fluid to the back of her hand. Then they shot her with something for the nausea and vomiting, which soon made her sleepy. Then in came a woman from the laboratory and started drawing vital fluids for all the tests that young doctor had ordered.

When they finally left her alone, Hazel Marie lay there, looking ashen with dark circles under her eyes. I didn't know what to do. I didn't want to leave her alone, yet I needed to get home and let Sam and Lillian know what was happening. And I needed to get her some decent night-clothes.

"Miss Julia?" Hazel Marie whispered.

"I'm right here, Hazel Marie. What do you need?"

"You'll look after Lloyd, won't you?"

"Of course, I will. Don't I always?"

"No, I mean," she said, her eyes barely open, "if I die."

"Hazel Marie! Don't be thinking like that. You're not going to die, at least, not any-time soon. You just concentrate on getting well and put such thoughts out of your mind. I'm thinking of going on now since Lloyd'll be home soon. I'll bring him up to see you tonight." I patted her arm and leaned over to look at her. Her eyes were half-open, but I don't think they were see-ing anything. "Hazel Marie?" I whispered. "Are you awake enough to answer one question? You want me to call Mr. Pickens and tell him you're here?"

My only answer was a soft snore, so thinking, *I guess so,* I tiptoed out of the room and went home.

Chapter 3

"Lillian," I said as soon as I stepped into the kitchen, "where've you been?"

"To the grocery store, the post office, the dry cleaners an' the shoe shop to pick up Mr. Sam's ole boots. Jus' like I tol' you."

"Oh, that's right. I'd forgotten. Well, too much has happened while you were gone. I have to sit down." And I did, collapsing onto a chair by the table and rubbing my hand across my brow. "You won't believe this, but I just put Hazel Marie in the hospital."

Lillian whirled around, her eyes wide. "What you mean, in the hospital?"

"She's sick, Lillian, and I took her to the doctor, but don't get me started on that. Anyway, he admitted her and she's over there all hooked up to this, that, and the other. And they've stuck her with so many needles it's a wonder she's survived them all. And put her in a skimpy little hospital gown that has to be replaced." I looked around as if someone else should be in the room with us. "Where's Lloyd?"

"He stayin' late at them tennis courts to practice. 'Member? He tell about it at breakfast. He oughta be home pretty soon."

"Well, I'd forgotten that, too. I tell you, Lillian, this has not been a good day, and it started out so well." I got up to get a cup of coffee. "I guess they all do, don't they? And I guess it's a good thing we don't know what's coming our way when we get up every morning. Otherwise, many of us would just stay in bed."

"Not if they have work to do, they don't. Now tell me what be wrong with Miss Hazel Marie."

"That's the thing, Lillian, I don't know. And neither, it seems, does that substitute doctor in Dr. Hargrove's office. When we left to go to the hospital, I almost kept on driving to Asheville. Except I don't know any doctors over there. But I am not happy with that young man. Any real doctor could've listened to her symptoms and looked in her eyes and down her throat and come up with some answers. But not him. He just said he didn't know what was wrong with her and brought up such awful possibilities as infections and parasites, of all things, that she might've picked up in Mexico or San Francisco. That simply does not engender a whole lot of confidence as far as I'm concerned. He could've taken a stab at it, if for no other reason than to offer a little comfort. I mean, they blame everything else on the flu or old age or some kind of female problem, so why not this?"

"I don't know, Miss Julia. But I tell you one thing, I been noticin' how she pick at her plate. She hardly touch anything I fix. An' she lookin' pore, too, like her eyes too big or something."

"I wish you'd said something, Lillian, before it came to this. I'm ashamed that I didn't notice anything." I poured the coffee into the sink, realizing that I didn't want it. "Where's Sam? Have you heard from him?"

"He settin' in there in the livin' room."

"Why, what in the world . . . ?" I turned and started out of the kitchen. "What's he doing home in the middle of the day?"

I pushed through the door into the dining room and continued on into the living room where Sam was sitting on the sofa, pen in hand and a yellow legal pad propped on his knee. A stack of papers was on the lamp table beside him.

"Sam?" I said, hurrying toward him. "I'm so glad you're here. Hazel Marie's in the hospital and nobody knows what's wrong with her."

Sam looked up over his glasses and quickly put aside his pen and pad. "What happened, Julia? Is she all right?"

"I don't know. Nobody does." I sat down beside him as close as I could get. "I'm so worried about her I don't know what to do."

"Tell me," he said, slipping his arm around my shoulders.

So I did, from start to finish, not leaving out one thing, even touching on female trouble in a delicate way and including especially my concern over that untried doctor. "We have to get her to somebody who'll know what he's doing, Sam. Why, that ponytailed doctor doesn't even know enough to put on a pair of socks."

"All right," Sam said, "here's what we do. Let's let him run his tests, then we'll see what he says. If he still doesn't know, why, then we'll take her to Bowman Gray or down to Duke. It could just be a touch of flu."

"That's what Dr. Hargrove would say. He wouldn't make such a fuss about it and worry us half to death with thoughts of imminent, well, you know. Oh, Sam, Hazel Marie's had such a hard life and now, just when things are easing off for her, this has to happen. It's not fair." I clutched at him. "For all we know, that child could end up an orphan."

"Now, Julia, Lloyd's not going to be an orphan anytime soon. Besides, he has you and he has me. And Pickens, too, for that matter. Which reminds me, does Pickens know about this?"

I shook my head, unable to speak for being so choked up. "I asked her if she wanted me to call him, but she was too far gone to answer." I looked up at him. "But I guess we should, don't you think?"

Sam unhanded me, reached for his papers to straighten them before putting them in a folder. "Why don't you do that while I run this stuff back over to my house and tell James to go on home."

"Well, that reminds me," I said. "I was so glad to see you here that I didn't think to ask why you're home so early. I thought you'd still be working. Is anything wrong? Anything else, I mean?"

"Not really," he said with a trace of a smile. "I've just had a few things on my mind, so I came home to think them over. Besides, James took a notion to clean out the garage, and he kept coming in to ask if he should keep one thing or throw out another."

"James gets on everybody's nerves when he starts talking," I said, but was somewhat brought up short by realizing that I could possibly have been neglectful of Sam here lately. To think that he had something on his mind so worrisome that he needed peace and quiet to ponder it made me feel guilty for showing so little interest in his work. I rarely asked what he was doing, assuming that it filled his time, now that he was retired, in a productive way. "So what was on your mind? Anything interesting?"

"Oh, this and that." He nodded toward the folder in his hand. "Trying to organize my thoughts. And some of the records I've found."

Sam had been working on a legal history of Abbot County for some few years now, ever since he'd retired from the practice of law. He'd spent untold hours in the courthouse tracking down ancient records, deeds, and court cases, then putting the information into some kind of order in the office at his house—the house he'd moved out of when he came to live with me. *Legally* live with me, I might add. I was proud of him and completely supportive of his effort to write the definitive book on lawyers, judges, prosecutors, and some of the more nefarious cases tried in our county from the earliest times to the present. Just think how many people would buy a copy, if for no other reason than to see if their names were in it.

Putting aside my concern for Hazel Marie for the moment to concentrate on him, I asked, "How far along are you?"

"I'm well into the sixties now."

"The sixties! Why, Sam, that's remarkable. You're really moving along."

"I'd like to think so," he said, "but I'm just getting to the time when there's almost more material than I can manage." He smiled somewhat ruefully. "We are a contentious people, Julia. That courthouse is bulging with records on paper, microfiche, and computer disks."

"I thought the new courthouse was supposed to be able to handle everything. Don't tell me we're going to have to build another one."

"Oh, I don't think so," he said. "It's just that tracking these things down and putting them into some kind of order so I can tell exactly what went on is no easy task."

"Well, I'm sure you can do it. There's certainly no one else who could." *Or who'd want to*, I thought but didn't add. A good wife always encourages her husband in his interests. For one thing, they keep him occupied and out from under foot most of the day.

Then, satisfied that I'd exhibited the proper amount of interest in his affairs, I said, "Well, you better run on, but do hurry back. Lloyd'll be home soon, and I know Mr. Pickens is going to be beside himself when he hears the news. We're going to need you here."

⚮

I walked Sam to the door, urging him again to hurry back, and went to the kitchen. "Lillian," I said, "will you get out Hazel Marie's gowns and whatever you think she'll need? I'll pack up her best ones to take over a little later on."

"Yessum," she said, wiping her eyes, "that's what I was gonna do, anyway. An' she prob'ly want all her beauty aids, too, if she able to use 'em."

"Now, Lillian, we have to be optimistic about this. For one thing, I don't want Lloyd to see us so concerned. He's going to worry himself sick as it is."

"Well, me, too," she said as a fresh track of tears streamed down her face. "Lotsa folks go to the hospital an' don't never come home again."

"Don't say that! My word, Lillian, she can't be that sick." I had to hold onto the counter. "Can she? I don't know what I'd do if. . . ." I took hold of myself but hardly knew what I was doing. "On second thought, I'll go get her things together. It'll give me something to do. Oh, and I have to call Mr. Pickens. I declare, I don't know if I'm coming or going."

I trudged upstairs to Hazel Marie's room, but before collecting what she'd need in the hospital, I sat on her bed and reached for the telephone. Mr. Pickens had always been a good man to have around in a crisis, but I didn't know how he'd handle this one. I knew he'd come flying over to sit by her bed, though, and be there to help me pin that flighty doctor down.

After placing the call, I hung up the phone, thinking that if any pinning was going to be done I'd have to do it. I'd learned, to my dismay, that Mr. Pickens was unavailable, out of town on a case and not expected back anytime soon. "This is an emergency," I'd told the answering service woman. "I need to get in touch with him." But she was no help at all. I didn't believe her, for what private investigator goes out of town without leaving some notification of where he'd be or how he could be reached? But try as I might, I couldn't budge her.

So I got out Hazel Marie's overnight suitcase and began packing some gowns, a robe, and her bedroom slippers. That's what you call being optimistic, I thought to myself, making preparations for her to be up and out of bed. At the sight of all her beauty products in the bathroom, though, I threw up my hands and decided to let Lillian determine which ones to take.

Hearing a slight commotion downstairs, my heart gave a lurch and I hurried out of the room. Lloyd was home, and I was faced with telling him the sad news. Then it would be up to me to comfort and reassure him when I, myself, had little comfort or reassurance to give.

Chapter 4

I hurried downstairs, stewing not only over Hazel Marie's condition but also over Mr. Pickens's thoughtlessness and my coming talk with Lloyd. Lord, that child would be overcome with worry when he heard about his mother.

I stopped for a minute in the dining room, collecting myself so I could talk to him in a reassuring fashion. I wanted him to know that people go to the hospital all the time and come home again in much better shape. I would present the situation to him calmly and with full confidence that Hazel

Marie was in good hands and being well cared for.

So what did I see when I pushed through the swinging door into the kitchen? Lillian, her face streaming with tears, crushing the boy to her bosom.

"Oh, you pore little thing," she crooned, sobbing between the words. "It gonna be all right, don't you worry. She be well 'fore you know it, an' be back home with us, singing' an' flittin' 'round like she always do."

Lloyd struggled out of her grasp, looking with alarm all around the room. "What is it? What's happened?"

"Lillian," I said, "get hold of yourself. You're scaring him to death." The truth of it, though, was that she was scaring me, too. I'd never seen her break down in that way, and I feared she'd understood the situation better than I had. "Come sit down, Lloyd. Lillian's just upset, as we all are, but things aren't that bad. The doctor's put your mother in the hospital and. . . ." At his gasp, I hurriedly went on. "Just for some tests, that's all. She's not been feeling well, and he wants to make sure that everything's all right. It's really nothing to be too worried about."

"Mama's sick?"

"To tell you the truth, Lloyd, I think it's just a touch of flu. She has all the symptoms—a fever, loss of appetite, and so forth. It's almost the season for it, you know. The summer kind, anyway, and every year we have some kind of Asiatic bug that makes a transatlantic or transpacific flight. One or the other." I wasn't telling him the unvarnished truth because I was still hoping that Hazel Marie's malady had to do with female matters. But that wasn't something to be discussed with a child on the verge of adolescence, the age when they know nothing and imagine a lot.

The boy's face was so drained that his freckles stood out to an alarming degree. His hands shook and he looked as if he'd throw up any minute. So maybe Hazel Marie did have the flu and it had started to spread.

"Look at me, Lloyd," I said, my voice calm and soft. "We have to stay strong so we can do all we can to help your mother. After supper, Sam and I'll take you to the hospital to see her. When I left this afternoon, she was already feeling much better. Sleepy, but better. So pull yourself together and we'll get through this all right."

"Yes, ma'am," he said in a tremulous voice, "I will. But I think I'll go upstairs and, maybe, pray a little."

I watched him trudge out of the room, his thin little legs sticking out of his tennis shorts, and realized that I'd not reassured him in any way. I looked over at Lillian who was wiping her face with her apron. "I expect it'd be well for us to do the same," I said and walked over to pat her shoulder. "Pray, that is. But we have to be strong, Lillian, and not frighten the child."

"I know, Miss Julia," she said, "an' I'm tryin'. Maybe I better cook something, that always he'p me. I have us a early supper, 'cause I know you didn't have no lunch and I know y'all goin' over to the hospital again. An' I know you didn't finish packing 'cause you didn't bring down her suitcase an' prob'ly didn't put in what she want anyway. I know she want her best gowns, 'specially that lacy one Mr. Pickens give her."

"Lord, Lillian, not that one. She has a young doctor, and we wouldn't want to distract him. He might never let her come

home. Besides, I don't need to be reminded
of how inappropriate a gift that was. Victoria's Secret, of all things. But, yes, an early
supper would be fine so we can all go over
to the hospital. Thank you for thinking of it."
I patted her again. "Are you all right now? I
need you to help keep us on an even
keel."

She nodded, wiped her face again, then
said, "I will. I jus' have a little sinkin' spell. I
be all right in a minute soon's I put something on the stove."

I wandered out of the kitchen and through
the house, starting twice to go upstairs to
comfort Lloyd, but coming back down again.
What could I tell him when I knew nothing
myself? I certainly wasn't going to mention
parasites or an all-out infection to him. He
was a worrier, just as I was, and smart
enough to know that being suddenly put
into a hospital didn't bode well for anybody.
For a doctor to run tests on a patient meant
one of two things: Either he wanted to confirm something awful that he suspected or
he didn't have an idea in the world what
was wrong and hoped the results would
give him a clue. Either was disturbing and
not easily discussed with a child.

I couldn't stand it any longer. Maybe that doctor had come back in. Maybe the nurses could tell me something. Maybe Hazel Marie was, indeed, better. Or worse, and needed me.

I marched through the kitchen, telling Lillian I'd be back in thirty minutes, and went out into the drizzle and drove to the hospital. It would be well, I told myself, to check on her again before bringing Lloyd up to see her. It wouldn't do him any good to walk in and see her in the active throes of whatever ailed her.

I hoped, of course, to catch Dr. McKay—pardon me, Rick—on his afternoon rounds. As I parked and walked into the hospital I realized that most of my anxiety was rising from being dependent on a young man barely old enough to shave. I mean, he didn't know who we were. Here, he'd come to town, not knowing a soul, thinking he could dispense medical care to whoever showed up. Why, he probably thought that Hazel Marie and I had just walked in off the street. With Dr. Hargrove, I knew we'd get the best the profession had to offer, or I'd know the reason why. He'd known us for years and knew we wouldn't stand for less than the best. Besides, he was a Presbyterian, too, and understood that he'd have to sit in church with us every Sunday that rolled around. That sort of fellowship with one's physician can make him very particular in how he dispenses medical care.

❧❦

Foiled again, I thought as I turned away from the nurses' desk. Not only was the doctor not around, neither was Hazel Marie. She had been trundled to some department for a lengthy test, which I was assured would be finished by the time regular visiting hours began. There was nothing to do but go home again, uninformed and unsatisfied.

On my way home, I suddenly veered off and drove to Sam's house, hoping to catch him there. I simply needed to talk and, with Lloyd in the house, I couldn't voice my concerns for fear that he would hear them.

I pulled into the driveway at Sam's house, stopping short of the open garage door. I got out of the car and saw James up on a stepladder handing boxes down to Sam.

"Sam?" I said, entering the garage.

"Well, hey, Julia," Sam said, with the surprised and delighted smile that he always gave me. He set the box down and dusted off his hands. "What brings you here?" Then he frowned, remembering Hazel Marie. "Is everything all right?"

"Hey, Miss Julia," James said from atop the ladder. "You come to he'p us?"

"Hardly. We'll leave it with you, because I have to take Sam away for a few minutes. Walk into the house with me, Sam. I need to talk to you." James was the biggest gossip in town, so I certainly wasn't going to talk about Hazel Marie in his hearing.

Sam and I walked into his kitchen where James couldn't hear us, but I closed the door just in case.

"What's going on, Julia?" Sam asked, as he went to the sink to wash his hands. "Have you heard anything?"

"Not a thing. I just went to the hospital to, you know, check on her, but they'd taken her off somewhere for some kind of test. What in the world could they be doing to her?"

"Maybe they're doing an MRI or some kind of scan. I wouldn't worry about it, Julia. It'd all be part of the tests the doctor is running." He dried his hands with a paper towel and came to my side. "Have you told Lloyd? How's he taking it?"

"Oh, Sam, that child is scared out of his wits, as I knew he would be. He went straight upstairs to pray, which I would do myself if I could sit still long enough. But you need to come home now and help me with him. What are you doing, anyway? I thought you just came to put up some papers. This is no time to be cleaning out a garage."

"I know," he said, putting his arms around me. "I'm sorry. It's just that James had such a mess out there that I had to get into it myself. If I'd left it with him, I'd never find anything again. But I'm sending him home right now, and I'll be along in a few minutes."

"Good. I need you there and so does Lloyd. Oh, and, Sam, I tried to get Mr. Pickens, but he's out of town and not expected back anytime soon. I could just sit down and cry at the thought of it, because when Hazel Marie hears that she may have some sort of crisis or something."

"No, she won't," Sam said in a soothing tone. "I expect she knows where he is and she can tell you how to reach him."

"Oh, of course," I said with relief. "I hadn't thought of that. To tell the truth, I'm not thinking straight about anything. You'll go with us tonight to the hospital, won't you?"

"I'm planning on it. Now, you run on and let me lock up here. I'll be right behind you."

He hugged me close for a minute, my first calm minute of the day, then I left.

Chapter 5

It was still early when we arrived at the hospital after supper, but because of the damp, cool day and the low clouds overhead, it felt late. Sam drove us and, after parking, carried Hazel Marie's suitcase, with me following with Lloyd. Lillian brought up the rear, a huge paper sack in her arms. Nothing would do but she had to come with us and I was just thankful that she'd put Latisha, her great-granddaughter, in the care of a neighbor. Hazel Marie was in no condition to put up with the child's constant questions and comments about everything she saw.

So in we trooped through the lobby, into

the elevator, and up to the second floor. The hall was dimly lit and a few visitors were going in and out the doors. One scantily clad man, clutching a robe together, pushed an IV pole as he walked up and down the hall. Lord, it was a depressing place, and I couldn't wait to get Hazel Marie out of it.

I tapped on her door, then pushed it open and we all filed in. She turned her head toward us, but I could barely see her. Only one small crooked-necked lamp was on, so the room was dark and edged in shadows.

"Mama!" Lloyd said and ran to her bed.

She reached for him and pulled him close. "Oh, Lloyd, I'm so glad to see you."

"What's wrong with you?" he asked. "Why'd they put you in here? When're you coming home?"

She smiled and brushed back his hair. "Just as soon as I can. Maybe tomorrow if they get through with the tests. Hey, Mr. Sam, Miss Julia." She sighed as if greeting us had taken all her strength, but then she managed a weak smile. "Lillian, my goodness, I didn't see you. Y'all didn't have to come. I'm all right, really I am."

"You don't look all right to me," Lillian said, stating a fact we could all see, but which I'd as soon not have had put so bluntly. One must encourage the sick, even if it means telling a story or two. "Now, Miss Hazel Marie," Lillian went on as she put her paper sack on the dresser. "I brought you some soup an' cornbread an' a piece of lemon pie. I know they don't have good home cookin' here, so you get them nurses to heat this soup up for you whenever you have a mind for it."

"Thank you, Lillian," she managed to murmur, but a definite greenish tint passed over her face.

"I'm gonna make you some bran muffins, too," she went on. "To clean out yo' system with. Then you feel better."

At Hazel Marie's desperate glance at me, I said, "That's the last thing she needs, Lillian. Let's think more along the lines of Jell-O or a clear broth. Something soothing like that."

Lillian nodded. "I do that, too."

There weren't enough chairs in the room, so Sam went out to the nurses' desk and thanked them for the use of a few of theirs. Lloyd remained by his mother's bed, glancing occasionally at the IV in her arm and staying far from it. Hazel Marie asked for her bed to be raised slightly, which I took to be a good sign. Sam called in a nurse to do it, since none of us wanted to risk causing a sudden jolt.

So after a while, we were all sitting around with nothing to say. Hospital visits are not the most conducive to conversation in the best of circumstances, which this wasn't. It's hardly the most encouraging thing to the sick and ailing to discuss how things are proceeding along at home without them, and, after you've asked how someone is feeling and told a few stories about how well they look, there's little else to say.

Sam started in telling about straightening his garage and some of the remarks James had made about people being pack rats, and after we'd congenially laughed a little, silence fell again. Lillian didn't help matters, because she looked ready to break down any minute. Hazel Marie herself was making little effort to entertain us, a sure sign of a weakened condition. Every time there was a lull in the conversation, her eyes started closing and she'd blink them, trying to stay awake.

"Hazel Marie," I said, finally hitting on a subject that might interest her, "did you get a chance to watch your programs this afternoon?"

"No'm, I kept falling asleep, even when *All My Children* came on."

Well, that was certainly a bad sign, but I didn't comment on it. I glanced at Lillian, who had begun putting Hazel Marie's nightclothes in a dresser drawer and saw her wipe tears from her face, and that wasn't a good sign, either.

"Sam," I said, "I think we'd better go. Lloyd has an early morning, and Hazel Marie needs her rest." I walked up behind Lloyd and put my hands on his shoulders. "We'll take care of him, Hazel Marie. You just concentrate on getting well. Has that doctor been in tonight?"

She nodded against the pillow, her hair getting more entangled than it already was. "A little while ago. He just said he might know something tomorrow."

My mouth tightened at that, but it wouldn't do to undermine a patient's trust in her physician, so I said nothing. But I thought a lot, little of it very complimentary. "Say good night, Lloyd, and run along with Sam and Lillian. I need to speak with your mother for a minute."

He leaned down to kiss his mother, and she wrapped her arms, one hand encumbered with tape, needle, and tubing, around him. My stomach clenched up at the sight, and I had to turn my head.

I let them all go out before me, then leaned down to Hazel Marie. "Hazel Marie," I whispered, "I tried to get Mr. Pickens, but he's out of town and his answering service was no help at all. Tell me where he is and I'll keep trying, because he'll want to know. I expect he'll come flying in from wherever he is."

She turned her face away and murmured something.

I leaned closer. "What?"

"He won't," she whispered.

"Why, why ever not? Of course he will, Hazel Marie. He'll be so upset at the thought of you being ill."

"I didn't want to tell you," she said so low that I could hardly hear her. She turned her head to look up at me through half-closed eyes. "He's probably in Charlotte. That's where he's moving to."

"*Moving*?" My heart dropped at the

thought, because that meant Hazel Marie and Lloyd might go with him. "My gracious, he can't do that. Why would he want to?"

"Because it's over," she mumbled. "We broke up."

"What! Hazel Marie, I don't believe it. *Why?*"

"Because I couldn't stand it anymore." She reached up with her taped hand and brushed tears from her cheek. "And please don't tell Lloyd. He doesn't know yet. But I had to do it, Miss Julia. All I've ever been is somebody's girlfriend my whole life, and it won't ever change with him."

Well, I expect she was right about that since he'd already tried two or maybe three wives and hadn't kept a one of them. Or maybe they'd left him, who knew? But Hazel Marie had known his unsavory history, and I'd thought she was reconciled to his skittishness when it came to marriage. So I was shocked that she'd had the gumption to put an end to it.

"You mean," I asked, "*you* were the one to break up?"

She nodded, making the tears flow faster. "It really upset him."

"Well, I guess so. I doubt Mr. Pickens

has ever been on the receiving end of something like that. Well, Hazel Marie, I don't know what to say. In one way, I'm proud of you, and, in another, I'm going to miss him."

"Oh, me, too," she sobbed.

"Oh, my goodness, this won't do at all. It's not good for you to get emotional while you're sick. Just stop thinking about it, Hazel Marie, it'll work out. And this might bring him to his senses."

Her head went back and forth on the pillow, doing less and less for the state of her hair. She didn't seem to mind, which just goes to show how sick she was. "No, I don't want him here. I don't ever want to see him again. So, Miss Julia?" She grabbed my hand. "Don't call him. All it'd do would be to drag things out and make them worse. Promise you won't call him."

"Well," I said, doubtfully, "if you insist. But I think he'd like to know you're in the hospital. He could at least send flowers."

"No, I'm about to get over him, and I don't want to start anything up again. And I don't want Lloyd to be in the middle of it. He'd be so upset."

"You're certainly right about that, and

you know I'll support you in whatever you do. But we can talk about this later on. Right now, I want you to rest and get well. I'll be back over first thing in the morning. I want to talk to that doctor." Fearing that her stirred-up emotions would cause a relapse, I was anxious to leave so the medications could do their job. And so I could tell Sam about this unexpected development. "Sleep well, Hazel Marie, and don't lie awake worrying."

The door swung open just as I stepped away from the bed and a nurse bustled in, or rather, she would've bustled if she'd had on a starched uniform instead of a nylon one, which only swished. "She's not going to lie awake," she said in a voice too loud for the surroundings. "Here you are, Hazel Marie, let's see if you can keep it down so you won't need an injection. Down the hatch now."

As Hazel Marie took a tablet from her, I thought to myself how it seemed that the entire medical community from the lowliest receptionist to the highest-powered specialist conspired to make patients feel like children. Frankly, I didn't like being addressed by my first name by complete strangers, and the one time a bank teller right out of high school presumed to be a close acquaintance, I took it as my duty to teach her some respect for her elders.

But it wouldn't have been prudent to incur the wrath of those who were caring for Hazel Marie, so I waved and slipped out the door, my heart pounding with anxiety. Not only was Hazel Marie sick with who-knew-what, but she'd cut off Mr. Pickens and I hadn't even known it. I needed to talk to Sam. And Lillian. Between the three of us, surely we could figure out something.

Chapter 6

Sam drove us home in near silence, broken only by Lillian in the backseat trying to allay Lloyd's worries. I didn't think she was succeeding since she kept crooning, "She be all right now. Don't you be worryin' yo'self sick, you pore little thing, you."

Sam reached over and took my hand, knowing that I was as tense as a stretched rubber band. We dropped Lillian off at her house, then proceeded on to ours. I went upstairs with Lloyd and tried to comfort him. I wasn't much better at it than Lillian had been, since I went to the other extreme by telling him that doctors put people in the hospital these days just to run expensive tests. "Liability, Lloyd," I said. "They have to eliminate everything under the sun so they won't get sued if they miss something. Your mother just has a touch of the flu or it could be food poisoning. But don't tell Lillian I said that."

With a weak smile, he began to get ready for bed. I didn't say a word about doing any reading, since his summer list was as long as my arm and he'd probably already done more than any of his classmates. And I most certainly didn't mention the state of affairs between his mother and Mr. Pickens. The child had enough on his plate without adding another concern. That was all I could think of, though, and I couldn't wait to unload this new worry onto Sam.

When I got back downstairs, I practically flew to Sam on the sofa in the living room. "Oh, Sam, the worst thing in the world has happened. Almost the worst, I mean."

"Now, Julia," he said, putting his arm around me. "She didn't look that bad to me. A little washed out, maybe, and tired, but not *sick* sick. And she's not in pain,

and the doctor hasn't found anything obvious—he wouldn't be running screening
tests if he had."

"I know all that, Sam, and of course I'm
worried about Hazel Marie's health, especially that fever. But this is something else."
I patted my chest, realizing that Hazel Marie's sudden about-face where Mr. Pickens
was concerned had truly shaken me.

He put his hand on my throat, then ran
it around the back of my neck. I shivered
just the slightest little bit. "What else is
bothering you?" he asked in that soothing
way he had.

"She told me right before I left that she
broke her engagement to Mr. Pickens."

Sam reared back to stare at me. "I didn't
know they were engaged."

"Well, of course they weren't. *Officially,*
that is. But after several years of seeing no
one else and going off to San Francisco
together, to say nothing of Mexico, I don't
know what else you would call it. Be that as
it may, though, and whatever it was, she's
ended it. Can you believe that? Sweet, go-
along-with-anything Hazel Marie just up
and told him she wasn't going to be a girlfriend all her life."

"Well, my goodness," Sam said. "That's a pretty come off."

"It's worse than that. Who else is she going to take up with, I ask you. I'm just convinced that Mr. Pickens would have come around eventually, and her being sick could've been just the thing to galvanize him into action. But she doesn't even want him to know she's sick. She made me promise not to call him." I grasped Sam's hand. "And I couldn't get him anyway because nobody knows where he is. I can't help but believe if. . . ."

"Julia," Sam said. "If she doesn't want him to know, then we can't call him. It's not up to us to go against her wishes."

"Well," I said carefully, "Lloyd could call him, don't you think? I mean, it wouldn't be us doing it. And if Mr. Pickens is still out of touch, he could leave a message. That would be a perfectly normal thing to do, if Lloyd would just think of it on his own."

"*If* he does," Sam said, "but not if somebody gives him the idea."

"Oh, I wouldn't do that." But, I thought, Lillian could, and if I just happened to mention the possibility in her hearing . . .

"Well," I said, untangling myself from

Sam's arms, "I need to go to bed. I want to be at the hospital early enough in the morning to ask that doctor a few questions. And you know some of them make rounds at the crack of dawn just to avoid being pinned to the wall by family members."

Sam laughed. "Okay. I'll get the lights."

A little while later when Sam and I were in bed, drifting off to sleep wrapped around each other, I thought to myself how comforting it was to have this warm and safe place next to him. It was the best part of being well married. Almost.

The following morning I left Lillian and Sam to get Lloyd off to his tennis clinic and arrived at the hospital a little after seven, only to learn that Dr. McKay had come and gone.

"You mean he's already been here?" I looked from one nurse to the other as they stood and sat around a desk midway in the hall. "Well, what did he say about Ms. Puckett's condition?"

One of them, probably the head nurse since the others looked to her, said, "You'll have to speak to him. We can't give out that information."

"Well then, how was her night? Did she sleep well? Is she still throwing up?"

The nurse stared at me for a minute. "We can't . . ."

"I know, I know," I said, pursing my mouth and doing an about-face. "It's all classified information." And walked off.

I went to Hazel Marie's room, expecting any moment to be called back and told to wait for visiting hours. But I reached her door without being stopped, tapped on it, and pushed it open. "Hazel Marie?"

She couldn't answer because she was leaning over a curved basin on the bed, trying to throw up from an empty stomach.

I dashed out to the nurses' desk and broke into the circle around it. "She's sick again. Come quick."

One of the nurses followed me into Hazel Marie's room. She took a wet washcloth and wiped Hazel Marie's face, which I could've done myself if I hadn't expected something more therapeutic than that.

Then the nurse told her to lie back down and not move around so much, giving me the eye as she said it. I wanted to tell her that I'd just gotten there and had not been the cause of an upset stomach. I held my peace, though, when the nurse said she'd bring an injection for the nausea.

Hazel Marie lay on the bed, looking exhausted, while I drew up a chair. I wanted to talk to her, wanted to hear more about her decision to cut off Mr. Pickens, but she was in no shape for conversation. When the nurse came back in with a syringe, I turned my face away, not wanting to see the actual procedure.

When the nurse left, Hazel Marie managed to turn her head toward me and murmur, "Lloyd's all right?"

"He's worried about you, but other than that, he's fine."

She nodded, her eyelids heavy with fatigue, and as the room quieted, she drifted off to sleep.

I stayed so long that I found myself about to nod off, too. But after a while, I got up and looked down at her to be sure she was deeply asleep. Then I tiptoed out and went to Dr. Hargrove's office.

❦

"I want to see Dr. McKay," I told the receptionist. "And, no, I don't have an appointment. I'll just sit here until he can give me five minutes of his time. I want some answers from him, and I'll wait all day if that's what it takes."

It didn't take all day, but it did take almost an hour before I was ushered back to Dr. Hargrove's office, which Dr. McKay had taken over.

"Mrs. Murdoch, is it?" He had the courtesy to stand when I entered and motioned me to a chair in front of the desk. "What can I do for you?"

My mouth tightened at the question. What did he think he could do for me? Did he think I'd just dropped in for a chat? There was a sick woman over in the hospital, and he wanted to know why I was here?

"You can tell me what's wrong with Hazel Marie," I said, holding my pocketbook on my lap. "What kind of tests are you conducting on her, and what have you found out about her condition?"

"Well, now," he said, pulling out a desk drawer and propping his feet on it. He leaned back in his chair and clasped his hands behind his head in a casual manner that irritated me beyond words. "There's still a number of tests to be run, so I don't have anything to tell you at the moment. And frankly, I wouldn't even if I knew anything. I'd be running into ethical problems if I discussed the case with anyone but the patient herself." He smiled to take the sting out of his words. "I'm sure you understand."

"I do understand and I appreciate your high standards. However, Hazel Marie means the world to us, and we feel, in ways of which you are unaware, somewhat responsible for her. I don't mean to imply," I quickly added, "that she's unable to care for herself. In fact, she's more than able. I'm only wondering if you couldn't discuss the possibilities, let us say, *in general,* without specifically discussing her case. I wouldn't want you to get in trouble with the Board of Ethics or whatever." Actually, I didn't care if he got in trouble or not. I wanted some answers so I could stop imagining the worst.

"Well, just being speculative and non-specific," he said, his eyes roaming around the room before coming back to me. "And if you won't hold me to anything, I'll just mention again that a generalized infection or an intestinal parasite of some kind has to be considered when a patient has been out of the country and presents symptoms of severe gastrointestinal involvement. A complete blood workup will help determine that. Also an upper GI series might be called for to rule out a couple of things. Then possibly some allergy tests. That'll all take time, so we'll just have to be patient."

Be patient! I thought. How could I be patient while she was over there wasting away to nothing?

"Well," I said, "can you think of anything else in this hypothetical situation we're talking about? We're all worried sick, so if you're completely in the dark, tell us and we'll take her somewhere else."

"Oh, I don't think that'll be necessary," he said, suddenly sitting up in his chair.

"Maybe not," I said, my back so stiff I couldn't lean back. "But it's always an option. Dr. Hargrove wouldn't mind us getting a second opinion, or three or four if that's what it took, even though we've been friends for years. Of course," I went on, "he never needed any extra help with a diagnosis."

A slight smile slipped across Dr. McKay's—pardon me, *Rick's*—face and he began playing with a pen. "I don't mind a second opinion, either, and we'll get one if the tests are inconclusive. But what I'm doing is exactly what any other physician would do. So why don't we wait for the results, then talk again?"

"Well, can't you tell me what you *think* it is?" I said, trying my best to get something out of him. "Surely you have some possibilities in mind."

"Speaking hypothetically, the first thing you think of with vomiting and a low-grade fever is dehydration, which is symptomatic and not particularly indicative. That could be caused by a number of things. Gastric ulcer is one possibility."

"An ulcer! Why, whatever for? She doesn't have a worry in the world." I stopped and reconsidered. Maybe she did. Maybe she was so worried about getting rid of Mr. Pickens that it had begun to eat away at her. But as far as I knew, that had just happened, not long enough to give her physical problems. "How fast does an ulcer come on?"

"Not fast, usually," he replied. "So without other long-term symptoms, I'm not convinced it's an ulcer. An allergy of some kind should also be considered."

"Why, I don't see how. She rarely ever sneezes unless she has a cold."

"Could be a food allergy," he said. "Like from dairy products or certain grains."

"Well, if that's what it turns out to be, let's don't tell Lillian." At his frown, I went on. "She'd be devastated if she'd been the unwitting cause of all this trouble. But I'll tell you frankly that this all sounds like guessing to me. I don't mean to hurt your feelings, but you'll have to do better than that."

"Well, in a way you're right," he said. "At this point, without the test results, it is a matter of guessing. But like I said, we should be getting a few results back later today."

"We can only hope, can't we?"

He nodded, looked at his watch, and I knew he wanted me to wrap this up and be gone. So I stood.

"Thank you for seeing me," I said. "I just wanted you to know that Hazel Marie is precious to us, and that we'll do whatever it takes to get her well. I'm glad to hear that you're not thinking in terms of some horrific disease or condition, although your earlier mention of a parasitic infestation has made my skin crawl. On the other hand, I hope you won't overlook anything that could be worse than ulcers or allergies." My face flamed for an instant. "Given her age, female trouble should be considered, too, you know."

At his smile, I turned away and headed for the door. Behind me, he said, "I assure you that I'm not discounting anything at this point. She needs to be rehydrated and that fever brought down, so I'll keep her in the hospital another night. Then if all goes well and nothing else crops up, I'll discharge her tomorrow."

I kept walking out the door, down the hall, and out into the parking lot, knowing little more than when I'd gone in.

Chapter 7

I parked the car in the driveway and went in the back door, as was my wont, knowing that I hadn't accomplished a thing other than to put Dr. McKay on warning. Maybe that was enough to stir up some action on his part. Frankly, I didn't think I could stand the anxiety of waiting another several days before knowing something conclusive.

I walked into the clean and shining kitchen, my mouth already open to lay my concerns onto Lillian. But the kitchen was empty. Assuming she was upstairs, I took off my raincoat and proceeded farther into the house, looking for her. Instead, I found Sam in the living room.

"Why, Sam. I thought you'd be at your house, working. Is anything wrong?" If I hadn't had my mind on other things, I would've taken more note of his uncommon presence at home two days running.

"No, sweetheart," he said with a distracted look. Then he put aside the yellow legal pad he'd been writing on and gave me his full attention. "Just trying to work a few things out."

"Oh, my goodness," I said, hurrying to sit beside him. "What is it? Have you thought of what could be wrong with Hazel Marie? Tell me, Sam, I'm about to lose my mind with worry."

"Those tests take time, Julia," he said, holding me close. "You have to allow for that and not get yourself all worked up. I know it's hard, but for her sake, and Lloyd's, too, we have to wait it out."

"You're right. I know you're right. I just keep thinking that if Dr. Hargrove were here, we wouldn't be going through all this. Well, anyway," I said with a sigh, "I guess we'll know soon enough. But it doesn't help that she's thrown Mr. Pickens over. I'm still so shaken that she sent him packing that I can hardly comprehend it. And she didn't even tell anybody, not even Lloyd. Maybe that's what's wrong with her. She just kept it bottled up so long that it had to come out some other way."

"When did all this happen?"

"I don't know. I was so stunned I didn't think to ask her. And she didn't much want to talk about it." I sat still for a second or two, then raised my head from his shoulder. "You know what I think? I think she's been sick longer than we've realized. If she'd been feeling herself, she'd never have cut him off. Maybe I ought to tell that doctor. It could be an important symptom."

"Julia," he said, pulling me back closer. "If it is, let her tell him. It's not our place."

"Well, people do make bad decisions when they aren't feeling well. Life-changing decisions, too." And speaking of that, I still wondered if Hazel Marie's problem didn't have to do with the change of life. Dr. McKay hadn't even mentioned that, but I could've told him of three people I knew who'd gone off the deep end during those times in their lives. One had gone into a steep decline and stayed in bed for the next seven years, and another refused to recognize her own children, and the other had taken after her husband with a butcher knife.

You can't be too careful when certain internal changes begin to occur, and *Rick* should've had that uppermost in his mind.

I guess, though, if all Hazel Marie did was throw up all over the place and tell Mr. Pickens to take a hike, maybe we were getting off lightly.

∞

It didn't take long for the word to get around town that Hazel Marie was in the hospital. Nurses talk, too, you know. So the phone started ringing off the hook with everybody wanting to know what was wrong, how bad it was, and what they could do to help. It just did me in to have to keep saying that I didn't know what she had and neither did her doctor. That opened the door for all kinds of speculations.

Mildred Allen said, "You remember Mamie Harrison? They put her in the hospital without knowing what was wrong and you know what happened to her. She was never the same again."

And LuAnne Conover phoned, wanting

to know why I hadn't called her with the news. "I can't believe you, Julia. You *know* I'd want to know and I had to find out at the post office. I'd've been by your side every minute if I'd known. Now listen, I heard about this new treatment that some clinic right outside of town is offering. I'd look into that if I were you."

Betsy Harris called wanting to know if we'd thought of a chiropractor. "You wouldn't believe how much better I felt after having my back aligned," she said.

And, Lord help us, Margaret Benson from the Lila Mae Harding Sunday school class called wanting to know if Hazel Marie would consider acupuncture. "You'd be amazed, Julia," she said. And I probably would if anybody ever got me near that many needles.

Etta Mae Wiggins called, very distressed, offering whatever help we needed. "I just love Hazel Marie," she said. "I'll drop everything and do private duty on her. Or take care of her when she comes home. Whatever she needs."

And of course, Emma Sue Ledbetter called to say that she was holding Hazel Marie up in her prayers.

"Well," I told her, "hold up the rest of us while you're at it." Then, as much as I hated to start something I couldn't stop, I asked her to activate the prayer chain. There was no telling what the talk would be by the time everybody passed the word along the telephone lines, but we needed all the help we could get.

"Lillian," I said, hanging up the phone again, "people are kind but, I declare, it gets to be too much sometimes."

"Yessum, they start bringin' covered dishes pretty soon you don't watch out."

I shuddered, thinking of the last time the town turned out with covered dishes. It was for a funeral that, thank goodness, never occurred since Horace Allen turned up alive and well, but the thought of the same outpouring for Hazel Marie made me want to weep.

I took my time that morning before going to the hospital. Having missed Dr. Mc-Kay on several occasions when I'd tried to time my visits to his, I'd just about given up on catching him on his rounds. So I ended up stepping out of the elevator in midmorning, only to run right into him as he was leaving.

"Why, Dr. McKay," I said, delighted to catch him unawares, "how nice to see you. And how is our patient this morning?"

"Doing well," he said with the beginnings of a smile. "Her fever's down this morning, and she's been able to take a little dry toast and liquids by mouth. So if all goes well, she'll soon be on a normal diet. When she gets home, I want her to take it easy for another week. Give her several small meals a day instead of three big ones, and make sure she gets plenty of rest. Let's give it one more day here to be sure the vomiting has stopped and she's fully rehydrated. You can take her home tomorrow."

"Well, that is good news and a great relief to me. But we certainly don't want it to happen again. So what's your diagnosis? Or do you have one? Or can you even tell me?"

"Oh, I have one, all right," he said, this time with a broad satisfied smile on his face. "Actually, and I don't mind admitting it, one of the nurses put me on the right track. The only thing wrong with Hazel Marie is a touch of *hyperemesis gravidarum*."

My hand flew to my throat and I rocked back on my heels. "Oh, my," I gasped, "that sounds . . . grave."

"Not at all," he said, turning toward the stairs. "It's under control now and her condition is completely curable." He glanced at his watch and moved off. "In time, that is. I'll let her tell you about it."

As he left, I had to put my hand against the wall to steady myself. He was certainly treating Hazel Marie's condition lightly enough—even cavalierly—but I knew that anytime an illness had a Latin name, it had to be serious. So I stumbled down the hall, tapped on Hazel Marie's door and peeked in, prepared to offer succor and comfort and a consultation with another doctor.

"Hazel Marie?" I whispered, easing into the room.

She took one look at me, then grabbed the sheet and flipped it over her head. Turning toward the wall, she pled, "Don't look, Miss Julia! Please don't look at me. I can't stand it."

"Why, Hazel Marie," I said, hurrying to the bed. "What is wrong with you? Listen, it can't be that bad. I just saw Dr. McKay out in the hall and he said you'll soon be well and eating as normal as anybody. That's good news. You have to be happy about that."

"I'm not happy about anything," she mumbled, huddling under the sheet, her feet drawn up and her whole body curled away from me. "I'm so sorry, Miss Julia. Just so sorry, and I'll leave just as soon as I can."

"Now, Hazel Marie, we'll have you out of this place in no time, so don't worry yourself about when you leave. Sam and I will take care of everything. We all want you home, and Dr. McKay said that the Latin condition you have is completely curable."

She drew herself up tighter, her shoulders trembling as she began sobbing into her pillow. "No, it's not," she moaned. "It's awful, and, Miss Julia, I didn't mean to. I'd give anything for this not to happen. I'm so ashamed."

"You don't have one thing to be ashamed of," I assured her, distressed that Dr. McKay's diagnosis and prognosis had sent her into such a tailspin. "After all, you didn't do it to yourself. Turn over now, and tell me what has you so upset. The doctor seemed pleased with your progress."

"Easy for him to say," she snuffled into the pillow. "He doesn't have to look you in the eye, knowing what he's done."

"Well, believe me, he doesn't have much to be proud of, the way he's conducted himself. But, Hazel Marie, honey, please turn over and tell me what he said. I don't understand Latin, so I don't know how to help you."

She pulled the sheet down, using it to wipe her face, but she didn't turn over. Speaking to the wall, she said, "He didn't tell you what caused it?"

"No, just that you'd explain it."

"Oh, Lord," she moaned, burying her face again. "I don't think I can. But I'll leave, Miss Julia. I promise I'll go somewhere far away so nobody'll ever know."

"Hazel Marie!" I said, a bit sharply. "Stop this talk of leaving. If you have something catching, we'll put you in isolation, but you're not going anywhere. Now tell me what we need to do to get you home where you belong."

I didn't think she was going to answer, but suddenly she turned over and sat up in bed. Her face was blotched, her hair a rat's nest of tangles with black roots and

her eyes still overflowing. She drew her knees up and rested her forehead on them, hiding her face from me.

"I guess you might as well know," she said, her voice muffled, but determined. "You'll find out sooner or later anyhow. I . . . Miss Julia, the doctor said . . ." Her shoulders hunched together and her voice dropped to a whisper, "The doctor, he said I'm . . . expecting."

"Expecting what?" As soon as the words were out of my mouth, I drew a sharp breath as it hit me. "A *baby*?"

I felt for something to hold on to, my hand lighting on the back of a chair. "Hazel Marie, are you expecting a baby?"

She nodded and swallowed hard. "That's what he said, but I don't see how."

Well, Lord, if that was the case, she was worse off than any of us knew.

I stood there a few minutes, as all the implications of this news seemed to hover over my head. I'd been struck dumb a few times before in my life, but even when my tongue wouldn't move, my mind had continued to function. But not this time. I couldn't speak and I couldn't think. I just stood there and looked at her, a white noise in my brain. And the first thing that came into my head? A change-of-life baby, a distressing event for most couples and even more so for Hazel Marie who wasn't even a couple.

"Hazel Marie," I finally managed to say, "you do know how babies are conceived, don't you?"

"Yes, ma'am, it's just that I didn't think it would happen. I mean, I thought I was past the age. So," she whispered, still unable to look at me, "so that's why I have to leave. I'll go somewhere where nobody'll know you or know . . . how bad I've let you down. I'm just so sorry."

As she dissolved into tears again, my mind jumped back into gear. And the first thing I thought of was that, as shattering as the news of a baby was, it probably wasn't as bad as having a tropical parasite. "Well," I said, "I'll admit that this has set me back a little, but it's fixable. I'll get Mr. Pickens back here if I have to drag him by the hair of his head. Then we'll get you married and nobody'll be the wiser. See? It'll work out, so you put aside any thought of leaving." Then with a supreme effort of will, I went on. "We'll have things to do to get ready for a baby. Just imagine, Hazel Marie, a new little baby! Why, everybody's going to be so happy for you, and Mr. Pickens most of all."

She shook her head. "No, he won't. And, Miss Julia," she said, finally turning those big eyes on me, "I have to do this myself. I'm the one to blame and I don't deserve anything but to bear the awful shame of it." A great sob shuddered through her. "For the second time in my miserable life."

"Oh, my goodness!" I cried. "Hazel Marie, don't think like that. Why, Lloyd is no cause for shame. He is the light of your life, and mine. You've raised a fine boy, and I'm sure you'll do just as well with this one, whatever it is." Then recalling that she'd said she had to do it herself, I trembled. "Hazel Marie," I whispered, "you're not thinking of . . . *doing* something, are you?"

"You mean . . . ?"

I nodded, unable to say the word.

"No," she said, shaking her head, "I couldn't do that. That's why I have to go off somewhere, pretend to be a widow or something. And try to make a life for it."

"No," I said with conviction. "No, we'll get you and Mr. Pickens married, and that'll solve all your problems." I bit my lip, then proceeded. "I hate to ask this, Hazel Marie, but I guess I better. It is Mr. Pickens's, isn't it?"

Her head flopped down on her knees again, and she began weeping as if her heart would break. "You must think I'm terrible!"

"Oh, no. No, I don't. I just don't want you marrying the wrong one, that's all."

Trying unsuccessfully to dry her face, she said, "There's never been anybody but him. And there never will be. But, Miss Julia, there won't be a wedding. There's only going to be another little bastard—excuse me for saying an ugly word, but that's what everybody else will say. Because J.D. won't marry me. That's why we broke up in the first place."

"You mean he *knows* about this?" I was shocked. I knew that Mr. Pickens danced to his own tune, but even he couldn't be so callous.

"No," she said, shaking her head. "No, he doesn't. I just found out myself when Dr. McKay told me the test was positive.

But he's not *going* to know, because I never want to see him again as long as I live. If J.D. won't marry me for myself, I don't want him marrying me for a baby."

Well, I didn't see why not. As far as I was concerned, that was the best reason of all to marry, and it didn't matter to me how many movie stars had babies out of wedlock. Their example didn't make it right, and I determined then and there that Mr. Pickens was going to do the right thing, come hell or high water, although I am not a cursing kind of woman by any stretch of the imagination.

Chapter 8

I don't know how in the world I got home in one piece, the way thoughts were flitting in and out of my head like a swarm of bees. Could that doctor have gotten it wrong? How could he have mixed up an ulcer or a parasite with a baby? What kind of test had he run? Maybe the test was wrong. Was he so young and untried that he needed help to diagnosis something that should've been obvious? Not to me, you understand, but to a doctor. Dr. Hargrove wouldn't have had to rely on a nurse, but thank goodness for the woman's common sense.

And, if Hazel Marie continued in her resolve to reject Mr. Pickens, what were we going to do with another illegitimate child? It had taken every favor and every cent owed to me to get the town to accept Hazel Marie and Lloyd, but even I couldn't expect them to overlook a second slip.

I pulled into the driveway, turned off the ignition and just sat there, thinking. The last thing Hazel Marie had done before I left the hospital had been to beg me not to tell Sam and Lillian.

"I don't want them to know," she'd said. "I'm too ashamed."

"Hazel Marie," I told her, "I have to. They are worried sick about you, and you know they'll keep on after us and after us, wanting to know what's wrong. By the way, what *is* wrong? I mean, I never heard of being with child turned into Latin before."

"Oh," she mumbled, "the doctor said it meant a lot of vomiting due to pregnancy. Something like morning sickness all day long." She sniffed, then blew her nose. "And I didn't even know there was such a thing."

"Well, me either," I'd said, amazed at what you can learn if you just listen. "Now,

Hazel Marie, I want you to let me tell Sam and Lillian before you get home. That way, you won't have to do it yourself, and they'll have time to get used to it. But not Lloyd. I'll let you do that in your own time and in your own way. And when you get your strength back, we'll sit down and figure out what to do."

She'd finally agreed and I'd left, only to find myself still sitting in the car trying to figure out the next step.

"Lillian," I said as I walked through the door and into the kitchen on my way to the living room, "is Sam here?"

"No'm," she said, wiping a pan with a dishrag. "He at his house."

I didn't stop, just turned in a half circle and headed back to the door. "He's always somewhere else when I want him."

I got to the door, but, on second thought didn't open it, just turned in another half circle and walked back into the kitchen. "Well, I wanted to tell him first, but since you're here and he's not, I'll tell you. You were second on my list, anyway. You might better sit down, Lillian."

"*Oh, Lord!*" she cried, flinging the pan in

the sink and throwing the dishrag in the air. "I knew it, I knew it! Oh, my sweet Jesus, Miss Hazel Marie got something awful! What we gonna do, Miss Julia, what in the world we gonna do?"

"Lillian, Lillian," I said, taking her by the arm and leading her to a chair at the table. "Sit down now and listen to me. It's not something awful. Well, I mean it is, but not the way you're thinking. Just listen to me now because we're all going to need your help."

Tears were gushing from her eyes and I could feel her trembling as I sat beside her. "Oh, that pore little boy without no daddy and now no mama, neither. They say good folkses die young, and nobody better'n Miss Hazel Marie. Oh, that sweet little thing, she too good for this world."

"I know, I know," I crooned, handing her a dish towel since the Kleenex box was out of reach. "But she's not dying, not even close to it. No, listen now and pull yourself together. That's not what I have to tell you. Are you listening?" I pulled the dish towel from her face, looked her in the eye, and took a deep breath. "Hazel Marie's going to have a baby."

Lillian's eyes got wider and wider as she took in the news. She stared at me in wonder, then she sprang from the chair and let out a shout that could've been heard on Main Street. "A baby! She gonna have a baby? Thank you, Lord! Oh, thank you, Jesus! We gonna have us a baby in the house!"

Then she spun around and stopped. "We need us a new dryer, Miss Julia, for all them diapers. That ole one gettin' finicky on me. Oh, thank you, Jesus, a new little baby!"

I didn't remind her that nobody washed and dried diapers anymore. I just let her enjoy planning for the addition to our family, while waiting for her elation to run its course. In fact, I couldn't look far enough ahead to worry about diapers, since we had to get through the next few months first.

"Lillian," I said, "one thing to keep in mind. We cannot tell Lloyd. His mother needs to do that, so we have to keep it to ourselves. I'll tell Sam, but it'll only be the three of us who knows. Well, and Hazel Marie, of course."

Lillian's eyes squinched up as she

thought it through. "What about Mr. Pickens? He make another one what knows."

I shook my head. "No, apparently he doesn't, and furthermore she doesn't want him to know. Have you ever heard of such a thing? I can't get over it."

Lillian's voice dropped low as she asked in wonder, "He don't know?"

"No, and I'd think a man of his knowledge and experience would know that when you play with fire you're likely to get burned. I am very upset with him, Lillian, and I don't care what Hazel Marie says, he is going to get himself back here and accept his responsibility. This new baby will have a father if it's the last thing I do."

"Oh, he do that, Miss Julia," Lillian said, nodding her head in complete confidence. "Mr. Pickens, he a fine man an' he get her married 'fore you know it."

"I'm not so sure, Lillian, because there's another fly in the ointment. I guess I haven't told you, but Hazel Marie has broken up with him and he's moving to Charlotte. She made me promise not to call him and says she never wants to see him again. I am just heartbroken over it, especially with a baby on the way."

Lillian was rarely speechless, but this time she was. She stared at me with her mouth wide open, then she snapped it shut only to open it again to speak. "You don't mean it," she said in utter awe. "Why, that pore little thing don't know what she doin'. No wonder she sick. Miss Julia, they's only one thing to do. We got to get Mr. Pickens back here, an' tell Miss Hazel Marie she don't have to see him, she jus' have to marry him."

"My feeling, exactly. Be thinking how we can get him here, especially since she made me promise not to call him."

"Oh, I already figure that out. I know how to use the telephone, an' nobody make me promise nothin'.'"

"Lillian," I said, as a great weight rolled away, "I don't know what I'd do without you."

"Me, neither," she said, and we smiled at each other in complete agreement.

☙❧

By the time I got to Sam's house to tell him the news, I'd worked myself into a fiery state over Mr. Pickens's careless ways. He'd taken advantage of Hazel Marie, then walked off, leaving her with the consequences. The very idea, I fumed, strewing seed hither and yon, then leaving before the harvest. I was not going to have it.

And Hazel Marie could just get herself off her high horse and walk down the aisle like many another had done before her. Those two had more than themselves to think of, namely Lloyd and the new little bundle of joy or whatever it was. They'd made themselves a family, so now they could just act like one.

The garage door was closed, so I got out of the car and walked up on the porch, taking care not to slip on the wet leaves that covered the steps. I rang the doorbell, still reluctant to just barge into another woman's house, even though Sam's first wife had been dead and buried for longer even than Wesley Lloyd Springer.

James opened the door and immediately stepped back. "Miss Julia, how you do? Come in, come in an' dry off. It gettin' airish out there, don't you think?"

"I hadn't noticed," I said, walking into the wide entrance hall. "If you've finished with the garage, James, you need to get those wet leaves raked off the steps and the walk."

"Well, I ain't 'zactly finished with the garage. They's still a heap to do in there."

"Take time out like you're doing now and get rid of those leaves. Somebody's going to fall and break something." Sam was entirely too lenient with James, who could look at work to be done and never see it. "Is Sam in his office?"

But just then, Sam opened the door into the hall and my heart lifted as it always did at his welcoming smile. "I thought I heard somebody out here. Come in, Julia, I'm glad to see you." Then his face sobered. "Has the doctor . . . ?"

"Yes," I said, cutting him off, aware of James standing there, listening. "And it's nothing but a touch of flu. She'll be coming home tomorrow for a few days of rest. No visitors and no running around until she gets her strength back. I am so relieved."

I marched into the big front room that was Sam's office, waited for him to follow me, then turned to James. "Now's a good time to rake those leaves." Then I shut the door.

Sam's eyebrows went up, as he gave me a questioning look. "Just the flu?"

"That's right," I said, slightly louder than

usual in case there was an ear pressed to the door. "One of those new strains, it seems." That would buy us a little time, I thought, as I pressed my own ear against the door until I heard James's footsteps going into the kitchen. It took some little while since an Oriental rug covered most of the hall. Satisfied that he was gone, I nodded and made sure the door was tightly closed.

"Julia, what are you doing?" Sam asked, torn between laughing and worrying about my unusual behavior.

"Waiting for James to get out of earshot. He'd have everything I say spread all over town by nightfall. And, Sam, we have to keep this to ourselves. Only you and Lillian will know it. Well, and me, too, of course. But nobody else."

"All right. Come sit down and tell me. I take it, it's more than the flu?"

"I should say it is," I said, flopping down on the leather sofa. "I had to beg Hazel Marie to let me tell you and Lillian, because she didn't want anybody to know. As if," I continued with a sniff, "everybody in the world won't know eventually. There's no easy way to tell you, Sam, so I'll just say it. Mr. Pickens, that reckless, three-time loser in the marriage market, has put her in the family way."

"Well," Sam said, laying his head back on the sofa and gazing at the ceiling. "Well, this is a surprise. There's no doubt? She really is pregnant?"

I nodded. "As she can be. And even with all that morning sickness, she didn't have a clue. Although," I went on, "you'd think she might've suspected, especially since, after having Lloyd, she obviously knows what causes it. Although I will admit that because of her age, if nothing else, it didn't occur to me." I paused to draw a breath. "And apparently it didn't to that young doctor, either. A nurse had to suggest it to him and thank goodness she did before he ran up a horrendous bill doing all those tests. And I tell you, Sam," I went on, right on the verge of outrage at the thought, "it looks like they just turn young, inexperienced doctors loose on the public with their minds so filled with esoteric classroom ailments like parasites and generalized infections that they can't even think of common, everyday conditions like being with child. Obviously, Dr. McKay knew Hazel Marie wasn't married, but he should've also known that being unwed hasn't stopped anybody yet."

"Well," Sam said again, apparently unable to quickly come to terms with the news. "I would've thought Hazel Marie might be a little, well, maybe old to have to worry about such a thing."

"She did, too! That's what got her in trouble. But it's all those vitamins that people take, Sam. Change-of-life babies are quite common these days. Actually, though, I thought she'd passed the danger zone, myself. But," I sat up straight to look at him, "it was San Francisco that did it. You remember that trip they took with another couple to chaperone? Well, a lot of good that did. I knew she shouldn't've gone off across the country with him, but what could I do? I thought they both had enough sense not to get in this predicament. And, now, it's left to us to make the best of it. Sam," I said, grasping his arm, "we've got to find Mr. Pickens and get him back here before her condition begins to show."

"I hate to ask this, Julia, but are we sure Pickens is the father?"

"Why, Sam, how could you ask such a

thing! Of course, he's the father. Hazel Marie is not a loose woman, and she's been as true to him as any wife. No, I don't have a doubt in my mind that he's the guilty one. Besides, she told me he is, and what is that sorry thing doing? Moving to Charlotte, that's what."

Chapter 9

"He's moving?"

"That's what she said."

"Well, that's hard to believe," Sam said, frowning. "It's not like him to shirk a responsibility like this."

"He's shirking because he doesn't know it. Which I intend to remedy just as soon as you help me locate him."

"Now, Julia," Sam said, turning his frown on me. "We ought not get in the middle of this. Didn't you promise her you wouldn't call him?"

"Things have changed since then, but, yes, I did. I was hoping Lloyd would do it, but of course he doesn't know about the baby. So even if he did call Mr. Pickens, he wouldn't have the best of all arguments to get him here. So, Lillian's going to do it. And don't frown at me, Sam Murdoch, I don't have any control over what Lillian does. She's her own woman, and if she thinks he ought to know what he's done, why, I say more power to her."

"My goodness," Sam said, trying not to smile, "you are a devious woman."

"Not devious at all, just determined. See, Sam, I am less concerned about Mr. Pickens and Hazel Marie and what *they* want than I am about what Lloyd and that new little baby need. I mean, Hazel Marie and Mr. Pickens are adults and they've *had* what they wanted, so now they can just think about the innocent ones in this mess. And when you think of it that way, you can ignore promises, and you can forget about Hazel Marie saying she never wants to see him again, and you can make Mr. Pickens get himself here so he can do the right thing. And furthermore, we don't have a lot of time for fiddling around. Hazel Marie's so skinny now that she's going to be in maternity clothes before we turn around good."

"Well, when you put it that way . . ."

"It's the only way to put it. Now, the thing for you to do is track down Mr. Pickens. His answering service doesn't know where he is and Hazel Marie says she doesn't either. So I'm thinking that you should see if he has his house up for sale. If he does, a real estate agent will know how to reach him. And if that doesn't work, you can call that insurance company that has him on retainer. They'll know, unless he's thrown all common sense to the winds. Which I doubt. But in that case, we'll ask Coleman to track him through the Charlotte police department."

Sam looked at me in an indulgent, but admiring, way. "You've really thought this through, haven't you?"

"Yes, I have. I am not going to have Hazel Marie going through another pregnancy alone and unwed, and I'm not going to have Lloyd suffering any shame or ridicule because of their precipitant and careless actions. And," I went on after a moment's thought, "I am not going to be put in the position of having to defend the indefensible to everybody in town. To Pastor Ledbetter, in particular."

Every friend I had, along with their probable responses to another child unblessed by legitimacy, passed through my mind. LuAnne Conover would be shocked to the core, and she'd lambast me for what she'd see as my complicity in the situation. Appearances were so important to her that she had little sympathy for any deviations. On the other hand, if everybody else accepted Hazel Marie, she would follow along, not ever wanting to be the only holdout on anything.

Helen Stroud would never let anyone know what she thought. She'd treat Hazel Marie as politely as she always did, but you'd always wonder what was going on in her mind. Emma Sue Ledbetter would agonize over forgiving the sinner while condemning the sin, putting a great strain on her testimony as she tried to figure out where the lines were drawn. Mildred Allen was the only one whom I figured would wave off the whole matter. But, of course, she almost had to since she'd fairly easily come to terms with her only son having had a remarkable and surgical transformation into a woman.

I couldn't even imagine what the verdict

would be among the members of the Lila Mae Harding Sunday school class, to say nothing of the garden club and the book club, all of which Hazel Marie belonged to. It's a settled fact that groups of women were influenced by the loudest and most unforgiving talkers among them.

Of course, I thought, as I rubbed my forehead almost in despair, none of that spoke to my own feelings. I was as rigorous and unbending as the worst of them when it came to expecting others to do as I did, which entailed following the rules and traditions of a moral society. But when it came to people I cared about who'd started down that slippery slope, why, I could find all kinds of excuses for them. Fact of the matter, I was swinging back and forth between being torn in two with anger at Hazel Marie and Mr. Pickens, but mostly at him since he ought to've known better, and being protective of her and that innocent baby.

"Julia?" Sam said, sliding an arm around me and pulling me close. "Are you all right?"

"I'm not sure. I'm having trouble taking it all in, plus trying to figure out how to handle those two bullheaded people. Mr. Pickens

is moving away, if he hasn't already, and
Hazel Marie wants to move somewhere
where she can pretend to be a widow. I
ask you, Sam, is that a solution to anything? I'd be tempted to help Hazel Marie
do exactly that, if she wouldn't take Lloyd
with her but you know she would. And what
would that do to him? He'd be leaving the
only decent home he's ever known, changing schools, and having to aid and abet his
mother's pretense. I can't have it, Sam, I
just can't. We have to get Mr. Pickens back
here and lay down the law to him."

"I agree," he said, running his hand up
and down my back, a gesture that soothed
my soul. "But there'll be no need to lay
down the law. Pickens won't have to be
forced to do the right thing. My concern is
Hazel Marie. She's raised one child on her
own. She may feel she can do it again, especially since she has money coming in
from Lloyd's inheritance. It would be a whole
lot easier this time."

"I'll take care of Hazel Marie, don't worry
about that. You handle Mr. Pickens.
Frankly, I don't care if they never live together or even see each other after they're

married. They can divorce the day after the wedding for all I care. But they're going to put things right for the sake of that baby and for Lloyd or I'm going to know the reason why. And if either of them balks at a shotgun wedding, I can point out three or four couples in town who had seven-pound premature babies—Binkie and Coleman, for one—and their marriages are still going strong. I mean, you do what you have to when the circumstances demand it, and these circumstances certainly demand it."

"All right," Sam said, shifting to stand up. "Let me get started trying to find Pickens, while you get Hazel Marie ready to see him. But I'm only going to locate him, not tell him anything. She'll have to do that. Anyway, I don't think there'll be a problem with him, but, like I said, I'm not so sure about her."

I waved my hand. "All Mr. Pickens has to do is be sweet to her, tell her he loves her and ask her to marry him. Believe me, she'll fall all over herself agreeing to anything he says. After all, that's what got her into this condition in the first place. You just make sure that he knows he might have to do a little courting, but she'll come around."

"I hope you're right, and I hope we're doing the right thing. I'm never comfortable interfering in the lives of other people."

"Well, I'm not either, and, as you know, I rarely do it. It's only when I'm absolutely sure of what's best that I dare to step in. But this is surely just such an occasion."

⊛⊛

I left Sam to his telephoning and went home, noting as I left that James had done a fairly decent job of clearing the steps and front walkway.

As soon as I stepped into the kitchen, Lillian's eyes swept the room as if she expected someone to be listening in. Then she tiptoed over to me and whispered, "How Mr. Sam takin' it?"

"Just as he always does," I said, ridding myself of my raincoat. "He takes anything that happens right in stride. And, Lillian, there's no need for you to try to find Mr. Pickens. Sam's doing it for us, since he has contacts we don't have. I expect we'll hear from him most anytime now."

"Well," she whispered, "I didn't know he gonna do it, so I call his house and his office but didn't get no further than you did. Then I call that operator down in Charlotte an' ask do he have a telephone an' he do. The number right over there by the phone, but nobody home there, either."

"Why, Lillian," I said, looking at her in amazement, "that is outstanding. I never would've thought of that. Well, I probably would have eventually, but you did it. Is this it?"

I picked up a scrap of paper with a number in a different area code just as the back screen door slammed.

"Lloyd home," Lillian said, as I crammed the slip of paper in my pocket.

"Not a word to him, Lillian, about any of this. Just that his mother's coming home tomorrow. That's all he needs to know."

Lloyd walked into the kitchen, propping his tennis racket against the wall as he headed for the counter and the snack that Lillian had put out for him. "Who needs to know what?" he asked. "Is mama all right?"

"She's fine, getting better all the time. We were just talking about that new doctor who's proved that he knows all he needs to know." Quickly changing the subject, I went on. "We'll be bringing your mother home in the morning."

His face lit up. "Tomorrow? Oh, wow, I'm glad about that." He put down a half-eaten banana and pushed back his wet hair. "We had to play indoors again today 'cause the courts were too wet to use." He reached for his racket, then struck with a sudden thought, said, "Is it all right if I walk downtown and buy some flowers for her room? The rain's about stopped and I've got some money."

"That's a wonderful idea. She'll have to stay in bed for a few days, so flowers in her room will be perfect. Here," I said, searching in my pocketbook for a couple of twenties, "take this with you and get something bright and pretty from Sam and me. If they're too awkward to carry, just have them delivered this afternoon. I know it's late in the day, but don't let them put you off. I've done enough business with that florist for them to go the extra mile for me."

ॐ

The next morning dawned hot and cloud-less with everything looking fresh and green from the rain, a far cry from the usual dog days of August. Before going in to breakfast, I went up to Hazel Marie's room to open the draperies and to turn down her bed. Looking over our preparations for her return, I couldn't help but think that she'd have to realize how important she was to us.

When I got to the dining room, I found Lloyd so excited about his mother's imminent discharge from the hospital that he could hardly sit still long enough to eat a decent breakfast. He kept saying how glad he was that it was a Saturday, so he didn't have to go to his tennis clinic.

"I wouldn't learn a thing," he said, grinning across the breakfast table at me. "My mind would be on Mama coming home, and everybody'd be acing me right and left."

I agreed, realizing that I had the same excited expectation of Hazel Marie's return as he had. Ignoring the nagging worry of what our next step would be, I turned to Sam, "Sam, her bedroom looks like a florist's shop. You should peek in and see. Everybody we know has sent flowers or cookies or books or something. Lillian has the best sheets on her bed with half-a-dozen pillows propped up on it. A few days of bed rest won't be a hardship at all. And," I went on, meeting Sam's eyes over my coffee cup, "bed rest means just that. No visitors, no phone calls and nobody asking personal questions."

"I can visit, can't I?" Lloyd asked. "I won't ask any questions, except maybe, 'How're you feeling?'"

"You're not a visitor," Sam said, with a pat on the boy's arm. "You're family, and family doesn't come under the no-visiting rule."

Lillian pushed in from the kitchen, bearing a basket of hot biscuits. Just as I reached out to take it from her, a jolt of fear brought us all to a sudden standstill— my hand hanging in the air, Lillian holding out the basket, Lloyd's water glass halfway to his mouth and Sam's fork clattering to his plate.

An eerie wail like "Whoo-oo, whoo-oo," then "Whoo-oo" again, reverberated from a distance, but closing in fast. "What's that?" Lloyd cried as he sprang out of his chair.

We stared at each other, our eyes getting bigger as the ululation neared the house. Then a flash of dark clothing zipped past the dining room windows, and we heard the slap of outsized running shoes on the paved driveway. Then someone began banging on the back door, hitting it so hard that the screen rattled on its hinges.

Sam was on his feet, heading for the door, with Lloyd right behind him, as Lillian, her eyes big with fear, dropped the basket, scattering biscuits everywhere. I clasped the edge of the table with both hands, not knowing whether to get under it or go see what the trouble was.

"Lord he'p us!" Lillian cried, as a loud voice bellowed "Mr. Sam! Mr. Sam!" out in the kitchen. "That nobody but that worthless James! What he doin' scarin' everybody out of they wits?"

We pushed through the swinging door into the kitchen to see James leaning over, his hands on his knees, trying to catch his breath, while Sam tried to get a straight answer out of him.

"Mr. Sam," James puffed, "you got to come quick. I never seen the like. Ever'thing all messed up and broke into and strewed all over the place. You got to come quick."

"James," Sam said, leading him to a

chair. "James, calm down and tell me what happened."

James sank heavily into a kitchen chair, mopped his face, and looked up at Sam. "Somebody done broke in yo' house, Mr. Sam, an' I don't know but what they still in there."

Chapter 10

"Call nine-one-one, Julia," Sam said. "Come on, James, let's get over there."

"Sam, no!" I cried. "Not if somebody's still there."

"If they were, they'll be gone by now. Tell the officers to meet us there. Get up, James, and let's go."

James wasn't all that eager to leave the safety of our house, but he dragged himself up and followed Sam out the door. And, just as I punched in the emergency number with shaking hands, Lloyd dashed out after them.

"Lillian," I said, motioning to her to stop

him, but my call was immediately answered and I had to report the breaking and entering at Sam's house.

I hung up the phone and turned to scold Lillian for letting Lloyd go, just in time to see her crawl into Sam's car with the rest of them. It backed out of the drive and was gone.

"Well," I said to nobody, "I guess I'm left behind to clean up the kitchen." Which was just as well, since bringing in dishes from the dining room and stacking them in the sink gave me time to calm my nerves. Hearing sirens converging a few blocks away, I could only hope that Sergeant Coleman Bates was one of the responders. As a personal friend, he would make sure that a thorough investigation was carried out.

But who could've broken into Sam's house? And why? Sam didn't keep any valuable items there, so what could they have wanted? Well, I sighed, it was vandals, most likely, or somebody just looking for empty houses to rob. It had become common practice to have a friend stay in a house just so it wouldn't be empty during the time a family was participating in a wedding or a funeral—a poor commentary on the current state of the world in my opinion.

After clearing the dining table of crumbs, picking up biscuits from the floor, and putting the centerpiece back into place, with still no call from Sam, I decided to go see for myself what was going on. Then, glancing at my watch, I realized that time had gotten away from me.

"Goodness," I mumbled, searching for the car keys and my pocketbook, "if I'm late getting to the hospital, no telling what Hazel Marie will do. She could think we don't want her home, get her feelings hurt, and take off for parts unknown."

So as concerned as I was about the goings-on at Sam's house, I had no choice but to go to the hospital and bring Hazel Marie home. And it was a good thing I made that decision, for I found her already dressed and waiting for me in a wheelchair.

"Hazel Marie!" I exclaimed. "Honey, are you too weak to walk?"

"I don't think so, but it's hospital policy. Everybody has to be wheeled out." Then, looking away from me, she mumbled, "I thought maybe you weren't coming. I thought you'd changed your mind about me coming home."

"Oh, Hazel Marie," I said, immediately contrite for being even a few minutes late. "You mustn't think that. Of course, we want you home, everybody is so excited to have you back. It's just that the strangest thing happened this morning. Somebody broke into Sam's house during the night, and James came running over, scared to death. You can imagine how upset we all were, so naturally my schedule was completely disrupted."

"Somebody broke in? What for?" Hazel Marie's face, already strained from worry and digestive upsets, took on another layer of concern.

"I don't have an idea in the world. Sam and Lillian and Lloyd took off with James while I was calling for help, so I came here instead of going there. Now, Hazel Marie, where's your suitcase and what're we going to do with all these flowers?"

"They said an orderly would bring everything on a cart, but I told them to give most of the flowers to the other patients. Was that all right?"

"Of course. It's a lovely thought, but we better take that dish garden LuAnne sent. You know she'll ask about it."

Hazel Marie's hand immediately covered her face, as she bowed her head. "I don't want LuAnne to know about me," she said as tears began to flow.

"LuAnne's not going to know a thing, and nobody else is, either. I've already put out the word that the doctor ordered complete bed rest with no visitors, which he should've done even though he didn't. But that'll give you time to recuperate at your own pace, and time for us all to make the appropriate decisions. And time, too, I might add, for you to build up your strength. I declare, Hazel Marie, you're no bigger than a minute. I hope you've gotten your appetite back. You're eating for two now, you know."

While getting her home and settling her in bed, I kept up a constant stream of chatter, not only to keep her mind off her situation but also to keep mine off what was happening at Sam's house. No one was at home when we arrived, so I remained in the dark about the break-in and wasn't too happy about it. Still, Hazel Marie was my first order of business, so I proceeded to impress on her the importance of her health and well-being.

Drawing a chair close to her bed, I said, "Now, Hazel Marie, I know that women in your condition need exercise as well as a nourishing diet. However, I think you should confine yourself to your room for a while and not be out walking around. We don't want people thinking they can drop in and visit, and we don't want them wondering why you're not at the book club or at church or in Sunday school if you're seen moving about. We'll just let it be known that you have a long recuperation period. But the longer you lay around, the less likely you are to want to eat. Remember that old saying about women losing a tooth for each child they have? We don't want that to happen, so I want you to go heavy on milk and cheese and things like that. And vegetables and fruit, of course. Lillian will know what all you need."

She turned her head away from me and whispered, "What does Lillian think of me? And Mr. Sam?"

"I'll tell you the truth, Lillian is walking on air. She is thrilled at the thought of a new little baby in the house. And Sam, well, you know Sam. He is the least judgmental man in the world, and he's absolutely convinced that Mr. Pickens will be back here any minute to take care of you."

"I don't want him back," she said with a quiver in her voice, as well as a trace of determined will. "I don't want to see him. I don't even want to hear from him. He had his chance, and, Miss Julia, I've learned a few things from you. I know now that everybody has to look after themselves. And that's what I'm going to do. I got myself in this fix by depending on somebody else, but no more and not ever again. I'll take care of myself. And Lloyd. And this baby. As soon as I get over this hyperemmy-whatever-it-is, I'm going to move away and do it on my own. I've learned that there're times when you just do what you have to do, whether you like it or not."

I let her words hang in the air, as I gathered myself to deal with her new commitment to independence. Finally, feeling my way, I said, "I think that's commendable of you, Hazel Marie, but I hope you'll let us help you any way we can."

"Well," she said, a little more subdued

by my seeming agreement with her plans, "I just don't want to bring any shame down on your head. Can you imagine me staying here as I get bigger and bigger and the talk gets worse and worse? I know they'll cut me off, but I don't want them to do it to you. So the best thing is for me to go somewhere else. We can tell people that I've taken a job in, I don't know, maybe Florida." Her face took on a dreamy look. "I've always wanted to live near the beach."

"That's what we'll do, then," I said, crossing my fingers as I said it. "But I hope you'll at least consider leaving Lloyd here during your confinement. I mean, what would you do with him when you have to go to the hospital for childbirth? And this coming school year may be his best yet. He'll be in the honor society and he has a class office. It'd be hard on him to move to another school."

She started crying again, moved by the realization of all the lives she'd be changing and uprooting. "I don't know if I could leave him. I'd miss him so bad, but I do want to do the right thing."

A little late for that, I thought, but, of course, didn't say. I was pleased enough that she was at least considering the possibility of leaving Lloyd with us. And I might say at this point that I had no intention for her to leave at all, much less take Lloyd with her. But there's more than one way to skin a cat, and my intention was to keep her here and happy until Sam could find Mr. Pickens. And if it took agreeing with her plans to move, even seeming to aid and abet her with them, why, I was willing to do just that.

And don't tell me that I was engaging in deceit and deception, or that the ends never justify the means. Like Hazel Marie said, and as I myself had said many times before, you do what you have to do.

Hazel Marie shifted in bed, propping her pillows so she could sit up straighter. I knew she had expected me to put up a bigger fuss over her plans to leave, but I was after larger game.

"Well, right now," she said, watching me intently, "I think I have to take Lloyd with me. I could send him back when the baby is due, if you wouldn't mind."

My heart gave a lurch, but I just nodded. "Whatever you think best, Hazel Marie. See that bud vase on your dresser? He bought those two roses with his own money just for you."

She smiled as her eyes filled with tears again. I handed her the Kleenex box. "He is so sweet," she said. "I just couldn't go off and leave him."

"I know," I murmured agreeably. "But you do need to think carefully how you're going to tell him about your condition."

That brought on a full-scale crying fit, but finally she pulled herself together. "It's all my fault," she said. "And now so many people're being hurt. I'd do anything, Miss Julia, anything in the world to make this right."

"Well," I dared to venture, "one thing that would make it right is for you and Mr. Pickens to marry."

"No," she said, shaking her head. "Anything but that. I am not going to chase after him to make him do what he doesn't want to do. I know it's a bit late to be standing on principle, but I have to some time or other."

Principle, I thought, *huh.* She was standing on sinking sand, if she wanted my opinion. But she didn't, so I didn't give it.

"So," she went on, "please don't tell him.

Promise me that you won't. I'm serious about this, Miss Julia, please promise me."

"I do promise you, Hazel Marie. Besides, he's unavailable at any of the places I know, and nobody seems to know where he is. So you have my word. I will not contact him in any way, shape, or form."

Of course, I am never comfortable saying one thing and doing another, or of telling stories, or of letting someone believe what they wanted to, but I deemed it judicious of me to placate the sick, which Hazel Marie was.

My promise, so readily given, seemed to ease her mind, and mine, too, as well as my conscience, for I had no intention of contacting Mr. Pickens. Sam and Lillian had that job well in hand, and I was pleased enough to leave it to them.

Chapter 11

Hearing a commotion downstairs, I got up and went out in the hall to look over the stairwell. "Lloyd," I called. "Your mother's home."

I heard the thud of his feet running through the house and clamoring up the stairs. "She's home? Where is she? Mama, where are you?"

"She's in bed, Lloyd," I said as he gained the upstairs hall. "And she's feeling a lot better. Run in and stay with her a while. I need to talk to Sam."

"Mama, wait till you hear what happened,"

he said as he flew past me, running to his mother's bed.

Hearing them greet each other as if they'd been separated for months, I had a sinking feeling that my plan to keep him with me might not be the best one I'd ever had. How could I even consider letting Hazel Marie go away without him? Those two had faced shame and censure together; yet for all of that, Hazel Marie had raised as fine a boy as ever lived.

So, if she absolutely rejected Mr. Pickens's proposal—if we ever got him to his knees in the first place—maybe she and Lloyd could manage on their own again. Hating even to consider losing them, I resolved to hound Mr. Pickens to the ends of the earth if that's what it took.

"Julia!"

Sam was at the bottom of the stairs, calling, so I hurried to meet him. "What happened, Sam? Is everything all right?"

"As all right as it can be, considering. You got Hazel Marie home?"

"Yes, she's upstairs. But tell me about the break-in."

He took my hand and began to lead me

into the living room, just as Lillian came by with a tray of food for Hazel Marie. "We got to fatten that little woman up," she said. "She eatin' for two now."

"Lillian," I said, stopping her, "the doctor said she shouldn't have anything spicy or rich until we're sure her stomach has settled. Just small portions of bland food several times a day."

"Yessum, I know. You done tol' me."

"Well, so I did. But listen, do be careful what you say in front of Lloyd. Remember, he doesn't know about the you-know-what."

"Oh, that's right. I be careful, don't you worry. He won't know a thing from me. But sooner or later, he gonna know."

I followed Sam into the living room and we sat in our usual place on the sofa. For some reason, perhaps because I'd been thinking of Hazel Marie and her first foray into illegitimacy, I thought of how Wesley Lloyd and I had never sat together. He had always taken the chair to the right of the fireplace and I'd taken the opposite one, with never the twain meeting.

No longer, though, for Sam and I just naturally flowed together. Where one went, the other was sure to follow. He was the kind of man who liked to touch, sometimes with his hand on mine or an arm around my shoulders or waist or sometimes with just a meeting of the eyes. It had taken me some little while to become accustomed to such demonstrations of affection, public and otherwise. Now, though, I'd be lost without them.

"Tell me what happened, Sam," I said. "I've been so worried about your house."

"Well, first off, let me say that I'm sorry you had to get Hazel Marie on your own. I fully intended to go with you, but I tell you, Julia, that house is a wreck. The back storm door had been taken off the hinges, and the window in the back door itself was broken. Then whoever it was just reached inside, unlocked it, and walked right in."

"Oh, my. I was half hoping that James was exaggerating, since he's fairly well known for doing that."

"No, he wasn't exaggerating. Everything in the kitchen cabinets was strewn all over the floor, chairs turned over in the living and dining rooms, mattresses upended and slashed and papers and books thrown everywhere. I can't tell you how disheartening it is to see it."

"Did they steal anything? Or could you tell?"

"Not anything obvious. But I don't keep anything really valuable there."

"But, Sam, you have some fine pieces of furniture. None of that was gone?"

"No, but I might've overlooked something small. Coleman and several deputies got there right after we did, and they sorta took over, trying to figure out who might've done it. There's not much I can do till they're through."

"Oh, I'm glad Coleman came. I'd rather have Coleman on the job than anybody. Unless," I said, sitting up with a sudden thought, "it's Mr. Pickens. That's what you can do, Sam! Hire him to solve this case. He'll come back to help you, I know he will."

Sam smiled and pulled me back closer. "I don't think we'll need a case to entice him back, but I'll keep it in mind. But what I've got to do now is get over there and begin straightening things. Coleman wants me to go through everything as soon as they're finished and be sure nothing is missing."

"I'll help you with that."

"I hope you will. I've already got James calling around to get the doors fixed, and I told him to start on the kitchen as soon as the deputies're through."

"We should've put burglar alarms on that house," I said, "and this one, too. But that one stays empty every night, and I'm sorry we didn't think of it before. Now it's like locking the barn door after the horse is gone."

"It is that," Sam agreed. "But you're right. We should have both houses wired to an alarm in the sheriff's department. I'll take care of that today." He stood up, then said, "I'll run up and speak to Hazel Marie first, though."

"No, Sam, better not," I said, putting out a hand to stop him. "She'll make you promise not to contact Mr. Pickens, then where would we be? In fact, to keep that from happening, maybe you should stay away from her until you find him."

Sam nodded. "You may be right. Well, tell her I asked about her, but that Coleman needs me at the house."

While we were eating lunch, Coleman called to tell Sam that they were through with their clue-searching business and that he should get started on a list of anything missing. After running up to tell Hazel Marie that we'd be at Sam's house for the afternoon and ask if she needed anything, I asked Lillian to stay with her. Lloyd was torn between staying with his mother and accompanying us to the burglarized house. He ended up going with us, since investigating a burglary was more exciting than watching Hazel Marie take a nap. He felt bad about it, though, and ran back several times during the afternoon to look in on her.

To say that the sight of Sam's elegant home so torn up was disheartening is an understatement. I could've cried as I surveyed what had been done to it. As we waded into the shambles and began to set chairs upright and replace cushions, it looked more and more as if the perpetrators had destroyed just for the unhealthy thrill of it. Cushions and mattresses had been sliced open and the foam pulled out. A layer of down feathers was all over the living room, causing James to sneeze his head off. When I couldn't stand the eruptions any longer, I sent him back to the kitchen and told him to stay there.

I was purely sickened by the senseless damage, realizing that we'd have to have almost everything reupholstered. But other than that, the only real destruction was a couple of smashed television sets and a French porcelain lamp that lay in shattered pieces in the front hall. I did tear up a little when I saw it, for I'd kept meaning to take that lamp home with me and had never gotten around to it.

Finally, after we'd made some headway in the straightening process, Lloyd and Sam began to pick up the books and papers that were scattered all along the hall and especially in Sam's study where the worst of the destruction had taken place. His desk drawers had been pulled out and the contents dumped, books thrown off the shelves, and his computer kicked in with wires left dangling.

I walked up behind Sam as he stood with slumped shoulders, gazing at the ruined computer. I put my arms around him and laid my head against his back. I knew he was looking at the loss of all he'd worked on for so long.

"I'm so sorry, Sam," I said. "This is just awful. Who could've done such a thing?"

He put his hands on my arms where they wrapped around him. "I don't know, Julia. At this point, I can't even guess who or why."

"But all your work, Sam! Years of research and writing and putting things together—it's all gone. But, listen," I said, turning him to face me as I struggled to reassure him, "you can do it all again. You've got all that information in your head, and that's a better computer than anybody can make. Please don't be discouraged, and don't let this deter you. I know you hate to have to start from scratch, but you can do it."

"Well," he said, looking somewhat pleased with himself, "hardly from scratch." He reached into his pocket and pulled out a tiny black tube. "See this? It's a flash drive and it has every word that was on the computer in it."

"Everything? In that little thing? Oh, Sam, if that's true, you are the most fore-sighted man I've ever known."

"Oh, I doubt that. It's common practice to back up your work with one of these things. But," he went on, glancing around at the paper- and book-strewn room, "there's all this to deal with. My reference notes, my sources, and most of all the copies I made of public documents—most of that wasn't on the computer to begin with. I've got to get them in order, or I'll be going back and redoing a couple of years worth of work."

It was going to be a job, for papers—yellow pages torn from legal pads, smudged photocopied sheets, and torn scraps with notes jotted down—practically covered the floor of the study and the front hall. Some pages had been wadded up and thrown aside, while others had been ripped in two and strewn around. It was plain to see that many had been stepped on, but who knew if they were our footprints or those of the deputies or of the villians, themselves? It was purely a shame because Sam was such a neat and orderly soul who took pleasure in knowing exactly where everything was.

"Let's get to it then," I said, bending down to scoop up an armful of papers. "You sit down, Sam, and Lloyd and I'll do the picking up and bring it all to you. You can begin arranging the pages into some kind of order since we can't help you with that."

"Okay," he said with a heavy sigh. "That's

probably the best way to tackle it. Thank you, Julia, but don't overdo it. When you get tired, just say so and we'll stop."

But how could I ever get tired of helping this wonderful man? I was happy to be able to do something for him, although I admit that by the time we crawled into bed that night my back was aching from all the bending over and lifting I'd done throughout the afternoon.

But we had made a dent in the mess, although it would be some time before Sam's house was back in its original condition. To my mind, though, the break-in was merely a distraction from the real problem, which was Hazel Marie upstairs, growing by the minute, and Mr. Pickens going blithely on his way with no conception of what he'd left behind.

Chapter 12

"Sam?" I said, sighing as I put aside the Sunday edition of the *Abbotsville Times* where Maureen Dowd's column ran about once a month. I looked forward to reading it because the woman couldn't find a kind word to say about anybody in politics. Even though her column brought forth a spate of complaints to the editor about rampant liberalism, I enjoyed her waspish comments as long as she aimed at somebody I didn't like. Otherwise, I could take her or leave her. This Sunday afternoon, I left her and turned my attention to the vexatious matter of Hazel Marie.

"Hm-m?" Sam answered, his mind on the front page articles. He had been at his house all morning trying to make greater inroads on the disorder. He'd bypassed both Sunday school and church, since his ox was truly in the ditch in spite of Pastor Ledbetter's frown at my explanation of his absence.

"I've been thinking."

Sam lowered the paper. "Uh-oh."

"No, now, listen. I'm thinking that when you locate Mr. Pickens, you shouldn't even mention Hazel Marie and certainly not her condition. Just make it purely business. And by the way, what have you done about finding him? We don't have all the time in the world, you know. That baby'll be here before we know it."

"I'm on it, Julia. I called the phone number Lillian got this morning, thinking it was a good time to catch him in. Nobody answered and there's no answering machine."

"I suppose it's too much to hope that he was in church somewhere."

"I expect so," Sam said, smiling. "But I was able to find out that it's a residential number, so I got an address. Sounds like an apartment of some kind, which makes sense if he's just moved. The next thing I'm going to do is what you suggested and contact his real estate agent. He does have his house on the market, which I'll admit surprises me. So it looks as if they really have broken up." Sam shook his head in disbelief. "It's hard to take in, him just giving up and moving off without a word to any of us."

"He's hurting, Sam, that's why. He thinks if he can get far enough away, he can deal with it better. But," I said with a knowing nod, "Charlotte's hardly far enough, in my opinion. But, Sam, here's the thing. When you do talk to him, don't tell him why we want him back here. We don't know what's gone on between those two, and he might think she's really through with him. Or, who knows, he might have his back up so much that he's through with her. He could turn you down flat."

"I don't think so, Julia. Pickens'll do the right thing. All he needs is to know that the right thing is called for."

"Maybe so, but I don't want to risk it. He's just as liable to run amok as not. So I think you should leave Hazel Marie out of the conversation entirely. Just tell him that you need him to look into the break-in at your house. Hire him, Sam. Sign a contract or whatever you do when you put a private investigator to work. He won't turn you down, he thinks too much of you. And," I went on, getting into my story, "even if nothing's missing at your house, make up something that you need him to look for. Anything will do, just so there's some urgency about finding it and, of course, finding out who did the breaking and entering. Offer a reward if you have to. I just think that if you put it to him that this is a purely business proposition, he's more likely to respond. And once he's here, why, then we'll just see what happens. But you have to impress on him that you need him right away. Time is of the essence, you know."

Sam stared off into the distance, which ended at the opposite wall of the living room, until I had to give him a little nudge with my elbow. "Sam?"

"I'm thinking, Julia," he said, "and, as it happens, I don't have to make up something. It's looking more and more like a few things are missing." He sighed and brushed his hand over his thick white hair that so distinguished him. "Of course, I haven't completely brought order out of all the chaos, but there were some papers that I was specifically looking for. And, so far, I haven't found them."

"Oh, surely you will, though. I don't know how you could find anything in all that mess, but we stayed at it long enough last night." It had been close to midnight the evening before when we'd gotten home from his house, having left everything but his papers in a semblance of order. "To say nothing of the work you did this morning. Do you want to go back over there now? Just tell me what you're looking for, and I'll help you find it."

He shook his head. "No, I'm pretty sure those papers are gone. I had them in a special folder, a red one that I used specifically for them. It would be easy to find if it was there. The only thing I know to do is go back to the courthouse tomorrow and start recopying."

"That's too bad, but at least they're not irretrievably gone."

"No, it just means some lost time, repeating what I've already done."

"Well," I said, patting his hand, "you have plenty of that, so it'll work out."

He smiled. "Yep, time's what I do have, but it'll be tedious. What I found was in several different files and cases, which I'm not sure anybody has ever put together before, or seen the connections. The same two names run consistently through them all."

"Two people?" I sat up straight and looked at him. "Then that's who broke in. Who are they?"

"Well, that's just it. They're both dead."

"Oh, Sam," I said, grabbing his arm, "a mystery! It's a perfect case for Mr. Pickens to investigate. You won't have to make up a thing. You really do need him."

❦

Later in the afternoon, I walked up the stairs to Hazel Marie's room to visit the sick and ailing. I found her out of bed, sitting in one of the pink velvet slipper chairs beside the front window.

Her door was open so I walked in. "How're you feeling, Hazel Marie?"

"All right, I guess," she said. She smoothed her hand down the silk peignoir she was wearing, her eyes downcast. "At least, my appetite's coming back a little."

"And you're keeping everything down?" I sat across from her in the matching chair.

She nodded. "So far, so good." She turned away from me to look out the window. She still found it hard to meet my eyes. "The medicine helps even though it makes me sleepy. But I should be able to leave in a day or two if you can put up with me that long."

"Oh, Hazel Marie, please don't say that. I don't want you to leave at all. If you'd only reconsider, we could come up with something that would make it easier for you."

She gave me a quick glance, then turned her eyes away again. "There's nothing that'll make it easier."

"Well, let me think about it." So I did for a second or two. "How about this? What if we say you married an old friend but didn't tell anybody because you realized right away that you'd made a mistake. You're in the process of getting a divorce and, that way, Hazel Marie, everybody will admire you for having the baby even though your heart is broken."

She managed a faint smile. "I can see us spreading that around. LuAnne and Emma Sue would want to know the details—when we were married, how long we lived to-gether, and why you didn't know anything about it. They'd be counting on their fingers and coming up with more questions. They all know about J.D., too, and they'd be ask-ing what happened to him." She took a Kleenex from her pocket and dabbed at her eyes. "Besides, I'm not very good at telling stories. Somebody would ask me some-thing and I wouldn't know what to say."

She was right about that. Hazel Marie was as open and honest as the day is long, and I knew there was no way she could carry off an involved story like the one I'd just dreamed up. Emma Sue, with the best will in the world, would ask her a question and Hazel Marie would be like a deer in the middle of the road, too stunned to move, much less answer.

"Well," I said, "maybe that's not such a good idea, but I'd be willing to try it if it would keep you here. I want you to know how much we all care for you."

That brought on a full-blown spate of sobs and more apologies for letting me down and bringing shame on my head.

"Listen, now," I said, when she was able to listen. "Just don't do anything for a week or so. Say, two or three. You're still recovering, and it would be awful if you went some place far off and got sick again. You shouldn't even think of moving until you're strong and healthy and able to make some wise decisions. I mean, you'll need to decide just where you'll go, and then make arrangements for a place to live and find out what kind of doctors are there." I stopped and did a little looking around myself as I approached the subject of greatest concern. "What have you told Lloyd? Have you talked to him?"

She shook her head. "No'm, not yet. I'm not sure I can, I'm just dreading it so. Because as soon as I do, he'll know what kind of mother he has."

"Now listen to me," I said, leaning toward her. "All he needs to know is that you were in love and planning to be married. Eventually, at least, because you were. Lloyd and everybody else knows how much you loved Mr. Pickens, so they're not going to blame you. Lloyd certainly won't."

I could hardly believe I'd said such a thing, and further, that I firmly believed it. Never before had I been known to offer any excuse for such behavior as Hazel Marie had so obviously indulged in. Yet here I was, not only excusing it, but finding justification for it, and using *love*, of all nebulous and unreliable things, to justify it. There was a time, not so long ago, when I would've averted my eyes and walked on past any unmarried mother-to-be. There would have been some pity in my heart, knowing what the mother and her unborn child were up against, but my basic feeling would've been that she was reaping what she'd sown, and getting exactly what she deserved.

Well, you do live and learn, or at least, I do, especially when someone you care for finds herself in that kind of predicament. Things look a little different on the other side of the fence.

"Miss Julia?" Hazel Marie said, bringing me out of my reverie. "I've been thinking that there's something I could do. If I could bring myself to do it. I know other people have done it and been all right with it. I just don't know if I could."

"What's that, Hazel Marie?"

"Well," she said, needing the mascara-smeared Kleenex again for her eyes, "I could make up some story for Lloyd and leave him here. Then I could go off somewhere and have the baby and then . . ." She stopped, her voice hoarse with tears. "And then put the baby up for adoption." The Kleenex covered her face by this time as her shoulders began to shake. "Then I could come back and get Lloyd. He wouldn't have to know anything about it."

My first reaction was to lean over, put my hand on her arm and try to talk her out of such an extreme solution, so I did. "Oh, no, Hazel Marie, that would be too terrible. I can't bear the thought of you giving up that tiny baby and never knowing who it was or where it was. None of us would ever have a minute's peace if you did that. Please, let's think of something else."

But my second reaction, which I kept to myself, was that adopting that baby out would solve a multitude of problems. But only for us and only in the short run, not necessarily for the baby. Who knew who would adopt it? Who knew what kind of life it would have? The thought of a little one with Mr. Pickens's black eyes and Hazel Marie's sweet nature in the care of strangers filled me with an overwhelming sadness. What it would do to Hazel Marie, I couldn't imagine.

Then it hit me. The only reason either of us was thinking of hiding the existence of that baby was to keep us from being the topic of whispers and gossip. Well, and to keep a little immorality under wraps. But what if Hazel Marie stayed home, grew noticeably and publicly larger, and gave birth at Abbotsville General? Would the world come to an end? No, it wouldn't. Oh, there'd be talk, all right, and she'd be snubbed and excluded from parties and clubs and whatnot, as I would be, too, since she'd be doing it with my approval.

Well, I was getting tired of the same old social whirl anyway. All it was was the same people saying and doing the same things over and over. I could do without that. Pastor Ledbetter might drum us out of the church, but there were other churches that would welcome us and our tithes with open arms.

The more I thought about it, the better it seemed. Contrast a little snubbing against a child turned out to fend for itself, and there was no contest. All Hazel Marie would have to do was hold her head up high and go right on with her business, knowing that she was accepting the care and the responsibility for what she had put in play.

The only one who might suffer from having a mother who was having a second illegitimate slip was Lloyd. I hated the thought of him being the brunt of jokes and jeers, but if it got too bad, there was always boarding school. Although that was another extreme solution I could hardly bear to consider. Still, I suspected that he'd weathered the same responses to bastardy before this and he'd come out, as far as I could see, unscathed.

By this time, I'd about convinced myself that if the boy were told everything, given all the options to consider, that he'd come down on the side of keeping his little brother or sister and riding out the storm.

But it wasn't my decision to make. It was Hazel Marie's. She, however, could be swayed and I might try to do just that. I mentally shuddered at the thought of going about my usual activities around town with Hazel Marie in tow, and her as big as a house, and everybody shaking their heads in dismay at our blatant disregard for appearances. It wasn't something I would look forward to, but I could do it if it meant keeping Lloyd with us and that baby out of the hands of a stranger.

But first, we had to give Mr. Pickens a chance. If we could find him, and if Sam was right that he would do the right thing.

Lord, my head was reeling with just the thought that Hazel Marie might give that baby up for adoption. I'd played along with all her proposals for solving the problem so that she would continue to confide in me and so that I would know how to talk her out of some of her more drastic schemes. It seemed to me that her head would be reeling, too, thinking up first one thing and then another and none of them worth a lick, especially when there was a simple, quick, and perfect resolution to everything. I was convinced that if I could get Mr. Pickens delivered before that baby was, Hazel Marie would snap him up and never look back.

"Hazel Marie?" I said, lowering my voice and leaning close. "If Mr. Pickens . . ."

She jerked upright. "No. No, ma'am, I just can't." Then she covered her face with the Kleenex and folded up on herself. "Oh, I'm sorry, Miss Julia, I didn't mean to snap at you. I'm really sorry. It's just that I can't . . . I mean, I don't want him anywhere around.

I just hate him, and he's no help, anyway." She lowered the Kleenex and took a deep breath. "It's my problem, and he doesn't have anything to do with it."

Well, it seemed to me that he'd already had plenty to do with it, but I'd just learned my lesson: Stay off the subject of Mr. Pickens. At least until we could get him here, which had better be soon or she'd be so wedded to the idea of going it alone that not even his black-eyed charm would be able to deter her.

Chapter 13

Late the next morning, I was back in Hazel Marie's room, chatting with her. Trying to keep her spirits up, I described the break-in at Sam's house and what a trial it was proving to be to get things back in order. She was properly dismayed at the thought of such heedless destruction, but plainly it was not a matter of immediate concern to her. Too much else on her mind, I supposed, even though I was doing my best to distract her by listing off the problems that other people were facing.

And one of those problems was having everybody in town knowing about the break-in and having to fend off the result-ing phone calls. Wouldn't you know that the *Abbotsville Times* ran it on the front page? Lawyer's home vandalized the head-ing read above two paragraphs and con-tinued on the back page. The article said no more than we already knew, namely that the sheriff had no suspects and the investigation was ongoing. The whole thing vexed me because that house was no lon-ger Sam's *home*. Since he now lived with me, it was his *former* home and now only his *house*. I wished they'd get the particu-lars right.

But hearing Sam come in downstairs, I hurriedly went down to join him.

"Sam?" I said, meeting him in the hall. "You're home early. Have you finished?"

"I think I have," he said, wiping his hand across his face. He looked more tired and dispirited than I'd ever seen him. "It's no use, Julia, more than papers are missing. I had five cassettes of interviews that weren't transcribed, and they aren't there. I doubt I can replace them. Now that this has hap-pened, people will have second thoughts about talking to me."

"Oh, Sam, surely not."

"'Fraid so," he said with a shake of his head. "I called one woman this morning and she hung up on me. And remember Rafe Feldman? I interviewed him a while back, but his mind is completely gone now. And even worse," he said, slumping into a chair, looking beaten, "I just spent an hour or so at the courthouse and the records I needed to replace what's missing are gone, too."

I stood over him, unable to take in what I was hearing. "You mean, somebody has taken them from the public domain? That's not legal, is it?"

"Hardly," he said with a rueful smile. "Somebody has been awfully busy wiping out what it took me so long to put together." He leaned over, resting his arms on his knees. "Actually, it'd be hard to walk out of there with an armload of files, so chances are they're still there, just misfiled. But Lord, it'd take forever to find them. I mean, we're talking records from a period of over ten years, Julia, and they were filed some forty years ago."

"Can't you find them on a computer somewhere? I thought that was where everything was these days."

He shook his head. "No, they haven't got that far back yet. Everything current is computerized, but it's taking years for the clerks to enter the back records."

"Maybe you can do without them. I expect you remember most of whatever was in the records."

Sam smiled at me. "I need the documentation, honey. I can't just write what I think, or even know, without backing it up with citations of case numbers, dates, and so on. It's looking more and more like I'll have to give it up."

"Oh, no, Sam, you can't do that. You've put too much time and effort into it. And, listen, this theft is proof positive that what you're doing has value. Why else would anybody want to keep you from doing it?" I stopped and sat down beside him. Taking his arm, I went on. "Two things, Sam. One, figure out who wouldn't want you to write whatever you were writing and that's your thief. And, two, you really do need Mr. Pickens."

"Well," he said with a pleased smile, "that's what I came to tell you. Pickens is on his way."

I flopped back against the sofa, relief

flooding my soul. "Well, thank the Lord." My relief didn't last long, for I sat up with a jerk. "You didn't tell him about Hazel Marie, did you?"

Sam shook his head. "No, I made him a business proposition and he took it. He's going to stay at my house while he looks into the case."

"Oh, but that's perfect, Sam. Lloyd will be in and out over there, so he'll certainly see him. Then *he* can tell his mother, and you know he'll tell Mr. Pickens that she's been sick. So they'll both get to know about the other. And that way, you and I won't have a thing to do with it. There's no way she can be upset with us. Well, with me, since I'm the one who did the promising.

"Now," I went on, doing a little distance gazing myself, "we'll have to think of some way to get them together. I've never known Hazel Marie to be so adamant about anything, but she insists that she's through with him. I mean, ordinarily she's as pliable as she can be, always willing and eager to please." I thought about how Hazel Marie had expressed such a sudden and unusual antipathy toward Mr. Pickens. So unlike her normal self. "You know what

I think it is? I think it's all those hormones that women in her condition have to deal with. You may not know this, Sam, but a lot of women are just completely turned off of their husbands the whole time they're expecting."

Sam's eyebrows went up, but I couldn't read the expression on his face. "Is that right?"

"Yes, but the thing is, as soon as the baby comes, why, the mother's attitude changes right back to the way it was before."

"I guess that's why they generally have more than one baby."

"Oh, I think you're right about that. But what I'm getting at is that Hazel Marie may be one of those women, and if we let her run Mr. Pickens off for good while she's this way, why, she'll regret it in nine months. Eight months, I mean, or is it seven? I better find out how long we have."

Sam nodded. "Shall we tell Lloyd that Pickens is coming?"

I had to think for a minute, then I said, "I think not. At least, not right away. Let's let Mr. Pickens get here, get settled at your house, and firmly involved in the case.

Then we can tell Lloyd, or just let him discover Mr. Pickens's presence on his own. Because you know he'll run tell his mother as soon as he knows. I don't want to take the chance on her getting all upset before he even gets here. She might get it in her head to pack up and go off somewhere, or, who knows, she could get so perturbed that the baby would be endangered or marked in some way. You see, Sam, women in her condition have to be sheltered from any kind of distress or strong emotional upheaval."

I knew, since Sam and his first wife had had no children, that he was unfamiliar with how to deal with expectant mothers, so I felt it necessary to enlighten him. Of course, I had had no personal experience with such matters myself, but that didn't preclude my having heard them discussed at innumerable parties and meetings and in general discussions wherever women gathered together. After all, it didn't take actually having a baby to know all one needed to know. Just look at all the male obstetricians.

"So," I went on, "when is Mr. Pickens supposed to get here?"

"Tomorrow night. He has to wrap up a couple of things he's been working on in Charlotte, then he'll be on his way."

I thought for a few minutes. "Shall we ask him to dinner? You know he'll expect it, since he's never been in this town without Lillian feeding him something."

"No, he'll be late getting in. But we, or rather, you will have to decide about the following night. Are you going to just spring him on Hazel Marie or will you warn her beforehand?" Sam cocked an eyebrow at me. "Either way, she's going to have a fairly strong emotional upheaval."

"I think," I said, ignoring his last remark, "that I won't do either one. As far as Hazel Marie will know, I've been in the dark as much as she has. Why, Sam, I didn't have an idea in the world that you were calling on Mr. Pickens to investigate the break-in. You didn't say a word to me about it, and first thing I knew, here comes Mr. Pickens, all housed and contracted for. And, as far as having him for dinner every evening he's on the case, why, that's just my normal, courteous way of doing things." I looked wide-eyed and guileless at Sam, then broke into a smile. "How does that sound?"

He laughed. "Sounds fine to me. If you can pull it off, and if she'll believe you."

"Oh, she'll believe me because I promised her I wouldn't contact him. And I haven't, as you well know. Besides, if she can't bring herself to be in the same room with him, why, Lillian can take her a tray like she's been doing. At least we'll have them both in the same vicinity, and Lloyd can carry reports from one to the other, because I'm staying out of it." I stopped and cogitated for a minute. "Of course, that's not going to solve anything because she hasn't told Lloyd about the baby yet. So, for all intents and purposes, he's not going to have that much to report. You think we ought to tell him?"

"Us? Tell Lloyd about the baby?"

"Yes."

"No," Sam said, shaking his head. "Absolutely not. We have to leave that to her."

"Well, you're right, I guess. It's just that I can see both of them keeping their distance, with neither of them knowing the real reason he's been called back. How long can that go on? Mr. Pickens'll solve your case, I have no doubt, then he'll leave without even seeing her, much less marrying her. We'll really be up a creek then."

"I'll tell you what, Julia. Let's take it one step at a time. Have Pickens to dinner as often as you want. Hazel Marie will know he's here and he'll know she's here, so I think we can leave the rest of it up to them. And keep in mind that marriage might not be the best thing for them."

"Maybe," I said, *but maybe not*, I thought. One thing I knew for sure, if Mr. Pickens came just for dinner every night and Hazel Marie kept to her bed to avoid him, it would be up to me to think of a way to facilitate some movement from one to the other. Marriage might not be the right thing for those two, which I didn't believe for a minute, but it certainly was for what they'd engendered.

Chapter 14

LuAnne Conover, bright and cheerful, showed up at my door later in the day. She was laden down with a huge basket of fruit and a plastic bag full of magazines.

"My goodness," she said as she plopped the basket down on the floor. "That thing's heavy. How are you, Julia? We missed you in Sunday school yesterday, but I saw that you made it to church. I wanted to speak to you but you were out of there like a flash."

"Yes, I needed to hurry back to check on Hazel Marie. I felt I couldn't leave her for more than an hour, which was why I wasn't in Sunday school."

"Well, we were all glad you weren't. We discussed taking up a collection to buy this fruit basket for Hazel Marie, and it would've been awkward if you'd been there. Some," she said as she walked over to the sofa, "thought a fruit basket was too expensive and we ought to stick to a potted plant. Don't ask me who they were because I'm not going to tell you."

She sat down, and I joined her.

"I wouldn't ask for the world," I told her. "Besides, I can pretty much guess who they were. But I really do appreciate the thought and I know Hazel Marie will, too."

"Well, I hope she enjoys the fruit, too," LuAnne said, "because, believe me, it was expensive. But we all love Hazel Marie to death, and everybody is so concerned for her. But, tell me, Julia, what's wrong with her? I've heard all sorts of things from anemia to leukemia. You know how people are when they begin guessing and speculating."

Don't I ever, I thought. But I said, "I hope you can put a stop to those rumors because the doctor said it's some kind of condition with a long Latin name that causes digestive upsets. But it's curable with proper nutrition and bed rest for a considerable length of time. So that's the good news."

"What's the bad news?"

"Oh, there isn't any, just that she's lost a lot of weight and feels really tired. But we're all seeing to it that she gets plenty of rest and isn't disturbed in any way."

"Well, I certainly won't disturb her. I'll just tiptoe upstairs and speak to her. Everybody's expecting a firsthand report from me. That's why I was selected to bring the fruit basket. I'm so close to her, you know."

"Oh, LuAnne, I'm so sorry, but she really can't have visitors. Why, they even put a no visitors sign on her door at the hospital, and Dr. McKay was very firm about it when he let her come home. And, you know, if I let one person go up, everybody else will expect to, too. Please understand, because Hazel Marie would love to see you even though she can't."

"I won't tell anyone," LuAnne said, preparing to get to her feet. "Why don't you go up with me, and I'll just stick my head in the door and speak to her. Surely that wouldn't disturb her."

Lord, what else could I say to head her off?

I took a deep breath. "Well, LuAnne, if you want to know the truth, one quick visit from you probably wouldn't do any harm. But she has felt so bad for so long that she hasn't been able to keep up her appointments with Velma." I leaned toward her and whispered, "See, she hasn't had color for so long that all her dark roots are showing."

LuAnne laughed and settled back onto the sofa. "Well, bless her heart, I can certainly understand that, and I wouldn't embarrass her for the world. Besides, if she's well enough to worry about hair color, then I can give a good report on her condition. Now, listen, Julia," she went on, picking up the plastic bag she'd brought, "I did this on my own, so I want you to tell her that it's from me and not from the class. I wasn't sure what to get, so I brought her two of my favorites and two that I know she likes."

LuAnne pulled out two magazines: *People* and *Vanity Fair*, and placed them on the coffee table. "These shouldn't tax her strength too much," she said, "unless she starts reading some of the long articles in *Vanity Fair* about murders and drug use and so forth. You might caution her against those, but generally it's an interesting magazine, although the print's so small you can hardly read it."

"I'm sure she'll love them. You're very thoughtful, LuAnne, and I'll see that they're right beside her bed."

"Well, I'm not through. See," she said, pulling out two more magazines, "here's *Modern Bride* and *Martha Stewart Weddings*, because I know she loves to plan her wedding, even though it's doubtful she'll ever have one. But everybody needs a dream, don't they? I do hope hers will come true someday."

"Oh," I said fervently, "so do I." *More than you know,* I thought.

"You know what I was tempted to buy? *The Examiner, The Globe,* and *The Star*, because I've seen her at Velma's and that's all she reads. But," LuAnne said with a long-suffering sigh, "I knew you wouldn't approve, so I didn't."

"Why, I wouldn't care, LuAnne, even though they've been sued up one side and down the other for false reporting. But anything that would lift her spirits is fine with me." Although gossip-spreading tabloids were not my cup of tea, I knew that Hazel Marie loved them. In fact, along with wedding and decor magazines, they were about the extent of her regular reading material, but you can't expect everybody's taste to run along the same lines as your own.

"Well then," LuAnne said, "if that's the case, tell her I'll bring the new ones as soon as they come out. In a couple of days, I think it is. And you, Julia," she continued with a smile, "can keep your opinions to yourself. Now, I better get on home. Leonard'll be waiting for his lunch."

I thanked her again, then saw her out. Picking up the magazines and the fruit basket, which was indeed heavy, I struggled up the stairs to tell Hazel Marie how I'd averted an unwelcome visit to her room.

"You told her what?" Hazel Marie's face lit up with a smile, the likes of which I hadn't seen in some while.

So I repeated the tale of the dark roots, and we had a good laugh about it. But then she sobered and ran her hand through her hair.

"I do need color," she said. "I just hate it

when I let it go so long. But I can't face going to Velma's, even if I felt like it."

"No, you're not up to it and you shouldn't go. I mean, Hazel Marie, nobody would ever guess that you're expecting. It's much too early for anything to show. But physically you're too weak to be gallivanting around town. And if you did, everybody would think you're well and expect you to resume your usual activities." I watched her carefully as she lay in bed, propped up by a couple of pillows. It pulled at my heart to see how gaunt her face was and how thin her arms. "Were you able to eat much breakfast?"

"I did. Lillian brought me some oatmeal with raisins and I ate most of it. I think it'll stay down if I don't move around too much. But you know," she went on, "I hate that my hair's such a mess. And it's only going to get worse the longer I stay in this bed."

Knowing that the state of one's hair affects one's whole outlook on life, I said, "Would you be up to coloring it yourself? I'll go to the drugstore if you'll tell me what to get, and Lillian and I can help you."

"Oh, would you? I'd feel so much better to have it done."

"Well, wait, Hazel Marie," I said, caution signs going up in my brain. "Is it safe to use dye when you're expecting? I mean, it could seep into your scalp and do some kind of internal damage, couldn't it?"

She laughed. "No, but I worried about it when Lloyd was on the way, and I called every hairdresser in town and talked to my doctor, too, and they all said it was all right. The only problem is that the dye might not take or it could turn out a different color." She pulled a strand of hair down across her forehead and looked at it with slightly crossed eyes. "Hormones, I guess. But it couldn't look any worse than this, regardless of how it turns out. I'd feel so much better if I didn't look so awful."

"You don't look awful, Hazel Marie. You just look tired, which is what you are. So tell me what you need, and we'll have you back to your old self in no time."

After writing down what she wanted, I left to go to the drugstore but first to ensure Lillian's help with a do-it-yourself dye job.

"I hope we don't ruin her," I said, expressing my doubts to Lillian. "I don't know how to color hair."

"Nothin' to it, Miss Julia. You just get what she want, an' I do the rest."

"Oh, good. If you've done it before, then we'll be in good shape."

"Well, I never done it before, but I seen it done."

I rolled my eyes and decided to change the subject. "There's something else, Lillian, that I need to tell you. But not a word to Hazel Marie about it, but Mr. Pickens is on his way. Wait now," I said, holding up my hand as her face lit up, "He won't get here until late tonight, and he'll be staying at Sam's house while he investigates the break-in. But he'll be here for dinner tomorrow night."

Lillian could be light on her feet when her spirits were up, and she looked as if she were almost floating. "He comin' up here to marry her! I knowed he would."

"Don't get too happy because he's not. At least not yet. He doesn't know a thing about anything, and Hazel Marie doesn't know he's coming. And it has to stay that way, so we can't say anything to either one of them."

"Well, why can't we? I thought gettin' them two together was what you wanted."

"It is, but, Lillian, if we push too hard, it could backfire on us. So, I'm going to let nature take its course, with a little help maybe from Lloyd. All unbeknownst to him, of course. See, I can't break my promise to Hazel Marie, and Sam doesn't believe in interfering in other people's personal problems. So just getting them in the same town and in the same house at the same time is all we can do. I'm leaving the rest of it up to them. It wouldn't be right for me to try any kind of manipulation, and you know I never interfere in personal matters, myself." I stopped and eyed her suspiciously. "Don't look at me like that, Lillian. My conscience is clear and it's going to stay that way."

Chapter 15

Pretending that I didn't see all the eye rolling she was doing, I left for the drugstore to get a box of Clairol's Nice 'N Easy Root Touch-Up in the Light Blonde shade. On my way, I began to think over again our options to protect Hazel Marie from the town's wagging tongues in case the plans for Mr. Pickens didn't work out. Something had occurred to me while talking to her, and this was a good time to give it some serious thought. What if we could send her to a sanitarium or a sanitorium, or whatever it was, of some kind? Celebrities were forever going off to get rehabilitated, so why not Hazel Marie as well? There used to be Florence Crittendon homes for unwed mothers, but I didn't know if they still existed since nowadays unwed mothers paraded themselves around instead of hiding away somewhere. But if they did exist, Hazel Marie would have constant care and not be in an apartment alone in a strange city.

If I could find such a place, all we'd have to do is keep her out of sight—and out of Velma's shop—for a little while longer, then send her off. We could tell it around that she needed a long recuperation in a dry climate.

Of course, that wouldn't explain the appearance of a sudden addition to the family, unless we said that Hazel Marie took pity on an unwanted baby and decided to adopt it herself.

Yes, and how many people would believe that?

Well, first things first, I thought, as I pulled into the parking lot next to the Rite Aid drugstore. Hazel Marie had suggested I go to Walmart, but I'd rather pay a few cents more than walk a mile once I got inside that huge store.

As I walked into the store and turned down the aisle with hair products on the shelves, who should I see but Emma Sue Ledbetter? I would've turned around and studied the cold remedies if she hadn't seen me at the same time.

"Julia," she said, straightening up from her perusal of the lower shelves. "Just the person who was on my mind. Have you ever had that experience? I mean, running into the very one that the Lord has put on your mind to pray for? It's more than coincidence, don't you think?"

"Um, probably so, Emma Sue. But why would you think I'm in special need of prayer?"

"Why, what with the worry over Hazel Marie, her being in the hospital and all, and that awful home invasion at Sam's house, I would think that you'd need more than the usual amount of prayer."

"Well, you're right. I have been beside myself with all that's happened, and I thank you for thinking of me."

"Oh, I always include the caregivers in my quiet times with the Lord," Emma Sue said. "They're often quite forgotten, but I know they need help and support just as much as whoever's the main topic. How is she, anyway?"

"Hazel Marie's still very weak, thank you for asking. She's still confined to her room, not even coming down for meals, and all this is on doctor's orders. The only thing that sustains us is that he says it's completely curable, although the cure is long in coming. So please do keep holding her up in your prayers." Waiting the appropriate godly moment, I added, "Prayer can be so uplifting."

"Oh, Julia, you do my heart good." Emma Sue got misty-eyed for a second, as she rejoiced in my spirituality. She wasn't always sure I had any. "But listen," she went on, "we're all praying for her and for you, but scattered prayer is not always so effective. What Hazel Marie really needs is the laying on of hands. It's usually done by the pastor and all the elders, especially on a new ordinand's head, but it can be done as a healing service, too. Why don't I tell Larry that Hazel Marie would welcome a healing service? He and I could come to your house and do it privately, since I know she won't feel like doing it in a regular church service."

Lord, the last thing Hazel Marie needed was Pastor Larry Ledbetter and his well-meaning wife coming into her bedroom intent on a prayer meeting. She would die of mortification, because neither the pastor nor Emma Sue would be satisfied with offering generalized and undifferentiated prayers. No, they believed in *specifics*. They would descend on her and question her as to her exact symptoms and want to know the name of her particular ailment and what the doctor recommended and on and on, as if the Lord needed a detailed list in order to address each item.

Hazel Marie would never be able to withstand their spiritual onslaught, and I just wasn't in the mood to lie to the pastor and before God. The laying on of hands, no matter how well meant, would be a disaster.

"I'd hold off on that, Emma Sue," I said. "Hazel Marie's breakfast is as likely as not to come gushing out under extreme spiritual stress. I think the best thing for her right now is some long distance praying."

"Oh, my goodness," Emma Sue said, "is she that bad off? I had no idea, and of course we should put it off for awhile. I'll tell you something, Julia." She glanced around, then went on in a whisper. "Not many people know this, but Larry has a delicate stomach. Sympathetic, I think it's called, so he might join right in if she started upchucking. Just tell her we're praying for her, and that we'll visit as soon as, well, as soon as things calm down."

Assuring her that I would relay the message, we parted ways, her to purchase a bottle of shampoo and me to scurry away from the hair dyes. No need to give Emma Sue further reason to offer Hazel Marie up in prayer. I dawdled among the face creams, the body lotions, and the bath salts until I saw Emma Sue pay for her shampoo and exit the store. Then I ran back to the dye aisle, quickly scanned the innumerable products to heighten, lessen, or completely alter the natural color of one's crowning glory, pounced on the Root Touch-Up in Light Blonde and made my purchase.

I declare, I thought when I was safely back in the car and on my way home, *no way in the world could I continue to protect Hazel Marie's secret condition with such lies as I'd told both LuAnne and Emma Sue.* Well, I wouldn't call them *lies,* exactly. They were more like highly creative stories in the service of a good cause. But the immediate question was: How many more could I come up with and how long would I have to keep spewing them out on the spur of the moment? My repertoire was about exhausted.

Well, I thought with some chagrin, the only savior on the horizon was Mr. Pickens, and a more unlikely one I'd be hard pressed to find. Still, he would solve all our problems if he'd get down off his high horse and submit to one more marriage. He could hold his nose if he had to, just so he made that baby legitimate and saved Hazel Marie and Lloyd from shame and disgrace.

Yes, I knew that bearing an illegitimate child was no longer considered a reason for shame and disgrace. I knew that many people did it these days without a lick of guilt or a tinge of embarrassment, flaunting themselves—clothed and unclothed—for all to see. But the fact of the matter was, Hazel Marie *did* feel guilt and she *was* embarrassed and ashamed, and I was proud of her for it. As far as I was concerned, she was showing character and good form.

Of course, she would be showing a

good deal more than that fairly soon, especially as thin as she was, so it behooved Mr. Pickens to get a move on and us to see that he did.

꧁꧂

"He got in a couple of hours ago," Sam said as he crawled into bed well after midnight.

I'd been dozing off and on, waiting for him to come home. I was anxious to hear if Mr. Pickens seemed any different after going through so many lifestyle changes. "Did he ask about Hazel Marie?"

"Not specifically," Sam said, yawning. "Just asked how everybody was."

"What did you say?"

"I said, 'Fine,' and that was it."

"Well, my goodness, Sam. What were the two of you doing all this time?"

Sam turned on his side and scrooched up close. "We discussed the case, honey. I showed him the scene of the crime, so to speak. Told him what Coleman's men were doing, explained exactly what's missing, that kind of thing. This is the first time I've seen him in working mode, and I tell you, he's impressive. Very professional."

"That's a relief," I said, snuggling up

close. "He's such a tease, always going on about something. I was afraid he might not take his work seriously."

"No fear of that. In fact, he put me off when I asked about his move to Charlotte. Just immediately went back to questions about the break-in."

My eyes were heavy by this time since I'd been holding off on sleep until Sam was next to me. But my eyes popped open as I thought of something else. "Did that new mattress get there?"

"Delivered this afternoon."

"Well, good. I'd hate for him to have to sleep on one that was cut to smithereens." Then in a few minutes I thought of something else. "Did James have fresh linens on the bed? What about the kitchen? Is there coffee and so forth ready for him?"

"He's fine, sweetheart. James went the extra mile for him, had the bedroom cleared out, the kitchen stocked, and even got one of the television sets replaced. Pickens is in good shape. You can check on him in the morning, well, later this morning, and see if there's anything else he needs."

"I don't know if I want to see him. What if I get so deranged at the thought of how he's shirking his responsibility that I just fly into him? I'm not sure I could hold my tongue if I see him going along as if everything's just fine and dandy. I'm liable to grab him up and shake him till his teeth rattle. I just hate having to wait for other people to do what they ought to be doing, don't you?"

I guess he did, for he didn't answer. He was sound asleep and after a few more minutes of worrying over how to make Mr. Pickens feel welcome, while at the same time letting him know I was not pleased with his behavior, I dropped off, too.

Chapter 16

By the time morning rolled around, it dawned on me that I wouldn't have to face Mr. Pickens right away. Dinnertime was hours away, so I had the whole day to prepare myself. Which was just as well, for the morning was taken up with coloring Hazel Marie's hair. We'd decided the day before that it was too late in the day to start the procedure, especially since Hazel Marie was noticeably more active and alert in the mornings. By the afternoons, though, when she began to feel queasy, she'd usually sleep for the rest of the day.

So right after breakfast, Lillian and I

stocked Hazel Marie's bathroom with loads of towels, a chair for her to sit on, and rubber gloves to protect our hands from turning Light Blonde along with her hair. It was amazing to me to discover that a dye that turns hair yellow starts out as a brown color. In fact, the whole process was amazing to me. Especially when I discovered that even though the color would fade away or grow out of hair, it was set forever in my good towels.

I have to admit that we had a pleasant time doing it, laughing with Hazel Marie and hoping that we weren't ruining her. As it turned out, Lillian didn't know much more than I did about dyeing hair, but the directions were good and Hazel Marie was an old hand at it. She told us how and where to dab it on and kept a close watch on the clock.

"Y'all better not make my hair fall out," she said, laughing.

It pleased me to see her in a lighter mood. Maybe getting your hair done is a way to put aside your troubles for a while. But I'll say this right now, the next time she needed color, I was going to offer Velma whatever she wanted to make a house call.

While we waited for the color to set, Lillian brought up a mid-morning snack and we had a nice time sitting together, talking about everything but what was weighing on our minds. I noticed that Hazel Marie was completely off coffee. She said even the smell of it, which is usually the best thing about it, made her stomach act up. She stuck to fruit juice, which was better for her anyway.

Lillian helped her into the shower when it was time to rinse her hair and stood right beside the tub, in case, as she said, the pore little thing got to feeling weak. And she did get weak, unable to hold up her arms long enough to roll her hair once she was out of the shower. Lillian blew it dry for her and put in the hot rollers.

We were all pleased with the results, although in certain lights you could tell where our efforts began and where they ended, mainly because there was just the tiniest tinge of orange where her hormones had acted up. Still, the dark roots were gone, so I didn't think Mr. Pickens would notice the difference. Getting her to the point of looking her best for whenever we could bring about a face-to-face meeting was the whole purpose of the process. Well, and to make her feel better, too.

But after it was over and we'd had lunch, I had nothing to do but dither around, thinking up one ploy after another to get those two together. Sam was off somewhere, probably at his house helping Mr. Pickens find the trail of whoever broke in and stole the very papers he needed.

My mind veered off in that direction, and I began to wonder just who would know what Sam had been working on. I mean, it was certainly no secret that he was doing research and writing a legal history of the county, but he'd been fiddling with that for two years or more. So, what stirred somebody up just at this time? That's what Mr. Pickens should be looking into, and I decided to bring that to his attention that very evening while he was at our table.

And that thought immediately swung my mind back to Hazel Marie and the urgency of bringing about a peaceful and proper settlement between them. It was the strangest thing in the world to me that she had so completely turned him off. It seemed to me that he had done or said—or *not* done or *not* said—something that had truly altered her very nature.

So it was all his fault.

Well, I could fix that, I thought. Between us, Sam and I ought to be able to get him to march down the aisle by appealing to his sense of duty, if for no other reason.

And, Lord, what was I going to do about Lloyd this very afternoon, I thought, as my mind picked up on another worry. He might even stop by Sam's house on his way home from the tennis courts, and that would be it. As soon as he saw Mr. Pickens, he'd come running to tell his mother. She could be packing up to leave before sundown.

I looked at my watch, seeing that Lloyd would soon be home, then I set my mouth and walked upstairs. Hazel Marie was propped up in bed, flipping through the pages of a magazine.

"You look so nice, Hazel Marie," I said. "We did a good job on your hair. How're you feeling?"

"Oh, I don't know," she said, closing the magazine and putting it aside. "I'm trying to get my mind off it."

"Off what? Besides the obvious, that is?"

"My stomach's felt unsettled ever since lunch. I have to keep swallowing and swallowing. You know how you feel when you want to throw up and can't?"

I nodded, noticing again how thin she was. "Well, I was hoping that you could get off that medication, but you can't afford to be doing much more throwing up. You're down to skin and bones as it is. Why don't you take one of your pills and lie real still for a while? Take a nap, why don't you? You had such a nice lunch, and you need to keep it down."

"I guess I better," she said, reaching for the prescription bottle. "I don't want to get so that I can't even keep a pill down."

"No, we'd be taking you back to the hospital for injections if you do that. Go ahead and take it, then lie down flat and try to sleep. I expect you'll feel better when you wake up." *Just about the time Mr. Pickens would be coming for dinner,* I thought, as I checked the time again. "I'll keep everything quiet for you."

She swallowed the pill with a sip of water, looked uneasy for a minute, then she lay back down. "I'm really getting tired of this," she said. "I want to be up and doing, and making plans, anything besides lying here wondering how fast I can get to the bathroom."

I smiled at her and straightened the covers. I couldn't help but wonder if she'd been this sick when she was expecting Lloyd, but I didn't ask. If I knew that, I might have some idea of how long she'd have to put up with it this time, and also how long I had to get her married. But the fact that it had been my husband who'd put her in that situation kept me quiet. For me to ask something like that would certainly put her under great emotional stress, so I kept my thoughts to myself. We didn't often discuss Wesley Lloyd Springer, anyway.

As the afternoon wore on, I became increasingly anxious about seeing Mr. Pickens, knowing now what I hadn't known the last time I'd seen him. My goodness, since that time the man had started something he couldn't stop and broken up with Hazel Marie and put his house up for sale and moved away, and I wasn't supposed to know any of it. Of course, he didn't know some of it, either, but my problem was how to sit at the table with him, talk with him and entertain him, all without sailing into him about how irresponsible he was being. Lord, I didn't know how I'd do it.

"Lillian," I said, pushing through into the kitchen, "how's dinner coming along? Can I help? Is Lloyd home yet? He ought to be here by now."

"Dinner comin' 'long fine, an' no, I don't need no help an' no, Lloyd called, sayin' he stoppin' off at Mr. Sam's 'fore he come home."

"I knew it! That means he'll know Mr. Pickens is here and he'll come running in to tell his mother."

"Well, she gonna know sometime," Lillian said, as she stood at the sink, peeling little new potatoes to put around the roast. "I don't know how you 'spect to keep it a secret anyhow."

"I can't, I know that. But I can put it off as long as possible. I'm just afraid if she hears he's coming, she'll get all upset and leave before he gets here. And she's in no condition to be doing that. But, Lillian," I went on, "don't you think that all it'll take is for them to see each other, and they'll work something out?"

"Yessum, I do. I jus' don't know what that workin' out gonna be."

"Well, me either, but this is the best I can do. Oh, here's Lloyd now." I opened the back door and patted his back as he walked in. I couldn't help but touch him whenever I could.

Sliding his tennis racket bag off his shoulders, he immediately went to the counter for the snack that Lillian had put out for him. He pushed up his glasses and said, "I think I'll take this up to Mama's room and eat it there. I can't wait to tell her that Mr. Sam's hired J.D. to investigate and he's already on the case. Did you know he was coming, Miss Julia?"

"Well, ah, Sam mentioned the possibility, I think."

"I bet Mama doesn't know. I'm gonna run tell her."

"Wait, Lloyd, don't go up yet. She had a sickly spell a while ago and took some medicine. You know how that flu just lingers on. She's sound asleep now, so let's not wake her. She needs the rest. Have your snack down here, and maybe find something to do down here, too."

"Oh, okay," he said and quickly downed

a glass of milk and a few graham crackers with peanut butter. "I can read a little in the living room, but I'll bet she'll be surprised J.D.'s here because she thinks he's on a case out of town somewhere."

"Is that right?" I mumbled, watching as he put his racket in a corner and left the kitchen. Turning to Lillian, I said, "I don't know how long I can keep this up."

Lillian turned to stare at me, her eyes glinting. "Is Miss Hazel Marie really sleepin' like you say?"

"Why, she certainly is. I saw her take the medicine, and you know she always sleeps a few hours when she does."

"Uh-huh, an' who tole her to take it? She s'posed to be gettin' off that stuff."

"Now, Lillian, the doctor wouldn't've given it to her if he didn't mean for her to take it. Besides, this is the first time she's needed it in days. And which is better, taking one little pill or throwing up all afternoon?"

"You jus' want her sleepin' so she won't know Mr. Pickens comin'. You ought to know better'n to dose that little woman up like that."

"Well, I don't. I'd rather have her asleep

than getting all upset, anticipating his coming. I want him already in the house by the time she knows it, so I'm just thinking of her well-being."

"Uh-huh," Lillian grumbled. "An' lightnin' gonna strike you one of these days, so you better get that table set 'fore it do."

Chapter 17

There were times when I could view Mr. Pickens in a friendly, objective way and acknowledge the fact that he was a nice-looking man by anybody's standards—frisky, yes, but quite nice looking. He was handsome in what I think is called a Black Irish way—dark hair and eyes with a medium complexion. But handsome is as handsome does, and he didn't always stack up so well in that category.

There were other times, though, when I couldn't help but view him in a more personal way and it was a different story then. Oh, I still saw his good looks, all right, but added to that I'd find myself experiencing a strange and unlikely response to those black eyes and teasing charm that would take my breath away, and I was old enough to be his mother. Almost old enough.

No wonder Hazel Marie had fallen under his spell. She hadn't been the first to do so, as I've mentioned before. Against my better judgment but out of dire necessity, I'd hired him almost sight unseen to find Hazel Marie when she'd gotten herself abducted by a bunch of racing hoodlums. I should've known there was trouble ahead when Mr. Pickens took one look at her picture, then demanded a retainer fee that he foolishly thought would commit me to giving him free rein. But he found her with help from yours truly, which he stubbornly refused to acknowledge, and from the moment they laid eyes on each other the sparks began to fly. Hazel Marie looked on him as her hero, as I'll admit he was to a certain extent, and he seemed to adore her. Love was in the air, as they say, except it had never led anywhere. Mr. Pickens remained as skittish as ever about settling down, content to have his cake and eat it, too.

So here he came with Sam just as Lillian took the roast out of the oven, and the kitchen came alive with just his presence. He was so full of himself, you know. Lillian couldn't stop grinning and plying him with questions and little appetizers, and Lloyd flew in to be part of the welcoming committee. One of the most attractive aspects of Mr. Pickens, in my opinion and in addition to the more obvious ones, was his affection for that boy. I could somewhat overlook his aversion to marriage because he'd become a father to Lloyd even though he refused to become a husband to the boy's mother. So far, that is, because the final word on that subject had yet to be said.

I might as well admit that I'd been somewhat standoffish with Mr. Pickens when I first met him. He'd been too arrogant and too self-confident to suit my taste and much too taken with Hazel Marie to let me rest easy. The last thing she needed, then and now, was another man in no mind to marry her.

And didn't that prove prophetic? If she'd listened to me then, we wouldn't be in our present situation, would we?

But as time went on, I'd gradually changed my thinking about him. He was faithful to Hazel Marie, and good, even sweet to her, which goes to show that first appearances can be deceptive. But all that goodness and sweetness and handsomeness—he could make any woman's heart flutter—couldn't make up for his stubborn determination to remain single. Even if it'd taken him three previous forays into marriage to build up that determination. It just seemed to me that one more marriage shouldn't be that big of a deal to someone who'd been in and out of so many before. Especially when so much was at stake with this one.

So as I watched him shake Lloyd's hand, then draw him close in a hug, I could've smacked him to kingdom come just to bring him to his senses. It broke my heart to see how Lloyd loved him and, to give credit where it's due, how Mr. Pickens returned that love. Even though Mr. Pickens had never had children, as far as any of us knew, he was a father to that boy, teaching him by example—in spite of his rough-as-a-cob exterior—what it meant to be a kind and decent man.

And now, he was just going to let all that slip away? And Hazel Marie was bound and determined to throw him over? It beat all I'd ever heard, and I wasn't going to stand for it even if I had to lie, cheat, or steal to change their minds.

"And how are you, Miss Julia?" Mr. Pickens said, taking my hand with one of his and putting the other one around my shoulder. "You just get prettier every time I see you."

Now, see? That's the way he was, always carrying on so that you couldn't believe a word he said. Everybody knows that women of a certain age don't get prettier. They might get more handsome, but not prettier. But that didn't change the state of my knees when he smiled down at me, black eyes sparkling, and I'd take prettier from him over more handsome any day of the week.

I didn't have to answer him because Lloyd was chattering on, telling Mr. Pickens that he was helping with the beginners' tennis lessons. "I have to be at the courts practically all day, J.D." he said. "My clinic's in the morning, then I help with the little kids in the afternoon." From there, he jumped to telling how Sam's house had been ransacked, how the deputies had swarmed around and how he'd never seen the like.

And all the while, Lillian stood there glowing just from being in Mr. Pickens's presence.

"Y'all better get on to the table," she finally said, shooing us out of her way. "I'm about to bring it in."

As Lloyd took Mr. Pickens's hand and led him toward the dining room, I sidled over to Sam and took his hand. My feelings about Mr. Pickens were an aberration and no more than a temporary distraction from my darling Sam. "How's it going?" I whispered.

"You mean . . . ?" he said, his eyes drifting to the ceiling beyond which Hazel Marie lay in bed.

"Yes. Has he said anything?"

Sam shook his head. "Not a word, but did you notice how he kept looking at the door? Like he thought she'd come walking in?"

Well, no, I hadn't. Too taken up with my own emotions, I guessed. But it warmed my heart to hear that he was watching for her, even if he couldn't bring himself to ask about her.

I did notice, though, when we got into the dining room that he frowned at only four places set on the table. His head swiveled toward the living room as if he expected her to come from there. Smoothly recovering, though, he took the place I indicated without asking one question as to her whereabouts. Of course, he didn't have much chance to question anything, for Lloyd talked on and on—except for a brief respite as Sam returned thanks. Lillian began setting one bowl or platter after another before Sam, and Sam began helping the plates and passing them around.

Lillian remained standing between Mr. Pickens and Sam, clasping her hands in front of her, while accepting all the compliments on the food.

Then before I knew it, and just as Mr. Pickens put a huge piece of roast beef in his mouth, she came right out and said, "Mr. Pickens, I guess you wondrin' 'bout Miss Hazel Marie. But she right upstairs in the bed where she been ever since she got out of the hospital."

Mr. Pickens's eyes got big as he took a

startled breath. Then he began coughing and choking on that meat, trying to speak and chew and swallow at the same time. Hacking and choking, he shoved his chair back from the table and finally got control of himself, but not before Lillian thumped him hard on the back.

"In the hospital?" he finally managed to get out, his face red and his voice strangled. "What for? Is she all right?"

"Oh," Lloyd said, blithely, "she's fine now. She just had a bug from Asia and has to rest up from it."

Lord, the child had believed me! Well, what else did I expect? Lloyd wasn't accustomed to being lied to, but I'd done it to downplay Hazel Marie's condition so he wouldn't worry. And now my chickens were coming home to roost.

"Have a piece of bread, Mr. Pickens," I said, as he cleared his throat again. "Or drink some water. That'll help it go down."

He pulled his chair back to the table and picked up his fork. "Sorry, Miss Julia. Just swallowed wrong."

"It happens to the best of us," I assured him. "I hope you're all right."

"I'm fine," he said, and eyed the tiny bit

of broccoli casserole on his fork before putting it in his mouth. "I'm sorry to hear that Hazel Marie's been sick. But she's getting better?"

I glanced at Sam, then at Lillian, wondering if this was the time to tell him. But, no, I couldn't, not with Lloyd there and him not knowing what so far his mother hadn't seen fit to tell him. "We think she is," I finally said. "It'll be a long, drawn-out recuperation period, though—a few months, the doctor said. She's lost a lot of weight, too, but we expect her to put a good deal back on real soon. Why, you might not even recognize her by springtime, but then she'll level back to her normal size."

Lillian's eyes rolled back in her head— and after *she'd* started it—and Sam was giving me a quizzical look as Lloyd continued to eat like he hadn't had a bite all day. Mr. Pickens just sat there like a stump, frowning at another piece of roast beef, while I wondered just how dense the man could be.

By the time Lillian served dessert, Lloyd had steered the conversation back to the trouble at Sam's house. "J.D., how're you going to find out who went into Mr. Sam's house and messed everything up? I thought you'd be out tracking 'em down."

Mr. Pickens perked up at that, making me aware that he'd been somewhat subdued ever since being notified of Hazel Marie's illness. But his work was something he could get into without letting little things like a sick ex-girlfriend distress him. So off he took, explaining to the boy how he'd had Sam make a list of all the people whose cases were in the stolen files. Then they'd sorted out who'd been the attorneys, prosecutors, defendants, witnesses, and so on in each case.

"See, Lloyd," Mr. Pickens went on, as I listened intently. "It's better to do your homework first, find out just who is who by putting them in categories so you can see how and where they intersect. I use index cards to separate them. Then maybe you can see some patterns in the relationships among the names on the cards. Understand?"

Lloyd nodded, a frown on his forehead. "It sounds like what Miss Carleton tells us to do before we write an essay. Even to the index cards."

"That's about it," Mr. Pickens said, laughing and stretching an arm across the back of Lloyd's chair. "But don't worry, we'll be doing some footwork, too, soon enough. We just need to see where to start and in what direction to go."

That seemed a sound method to me, so I nodded and suggested we adjourn to the living room. Mr. Pickens, though, said he wanted another look at those lists and thought he'd go on back to Sam's house. Disappointed, but pleased for Sam's sake that he was taking the problem so seriously, I could do nothing but wish him a good night.

As we closed the door behind him, I turned to Sam and said, out of Lloyd's hearing, "We've got our work cut out for us, don't we?"

Chapter 18

"Miss Julia?" Lloyd called from midway up the stairs. "Can you come up? Mama wants you."

"I guess I'm in for it now," I said to Sam, then responded to Lloyd. "Tell her I'll be right there."

Detouring to the kitchen where Lillian was stacking dishes in the dishwasher, I said, "Lillian, Hazel Marie's awake and asking for me. Would you fix her a tray and bring it on up? I think I'm going to need a distraction or some help or something."

"That's what I was about to do," she said, closing the dishwasher door, "since she fin'lly wake up after bein' dosed up like somebody did to her."

I wasn't in the mood for a lecture, so I thanked her and turned to go face the music.

"Miss Julia?" Lillian said, stopping me. "I don't know what to think 'bout that Mr. Pickens. I 'spected him to jump outta that chair an' go runnin' upstairs to see her. But all he done was set there an' nearly choke to death."

"I know, Lillian, and it worries me, too. He seemed no more concerned than any normal acquaintance would've been. I can't imagine what's going through that head of his. Or hers, either." I sighed, then started out again. "Well, we've done all we can do for the time being, but now I've got to go explain myself to Hazel Marie. Wish me luck."

❧❧

I found Hazel Marie pacing the floor of her all-pink bedroom, her arms wrapped around herself and her pink robe billowing out behind her.

"Miss Julia," she said, stopping to face me as I came through the door. "What is J.D. doing here? I woke up and heard him talking and thought I was dreaming. Or having a nightmare." She was trembling so that her silk robe shimmered in the lamp-light.

"Wait, Hazel Marie," I said, closing the door behind me. "Lloyd's across the hall, watching television. He doesn't need to hear this. Now," I went on, going over to her, "let's sit down and I'll tell you what's going on."

She let me lead her to a chair and, as I did, I could feel the tremors running through her body. Her face was pale and stricken-looking, and I knew I was dealing with a strong emotional upheaval.

"I told you about the break-in at Sam's house," I began, soothingly enough. "And when Sam realized that some valuable notes and things were missing, he decided he needed a private investigator. So he called Mr. Pickens. On his own, I might add. He'll be staying at Sam's house for the du-ration, but he won't be bothering you. The only time he'll be here is just to run over and have dinner with us, since that's the least we can do for a visiting professional. So, see, you don't have to be concerned about him at all."

"But you promised," she said.

"And I kept my promise. I didn't call him, Sam did. And it's business, Hazel Marie, just business."

"Yes," she said bitterly, clenching her fists. "Monkey business, if I know him."

"Listen," I said, "I promise you, you won't have to see him unless you want to." At her fierce glare, I quickly corrected myself. "I know you don't want to, so all you have to do is stay up here when he's eating dinner. And see, he didn't linger even tonight. He just ate and left, and that's the way it'll be all the time he's in town. Besides," I went on, trying to lighten her mood, "I certainly don't want to be entertaining him for hours at a time. I'm happy enough to feed him since he's working for Sam, but I don't want him hanging around half the night, either."

"Well, okay," she said, straightening out a Kleenex to blow her nose. "It's just that I thought I might begin coming down to the table. At least for one meal, and now I can't."

"Oh, Hazel Marie, that means you're feeling better."

She shook her head. "I thought I was

until this happened. And now I'm going to be stuck in this room forever! And all because of him!"

"No, no, don't say that. You can come down anytime you want and I'll keep him out. Whenever you want to have dinner with us, just tell me and I'll send him to Hotdog House or the Burger King. You don't need to worry about him at all."

"Oh, Miss Julia," she said, covering her face with her hands. "You're all so good to me, and I know I've been hard to live with. It's just that my whole life has gone to pieces and I don't know what I'm doing, or what I'm going to do or when I'm going to do it. Or where, either."

Lillian tapped at the door right about then, relieving me immensely. She backed into the room, holding a tray filled with Hazel Marie's dinner.

"Here yo' dinner, little girl," she crooned. "I hope you like it. That Mr. Pickens, he 'bout eat it all up. I thought I have to slap his hand, he take any more helpin's."

To my surprise, Hazel Marie looked up at her, smiled, and began to wipe her face. "I wish you'd slapped more than that. He needs it, coming here like he's still part of

the family and acting like nothing's wrong."
She suddenly covered her face again.
"And *everything's* wrong!"

"Oh, Hazel Marie," I said, dismayed by
her relapse. "Please don't say that. Things
will work out, see if they don't. Lillian, pull
that table over here, please, and let's see
if she can eat something. Look, Hazel Marie, see what a lovely dinner Lillian's fixed
for you."

Lillian pushed a side table close to Hazel Marie and began to spread plates and
dishes on it. "See here," she said, patting
Hazel Marie's back, "here's a nice slice of
roast beef, jus' what Mr. Pickens choke
hisself on."

"He did?" Hazel Marie looked up at her
through red-rimmed eyes. "Would've served
him right if he'd strangled on it."

Then she laughed, or tried to. "Oh, me,
I've got to try to get him out of my system.
He's out of my life for good now, and I'm
not going to let him upset me anymore."
She took a deep breath and reached for a
fork. "Thank you for this, Lillian. I'll be coming downstairs a little tomorrow, so you
won't have to be carrying all this up here
much longer."

"Why, you know I don't mind," Lillian said, giving me a worried look. "I want you well again, an' I do whatever it take to get you well."

"I know and I appreciate it more than I can say," Hazel Marie said with only a small sniff. "But the time has come for me to start taking care of myself."

Lillian and I looked at each other over Hazel Marie's head, each of us staring at the other's concern. Did that mean she'd soon be leaving?

❦❦

Lloyd, dressed in white shorts and a navy polo shirt, came to the breakfast table the next morning and announced, "Mama's coming down. She's going to eat with us this morning."

"Why, that's wonderful," I said, pushing back my chair and getting to my feet. I took another place mat from a drawer of the sideboard and put it on the table, then went to the kitchen door to let Lillian know. "Put on another egg or two, Lillian. Hazel Marie's coming to the table."

I walked to the foot of the stairs and saw Hazel Marie, fully dressed, sliding against the wall as she stepped carefully down the stairs.

"Can anybody see me?" she whispered, as if she didn't want anybody to hear her either. "Has Mr. Sam gone?"

"No, he's still here."

She immediately turned around to go back upstairs. "I can't face him. Please, Miss Julia."

"Oh, no, Hazel Marie, come on and eat with us. He really wants to see you. He's been asking and asking when he can visit you. He loves you, Hazel Marie, and that hasn't changed."

"But he's ashamed of me, too, isn't he?"

"Not at all. He's already planning to take that baby fishing. Now you come right on. He'll be thrilled to see you." I held out my hand to encourage her. "And don't worry, I'll close all the curtains so nobody can see in. You look lovely, Hazel Marie, like you're feeling a lot better."

"I still feel a little weak," she said, taking my hand, "but I hope it's just from staying in bed."

"Well, we don't want to rush it, do we?" I led her to the chair that Sam had jumped up and pulled out for her and she took her place beside Lloyd.

"Welcome back," Sam said, patting her shoulder and smiling at her. "All fixed now? Anything you need?"

"No, thank you," she said, putting her hand on Lloyd's arm, perhaps for reassurance. "I'm fine, now that I made it down the stairs. Thank you all for putting up with me for so long."

Lillian pushed through the swinging door, just in time to hear her. "Why, Miss Hazel Marie, nobody 'round here puttin' up with anything," she said, placing a plate of scrambled eggs and grits in front of Hazel Marie. "When somebody sick, ever'body pitch in an' he'p 'em out, jus' like you do when somebody else be sick. Now eat all them grits, they set nice on your stomick, but I didn't give you no bacon or sausage. You don't need none of that greasy stuff."

Hazel Marie's eyes crossed just the slightest little bit at the thought of greasy sausage, but she gamely picked up her fork and began to pick at the food. Gradually, though, as her appetite grew and we stopped watching every bite she put in her mouth, she made fair inroads on her breakfast.

"Well," Sam said, putting his cup in the saucer, "if you folks will excuse me, I need to get over to the house and see what Pickens is up to."

Distressed that he'd brought up the forbidden name, I gave him a brief glare. He just smiled at me and went on, "I hope you have a good day, Hazel Marie. But take care and don't overdo it. I want to see you well and happy and back the way you were."

Well, didn't we all? But no chance at this point of reversing what had been done. Sam gave me a kiss, winked at Lloyd, and told him to work on his backhand. Then he was gone.

"Well, Hazel Marie," I said, putting my napkin beside my plate, "do you have any plans for the day? Anything you want to do?"

"No'm, but you know I have an appointment with the doctor this afternoon."

"Oh, that's right. Well, I'll drive you, because we still want to keep you under wraps for a while so everybody in town won't come visiting."

Lloyd looked at his mother. "You still can't have visitors? I thought, since you're up, you'd be well."

"She is, Lloyd," I assured him. "Or just about. But it takes a while to get over being sick, and your mother needs to take it easy and not get all social on us. And you know how people are in this town. If they think she's completely well, they'll be expecting her to lead a book discussion or do a flower arrangement or bring cookies for a Sunday school class or volunteer to walk for some cause. Why, she'd be bombarded with things to do and not get any rest at all. So it's better if people think she's still flat on her back in bed."

He grinned. "Yessum, I see what you mean. Everybody likes my mama so much, they can't leave her alone."

Hazel Marie's eyes filled as she leaned over to kiss his cheek. "I love you, Lloyd."

"Me, too," he said, sliding out of his chair, "but I gotta go." He left to get his tennis racket.

Hazel Marie lowered her head, then in a miserable voice, she murmured, "It won't be long before nobody'll like me, not even him."

"Nonsense, Hazel Marie," I said, briskly, although I thought my heart would break in two. "Don't let yourself get down. Let's go to the kitchen and visit with Lillian. She'll cheer us up."

Chapter 19

Lillian did her best, and so did I, but it was hard going to keep Hazel Marie occupied and on an even keel during her first day out of bed. It didn't help matters that we had all the curtains tightly closed, making the rooms dim and gloomy in spite of the bright sunshine outside. But neither Hazel Marie nor I wanted any passersby to see her up and dressed. They would've been knocking on the door, wanting to see her.

At one point, she decided she needed some exercise, so she walked throughout the house, around and around, through one room after another, then up the stairs and back down again, until she was winded and white in the face.

Finally, looking at her watch, she said, "I'd better get ready to go to the doctor. My appointment's at one."

Lillian gave us a light lunch, but Hazel Marie didn't do much damage to it. "I know he's going to tell me I've gained too much weight," she said.

"Why, you know not," I said, looking to Lillian for confirmation. "You haven't eaten enough to keep a bird alive, Hazel Marie, and half of that's come back up."

Nothing we said made much of an impression on her and, as I drove her to see that substitute doctor, I noticed her hands clenching and unclenching in her lap.

"I just hate this," she said as I turned into the parking lot at Dr. Hargrove's office. She pushed her hair back from her face. "I'd give anything if it hadn't happened."

"Now, listen," I said, pulling into a parking slot and turning off the ignition. "Regretting the past won't do you or anybody else any good. You can waste your entire life moaning and groaning over something that can't be changed. What you have to do is start right where you are and deal with whatever you have to deal with. Today is the first day of the rest of your life, Hazel Marie." I had to look away, unable to believe I'd come out with something so trite and silly. But she took it to heart, nodding her head in agreement, and seemed to feel better for it.

Of course, I was relegated to the waiting room where I sat and waited for an hour while Hazel Marie got weighed and examined and talked to by that doctor who needed a nurse's help to make a diagnosis. I could've been a taxi driver for all the note he took of me.

"What did he say?" I asked as soon as Hazel Marie and I were back in the car. "Is everything all right?"

"Well, you were right," she said with a sigh. "I have lost weight and he gave me a long lecture on nutrition and exercise and I-don't-know-what-all." She took some folded papers and brochures from her purse. "Here's what all I'm supposed to do, and I don't even feel like reading it."

"Oh, Hazel Marie, you have to keep your spirits up. Your emotional well-being is important to that baby, to say nothing of what you eat. My goodness, that baby could be losing weight, too, and we can't have that."

She shook her head. "No, he said the baby would get what it needs. It's just that my health would suffer. You know, hair getting thin and falling out, teeth getting loose. Things like that." She said the last in a monotone, as if the prospect was of little concern to her.

"Well," I said, trying to make light of such dire prospects. "I guess those old wives' tales are true. But you're not going to lose any hair or any teeth. You're going to eat right or Lillian's going to force feed you with me helping her."

"I know," she said with a weak smile. "And I'll try. He said I should soon be past the time of morning sickness—and evening sickness, in my case—and I think I am. I don't feel as sick as I did just a few days ago when I could hardly stand the thought of food."

"That's good. I'd noticed that you were eating a little better. Did he tell you when we can expect the baby?"

She held her head in her hand for a minute, then looked up, sighed deeply, and said, "He said Dr. Hargrove will be back next week, so he wants me to come back in to see him. He said I might be further along than he'd thought at first."

I took my lower lip in my teeth, thinking that I might've been too quick to blame San Francisco. But if so, then when and where? Not that it was any of my business, and I wasn't about to ask her, but I do like to know what I'm dealing with. As well, I might add, as *when* I'll have to deal with it.

Leaving that alone with some effort, I said, "So Dr. Hargrove will be back? That's good, Hazel Marie. We know him and he knows us. You'll be in much better hands then. Unless," I went on after a second thought, "you think you should see a specialist. You know, one who delivers babies all the time."

"I don't know," she said. "I'm dreading seeing Dr. Hargrove because, well, you know, he's in our church and all. I wish he didn't have to know."

"That's something to think about," I said, driving toward home. "But Dr. Hargrove has so many secrets in his head about the people in this town, it's a wonder he's able to sleep at night. It's up to you, though. If you'd be more comfortable going to some-body in Asheville, that's where we'll go. And Dr. McKay will be leaving, I presume, so nobody but us will know anything."

"He'll tell Dr. Hargrove, anyway. I mean, he'll report on the patients he's seen while Dr. Hargrove was away, so it doesn't mat-ter. He's always been so nice to me that I dread having to face him. But," she said with a heavy sigh, "the word's going to get around one way or another if I don't hurry and leave town."

Well, that didn't do my equilibrium any good, but I let it pass. "Let's just see how well you get along in the next week or so. You have plenty of time before anything starts to show, even if you're farther along than that halfway doctor thought."

I still wasn't happy with the way Dr. Mc-Kay had missed the obvious and missed it even though I'd told him he should con-sider female problems. And what's a worse female problem than being pregnant with-out a husband?

By the time we got home, Hazel Marie was dragging, so after she'd eaten part of a snack Lillian had prepared for her, she went upstairs to lie down. That gave me a chance to catch Lillian up with what the doctor had said.

"So," I said, finishing my report, "she may be farther along than we'd realized, and with Dr. Hargrove coming back, she's anxious to be leaving. I am so distressed because heaven knows where she'll end up."

"Miss Julia," Lillian confided in a low voice, "she can't look after herself all by herself and that baby, too. An' what she gonna do 'bout Lloyd? He goin' or he stayin'?"

"Well, that's the question, isn't it? I don't know which is worse, having both of them gone or her off by herself with nobody to get help if she needs it." I could feel my nerves going to pieces everytime I thought of the ramifications. "We've got to get Mr. Pickens to make a move."

"He be here for supper again tonight. Maybe we ought to jus' tell him. An' tell him what he got to do about it, too."

"I'm tempted, Lillian, I am really tempted. But I did give her my word, and I hate to go back on it. At least until there's nothing left to do but that." I blew out my breath, exasperated because no one was doing what they were supposed to do. "Well, we still have a little time. As long as she's not packing her suitcases, we can wait a while longer and hope something will give."

Dinner that evening was a repeat of the previous night, although without Mr. Pickens's choking episode. He came in, being his usual cheerful self, although I thought I noticed that it took a little more effort than usual. I hoped so. I hoped he was having trouble sleeping and trouble keeping his mind on his work and trouble making it through the day. He had no trouble eating, however, or engaging Lloyd and Sam in conversation. But, like the night before, he left as soon as dinner was over, expressing his apologies to me and his compliments to Lillian.

"Mr. Sam?" Lloyd said as soon as Mr. Pickens had left. "Are y'all finding out who broke into your house?"

"We're working on it," Sam said. Then with a look that included me, he went on. "I'm still trying to find some of those files that're missing at the courthouse. And trying to set up appointments to interview people again." He sighed, almost with resignation. "They don't want to talk to me, though. The word about the break-in has gotten out, and that's made everybody jittery. It doesn't make sense to me, but that's the reason they give." He managed a small laugh. "Those who'll even give a reason, that is."

"Which is most important, Sam," I asked, "the files you copied from the courthouse or the interviews?"

"The files, by far," he said. "They're copies of official records, while the interviews, well, they were what people wanted me to hear. Lots of excuses, omissions, and forgetfulness. I only did them hoping somebody would let something slip." He smiled ruefully. "Nobody did."

Lloyd, who'd been listening intently, said, "Why don't you let J.D. interview them? They might talk to him because they'd know he's not writing a book. I mean, he could say that he's protecting their privacy in case whoever stole your notes and things decides to do something with them—like write their own book."

Sam ran his fingers across his mouth, studying the boy's suggestion. "We've been talking about doing just that, Lloyd. If I stay out of it, and he approaches them— there're only four, not counting Rafe

Feldman—with, say, a concern for their interests, he might get somewhere. That's a good idea, Lloyd, but you better watch out. Pickens might offer you a job with that kind of thinking."

Lloyd grinned, delighted to have helped, then excused himself to get ready for bed.

I reached across the table and laid my hand on Sam's. "If we lose that boy, Sam, I don't know what I'll do."

"Time, Julia," he said, laying his other hand on top of mine. "Give it a little more time and see if Hazel Marie and Pickens can work it out themselves. They've both got to save face, I expect. Just remember, if they're still this far apart by the time Pickens is ready to leave—or Hazel Marie is— why, then maybe we'll think about forcing the matter."

I bowed my head in relief. "I'm so glad to hear you say that. I have held off and held off, but there's no way I can let them go their separate ways with Mr. Pickens no more aware of what she's going through than he is now." I looked up at him and smiled. "When I think of how obstinate that man is, I could just throttle him."

"Well," Sam said, smiling, "hold off on that for a while. He's got a bee in his bonnet about what those five people have in common. He spent the day in the Register of Deeds office at the courthouse, looking up every one of them. He's convinced that some sort of underhanded dealing went on, either among them or because of them. Follow the money, he says, and the Records room is a good place to start."

"Why, Sam, if those people paid their way out of trouble, I can't imagine they'd have it *recorded* somewhere."

He laughed. "No, of course they wouldn't. But he thinks it'll be helpful to know what was going on in the county during the sixties. He's just doing some screening to eliminate the possibilities."

"I just hope he doesn't overlook the obvious like Hazel Marie's doctor did when he started screening the possibilities. I couldn't take another surprise like the one we got."

Chapter 20

It wasn't two days later, right after break-fast, that Hazel Marie announced a monu-mental change of heart—a mood swing that took me by surprise and my breath away, as well. She'd come down that morn-ing fully dressed in a frilly summer dress and high-heeled sandals. To complement her attire, she'd put on her full amount of makeup, with maybe a tad more blush on her cheeks than usual.

"Miss Julia," she declared as soon as Lloyd and Sam left for the day. "I have had my fill of crying and being depressed over what I've brought on myself. Like you said, nothing's going to change things, so I'm going to pull myself together and deal with it."

"Well," I said, a little hesitantly, "that's good news, Hazel Marie. How do you plan to do that?"

She twisted her mouth, thinking, then said, "First thing I'm going to do is stay out of that bed. I love my room, but I'm about sick of it now. And then I'm going to open all the curtains and let whoever wants to come in and visit."

"Are you sure about that?" I could just see her sitting around chatting with Emma Sue or LuAnne, as if nothing were amiss. Hazel Marie just didn't have it in her to dissemble enough to fool anybody. She'd be struck dumb at the first probing question.

"Well, look at it this way," she said. "It's a settled fact that I have to move somewhere. No, now, Miss Julia, I am not going to put you and Mr. Sam through what would happen if I stayed around. I have to leave, that's all there is to it. Now, I could hide away for a little while longer, then sneak out of town after dark. But that would leave you to make all the explanations. You'd have to come up with some kind of story and I don't want to do that to you. I know it would just kill you to have to lie to your friends."

Bless her heart, she had a better opinion of me than I had of myself, because I knew I could do it and keep doing it, if it meant that she and Lloyd would come back to us. With the baby, of course. Though, Lord knows what kind of story I could come up with to explain that little presence.

"Well," I said, "let's not cross that bridge till we have to. You don't have to hurry off anywhere."

"That's just what I mean," she said, pleased that I seemed to understand her plan. "I'm the one who has to come up with a story and take that burden off of you. See, Miss Julia, what I'll do is get my strength back, see a few visitors, and begin telling people that I've been offered a job in, say, maybe Miami."

"Palm Beach," I said, recalling a certain trip I'd made not so long before.

"Okay, Palm Beach," she agreed, "which would make sense since you've been there. Maybe you met somebody who's offered me a job."

"What kind of job, Hazel Marie?"

"Well, I haven't got that far. I'll think of something. Anyway," she said, with a determined air, "the thing is, I'm facing this head on from now on. No more hiding away until I go into hiding for good. That's the only way I see to keep you and Mr. Sam from suffering because of my mistakes."

"Hazel Marie," I began, pleading.

"No, my mind's made up. This is the best way to handle it." She stopped, looked away for a minute, then went on. "The only thing I ask is that you help me out when somebody asks me something I can't answer. You know how tongue-tied I get when I'm put on the spot, and Emma Sue has a way of putting me there."

"You and everybody else," I said. "And of course I will. I won't leave you alone with any of them. But, Hazel Marie, I am heartsick at the thought of you being gone. And Lloyd, too. I could just sit down and cry."

"Well," she said airily, "don't do that just yet. I still have a lot of plans to make, and I haven't decided about Lloyd." Her eyes filled up with the thought of him. Then she shook her head fiercely. "I am not going to start crying again, I'm just not. It doesn't help a thing."

"No, honey, it doesn't. But it sure relieves the stress."

⊗⊗

We were just pulling out chairs at the table on the third night that Mr. Pickens came to dinner, when Hazel Marie made good on her decision to face things head on. She walked into the dining room, her head held high, looking neither to the right nor to the left.

"Evening, everybody," she said, breezing right past Mr. Pickens without a glance.

As he almost stumbled in his haste to rise from his chair, she passed right on by and came around the table to sit beside me. Then she reached out and slid the centerpiece off center so it would block her view of Mr. Pickens and his of her.

"Oh, Hazel Marie," I said, getting up. "Let me get a place mat and some silver. We weren't expecting you, but we're so glad you've come down."

After setting her place, I took my seat beside her and, for encouragement, patted her hand under the table. Then my eyes met Sam's and I knew he was thinking the same as I: This was the first step, and Hazel Marie had made it. I smiled with satisfaction.

Lillian backed into the dining room, bearing a large casserole of chicken and rice. She almost dropped it when she saw Hazel Marie at the table.

"Well, law, I was 'bout to carry you up something," she said to her. "You sure you feel like settin' at the table? You can't be too careful when you been sick as you been. Ain't that right, Mr. Pickens?"

As I cringed in fear that Lillian would let something slip, Hazel Marie answered the question calmly. "I'm feeling fine, Lillian, thank you. Since *company* has just dropped in, I thought I should make the effort."

As Lillian returned to the kitchen, Mr. Pickens angled his head to look past the centerpiece. "I'm sorry to hear you've been sick," he said. "I hope it was nothing serious."

Lloyd chimed in. "Oh, it was serious, all right. It took days for that doctor to find out what was wrong with her, and I liked to died with all the worryin' I did."

"Well, she looks fine now, doesn't she?"

Mr. Pickens said, wanting, I assumed, some warmth on that side of the table. "Better than fine, in fact."

And she did. She had changed into off-white pants and a matching silk blouse with, I think, every piece of gold jewelry she owned.

"Looks can be deceiving," Hazel Marie said coolly, taking the plate that Sam had filled for her. "I've often been surprised at what little character can be found behind them."

"Have some green beans, Lloyd," I quickly said. "Mr. Pickens, you need more tea. Sam, ring for Lillian, will you, please?" Lord, was Hazel Marie going to pick a fight right here at the table?

Mr. Pickens smiled to himself, then said, "You know, I've had just the opposite ex-perience. The more beautiful someone is, the sweeter she is underneath."

Hazel Marie delicately sniffed, then ap-plied herself to her dinner. Lillian came in to refill our water and tea glasses, and Mr. Pickens and Sam raved to her about the casserole. It was good, but I was too tense to properly enjoy it.

Especially when Lillian leaned over Mr. Pickens and said, "Don't she look good for somebody in her condition?"

My roll fell onto my lap and then to the floor. Lloyd jumped up and ducked under the table. "I'll get it, Miss Julia. We don't want anybody stepping on it."

"Here, Julia," Sam said, his mouth twitching, as he passed the basket of rolls to me. "Have another one, sweetheart. Lillian, we probably need a few more."

She took the basket and left the room, for which I was mortally grateful.

"Sam," I said, trying desperately for a change of subject, "Have you made any progress at the courthouse?"

"No, and it's the strangest thing. Those files have to be there somewhere, but I've not found a one."

I thought Mr. Pickens would take up where Sam left off and steer the conversation into safer channels—maybe tell us what, if anything, he'd found at the courthouse. Instead, he was too busy trying to catch Hazel Marie's eye over or between stems of late summer roses and baby's breath. Hazel Marie kept her eyes on her plate or on Lloyd or on Sam or me. As far as she was concerned, there was an empty place where Mr. Pickens sat.

"J.D.?" Lloyd said. "You remember saying you'd like to go to Boy Scout camp with me sometime? Well, my troop's going to Camp Daniel Boone in a few weeks, just for the weekend, and I hope you can go. I think I can get maybe three or four badges in just a couple of days, first aid's one of them and canoeing, too. Daniel Boone's got a lake and everything. 'Course we'll have to sleep in a tent, but you said you like camping out."

Mr. Pickens trained those black eyes on Hazel Marie, who totally ignored the plea I saw aimed her way. Then he said, "I'd like to go with you, Lloyd, but you know how things come up. I might still be on Sam's job, or somebody else will be needing help. And, uh, your mother may have different plans for you."

"Oh," Lloyd said, plainly disappointed.

"We'll talk about it, Lloyd," Hazel Marie said. Then continuing to ignore Mr. Pickens, she went on. "*Some* people make promises they can't, or won't, keep. The only thing you can do is just go on without them and do the best you can."

Sam cleared his throat. "I think Lillian can bring dessert in now."

"Yes," I said, pushing back from the table, "and to move things along, I'll pick up in here." Anything, I thought, as I took Sam's plate, to get out of the frosty air.

As Mr. Pickens prepared to eat and run, which is usually considered impolite but for which I was grateful that evening, he tried to corner Hazel Marie as she left the table. She was having none of it. She brushed past him as if he hadn't practically knocked his chair over getting to his feet.

"Early day tomorrow, Lloyd," she said. "Say good night to your guest and come on upstairs." And out she went.

Looking, I thought, somewhat wistfully after her, Mr. Pickens shook Sam's hand, thanked me for dinner and went out to the kitchen to praise Lillian. I followed him, listened for a minute to the foolishness he carried on with her, then walked out onto the back stoop as he took his leave.

"Mr. Pickens," I said, "tell me the truth. Is there any hope of discovering who disrupted Sam's book? He's had his heart set on that for ever so long, and he's worked so hard on it. I hate to think that it's all been for nothing. So tell me, are you any closer to a solution than you were when you started?"

Mr. Pickens stopped, considered for a minute, then said, "I'll find 'em. Might take a few days, but I've got a plan of action, now that I understand just what's missing. It's a matter of finding out why the information on those papers is so important, and who it's important to."

Well, that had been my thought all along, but I only said, "I just wanted you to know that Sam considers that unwritten book his life's work. His retired life's work, that is."

"I know it," he said, and started toward his car. Then he turned back. "I guess she's really mad at me."

"Why, Mr. Pickens," I said with a smile, pleased that he was showing some concern. "How ever did you come to that conclusion?"

He grinned a bit weakly. "I don't know why she should be. All I've done was what she said she wanted."

I just shook my head at his thickness. "I would think, at your age and with your experience, you'd know better than to believe everything you hear. Follow your heart, Mr. Pickens. It might lead you to something quite surprising."

At his nod, which I wasn't sure indicated agreement, he turned away, thanking me again for dinner.

"But," I called after him, "I wouldn't leave it too long. In fact, if I were you, I'd get cracking. Things around here are in flux, Mr. Pickens. Here one day and gone the next."

He waved without turning around and I went back inside, wondering if I'd had my last chance.

Chapter 21

But I hadn't, as I was about to get a few more, thanks to Sam. He came home during the following morning to ask if I would accompany Mr. Pickens as he attempted to interview the key people who would no longer speak to Sam.

"Of course I will," I told him. "But why me?"

"Because if I go, they'll clam up. And Pickens doesn't know the county. He'd be spending half his time looking for those folks when you could lead him right to them. You could save us a lot of time."

"Well, I can try, but I'm not sure I know

the back roads all that well. Do any of
them live in town?"

Sam shook his head. "Not a one. They're
spread out all over the place. I could draw
him a map, but a couple of them came to
my house for their interviews. I'm not all
that sure I'd know how to find them."

"It's the strangest thing, Sam. They were
willing enough to talk to you then, weren't
they?"

"Yep, seemed to enjoy it, too. But, not
now. I wish the newspaper hadn't gotten
hold of the break-in. Now, not a one I interviewed will have anything to do with me."

"Well, I expect between Mr. Pickens and
me, we can get something out of them.
Don't worry, Sam," I said, secretly pleased
to be wanted, "people like to talk, especially about themselves. We'll manage
fine."

Sam handed me a list of the people
whose interviews had been on the missing cassettes. "There're five of them, but
these two, Ted and Bob Tillman, are broth-
ers, well, half-brothers, I think. There're no
records on Bob, but I got the feeling that
whatever Ted did, Bob was involved. They
live together, so you'll be making only four

visits. I listed Rafe Feldman, too, in the Morningside Rest Home, but you can forget about him. He's out of it. But this one," he went on, tapping the paper with his finger, "I know lives somewhere off the Delmont Highway."

"I know that area fairly well," I said, glancing down the list. "This won't be so difficult. But, Sam, how will we know what to ask? We don't know what you got out of them to begin with."

"I've talked it over with Pickens and here's what we decided. He'll interview them, but not about their legal problems. See, all of them were involved in arrests, arraignments, and court appearances of some kind back in the sixties, which was what my interviews were about."

As a name I knew jumped off the paper at me, I said, *"Cassie Wooten?"* I was shocked.

"She wasn't a Wooten then," Sam said, smiling. "Anyway, the reason you and Pickens will be talking to them is to see if they know who might've stolen the cassettes. You need to stay away from anything in their past, although it will certainly be on *their* minds. I want you to approach them like you're concerned that the thief, whoever it is, will use the information in ways they wouldn't like."

"You mean, blackmail?"

"I wouldn't put it quite that way, but you can imply it. But leave that to Pickens. All you need to do is direct him to where they live. And, we also think that you showing up with him will keep them from slamming the door in his face. Everybody knows who you are, Julia, so it'll seem more like a social visit."

"Well, I don't know, because everybody also knows I'm married to you. I'm not sure how much help I'll be, but I'm willing to try."

"Just get Pickens inside, that's all you have to do," Sam said. "He'll handle the rest."

"I'm glad he knows how to handle something," I said, putting the list in my pocketbook. "He's certainly not doing so well with Hazel Marie."

❀

When Hazel Marie decided she needed to do something useful that afternoon after lunch, she went upstairs to straighten the linen closet—one of her favorite busy things to do. She was changing the scented shelf

liners and rearranging the sheets and pil-
lowcases in neat stacks. I was happy
enough to let her do it, while I sat in the living room reading the newspaper in more
detail than my early morning scan.

Hearing a car door slam, I looked out
the window to see Emma Sue Ledbetter
and LuAnne Conover coming up the walk.
I threw the paper aside and hurried up the
stairs.

"Hazel Marie," I said, puffing just a little,
"LuAnne and Emma Sue are on their way
in. Do you want to see them or are you still
in bed?"

The stack of sheets she was holding
started sliding from her arms and her face
went as pale as one of them. "I think I'm
going to throw up." I caught the sheets and
put them on a shelf as she leaned against
the wall for support.

"You don't have to see them," I told her.
"I'll tell them you've had a relapse or something."

"No," she said, straightening up, "no,
I've got to do it sometime. It might as well
be now. But, Miss Julia, don't leave me
alone with them. I don't know if I can do it
by myself."

The doorbell rang downstairs and I heard Lillian's scuffling footsteps as she went to answer it. "Buck up, Hazel Marie. You'll do fine. If they put you on the spot, I'll jump in. Why don't you wait up here till I call you. They may not even expect you to come down."

Well, that wasn't the case, because Hazel Marie was the first thing Emma Sue asked about as soon as I went down and welcomed them.

"How is Hazel Marie?" she asked, settling herself on the sofa. "We do hope she's well enough for a little visit. You know, it's been almost two weeks since anybody's laid eyes on her and we're all so concerned."

"We really are," LuAnne said. "Why, Julia, just this past Sunday at church, old lady Evans told me she'd heard that Hazel Marie has some kind of wasting disease and wasn't long for this world."

"Oh, for goodness sakes," I said with a wave of my hand. "The things that get around in this town. Hazel Marie is well on the road to recovery after a long bout with whatever-it-was. She's still a little weak and shaky because she'd let herself get run down before it hit. And you know how that stuff lingers on. But, other than still needing a lot of rest, she's fine." I stood up. "Let me call her. I know she'd love to see you."

After going up to get her, I let Hazel Marie lean against me as we walked downstairs and into the living room. "Pretend to be weak," I whispered. "Then they won't stay long."

She nodded, plastered a smile on her face, and wobbled to a chair. "It's so good to see you both," she said.

Emma Sue ran to give her a hug, but not before asking if she was still contagious.

"Oh, Hazel Marie," Emma Sue said, "you don't know how I've prayed for you. Honey, you've been constantly in my prayers."

Not to be outdone, LuAnne had to give her a hug, too. "You're looking so good. Why, I wouldn't know you'd even been sick if Julia hadn't told me. Although it took her long enough to say anything. I had to hear it at the post office."

Lillian brought in a tea tray and a plate of shortbread cookies. I busied myself serving each of them, as the conversation gradually veered away from Hazel Marie's looks and condition. Which was a good thing, because they didn't seem to notice how the cup jiggled in Hazel Marie's saucer as she took it from me. I looked straight at her and gave her an encouraging nod.

"Uh," Hazel Marie began as soon as there was a lull, "you'll never guess what's happened." She put her cup and saucer on a side table and clasped her trembling hands in her lap. "I've got a job."

"A job!" Emma Sue exclaimed.

"*Why?*" LuAnne demanded, staring at Hazel Marie.

"Well," Hazel Marie said, her eyes downcast, "the offer's too good to turn down. And, you know, I can't just do nothing for the rest of my life." She took a trembling breath. "It's not a good example for Lloyd, for one thing." She glanced at me, and I nodded. She was doing fine.

"Oh, that's so commendable," Emma Sue said, "although I do think that mothers should stay home with their children. But," she went on quickly, "it's different with you, Hazel Marie, you have Julia and Lillian to take up the slack."

LuAnne had a frown on her face, making me wonder if she was entertaining a few doubts. "What kind of job?" she asked, wanting, as I knew she would, all the details.

"Well," Hazel Marie commenced, her hands gripped so tightly it was a wonder that no one commented on them, "they want me to be an event organizer. At a hotel. In Palm Beach. That's in Florida."

My eyes widened, and my cup began to jiggle. How had she come up with *event organizer?*

"Palm Beach!" Emma Sue cried, almost sputtering. "You're moving?"

Hazel Marie nodded, glanced at me and said, "I guess so."

I chimed in then. "Hazel Marie wants to expand her horizons."

LuAnne sat there, her eyes narrowed. "Just what does an event organizer do?"

"Um, well," Hazel Marie said, her eyes darting around looking for an answer. "They organize events. At the hotel, like, well, they'll give me a training course."

I leaned over to make a point. "LuAnne, you know those big hotels are always having social occasions, like dances and balls and luncheons and so forth. I expect Hazel Marie will be organizing them."

"Which big hotel?" LuAnne asked.

Hazel Marie's mouth opened but nothing came out.

"The Breakers," I said, naming the only one I'd heard of.

"Oh, my goodness," LuAnne said, patting her chest. "The Breakers! Why, that's marvelous. I've always wanted to go there. You are so lucky, Hazel Marie. How'd you ever know to apply?"

"Well," I said, ready with an answer, "I met a few people when I visited Palm Beach." Which was certainly true, let LuAnne think what she would. She didn't know who I'd met, and who I hadn't.

"I will really miss you, Hazel Marie," Emma Sue said, moved almost to tears, which was not unexpected, "but this sounds like a wonderful opportunity. So glamorous and all, but I hope you won't let being around all that wealth change you."

"No, ma'am, I won't."

I thought we'd gotten past the worst of it until LuAnne asked about Lloyd. "He's going with you, I take it."

"Well," Hazel Marie said, her voice thick

and quivery with threatening tears. "I haven't decided yet."

We'd gotten to the touchy place where I needed to be careful. So I picked my way by saying, "It's a big decision, as you can imagine, LuAnne. We're concerned about changing schools since he's done so well here, so Hazel Marie may go on by herself and send for him when she gets settled. She wants to do the right thing by him."

Emma Sue nodded. "That sounds like the smart thing to do. But, oh, Hazel Marie, we are going to miss you. I don't know who we'll get to help with the Christmas pageant. But you'll be back for the holidays, won't you?"

Lord, I had to nip that in the bud, since Hazel Marie was suddenly struck dumb, realizing that by the time Christmas rolled around, she'd be in no shape to be seen. "Why, Emma Sue," I hurriedly said, "the holidays will be her busiest time. That's the season in Palm Beach, and you know how social those people are."

"Oh, I do," LuAnne said, her eyes glowing. "I read about them all the time. You wouldn't believe all the parties they have, Emma Sue, raffles and auctions and all kinds of things. The season in Palm Beach is just full of high society types and glittering celebrities." She leaned forward, eager to share now in Hazel Marie's good fortune. "Maybe you'll meet somebody while you're there."

I saw a shudder run through Hazel Marie and quickly came to my feet. "I think she needs to rest now. Come on, sweetie, you've done enough today." I put my arm around her as she stood, then addressed LuAnne and Emma Sue. "Excuse me a minute. I'll be back down as soon as I help her upstairs. She still gets these weak spells, but a little Florida sunshine ought to fix that."

Emma Sue and LuAnne immediately rose and, wishing Hazel Marie well, prepared to leave as I'd known they would. You can generally count on people with good manners, even when you've temporarily put aside your own.

Chapter 22

"Lord, Sam," I said that night as we lay in bed, talking in the dark. "How in the world she came up with *event organizer,* I don't know, but it was perfect. Emma Sue and LuAnne didn't know any more about it than she did, so they couldn't get into details. But Hazel Marie had seen something about event organizers in one of her magazines. *Vanity Fair,* I think, and apparently it had stuck."

Sam laughed low in his chest. "Pretty fast thinking, if you ask me."

"I think so, too. And a whole lot better than running a cash register at a 7-Eleven,

which I think is all she's ever done. I can't
see that as something to build a career on,
or to move to Florida for, either. And Emma
Sue and LuAnne certainly wouldn't have."
I shifted to get a little more comfortable.
"But, Sam, the whole thing was like driving
stakes in my heart. I mean, she's taken the
first step toward moving away from us. It's
like a door has closed against any other
solution, and I am just sick about it."

Sam pulled me closer, letting me know
that he understood the despair I was feeling. "Has she told Lloyd yet? About the
baby, I mean?"

I shook my head against his chest, then
moved to come up for air. "No, and I asked
her about it. She said she thought she
might not tell him at all, especially if she
can bring herself to leave him here. And
then she admitted that the real reason she
hasn't told him is because he'd tell Mr. Pickens. So she's going to wait at least until
he's gone."

My words hung over us in the dark as
we both thought about that. Then I went
on. "I keep thinking that maybe one of us
ought to tell the boy and let him go ahead

and tell Mr. Pickens. Sometimes that seems the only way to break the logjam."

"Not yet, Julia. We might lose her for good if we interfere."

"Well, I'll tell you this, every time I think of Hazel Marie off somewhere by herself, I get so distraught I can hardly see straight. You know how she is, Sam, sweet as she can be, but naive and gullible. Somebody could take advantage of her, as several already have, and we wouldn't be there to help her."

"All we can do is let her know that we're here if she needs us. And, remember, she is a grown woman."

"I know, but being grown doesn't always mean you can take care of yourself." I turned over in bed, almost ready for sleep. "Or that you have good sense, either."

※

Mr. Pickens, looking professionally serious, came by for me the next morning. He was noticeably quieter than usual, not even carrying on nonsense with Lillian. Instead, he kept casting glances at the dining room door as if hoping that Hazel Marie would come through it.

"You feelin' all right?" Lillian asked him. "You lookin' a little peaked."

"I'm fine, Lillian," he said. "Just got my mind on what we have to do this morning."

I took the time to show Lillian the list of people we'd be searching for, asking if she knew where any of them lived.

"These folks," she said, pointing at a name, "they live on the other side of the county, close up to Brevard. You won't have no trouble findin' 'em, everybody knows who they are. An' this one here, I think he live on Benton Creek Road."

"Near that Pentecostal church?" I asked.

"Yessum, but not that far. I don't know them others."

"This one," I said, tapping a pencil against a name, "I believe lives up that wiggly road off the Delmont Highway."

Mr. Pickens had had enough directional discussion. "Let's get a move on," he said and headed for the door.

Raising my eyebrows at Lillian, I hurriedly collected my pocketbook and followed him out to his car. It was a different, but little better, one than the car he'd driven when we first met.

"I see you have a new car," I commented pleasantly as I slid into the seat beside him.

"Had it for a while," he said, busily cranking it and backing out of the driveway. "Which way?"

"Well," I said, realizing that social chit-chat was not on his agenda, "Let me see." I took the list out of my pocketbook and studied it. "Let's look for the Tillmans first. Go west on Polk, then take a right on Sanders Street. Go about six blocks and pick up 68 West. Then veer south after a few miles on the highway and turn left after you pass McCleary's grocery."

He gave no answer, just drove according to my directions. When he turned onto the highway, he said, "You do know where we're going, don't you?"

"I know *about* where we're going. I'll know it when I see it."

He gave me a quick sideways look that would've been chilling if I'd let it bother me. "You know, Mr. Pickens," I said, uncomfortable with his snippy responses and constrained by good manners to make sociable conversation to fill in the gaps.

"You'd do well to invest in one of those global things. You can get a portable and put it right up there on your dashboard. Then you'd be able to find any place you're looking for."

"Yeah, well, I've got one."

"Well, my goodness, let's use it."

"Miss Julia," he said, as if it pained him to point out the obvious, "you have to have an address for the thing to work."

"I know that. My car has one built in."

"Tell me this, then," he said with the hint of a mocking smile. "How do you enter: Go south a few miles, turn left at Mc-Cleary's grocery, and drive ten miles up a wiggly road? Or how about: Somewhere between that apple orchard with a feed and seed sign and the crossroads, but not as far as the Pentecostal church?"

I looked straight ahead, not deigning to answer. His sarcasm was so unbecoming that I wouldn't stoop to respond. As he continued to drive, the silence, if there'd been any with the rumbling of the outsized motor, would've been deafening.

Then he glanced across at me. "Or what about: On that road that crosses the creek that floods every time it rains? No, ma'am," he concluded, "what do I need with a GPS, when I've got one sitting right next to me?"

"Mr. Pickens," I said as coolly as I could manage, "since we'll be working together for the next few days, I would recommend that you put aside your personal problems and not let them slop over into your professional business. It would improve your disposition immeasurably. There's the grocery. Turn left right past it."

"Personal problems? I've got no personal problems," he said as he bounced the car off the pavement and onto a well-scraped dirt road.

"An inability to recognize a problem is a problem in itself," I said, deciding that if he needed a lecture, I was willing to give him one. "There's enough ice between you and Hazel Marie that you could cut it with a knife. Now it seems to me that the two of you could come to some sort of pleasant compromise. There're other people who're being affected, you know." Well, of course he didn't know, but I'd gone as far as I could safely go.

He nodded, gave the car a little gas as we started up a hill, then said, "Yeah, I know, and Lloyd's right in the middle of it.

But I don't know what she wants me to do. She won't have anything to do with me, and I'll tell you the truth. I don't know what I've done."

"Well, if that's the case, you're in worse shape than I imagined." I sat up and pointed to a small white house set back off the road on a hill. "I think that's the Tillman house. Turn in and let's see." Then with a sharp glance at him, I said, "You might consider that it's something you *haven't* done."

That comment gained me a disparaging grunt as he applied himself to negotiating the narrow driveway.

As the car bounced up the steep drive, I took note of the weedy front yard, the sagging barbed wire fence on the right, a car up on blocks beside a weathered barn and the small farmhouse that badly needed a good scraping and a few coats of paint.

"Doesn't look very prosperous, does it?" I murmured, looking out the windshield.

Mr. Pickens parked near the front porch and took some index cards from his pocket. Studying one, he said, "Says here that the Tillmans're half-brothers and they've lived here alone since their mother died. Neither ever married, and one of them, Ted, was arrested several times, mostly in the sixties. Never served any time to amount to anything, just kept overnight a few times. He made a couple of first appearances in court, then was released on time served or for lack of evidence."

"Arrested for what?"

"Looks like petty theft, mostly. He took a lawn mower from a neighbor one time that was later found in his barn." Mr. Pickens looked up and nodded toward the leaning barn. "That one there, I guess. And Sam mentioned something about a mule, but couldn't remember the details. Apparently his mother pled that he was mentally incompetent, and the court released him. Sam thinks Bob looks after him now."

"Well," I said, seeing two old men standing behind the screen door, staring at us, "looks like there's the brother and his keeper. We better let them know what we're doing here."

"Right." Mr. Pickens opened his door and started to get out. He turned back and said, "Keep it as light as you can, and let me ask the questions. Sam doesn't want them any more hostile than they already are." He gave me one of his old wicked grins. "They might shoot us."

Chapter 23

"Morning," Mr. Pickens sang out, as he mounted the rickety steps to the porch where the two men stood in the doorway, one in front of the other. The one in front, holding the screen door, was the shorter. He was round in body and full in the face, with red cheeks and deeply embedded eyes. What hair he had was white, ringing the crown of his head like a ruff of fur. With a red suit, beard, and wig, I thought as I stepped up onto the porch behind Mr. Pickens, this Tillman could get a seasonal job at the mall. Now though, he was wearing pants from an old suit, scuffed brogans, and a checked shirt. He seemed friendly enough, though he didn't step back to welcome us into his home, which was just as well. I had no desire to go farther than right where I was.

The Tillman brother looming behind had a full head of dark hair shot through with a sprinkle of silver and a vacant look on his face. A tuft of hair stood up from the back of his head, reminding me for a minute of Alfalfa. His lean frame seemed lost inside his overalls, although one hand kept slipping inside the bib to scratch something. His general appearance wasn't helped by the way his tongue flicked in and out of his mouth, barely touching his bottom lip, then zipping back in again.

Mr. Pickens stuck his hand out to the shorter man, giving him a friendly smile "Name's Pickens, and this is Mrs. Julia Murdoch. How're you doing, sir?"

Eyeing me from around Mr. Pickens's shoulder, the short man opened the screen door and shook the proffered hand. Then he said, "Murdoch, huh? Don't 'spect y'all are selling something, are you?"

"Nope, not a thing," Mr. Pickens assured

him. "Just wanted to talk to you and your brother if you have a minute or two."

"If it's about that trouble Murdoch had, we ain't got nothin' to say. Have we, Teddy?"

Teddy said, "Uh-uh."

"Well," I said, stepping out from Mr. Pickens's shadow, "it stems from that, but it's not about that. You know me, Mr. Tillman. I've seen you and your brother many times on Main Street, and you've both been so very courteous. I just thought that you'd be kind enough to listen to Mr. Pickens for a few minutes because he understands the kind of stress you're both under. He may be able to relieve some of it." I motioned to the rocking chairs on the porch. "May we sit for a minute, Mr. Tillman? You're Bob, aren't you?"

Bob nodded. "Suit yourself," he said, shrugging his shoulders. But then he took a seat himself and Ted followed suit. "But we got no stress and no problem, so don't look like there's much to talk about. 'Cept the weather an' it's been pretty much the same here lately."

"Oh, I think you must have some worries,"

I said, sitting in a rocker that tilted to one side. "Everybody else whom Sam interviewed is quite upset. I mean," I went on, leaning toward him, "who knows who took those cassettes that had your interviews on them and, I remind you, your court records, too. Who knows what they intend to do with them? Tell him, Mr. Pickens."

"It's like this, Mr. Tillman," Mr. Pickens said in his best professional manner. "I'm a private investigator, and Murdoch hired me to look after your interests and the interests of the others he interviewed. He doesn't want any of that information to rebound on you, especially since you'd been so helpful to him. He was going to use that information in a way that would protect your privacy, maybe even your identity. But there's no way to know what somebody else—whoever stole it—will do with it."

Ted chimed in then, garbling his words so that I couldn't understand a thing he said. Bob, though, apparently did.

"Ted says he don't want nobody talkin' about him. An' I don't neither. You got any idee who took 'em?"

Mr. Pickens shook his head. "No, we don't. That's why Murdoch is anxious to see if you could help us out. The sheriff is looking into it, but we'd rather solve the matter ourselves and not have it come out in the open. And I think you would, too. So here's the question: Can you think of any-body who'd be interested enough in things that happened forty years ago to break in and steal that information?"

Ted spewed out something else, and Bob, smiling, said, "That's right, Teddy, I'll tell 'em. Sorry, folks, but we can't he'p you. Tell you the truth, though, me'n Teddy's just as happy to let them interviews an' things git lost and stay lost. We talk too much when we git started, and Murdoch got us started. So I say let sleepin' dogs lie."

"Well," I said, somewhat irritably, "let us hope they continue to sleep and don't jump up and bite you when you least expect it. Sam is trying to do you a favor. He's hired Mr. Pickens at his own expense, specifi-cally to protect you, and you're giving us no help at all. Now, Mr. Tillman, if you have any thoughts on the subject of who would've wanted to steal your brother's records, you'd do well to speak up."

Mr. Pickens sat back and rolled his eyes

at my tirade, and Ted Tillman's tongue went in and out even faster. Bob Tillman, though, took no offense. He smiled vaguely in my direction and said, "Tell you what. You see if anybody else knows anything, an' maybe we'll go along." His eyes, set deep in facial folds, seemed to twinkle. "An' maybe we won't. All depends on who an' why an' what for."

"Well, of course it does," I said. "That's why we're here and why we're going to visit all the others. I don't understand, Mr. Tillman, why you're unwilling to help us when you would really be helping your brother. Now, I don't have any idea in the world what was on those cassettes and neither does Mr. Pickens. All we know is what Sam told us. Namely, that he wants them back in order to protect the Tillman name and reputation. Do you think the thief is going to be concerned about you? I don't, and neither does Sam. It would be to your benefit, Mr. Tillman, both Mr. Tillmans, to help us to the best of your ability."

"Sorry," Bob said, though he didn't look it or sound it. In fact, he seemed rather complacent about the possibility of having his brother's arrest record spread out for all to see.

Then, as a fresh spurt of unintelligible sounds issued from Ted, Bob went on. "Teddy says things is all up in the air an' we better wait to see which way the wind blows."

"Well," I said, losing patience and showing it by standing up, "it's unlikely to blow any good this way. Do you have any more questions, Mr. Pickens? I think these gentlemen have said all they intend to say, and we should take our leave. Thank you, Mr. Tillman." Then with a nod in Teddy's direction, "Mr. Tillman."

And I stepped down the porch steps and headed for the car, just so put out that some people wouldn't accept help when it was offered at no trouble or expense to them. Mr. Pickens stayed behind long enough to hand Bob a card and urge him to call if he thought of anything that would help.

⊗⊗

"Well," I said as Mr. Pickens took his place in the car and slammed the door, "that didn't go so well. I declare, I don't know why they wouldn't cooperate. You'd think they'd see they have nothing to lose and everything to gain. And speaking of that, Mr. Pickens, why did you leave everything to me? I thought you had all these questions to ask and I thought you knew how to get them to talk."

"I hardly had a chance," he said as he turned the car around before heading down the rutted driveway. As he turned onto the main road, which hardly amounted to more than a paved track, he went on. "I thought we'd agreed that I'd do the talking and you'd stay out of it."

"I would've, if you'd ever gotten into it. But I couldn't just sit there and watch Bob Tillman rock and Teddy Tillman lick his lips and you not getting anywhere. *Some-body* had to say something."

He kept driving and after a few miles I realized that he wasn't going to respond. I expect he was put out with me, but I couldn't help that. It wasn't in my nature to sit and wait for somebody to speak when a pointed question would do the trick.

After a while I couldn't stand the silence any longer. "What else did Sam tell you about the Tillmans? I know it was Teddy who got in trouble, but wasn't Bob mixed up in it, too?"

"Just Teddy," Mr. Pickens said, marking, I hoped, an end to the standoff. "It was Bob or their mother who kept getting him out of trouble, so he was involved that way. Sam represented Ted one time, or almost did. Said the mother and Bob came in to talk to him, but when Sam recommended pleading mental incompetence, the mother hit the roof. Stormed out, saying nothing was wrong with her boy that a leather strap wouldn't cure, and Sam could go jump in the lake." Mr. Pickens grinned. "Probably said it a little stronger than that. Anyway, the lawyer they ended up with did plead mental incompetence and Ted never served any time. He was never convicted of anything, either, but he sure was arrested time and again, usually with the goods in plain sight."

"And this was all years ago?"

"Yep. His last arrest was in the late sixties, I think. Nothing since then."

"Hm-m," I said, thinking it over. "Wonder why he stopped?"

"Maybe it was a phase and he grew out of it."

I glanced sharply at Mr. Pickens to see if was making fun of me, but his face gave nothing away.

After a few miles, I ventured a change of subject. "Where're we going now?"

"Cutting north toward Delmont, hoping you know where the Wootens live."

"I do, I think. But coming at it from this direction may put me off. It'll depend on where we hit the Delmont Highway. May I see the list that Sam gave you?"

He drew it out of the breast pocket of his jacket and handed it to me. "There're more notes in my briefcase on the back seat."

"Cassie Wooten," I said, studying the list of names and the few notes beside each one. "I know her, but not well. Just to speak to in the Winn-Dixie occasionally. The only time we ever really had a conversation was at a Church Women United meeting a few years back. She seemed ill at ease, uncomfortable in a crowd, and grateful when I took the time to chat with her. Talked a blue streak for several minutes about nothing in particular, then we got separated during lunch and never got back together. I don't expect we'll have any trouble getting her to talk, if that was any indication."

"Delmont Highway coming up," Mr. Pickens said. "Which way do I turn?"

I looked up and around, trying to determine where we were. "Left, I think. Then left again on Staton Bridge Road. We'll be going back the way we came, but on a different road. The Wootens live in a little crossroads community near where Hazel Marie grew up."

He had no response to that, so I said, "I said, near where *Hazel Marie* grew up."

"I heard you."

"I thought you might be interested, but be that as it may. William, Cassie's husband, and it's not Will or Bill, used to drive a postal route in this part of the county. I expect he's retired now. I don't know him at all."

I declare, I couldn't get anything satisfactory out of Mr. Pickens, so I just looked out at the scenery, such as it was, as he drove the way I directed.

"This is it coming up," I said as we approached Staton Crossroads. "Nothing but a gas station and a couple of empty buildings. There used to be a little grocery store, but I guess it's gone out of business. Drive on past, Mr. Pickens, I think their house is a ways down, but go slow so I can read the mail boxes."

Studying the names on the mailboxes as we passed three or four houses set back from the road, I pointed at one. "There it is. That little white house. Pull in the driveway."

"Yes, ma'am," he said and did so.

We sat for a few minutes looking at the neat, well-kept house and lawn. There wasn't a leaf on the grass nor a weed sticking up anywhere. The house itself, white clapboard with a small front porch, looked as prim and square as the yard. It sat in the exact center of the lot with a straight-as-an-arrow walkway leading to the porch, where two porch chairs sat squarely on each side of the door. A pot of red geraniums was on each side of the steps.

"Looks quite military, doesn't it?" I murmured, wondering at the amount of work it would take to keep the place in such pristine condition. "Do they know we're coming?"

"Sam called, but didn't say exactly when we'd be here. Let's go in, and, Miss Julia, let me handle it this time."

"With pleasure," I said crisply, then under my breath, "Just see that you do."

But as we approached the porch, Mr.

Pickens said, "If Mrs. Wooten answers the door, I want you to play on the fact that you know her socially. Introduce us and get us inside, then I'll take it from there."

"Yes, sir," I said, and almost saluted. He ignored me, reaching around to ring the bell. He stepped back so that whoever opened the door would see me first.

Cassie Wooten, plain and stiff in a blue housedress, her thick, iron gray hair pulled back in a bun, opened the door. She stood there for a minute, looking blank. "Yes?"

"Mrs. Wooten?" I said. "Cassie? I'm Julia Murdoch, formerly Julia Springer, remember? This is Mr. J.D. Pickens, and we're wondering if we might come in and talk with you a minute."

A brief smile of recognition flickered across her face, but her head turned quickly toward a man's voice asking who it was. She hesitated, then nodded and stepped back. "Come in," she said and led us into a small living room that was as neat and unlived in as the front lawn. There wasn't a book or a magazine or a plant in the entire room, nor any family photographs. The only jarring note to the sterile decor was the television set that was on a table right in front of the fireplace—a big no-no in home decor shows according to Hazel Marie who jotted down such decorating pearls in her scrapbook.

A slim man in gray trousers and a white shirt with the sleeves rolled up stood as we entered. His face was creased, but not by smile lines. Rather, he looked grim, almost aggressive, the overall impression emphasized by the brush cut of his reddish-gray hair.

"Who is it?" he demanded.

Not one to be intimidated by a former clerk, I immediately held out my hand and said, "Julia Murdoch, Mr. Wooten. And this is Mr. J.D. Pickens. We're here on behalf of my husband, Sam Murdoch. Actually, though, on behalf of Cassie when you get down to it. I'm sure you've heard of the break-in at Sam's house and we're anxious to get to the bottom of it, as I expect you are, too."

William Wooten quickly changed his tune, asking us to have a seat and ordering Cassie to the kitchen for iced tea, which both Mr. Pickens and I refused. The two of us sat on the sofa in front of a window,

Cassie took a straight chair, and William resumed his seat in a Barcalounger.

"I wondered when you'd get around to it," William Wooten said expansively. "Soon as I heard about that break-in, I told Cassie that Murdoch would be sniffing around again. Didn't I, Cassie?"

Cassie nodded, I thought somewhat hesitantly. I also noted that she kept looking at her husband, waiting to follow his lead, which he seemed to think his right.

Mr. Pickens jumped in. "Murdoch wants to know if you have any thoughts on who might have stolen the cassettes and the records of the people he interviewed. You might also be interested to know that the original records are missing from the courthouse. He's anxious that they not be in the wrong hands, as you must be, too."

"As far as I'm concerned," William said, "all that stuff would be better off at the bottom of the river. Murdoch came in here when I was gone and, I'll tell you the truth, Cassie don't know what she's sayin' half the time." He glared at his wife. "Told him all kinds of things better left unsaid and forgotten. She knows better now."

Cassie's face reddened as she looked at her hands knotted in her lap.

"Oh," I said, wanting to reassure her, "but you know that Sam would respect anything that shouldn't have been said. The problem now is that we don't know if the person who has them will do the same."

Mr. Pickens frowned at me and said, "I assure you, Mr. Wooten, that we're not here to go over the past. We're here only to see if you have any idea of who might have that information now."

Mr. Wooten snapped up his recliner. "I'm gonna tell you something," he said in a belligerent tone, "and you can take it straight back to Sam Murdoch. I don't appreciate him coming in here to talk to my wife when I'm not here, and frankly I don't care if he never finds 'em. Cassie doesn't have the sense she was born with, and he took advantage of her." He raised a finger, then pointed it at Mr. Pickens. "And furthermore, you got no right to come in here, upsettin' her and wantin' to dig into things that're none of your business. Cassie's a different woman now." He leaned back. "Tell 'em, Cassie."

Shocked, I glanced uncomfortably at Cassie, embarrassed for her and angered by her husband's outburst. Her hands were twisting in her lap, splotches of red on her cheeks, as she murmured a few words.

"Speak up," William Wooten demanded. "You got nothing to be ashamed of."

She looked up, but not at us. Her eyes gazed at something in the distance. "I found the Lord," she said.

"That's right," her husband said, nodding with approval. "I led her to the Lord, and now she's a born-again, church-goin' woman. Washed in the blood of the Lamb. Except," he said with a glare at me, "when somebody like Sam Murdoch wants to rake it all up again. But Cassie knows better now, don't you?"

"Yes," she murmured, looking at her hands again. "I won't talk about it any more, William."

"Well," Mr. Pickens repeated, "we're not here to go over anything again. We just want to know if you have any ideas about who could've stolen the records and inter- views, that's all."

"You're barking up the wrong tree then,"

Mr. Wooten told him. "Cassie and me got nothing to say about any of it. Cassie's learned her lesson, haven't you, girl?"

"Praise God, I have," Cassie said, her voice gaining in strength. "I haven't put a foot wrong in forty years, have I, William?"

"Not if you don't count yappin' off to Murdoch," he said with a tight-lipped grimace that seemed to pass for a smile. "And not if you don't count that meatloaf you fed me last night."

Lord, I'd had enough of him. I stood, thanked them for their time and walked out. Mr. Pickens had no recourse but to follow.

Chapter 24

"My word, Mr. Pickens," I said as he backed the car out of the driveway and headed toward Delmont. "That was the most down-trodden, repressed woman I've ever seen. I felt like smacking William Wooten out of that Barcalounger."

Mr. Pickens nodded. "Too bad we didn't catch her alone like Sam did."

"That's true. But don't you know she's suffered because of it." After a few minutes, I went on. "You know what I think? I think William Wooten could be our thief. He certainly wasn't pleased that Cassie had talked to Sam, and I wouldn't put it past him to make sure her records never saw the light of day."

"I had the same thought," Mr. Pickens said, surprising me that the two of us could agree on anything. "But without any evidence . . ." He shrugged. "Anyway, I slipped my card under a coaster, so maybe she'll find it and call."

"Maybe, but I doubt it. But I'll tell you something else we can do. Or I can do. I'll try to get Cassie off by herself—invite her to lunch or something, and get her talking again. The woman is starved for a little kindness. I mean, Mr. Pickens, you should've heard her at that Church Women United meeting. I couldn't shut her up. Not that I wanted to, but still." I stopped, thinking of how needy Cassie Wooten had seemed that day. "And you know something else? I think I recall hearing Emma Sue Ledbetter talking about some kind of women's ecumenical counsel she helped form. That's my preacher's wife, you know. Anyway, she happened to mention that Cassie Wooten was on it, too, representing her church. I remember being surprised, not about Cassie but about Emma Sue, since Pastor Ledbetter is not at all ecumenically inclined."

Mr. Pickens didn't seem interested in anybody's church activities, ecumenical or not. He just kept driving, but I thought that, if the opportunity presented itself, I'd ask Emma Sue in a roundabout way what she thought of Cassie.

Unable to stand the silence, I tried another tack. "I really don't want to pry into private matters, but did Sam tell you what Cassie did? She just doesn't seem the type to get in trouble with the law."

"Look in my briefcase," Mr. Pickens said. "Sam wrote out what he could remember from the records." He smiled, a little grimly, I thought. "You might be surprised."

I reached back for the briefcase, unlatched it on my lap and drew out several sheets of paper filled with Sam's scribbled recollections of the information he'd gathered on each of the people we were to visit.

"Let's see," I said, flipping through the pages. "Here's Cassie's. Oh, my word. *Cassie? Cassie Wooten?* Mr. Pickens, I can't believe this. Sam's got down here that she was accused by a neighbor—this was in 1966—of harrassment. Making threatening phone calls and splashing paint on the house, and, oh, my goodness, she was arrested for being drunk and disorderly and being a public nuisance, too. Not once, but three times, and resisting arrest every time. This is unbelievable. Oh, wait a minute." I read through Sam's notes again, comparing one page to another. "Did you notice this? Ted Tillman had the same prosecutor and the same judge as Cassie. You reckon that means anything? Well, I guess not. They had different defense attorneys. Not that they needed defending since none of the cases went anywhere." I blew out my breath, just done in by what I'd learned about Cassie Wooten's run-ins with the law. "This is just so hard to take in. I can't imagine her, or any woman I know, being drunk and disorderly, and a public nuisance, too. It's so . . . unladylike. Of course, all of us have some regrets about what we've done in the past." I gave Mr. Pickens a hard look that he didn't notice. "How reassuring, though, that some of us can redeem those errors before it's too late. All it might take is saying you're sorry and that you'll try to do better."

I waited for a response and didn't get

one. So I tried again, since it's incumbent upon any well-behaved person to make conversation when in polite company, and to *carry* the conversation when in impolite company. "Well, anyway," I said, making the effort since he seemed bound and determined not to, "maybe it was the sheriff's fault that none of these people were convicted of anything. Have you thought of that? Maybe his deputies lost evidence or something."

"Could be," Mr. Pickens agreed, making this a most unusual day to have a comment of mine approved twice in a row. "Sam's thinking along those lines, too. But he knew the sheriff back then and finds that hard to believe. He told me he can't find any connection between the sheriff and these few people that would warrant the special treatment they got."

"As far as I can see," I said, shuffling through the pages again, "there's no connection among the people themselves. Let's see, there's four, no, five people counting Rafe Feldman, but we can't count him, and we've seen two out of the four, Ted Tillman and Cassie Wooten. As unlikely a pair as you could imagine. What would they have in common, except a lot of arrests and no convictions?"

"That's what Sam wants to know, and what, apparently, somebody doesn't want him to find out." Mr. Pickens turned onto the Delmont Highway and aimed the car back toward Abbotsville. "You hungry?"

"I could eat," I said, looking at my watch. "And no wonder. It's almost one o'clock. Lillian will have something ready if she hasn't given up on us." With a sidelong glance at him, I casually went on. "You're welcome to have lunch with us. Sam has his Rotary Club meeting today, so it'll just be Lillian and Hazel Marie. And me, of course."

Mr. Pickens's mouth twisted just a tiny little bit, then he said, "I better get on. James said he'd have sandwiches ready, and I need to make some notes on our visits this morning."

"Well, that certainly won't take long. All we got from the Tillmans and the Wootens was essentially 'No comment.'" Then, recognizing a captive audience when I saw one, I said, "Now I know it's none of my business, but I declare, Mr. Pickens, if you and Hazel Marie keep avoiding each other, nothing's ever going to be resolved. Couples break up every day of the week, and if they all avoided each other nobody would ever speak to anybody again. It seems to me that the two of you ought to be able to get along. You were certainly able to long enough in the past to know how it's done."

He just grunted, offering nothing else in response. I supposed I was to take that as a rebuke for meddling in his business. But he wasn't alone in that business, although he didn't yet know what was at stake.

I sighed, bemoaning the silent treatment he was giving me every time Hazel Marie's name was mentioned. If he would ever open up and talk about their differences, I could perhaps guide him as I was doing with her. But if there was ever a stong, silent type, it was Mr. J.D. Pickens, P.I. Keeping one's own counsel can be commendable, but not when somebody is right at hand, just waiting to help.

He steered the car to a stop at the curb in front of my house. "I'll let you out here, if that's all right."

"It's fine," I said. "Do you want to go

back out this afternoon? We could see at least one more person today."

"After this morning, I'm not sure what good we're doing, but we ought to see them all. About two-thirty suit you?"

"That'll be fine, but won't you come in?" I asked as I gathered my pocketbook and prepared to step out. "Lillian would love to see you even if no one else would."

He turned the full voltage of those black eyes on me as a little smile played around his mouth, acknowledging my attempt to get him inside. He just shook his head. Lord, but the man was attractive. No wonder Hazel Marie hadn't been able to resist him. As for myself, I got out of the car while I still could.

I went in the front door and on into the kitchen. "Lillian? I'm home. Where is everybody?"

"Oh, Law, Miss Julia," she said, coming to meet me in the middle of the kitchen. "I thought you never get here. Miss Hazel Marie upstairs packin' her suit satchel."

"Oh, no, don't tell me that." I sagged against the counter. "What does she say? Is she planning to leave right away?"

"No'm, I don't think so. 'Least it don't

look like it. She got clothes strung out all over the place, sayin' she can't decide what to take and what not to."

"Well," I said, straightening up with an effort, "I better go see about her."

"No'm, you set yo'self down and eat something. I already got a salat made, an' she won't be goin' nowhere anytime soon. Now set down."

"I think I will," I said, as I pulled a chair out from the table. "I'm about to cave in, and I'm not sure I have the strength to face another hard-headed person. I declare, Lillian, I am completely dismayed. What are we going to do with her?"

"What you need is something in yo' stomick, then you able to go at it again." She took a covered bowl from the refrigerator and began preparing a plate for me. "Here," she said, setting the plate before me. "This a good tuna salat I jus' made with a little fruit on the side. I'm heatin' up some rolls. You want coffee or tea?"

"Coffee, I guess. I don't really care, whatever's made. Oh, Lillian, we can't let her go off. What has she said about Lloyd? What's she going to tell him?"

"I don't know, Miss Julia. She don't tell

me nothin', 'cept she got to do something even if it wrong."

"Well," I said, eating hurriedly, "that's exactly what I don't want her to do. She's not thinking straight. How could she, with all she has on her mind?" I buttered a roll, as one question after another rolled through my mind. Had Hazel Marie decided where she would go? Had she made plans as to where she would live when she got there? And, again and again, what would she do about Lloyd?

I had to force myself to eat, knowing I needed it, but there was hardly any taste to it. Lillian kept giving me the eye as she worked around the kitchen, and at one point when she refilled my cup, she put a comforting hand on my shoulder. Tears sprang to my eyes, and I almost choked on a piece of cantaloupe. I didn't often give up once I'd set my mind to something, but this situation with Hazel Marie had about defeated me.

I looked up as the door from the dining room was pushed open and Hazel Marie walked in. I tried to smile but was stopped in my tracks at the expression on her face.

"Miss Julia," she said, grasping the back

of a chair, her face white and drawn. "I think I need to go to the doctor."

I sprang from my chair. "What is it? Are you throwing up again?"

"No'm, it's something else—bad. Worse, even. Please, would you take me? I don't think I ought to drive."

Lillian ran to her and put an arm around her. "Lord, lord, honey. Set yo'self down and don't be movin' too much. Miss Julia, we better get her on 'fore she lose that baby."

"Oh, my goodness, yes." I grabbed my pocketbook and looked frantically for the car keys. "Help her out to the car, Lillian, and let's go."

Lillian practically carried Hazel Marie to the car, even though she protested that she felt well enough to walk by herself. But Lillian got her settled in the front seat, then climbed into the back. "I'm goin', too," she said, and I was glad to have her.

Little was said on our way to the doctor's office, so intent was everybody to get there. At one point I mentioned the fact that Dr. Hargrove should be back by now and saw tears streaming down Hazel Marie's face.

"I was hoping I wouldn't have to see him," she whispered.

"And I was hoping you would," I said. "He will be nothing but professional. And *kind*, Hazel Marie. You will be in good hands."

There was no question of waiting our turn when we got there and told the receptionist the problem. Hazel Marie was immediately taken to an examining room, and Dr. Hargrove himself came out and ushered Lillian and me to his office.

"Wait in here, Miss Julia," he said. "You'll be more comfortable and I'll see you after I've looked her over."

If I hadn't been so worried I'd have been pleased. This was how a physician should treat a long-time patient, dinner companion, and fellow church member.

"Lillian," I murmured as we waited, and after I'd looked at the bookshelves, the family pictures on the desk, and the diplomas on the wall. "I hate to say this, but if Hazel Marie's in no danger, this could really solve all our problems."

"No'm, Miss Julia, don't say that. We don't wanta lose that little baby. Miss Hazel Marie might think she don't want it, but she do. If she lose it, she be worse upset than if she don't. When the Lord send a baby, he send the wantin', too."

I nodded, deciding to stop praying for either outcome and leave that to the one in charge, but my poor pocketbook got kneaded to death as we waited.

After a good half hour, the door swung open and Dr. Hargrove, still with that beard I couldn't understand why he'd grown or kept, walked in and took his seat behind the desk.

"Lillian," he said, "she's getting dressed and might need some help. She's in the second room across the hall."

Lillian jumped up, eager to be of help, and left.

"How is she, Doctor?" I asked, leaning toward him.

"She's fine for now. These things happen, Miss Julia, sometimes as a warning of worse to come and other times for no reason at all. There can be ups and downs in any pregnancy, as you know. Well, perhaps you don't. But right now, all we can do is wait and see." He propped his large arms on the desk and looked directly at me. "Now, I assume that Hazel Marie's condition has created some problems for all of you, and anytime you want to talk about it, I'll be glad to listen. But for now, my concern is for Hazel Marie. What I want you to do is take her home and put her to bed. I want her flat on her back for several days until we see what's going to happen. She can get up to go to the bathroom, but no going up and down stairs and no strenuous activity. If at any time she gets worse, get her to the hospital and call me."

I was nodding all the way through these instructions, yet when he stopped I hardly knew what to ask. "But she's all right for now?"

"She is," he confirmed, and I was reassured by his confidence. That's what a patient wants from a doctor, not any of this hemming and hawing and possible this and possible that. "Now, while I had her here, I went ahead and did a sonogram, but I'll let her tell you about that."

The last time a doctor said similar words to me, I got a shock I still hadn't recovered from. But I nodded agreeably, thinking that modern science was remarkable for being able to predict the gender of an unborn child a little more accurately than dangling

a pencil on a string. So Hazel Marie perhaps knew whether we were to have a little
Pickens or a little Puckett when the time
came to have it. Not that it mattered, since
I still didn't know what we'd do with either
one.

Chapter 25

"Two!" My foot slipped off the brake onto the gas pedal as I backed out of the parking slot. The car jolted to a stop with a shattering crunch, snapping my head forward. Metal scraped against metal, and Lillian ended up hung over the front seat, screeching her head off.

"Oh, sweet Jesus!" Lillian shrieked. "You done hit something." She had her arms wrapped around Hazel Marie, holding on tight. "You all right? Are you all right?"

"Oh, Lord!" I cried, thinking I'd ruined Hazel Marie as well as my car. I flung open the door and sprang out to see what the damage was. I knew what I'd hit. I'd seen it big as life before I started backing out. I mean, who wouldn't have seen something as big as a Dempster Dumpster?

Walking to the rear of the brand new car I'd purchased for my trip to Palm Beach only a few months before, I surveyed the result of a foot slippage. There was a huge dent in the trunk and the bumper was caved in with one end dangling on the pavement. The corner of the Dumpster where I'd hit it had only a little chrome and black paint on it, which would wash off in the first rain and nobody'd ever be the wiser.

I got back in the car, reassured myself as to Hazel Marie's welfare, and moved the gear shift into drive. Then I proceeded out of the parking lot, looking straight ahead as if nothing had happened, while one end of the bumper bounced up and down, scraping against the pavement with sparks flying everywhere.

"Hazel Marie," I said, "I will never forgive myself if you got jolted too much. How're you feeling? Are you all right? Lillian, is she all right?"

"I'm fine, Miss Julia," Hazel Marie said. "Really I am. It wasn't much of a jolt."

"It big enough to th'ow me over yo' head," Lillian said as she sat back and searched for the seat belt, which she should've had on to start with. "I better strap myself in good, what with people runnin' into Dipsy Dumpsters an' messin' up they cars."

"Don't worry about the car," I said grimly. "I'm worried about Hazel Marie. Besides, they don't make cars like they used to."

What was a repair bill, even of monumental proportions, in the face of not just one, but two, illegitimate babies? There'd be no way to explain away twins as Hazel Marie's sudden impulse to adopt a needy child, no way to let her go off by herself and deal with two plus Lloyd. All I could think of as the grinding, clattering bumper scraped along behind us was that Mr. Pickens had an awful lot to answer for. *Twins!* What had the man been thinking?

After I'd pulled into the driveway, Lillian and Hazel Marie walked behind the car to behold the wreckage.

"Law, Miss Julia," Lillian said, "that gonna cost you a mint to get fixed."

Hazel Marie moaned and began to tear up again. "It's all my fault. I'm so sorry, Miss Julia."

"It's nobody's fault," I said, not wanting to talk about it. "I got distracted, that's all. Now, stop worrying about it. I still have my little car, so I'll be driving it for a while. Oh, look, Hazel Marie," I went on as we got to the back door. "Here's Mr. Pickens's card. I guess he came by like he said he would."

"Well, he can keep on going," she said. "Besides, he came to get you." She turned to me, her mouth trembling. "I'm sorry I messed up your plans. I know you're doing something for Mr. Sam."

"Hazel Marie," I said, pushing open the door and walking in, "will you please stop being sorry for everything? We have to get you taken care of and nothing's more important than that, including doing something for Sam with Mr. Pickens. They can both take a backseat for a few days. Now, I want you to sit right down and rest. Lillian and I have some moving to do. I'm going to put you in our room, and Sam and I will move upstairs."

"Oh, Miss Julia, you don't have to do that."

"Yes, I do. The doctor said no going up and down the stairs. Come on, Lillian, let's get started."

It took the rest of the afternoon to get the job done, but before we started, I'd called Ralph Peterson to come get my car and tell me in dollars and cents what the damage would be. I urged him to get a move on before everybody in town saw what I'd done and never let me forget it.

Lillian and I changed the sheets on my and Sam's bed first and put Hazel Marie in it. Then we moved a few necessary clothes from one closet to another and exchanged toiletries in the bathrooms, going up and down the stairs a hundred times. I declare, though, like Lillian had said, Hazel Marie's room was covered in clothes she'd had out getting ready to pack. We got those hung back up and made a little room for what Sam and I would need for the next several days.

Hazel Marie watched the comings and goings from our bed, but I had to keep telling her to keep her head flat.

"But I feel all right," she said. "And nothing's happening now."

"Well, I'm glad," I replied, "but that's not the point. Dr. Hargrove said flat on your back, and that's the way I want you."

She turned her face away and murmured, "Maybe it would be better all around if . . ."

"No," I said firmly, "we're not going to think that way. Why, Hazel Marie, one or both of those babies could be president one day. Or they could discover the cure for a terrible disease, or one could be a famous musician or even a preacher." I stopped and considered for a minute, wondering what would impress her more than that. "Or just be fine and decent men or women, or man and woman, who would be a blessing to you in your old age." I leaned over and straightened her covers. "There's a purpose for every soul that comes into this world, and what you have to do is follow the doctor's orders. Then if you lose them, you can rest assured that that's the way it's supposed to be. And if you don't, then that's the way it's supposed to be, too. Just be Presbyterian enough,

Hazel Marie, to trust that whatever happens is what is supposed to happen. What will be, will be, you know."

She smiled a little. "I think that's a song."

✸✸

The back door slammed and Lloyd came running in, sweaty from his tennis exertions and highly agitated. "Miss Julia! Your car's all messed up!"

"Oh, my word," I said, meeting him in the hall. "Ralph Peterson was supposed to have that car in the shop. I'm calling him again."

"But what happened?" Lloyd asked. "Somebody wrecked it?"

Lillian walked out just then. "Wadn't no *somebody*," she said. "A Dipsy Dumpster did it."

So then I had to explain, but when I got to the point of telling him that his mother had been put back to bed, he lost interest in car wreckage. "Just a little relapse," I assured him, as he headed in to see her.

"Oh, Lillian," I murmured, leading the way to the kitchen, "I don't know how long we can keep this up. Something's got to give, sooner or later."

"Some lemonade be good right about now," she said. "Let me make us a pitcher."

"Gladly," I said, collapsing in a chair at the table. "Hazel Marie looks all right, doesn't she? I mean, she'd let us know if something happens, won't she?"

"Yessum," she said, getting out the sugar and the lemons. "Like I tole you, she don't want to lose that baby. *Them* babies, I mean. Law, Miss Julia, can you believe us having two of 'em? Think how many years this house have no chil'ren at all, an' now it gonna be crawlin' with 'em."

So I sat there and thought about the empty years. Then I thought about what it would be like with two more besides Lloyd. If they turned out to be as satisfactory as he was, I would have no complaints. None at all, regardless of what the town thought.

Lillian put a glass of lemonade in front of me, then left to take two more glasses in to Hazel Marie and Lloyd. I'd just picked up my glass when I heard Sam's footsteps outside.

"Julia," he said, coming in the door, "what happened to your car?"

"Oh, nothing much, Sam," I said, getting up to pour lemonade for him. "It's just a little ding, nothing to get upset about."

Sam's eyebrows went up. "You didn't get hurt, did you?"

"Nobody got hurt but the car and a Dumpster. But I've already called Ralph to come get it. So let's not worry about it."

I had had enough of the inordinate interest everybody was taking in the condition of my car. When something goes wrong, the polite thing to do is to pretend you don't notice and carry on with general conversation. I just hated having attention drawn to any little mishap that could've happened to anybody, but if Ralph Peterson didn't come on soon, half the town would stop by to tell me my car was wrecked. As if I didn't know it.

❦

"One good thing," I told Sam that evening after I'd related, out of Lloyd's hearing, the highlights of the afternoon, "she won't be going anywhere anytime soon. But can you believe twins? It's more than I can take in and just complicates matters that much more."

We were sitting in our accustomed place on the sofa in the living room. Lillian had gone home and Lloyd was in the back bedroom, formerly my and Sam's room, with his mother. Although I'd suggested to Hazel Marie that she begin preparing the boy for all the changes we were expecting, she was still reluctant to reveal her condition.

"Not yet, Miss Julia," she'd said. "I could still lose these babies, and there's no need to worry him beforehand in case I do. It may just be that he'll never have to know." Far be it from me to put any kind of burden on the boy or on her, either, so I could do nothing but assume that she knew best.

"What'd you tell Lloyd?" Sam asked, bringing me back to the here and now. "I mean, about why his mother's back in bed."

"We just said she'd had a relapse of the same old flu and the doctor ordered bed rest. He seemed to accept it well enough, though I can tell he's concerned." I leaned my head on Sam's shoulder. "Oh, Sam, what're we going to do with two babies?"

"Have a houseful, I expect." He patted my back. "Have you given up on Pickens?"

"Not really, except he's certainly being uncooperative. I think, if he were to come in here with a huge bouquet of flowers and tell her he couldn't live without her, she'd fall all over herself marrying him. But I can hardly get him in the door. Oh, he'll come for dinner, but after the way she gave him the cold shoulder the other night, I'm not even sure of that anymore." I sat up to look at him. "It's like he's lost all get up and go, Sam. Why, I can remember when he first met her, nothing could stop him. He courted her like few women have been courted, but now it seems he doesn't want to even try. Why would he act in such a way?"

"Probably because it means too much to him. Doesn't want to risk putting it all on the line."

"It would give me hope if that's true. But, of course, if he thinks that way, it's totally ridiculous. Every woman wants to be courted. Wants to be wanted, and as long as he makes himself scarce, the longer Hazel Marie is convinced he doesn't care. And the longer she has to pretend that she doesn't, either."

Sam covered a yawn with his hand. "Well, whatever happens, we'll deal with it. But for Hazel Marie's sake, I hope something works out. Even with our help, being the unmarried mother of three children will be a heavy burden to bear."

"Well, how do you feel about it, Sam? I mean, having a houseful of illegitimate children?"

"Oh, honey, I don't care. A child is a child, regardless of what its parents have done. Besides, it'll liven things up around here to have a few babies around."

I took his hand in both of mine, thinking again how fortunate I was to have him. Then switching subjects, I said, "How did Mr. Pickens do this afternoon? Did he see anybody?"

Sam laughed. "He got lost down in the Bear Valley area. Came in cussin' and car-ryin' on about no road signs and poor di-rections. He was looking for Ilona Weaver, and I was able to get him only so far. He had to stop and ask several times and kept ending up where he'd started from. He needs you with him, Julia. Think you'll be able to go tomorrow?"

"If Hazel Marie doesn't take a turn for the worse, yes, I think so. In fact, I'll take Lloyd's cell phone, in case there's trouble here."

"Pickens has a cell phone."

"Even better, then. I'll leave his number with Lillian, so if Hazel Marie needs me, he can take the call. That way, he'll get the full impact of Lillian's hysterics which, believe me, will get him moving if anything can."

Sam and I went together to wish Hazel Marie a good night and to reassure ourselves that all was well with her. It was all she could do to look at Sam, she was still so embarrassed to have him know what she'd been up to. But Sam was kindness itself, the most nonjudgmental man I've ever known. I left the little silver dining room bell by her bed in case she needed me in the night, then told Lloyd it was time for him to be upstairs in his bed.

It felt strange walking up the stairs with Sam to the room I'd slept in for over forty years with another man. I'd given it to Hazel Marie so I'd never have to sleep in it again, yet here I was, walking right into the pink and gold wonderland that she and her decorator had turned it into. There was nothing left in it of my first husband, possibly because Hazel Marie hadn't wanted any reminders of him, either. I wondered how well I would sleep, because even without any tangible items, the room itself might prove to be enough to give me a nightmare or two. Yet by the time I crawled in beside Sam and scrooched up close to him, any thought of Wesley Lloyd Springer had gone completely out of my head.

Chapter 26

So the next morning I took off again with Mr. Pickens on our search for leads in the case of stolen records and interviews. Before leaving the house, though, I'd gone to see how Hazel Marie had fared during the night. I walked in just as she was coming out of the bathroom, heading back to the bed.

"How're you feeling this morning?" I asked, looking carefully for any signs of distress.

"I feel really good," she said, as she sat on the side of the bed. "In fact, I don't think there's anything to worry about. Don't you

think I could sit in a chair for a while today?"

"No, I don't. Hazel Marie, you have to
do what Dr. Hargrove said and stay in bed.
But if you don't have any problems today,
I'll call him tomorrow and see if you can
get up for short stretches. How will that
do?"

"All right, I guess," she said, lying back
on the pillow with a sigh. "But I am so tired
of being in bed all day with nothing to do. It
gets lonesome with Lloyd out most of the
day and you gone and Lillian busy. I know
I shouldn't complain, but I just get so sad
when I'm by myself."

I was moved by pity, for Hazel Marie
was not one who could entertain herself
with her own thoughts. Especially not now,
when her own thoughts were undoubtedly
filled with recriminations and regrets. "I'll
tell you what," I said. "Mr. Pickens can go
on his own this afternoon, and I'll stay
home with you. But I have to go this morning since he can't find the place by himself." I laughed. "Sam said he was lost all
yesterday, going around and around in circles, and came back cussing and carrying
on. Serves him right, don't you think?"

That got a smile from her, but not much else. So I went on, "Now, Hazel Marie, I'll ask Lillian to come sit with you a while. You two can make a list of what we're going to need for these babies. Oh, and you'd better begin to think of some names, too."

Well, that wasn't the best idea I'd ever had for providing some distraction, because the thought of the babies' imminent arrival made her face cloud up again.

"I know I should," she said, wiping her eyes with the palms of her hands like a little girl. "I feel like I'm caught in something I can't get out of. And," she went on, her voice catching in her throat, "I guess I am and everybody'll know it. Miss Julia, I'm already beginning to show. When I got up a few minutes ago, it was like they'd grown overnight."

"Oh, my word, and we haven't even thought of maternity clothes. I guess I'd better start a list, too."

"I don't care about maternity clothes," she said, turning her face away. "All I want to do is crawl in a closet and hide."

"Now, Hazel Marie, you mustn't think like that. Let's just take one day at a time and not look too far ahead. We're going to work something out if every last one of us has to move to Arizona or somewhere." I switched off the lamp by her bed, then walked over to open the blinds for a little natural light. "I'm going to send Lillian in. You get her talking and you won't have time for worrying. Is there anything I can get you while I'm out?"

"Well," she began hesitantly, "I know it's not good manners, but would you mind getting me a pack of gum? I'd love some, and it's not like anybody'll see me chewing it."

"Why, of course," I assured her, although gum chewing wasn't something I could ordinarily approve. "Any special kind?"

"Oh, Juicy Fruit's my favorite. I can almost taste it now."

Well, that craving was easy enough to satisfy, but I wondered what else her changing appetite would be demanding before it was all over.

❧❦

As I settled myself in the passenger seat of Mr. Pickens's car, it occurred to me that I was experiencing a certain lifting of the spirits. With the threat of Hazel Marie's losing those babies, the burden of worry about her taking off on her own had been lifted without my realizing it. Of course, worry about how we'd handle *two* babies had taken its place, but it was a relief to realize that Hazel Marie hadn't said one word about leaving since their advent had been announced.

I smiled to myself but aimed at Mr. Pickens as he pulled away from the curb. "I apologize for letting you down yesterday," I said pleasantly, determined not to start off in a dead silence and stay that way. "We had a semi-emergency and I didn't have time to call you."

I waited for him to ask who'd had an emergency, but instead he said, "I heard about your car. You have to watch those Dumpsters, they'll jump out at you when you're not looking."

That was a topic I certainly didn't want to discuss, so I turned it back on him. "And I hear you had trouble finding the Weaver house."

He nodded, keeping his attention on the street. "I hope you know where it is."

"It's fairly close to the Bear Valley Baptist Church," I said, thinking *I think* to myself.

"That's what Sam said, but I drove all over that valley and never saw a Baptist church anywhere."

"Well, believe me, there's more than one. Whenever you have two Baptists, you're likely to have two churches. So just go back to the same area you were in yesterday, and we'll find it."

He was content enough to let the conversation lapse as the car hummed along, but of course I was not. "I don't know Ilona Weaver," I said. "Is she expecting us?"

He twisted his mouth. "She was. At least she was yesterday. Sam tried to get her this morning to let her know we were coming. Nobody answered."

"Well," I said, "I guess that means we may miss her even if we find the house. Which I fully intend to do, I assure you." Then, thinking that an opportunity had just presented itself, I went on. "Of course, she's *expecting* only one. Wonder how she'll take it when *two* show up? A lot of people expect just one, then they're amazed when they get two—doubling their pleasure, you might say."

Mr. Pickens cocked an eye at me. "What're you talking about?"

"Oh, nothing," I said, looking out the window at the apple orchard we were passing. "Just thinking out loud. But, Mr. Pickens, don't let me forget. When we're on our way back, I'd like to stop somewhere and pick up some Juicy Fruit."

He laughed. "You taken up chewing gum these days?"

"It's not for me. It's for Hazel Marie, who's had to be put back to bed. A relapse of some kind, the doctor said. And all she's asked for is gum, which to my mind is little enough to do for her."

I glanced over and saw the frown deepen on his face, but it took the longest for him to respond. Finally, as if reluctant to show any interest, he asked, "She's still sick?"

"She's not exactly *sick*. She's just having a few problems with a normally normal condition."

Let him turn that over, I thought, and if he doesn't get it, then he's thicker than I suspect. The long silence proved that he was. Unable to stand it any longer, I said, "Mr. Pickens, it would do her a world of good if you'd show a little interest in her condition. It wouldn't hurt you to be a little less standoffish."

"Miss Julia," he said with an long sigh, "she's made it clear that she doesn't want me around. So, in spite of your efforts—as well meant as they might be—I am not going to push in where I'm not wanted."

Well, that engendered a long silence from me. Not knowing how to respond, I kept my eyes on the country road we were now traveling. Then seeing a vine-covered sign for Ebenezer Baptist Church, I said, "Turn left here." Then I said, "Well, I don't see why not."

He made the turn, straightened the car, then gave me a questioning glance. "Why not what?"

"Why not push yourself in? You might be surprised at the reception you get."

He gave me a wry smile. "I'm not the pushy type."

"Huh. If that's the case, then I don't know who is. Take a right at the stop sign."

He did and we proceeded on in silence, in spite of my many sidewise glances at him in hopes of eliciting more of what he was thinking. Giving up with a sigh, I said, "So what mischief was Ilona Weaver up to in her young years? Did Sam say?"

"Embezzlement."

"*Embezzlement?* My goodness, I've never known anybody who embezzled." Then after a few minutes, I said, "Well, of course there was Richard Stroud, but other than that, I still don't, because I don't know Ilona Weaver. Maybe I'd better prepare myself. Do you still have Sam's notes?"

He jerked a thumb toward the backseat. "They're in my briefcase, but there's not much on her. Sam said she was the most reluctant to talk of them all. Hardly let him in the house and was fairly belligerent about it. No wonder, though, because embezzlement's a felony and she got away clean. No conviction, no sentence, no explanation."

"Well, that is strange. How much did she embezzle?"

"A few hundred dollars, but it was from a Girl Scout cookie fund or a bake sale for the PTA. Something like that."

"Maybe they let her pay it back," I said, scrounging among the papers in his briefcase. "I declare, Mr. Pickens, you need to get these papers organized."

He ignored my suggestion and said instead, "The prosecutor dropped the charges, so some arrangement was undoubtedly made. In fact, Sam said he almost didn't include her, and wouldn't have, except for her records being stolen along with the others."

"Hm-m-m," I said, finally finding the skimpy notes on the Weaver case. "He just has 'Embezzlement. No charges filed.' Maybe she didn't take as much money as they thought."

He smiled at my ignorance of the law. "Embezzle a penny, and it's still a felony."

"Slow down, Mr. Pickens. It's right up here, I think." I craned out the windshield, looking for the place that Sam had described. "There it is. And there she is, I think, on the front porch."

I pointed toward a double-wide trailer on a small knoll to our left. It looked long and firmly anchored to the ground with a wide railed porch and a ramp along one side, made of raw treated lumber, obviously added to it. As he guided the car into the driveway, I could see a woman I took to be Ilona Weaver wrapped in a heavy sweater and a quilt, sitting in a wheelchair, taking the sun. I almost melted, looking at her, for the day was already sweltering.

"I didn't know she was crippled," I whispered.

"Yeah, Sam said she's been in that chair for a few years now. Some kind of degenerative disease, not sure what."

"Bless her heart," I murmured sympathetically. "Let's hope she'll appreciate a little company."

My hope was dashed as we got out of the car and approached the brooding woman in the wheelchair. She was heavyset from what I could tell, reminding me of a turtle, as she sat slouched over and huddled under the quilt. Thick plaits of hair, black enough to be dyed, draped along each shoulder. The frown on her face deepened, and her deep-set eyes glowered at us as we reached the bottom step.

"You can stop right there," she said, a hand holding the end of a slender rope snaking out from under the quilt. The other end of the rope was attached to the handle of the screen door. Behind the screen stood a silent but alertly watchful dog. As its form took shape behind the screen mesh, I could see saliva oozing from its mouth and hear a low but ominous growl deep in its throat.

I nudged Mr. Pickens and stepped back. "You go ahead," I whispered.

"Mrs. Weaver?" Mr. Pickens coura-geously said. "Sam Murdoch called about us stopping by. We'd just like to ask if you have any knowledge of . . ."

"I got nothing to say to Sam Murdoch or to you," Mrs. Weaver said. "I told him not to come out here no more and not to send nobody. An' if you think I don't mean it, why, I'll just jerk this rope an' let my rott-weiler tell you."

"Don't do that, Mrs. Weaver," Mr. Pick-ens said, prudently keeping his feet on the ground and away from the steps. "We're not here to make trouble. We're just trying to find out if you know who could've been interested enough in your records to steal them."

"I don't know an' I don't care," she said, giving the rope a light snap, making the dog's shoulders bunch up, readying itself to spring as soon as she opened the door. "But I'll tell you this, whoever took 'em did me a favor. More power to 'em, I say. No-body's got a right to go mucking through the past, anyway, an' you can tell Sam Murdoch I said so. Or do you want Alvin to send him a message?" And she snapped the rope again, this time rattling the screen and causing Alvin to bare his teeth. "You better be glad I got me a dog that won't do nothin' till I tell it to."

"We are, I assure you," I said, plucking at Mr. Pickens's sleeve. "Thank you, Mrs. Weaver, we'll be going now."

As we got back in the car with the doors safely closed, I said, "Alvin?"

Mr. Pickens grinned as he started the car. "Yeah, and I wouldn't want to question it. But Sam didn't mention a dog. Wonder if she got it after he came to see her?"

"I don't know, but she sure didn't want to talk to us, did she? If she wasn't confined to a wheelchair, I'd put her down as another suspect."

Chapter 27

As we traveled back toward town, stopping briefly at an outlying convenience store for a pack of Juicy Fruit gum which Mr. Pickens insisted on paying for, we were no wiser than when we'd left the city limits. After asking him to turn the air-conditioning up a little, I occupied myself with thoughts of the uncooperative and unfriendly Ilona Weaver. I had hoped she knew something that would help us, but with Alvin standing ready to pounce, there'd been no way of getting her to open up. So it had been a wasted trip, which I couldn't help but point out to Mr. Pickens.

"Well, that little visit didn't amount to anything, did it?" I said just to be saying something.

He grunted, while I watched the scenery as we passed through the valley. It was a typical rural countryside with a range of low purplish mountains to the west that bounded the valley. On either side of the road there were rolling hills with pastureland enclosed by barbed wire fences. A few head of cattle or milk cows—I couldn't tell which—lazily grazed as tails switched at flies. We passed the occasional unpainted farmhouse with a cluster of outbuildings surrounding it. More often, though, the farmhouses were derelict, falling in and covered with vines and weeds, while the families luxuriated in newer single or double wides sprouting television dishes and antennas.

Mindful that unprecedented opportunities presented themselves while I had Mr. Pickens to myself in the car and that those opportunities were fleeting, I prepared for another attack on his stubborn refusal to make any attempt at winning back Hazel Marie. All it would take would be a little give on his part, for I was convinced that

Hazel Marie could not and would not hold out against his manly charm—if he'd ever turn it on again. The only reason they were in this hostile situation was his unwillingness to reenter matrimony, while she was holding out for a commitment and a wedding ceremony.

At this point, a ceremony was all I cared about—just a quickie by a magistrate would do. As far as I was concerned, any kind of long-term commitment could be worked out later on.

"Mr. Pickens?" I said, trying to recall the steps to leading a soul to the Lord that I'd learned years ago in a workshop on witnessing when Pastor Ledbetter had brought in a visiting evangelist who'd been trained by Billy Graham in one of his crusades. The evangelist had emphasized that we shouldn't embarrass, shame, or pressure anyone into coming forward. He said that the best way to reach a recalcitrant heart was to tell of our own personal spiritual journey.

So, if recounting my experience would work in that situation, perhaps it would work in the present one.

"Mr. Pickens?" I said again. "As you

know, I've been twice married, which I know doesn't equal the number of times you've taken the plunge. But, I want you to know that if I'd thought all marriages were like my first one, I'd never have married Sam Murdoch. I'd still be a dried-up, bitter, and resentful widow if I'd been unwilling to take another chance. And I'll tell you the truth, there was a lot of comfort in keeping my anger toward Wesley Lloyd Springer alive and just not trying for anything better. But I thank the Lord every day of my life that I married Sam and learned what a real meeting of minds and hearts can be like."

"Glad to hear it," he said and yawned.

"Well, but what I'm saying is that you can't always go on past experience. Why, when I think of what my life was like with Mr. Springer, I just shudder. It makes me wonder how in the world I had the courage to marry again, even to a man like Sam. And then I really shudder, because what if I'd turned him down? Think what I would've missed. Think of how empty my life would've been. He is the finest man in the world and I almost turned my back on him. The thought of it can jerk me out of a sound sleep."

He cut his eyes at me. "Why're you telling me this?"

"Why, Mr. Pickens, I'm giving you my personal testimony! He who has ears to hear ought to listen to it. And another thing, marriage is honorable in all and devoutly to be desired."

He smiled. "Uh-huh."

"You just have to be willing to try again and, after all, from what I've heard, you and Hazel Marie have lasted longer in an unmarried state than any of your actual marriages. Doesn't that tell you something?"

"Tells me not to rock the boat," he said, infuriating me because nothing I'd said had gotten through to him. "Here we are," he went on as we approached my house.

"Oh, look," I said as Mr. Pickens pulled into my driveway, "there's Sam's car. Why don't you come in and have lunch with us?" And, I thought to myself, you can see how well Sam and I get along.

He waited ever so long before answering, then he said, "I wouldn't want to upset anybody."

"Oh, for goodness sakes, you're not going to upset anybody. Hazel Marie is confined to her bed, well, my bed, since she's not supposed to go up and down stairs."

His head swiveled so fast toward me, it was a wonder it didn't put a crick in his neck. "Is she that bad off?"

"No, I told you. She just hit a little bump in the road, but we're expecting her to have smooth sailing from here on out. Now come on in. Lillian will want to see you."

So he did, climbing out of the car and following me through the back door and into the kitchen.

"Law, Mr. Pickens!" Lillian greeted him. "I been thinkin' you done th'owed us over, you not been here in so long. But you hit it at a good time. I got some homemade chili, hot enough to put hair on yo' chest if you lackin', an' some French bread and cole slaw, just settin' here waitin'."

Mr. Pickens grinned at her, then walked to the stove to lean over and smell the bubbling chili. "I believe you were expecting me."

"I always 'spect you anytime you in town."

"See," I said, relieved to be in the air-conditioned house, "didn't I tell you?" Then, disappointed that we weren't having a cool salad, I patted my face with a Kleenex and said, "But it's awfully hot today to be having chili."

Lillian gave me a knowing glance. "Miss Hazel Marie say she have a taste for it, so I fix it."

Tempted to lightly mention that cravings for certain foods were typical of certain conditions, I refrained for fear that Lillian would take it a step farther. Instead, I said, "That sounds like she's feeling better. Where's Sam?"

"He in there visitin' with her," Lillian said to me, but her eyes were on Mr. Pickens. "An' she do all right this morning, 'cept she awful tired of that bed."

"I don't blame her, poor thing," I said for Mr. Pickens's benefit, which unfortunately didn't seem to dent his calm demeanor. "Go ahead and sit down, Mr. Pickens. I'll get Sam and give Hazel Marie this gum. Then we'll eat."

I walked down the back hall and turned into the bedroom just in time to hear Hazel Marie tearfully say, "I don't know why y'all are so good to me."

Sam, who was sitting in a chair beside

her bed, looked up and smiled as I entered. "Hey, Julia, come on in, honey. We're making plans for a passel of little ones that'll turn this house upside down." He patted Hazel Marie's hand. "Now, you just stop all that worrying about us and take care of yourself and those babies. I need some more fishing buddies, anyway."

After giving Hazel Marie the gum and assuring myself that she was having no more problems, I followed Sam back to the kitchen where he and Mr. Pickens were already discussing the morning's activities.

I drew out a chair and joined the two of them at the table. "Lillian," I said, taking pleasure in doing something that would've given Wesley Lloyd a stroke if he hadn't already had one, "get a bowl for yourself and sit with us."

"No'm, I got things to do. Y'all go ahead and eat."

Mr. Pickens looked up at her. "You can sit on my lap."

She doubled up, laughing. "You somethin' else, Mr. Pickens."

As we began to eat, she prepared a tray for Hazel Marie, fixing a bowl of chili for herself as well, and left for the bedroom.

"Sam," I said, after Mr. Pickens finished telling him of our unproductive morning, "there's something I don't understand. How did you get those people to talk in the first place? Did they just come right out and tell you they stole and embezzled and acted up in public without suffering any ill effects?"

Sam put down his spoon. "Not really. I was careful with my questions, just asking in a general way about their experiences with the law back in the day. A few of them volunteered a lot of personal detail, always with a laugh and some smugness about lost or insufficient evidence. And hinting at having some pull with the powers that be. The older Tillman brother got a kick out of telling me how Teddy never served a lick of time in spite of stealing everything that wasn't nailed down."

"Well, that's interesting," I said. "Because they sure aren't eager to talk about any of it now. So it stands to reason that the theft at your house is what has changed their attitude. And it may be that every last one of them knows who did it and who it is that has their records now, and they're too intimitated or scared to say anything." I looked at Mr. Pickens. "Did you tell him how Ilona Weaver almost sicced Alvin on us?"

"Yeah," he said with a short laugh. "And I was right. She didn't have a dog when Sam was there."

"If she did," Sam added, "I sure didn't see it. But I have to say that she was the most reluctant to talk to me. I put it down at the time to her illness, having enough on her mind not to want to dredge up the past. She was friendly enough, though."

"Well," I said, "she certainly wasn't very welcoming this morning, and I have no desire to upset her again. We have a couple more to see, don't we, Mr. Pickens? I think we ought to arm ourselves with a few dog biscuits, just in case we run up on some of Alvin's littermates."

Chapter 28

While we ate, Sam told us how he'd spent the morning in the courthouse, searching unsuccessfully for the missing files. After several hours, he'd given up and left a list of the relevant names with the clerks, asking to be called if they ran across any of the mislaid files.

"I'm not holding my breath, though," he said. "They're too busy to do a search, so I'm hoping that somebody will find them while looking for something else."

"And while you're hoping," I said, "hope they'll turn them in at the desk instead of leaving them where they are."

We continued in this vein, bringing up random suggestions of how we should proceed to get Sam back on track with his legal history. Mr. Pickens had less to say than either Sam or me, and I couldn't help but notice how his eyes kept returning again and again to the dining room door. It was as if he were visualizing Hazel Marie pushing through it, eagerly laughing and talking a mile a minute, her face lighting up at the sight of him.

And to tell the truth, I would've loved to have seen her come frolicking through the door myself. As I thought about it, I realized how still and quiet the house had been these last couple of weeks. The joy that was Hazel Marie, before she turned sour on Mr. Pickens and before she knew what he'd left her with, was gone. I missed hearing her chattering around the house, missed listening to her sing a country song, missed her giggle at something that had happened at church or the garden club, missed her clattering down the stairs, calling, "Miss Julia, guess what!" I missed seeing the pleasure she expressed over a new dress or a slice of one of Lillian's cakes or the sun shining through the latticework in the gazebo. And I missed seeing the delight she took in her son and in Mr. Pickens.

I could've shaken him till his teeth rattled for doing nothing to lift the pall of sadness in my house. If I'd ever had the slightest regret for taking Hazel Marie to my bosom, these empty days of gloom would've confirmed for me how much she contributed to my own well-being.

"Well," Mr. Pickens said, putting his spoon beside the twice-filled bowl on his plate, "that was some good eatin'."

I noticed a fine sheen of perspiration on his brow, which was no wonder since Lillian made her chili so spicy. Delicately patting my own face with my napkin, I said, "I hope it's fortified you enough to go out again this afternoon. I'm anxious to get everybody seen as soon as we can. If Hazel Marie takes a sudden downturn, I won't be able to accompany you."

Mr. Pickens gave me a frowning stare, making me think he was going to ask a penetrating question. In which case, I determined to answer it as plainly and succinctly as possible, if for no other reason than to see what he would do. But he didn't ask any kind of question, just stared a bit longer, then nodded.

"Okay," he finally said, "Rosemary Sullins is the last one. We might as well go on and see her."

"Don't forget Rafe Feldman."

"I wouldn't bother with him, Julia," Sam said. "It'd be a waste of time. He's in the final stages of dementia, so you wouldn't get anything sensible out of him."

"Well, so far," I said, "we haven't gotten anything sensible out of anybody." I pushed back from the table and stood. "I won't be but a minute, Mr. Pickens. I want to check on Hazel Marie, then I'll be ready to go. You know where the powder room is."

Walking around the table, I put my hand on Sam's shoulder. "Don't be discouraged, Sam. When we sit down and put all this together, I expect something—one name or another—will jump out at you. Of course," I said, thinking of Ilona Weaver, "one of them isn't in any condition to steal anything, so I don't know what good it'll do. But we'll keep working on it."

Sam smiled up at me and put his hand

on mine. "I appreciate what you're doing, sweetheart. Seeing these people may not tell us anything, but it has to be done."

"Right," Mr. Pickens said. "Basic investigative work."

As I gave Sam a final pat and turned to leave the room, Mr. Pickens said, "Tell Hazel Marie I hope she'll be feeling better soon."

I stopped without turning around, thinking that I should urge him to tell her himself, but decided against it for the time being. Lillian was with her, and Sam and I right here, making too much of an audience for a reconciliation or a knockdown, drag-out fight or any kind of confrontation between two people at such cross-purposes.

"Yes, I will," I responded and left the kitchen, wondering if I'd made the right choice.

I knew I had as soon as I walked into Hazel Marie's room and saw Lillian sitting on her bed, holding a Kleenex box.

"What's wrong?" I asked, hurrying in. "Are you . . . ?"

Hazel Marie shook her head and wiped her streaming eyes. "No'm, I'm all right. It's just hearing *him*! He's just sitting out there, eating and talking like, like everything's *normal*. And I guess it is. For *him*! But there's nothing normal about the mess *I'm* in."

"Well, for goodness sakes, Lillian," I said. "Why didn't you close the door?"

"I did, but she want it back open."

"It gets too hot in here with the door closed," Hazel Marie said, defending herself. "Besides, I shouldn't have to close myself in just because *he* comes and goes as he pleases."

"That's exactly right," I said, soothingly, but thinking that this was another example of an extreme emotional upset. "But we're leaving now to go see somebody else on Sam's list. So I want you to get some rest. Lloyd'll be home in a little while, and you'll want to be cheerful and perky for him."

She looked up at me through red, tearful eyes. "Shouldn't he be coming home for lunch? He's over at the courts all day long."

"Don't you be worryin' 'bout him," Lillian said. "I ast him everyday what he have to eat, an' he goin' to that Country Club Grill an' orderin' they biggest lunch." Lillian laughed. "I 'spect you stop worryin' when that bill come."

I surveyed the tray on the bedside table. "Speaking of that, Hazel Marie. You've hardly eaten anything. I thought you were craving chili."

"I was," she said mournfully. "Then I just couldn't get it down. I'm sorry, Lillian, I know you worked hard on it. I don't know what's the matter with me."

"Oh, I expect you do," I said with a laugh, trying to lighten her mood. "Appetite changes are to be expected. It's nothing to worry about."

"That's right," Lillian chimed in. "You no diff'runt from anybody else. Why, you not even bad as some I knowed. That little girl, name of Precious Watson, when she 'spectin', she crave that white clay some like to eat. She out diggin' that stuff outta the creek bank with a spoon everyday. An' she be chewin' on it the whole time till that baby come."

Well, that took Hazel Marie's mind off her own erratic appetite, and mine, too, if you want to know the truth. Wishing her a restful afternoon, I hurried out to join Mr.

Pickens for our last visitation. And a good thing, too, for he was standing by the door, impatiently jingling the keys in his pocket.

❧❦

Before I got the door closed good and my seat belt on, he had the car cranked and was backing out of the drive. "Which way?"

"West. I mean, east. Go east. Turn toward town and go across Main Street. Then right on Old Wellburn Road. We'll follow that for a few miles to South Wellburn. You know where that is, don't you?"

"Farming community? Beyond that big manufacturing plant?"

I nodded.

Then he asked, "What do they manufacture, anyway?"

Pleased that he was willing to converse, I was nonetheless chagrined that I had no answer. "Law, I don't know, Mr. Pickens. They used to make blue jeans until the owners moved the business to China or Mexico or somewhere. I don't know what they do now."

He grunted.

Unwilling to leave it at that, I went on. "It really created hardships for a lot of families when they moved, though. I mean, that business was the basis of the whole county for years and years. Then they just up and closed it down. That plant sat empty for several years, and people were hurting. That's when the state started the technical college here. To retrain people for other jobs, you know. Then some other business bought the plant and hired a few workers back. But what they do, I don't know. But I'll tell you this, the place is just a ghost of its former self." I finally ran out of anything to say and waited for his response.

I didn't get one, so I summed up. "I guess that's what you call outsourcing, isn't it?"

"Not quite," he said, his eyes on the road. "That's what you call moving to a cheaper labor pool."

"Oh." Then, "I guess you're right. Well, tell me about Rosemary Sullins."

"You know her?"

"No, never even heard of her. Sam gave me her address, though, and I know about where that is. At least, she doesn't live out in the sticks somewhere, so we shouldn't have a problem."

It wasn't so easy, though, for it seemed that Rosemary Sullins lived in what was once a mill village—block after block of small, identical houses, most of them without house numbers. After stopping and asking a boy who was pumping up a bicycle tire, we found the house, which stood out from the others because of the chain-link fence around the front yard.

We parked by the curb, then got out of the car. Mr. Pickens, with admirable courage, walked right up to the gate and unlatched it.

I clutched at his sleeve. "She might have a dog."

"I doubt it. Look around."

I did, and saw what the practiced eye of an investigator had already noted. A plastic tricycle lay on its side, pails and shovels stuck up from a sandbox, and a red and yellow plastic sliding board leaned to one side on the uneven ground beneath a shade tree. A deflated basketball lay next to the porch steps.

"Kids," Mr. Pickens said.

We walked up onto the porch where there was one Adirondack chair with an open Coke can on the floor beside it. An air conditioner, dripping water down the wall, rattled loudly in the window.

Seeing no doorbell or knocker, Mr. Pickens opened the storm door and rapped on the wooden door. "You introduce us," he said, "and get us inside."

A thin, angular woman opened the door and stared at us. She had grayish hair with streaks of white running from both temples. It was pulled back so tightly from her narrow forehead that it added to the gauntness of her face. She wore a pair of blue polyester knit pants that ended at her calves, reminding me of a certain green pair I'd once owned. A T-shirt with the logo of Tweetsie Railroad—namely a locomotive—hung loosely from her shoulders. And, Lord help us, I couldn't help but notice her long toes with chipped polish gripping the flip-flops on her feet.

I opened my mouth to greet her, but her mouth flattened out into a thin line and she said, "I got a permit."

"What?" I was confused.

"I only got four, so that's home care," she said. "I'm not runnin' a day care, so I don't need no more permits."

Mr. Pickens picked up on her meaning

before I did. "We're not from Social Services," he said smoothly. "I'm J.D. Pickens and this is Mrs. Julia Murdoch. We'd like to talk with you about that break-in at Sam Murdoch's house. I'm not sure you know this, but some information relating to you and a few others was stolen in the break-in."

"Something of mine?" She looked as confused as I was feeling. "Who did it?"

"That's what we're trying to find out, Ms. Sullins," Mr. Pickens said. "The only things missing are some interview cassettes and some case files. Yours were among them."

She stood for some little while, staring at us, then her eyes drifted away. I was about to burn up on the hot porch, and the noisy air-conditioner was getting on my nerves.

"May we come in?" I asked, fanning the bodice of my dress. "The heat, you know."

"I reckon," she said, moving back so we could step inside what may have once been a living room. It was now a playroom with three toddlers playing on the floor and an infant asleep in a crib beside a green sofa that was propped up with a brick where a leg was missing. On a small yellow plastic table, there were a box of Ritz crackers and a jar of Jif peanut butter with a table knife sticking up out of it. One child's face was smeared with what I hoped was peanut butter. Cracker crumbs crunched under our feet as we walked onto the indoor-outdoor rug, and an odor of milk, both fresh and regurgitated, mingled with that coming from an overflowing trash can of previously worn diapers.

As Rosemary Sullins turned around, I saw a long, thick switch of hair, coarse and stringy, more gray than white that was gathered by a rubber band on the back of her head. A ponytail, I thought, so unsuitable for a woman of her age. I noticed something else as she turned, as well. Those figure-hugging blue knit pants were tight everywhere except in the seat, which bagged, both noticeably and unattractively.

"Have a seat if you can find one," she said, moving a full ashtray from the sofa to the top of a television set. Some sort of animated cartoon featuring chipmunks ran unheeded on the set.

I sat gingerly on the edge of the sofa, propping my pocketbook on my lap, and Mr. Pickens eased down beside me.

Rosemary Sullins pulled up a yellow plastic child's chair and sat down, her knees hiked up high. "Well?" she said, her eyes narrowing at us. "Who else's did they get?"

Chapter 29

Mr. Pickens leaned forward, readying himself to draw out whatever information he could from this person of interest. "Ms. Sullins," he began, then winced as a piercing scream cut through the air. The baby in the crib startled awake with a cry, its little arms waving. It must've been used to the uproar, though, for it settled down and went back to sleep.

I thought I'd have a heart attack from the fright, but Rosemary Sullins had heard it before. She sprang from the plastic chair and ran over to two children struggling over some kind of toy.

"Greg'ry!" she yelled. "Let her have that. You hear me, let her have it!"

"I had it first!" the boy screamed, as he tried to jerk it from the girl's grasp.

"I don't care who had it first. Let her have it. I can't stand that screechin', my nerves is already shot."

"But I got it first!"

Rosemary raised her hand. "You turn that thing a-loose or I'm gonna pop you one."

I made to move, but Mr. Pickens put his hand on my arm and shook his head. It was just as well, for Gregory had turned it loose, but not before shoving the girl out of her chair. She cut loose with another unearthly shriek, and Gregory got his pop. It wasn't much of one, I'll have to say, but it was enough to send him to a corner where he sat, hunched over with his arms folded across his chest. He glared at Rosemary, his face red and streaked with the unfairness of it all. The first step, I thought, of growing up sullen and angry at the world.

"Them kids," Rosemary said, resuming her seat. "They about drive me crazy. Where was we?"

"Ms. Sullins," Mr. Pickens began again,

"I'm sure you read about the break-in at Sam Murdoch's house. Whoever was responsible for it could've taken any number of things—television sets, computers, and so on—but they didn't. They only took the cassettes with interviews on them and copies of certain case files. Yours was among them. We're trying to find out who would've been that interested in information on five people, and five people only. Those five files were specifically taken. We know that because Murdoch had files on hundreds of people dating from the eighteen hundreds up to the present. Since yours was one of them, we wanted to ask if there's anything you can think of that would lead us in the right direction."

"You sayin' I done it?"

"No." Mr. Pickens shook his head. "Not at all. We don't think any of the five did it. If one of you had, I figure you'd've only taken your own. Or else, you'd have grabbed any files at hand to cover yourself. But these five cases all occurred within the same ten-year period, back in the sixties. Something or someone ties them all together. We want to know if you have any idea of who or what it might be.

"Because I'll tell you this," Mr. Pickens went on in a seriously professional manner, "Murdoch is concerned that the information could be used against you—harm your reputations in some way or held over you to extort money."

Rosemary Sullins considered that for a moment, her dark eyes staring steadily at Mr. Pickens. It came to me that she had a sharp native intelligence that was belied by her incorrect use of the language.

"Who was the others?" she asked again.

Mr. Pickens hesitated, then he must've decided that secrecy wasn't necessary. "Teddy Tillman, Cassie Wooten, Rafe Feldman, Ilona Weaver. And you."

I wouldn't swear to it, but I do believe I saw a glint of recognition pass across her eyes, but there wasn't a twitch on her face. She was giving nothing away.

I had to say something, so I said, "Do you know any of them? Personally, I mean?"

She switched her eyes to me. "Cassie, a little bit, long time ago. Them others?" She shrugged her shoulders. "I know of 'em, like everybody else in the county."

She was right about that. The county wasn't that large or that heavily populated. Live in it a few years, and eventually you'd hear of just about everybody else.

"Can you help us, Ms. Sullins?" Mr. Pickens asked. "And maybe help yourself? Whatever you can give us won't go any further. A name, a few names, anything that would help us recover what was stolen."

Her hand suddenly snaked out toward me. I reared back, frightened. I thought she was after my pocketbook, but her hand went down beside the sofa and came back with a pack of Marlboros and a box of kitchen matches. She lit up and contemplated. As smoke billowed from her mouth, I thought I saw a glint of sly amusement in her eyes.

"I can't think of nobody," she said. "Why don't Murdoch jes' do it all over again?"

"That's the bad part of it," I said. "The case files at the courthouse are missing, too. And every one of you refuses to do another interview. He called and asked you, didn't he?"

She did smile then, somewhat smugly, I thought. "Yeah, he did. But I'm done with all that mess. I got no reason to go back over it again. 'Specially now, after somebody showed they don't want me to."

Mr. Pickens, beside me, took a deep breath. "Aren't you a little concerned about what that somebody will do?"

"Naw," she said, looking around. "What'd I do with that blamed ashtray? Them kids like to play in it, an' I have to keep movin' it." But it was too late. The long ash fell on the rug. She looked at it a moment, then rubbed it in with her flip-flop. "Naw, I ain't concerned a bit. I figure they did it to keep Murdoch from tellin' stories outta school. They ain't gonna turn around and do the same thing."

"But you talked to him!" I protested. "You and all the others. Why'd you let him interview you in the first place if you cared about telling stories out of school?"

"Well, I guess we didn't think it mattered after this long of a time." She drew deeply on her cigarette, then got up and mashed it out in the ashtray she'd finally spotted on the television set. "But looks like we found out it did."

"But to who?" I almost screeched. "Whom," I corrected myself, as if that mattered under the circumstances. "You *know*, don't you, Ms. Sullins? Or at least you have an idea of who it was."

"I got no idea," she said firmly. I could see her thin face set itself in rigid lines and knew we'd get little more out of her. Then she surprised me. "But if I got to guess, I'd guess it was that stuck-up know-it-all that Cassie married. It's likely him. That's who I'd go after, if I was you."

⟨⟩

"You think she's right?" I asked as Mr. Pickens guided the car away from the curb in front of Rosemary Sullins's house.

Mr. Pickens rubbed one hand down his face, squinched up his eyes in the bright sunlight and sighed. "Who the hell knows? Sorry, Miss Julia, I feel like we're running around in circles."

"Well, if you don't turn around we will be or else on our way to Charlotte. Take a left at the next street and let's go home. Like you, I am sick and tired of these people giving us the runaround. I think they all know who did it. Every last one of them, don't you?"

"Hard to tell." He fiddled with the air-conditioning vents with one hand while guiding the car with the other. "But the thing that strikes me is that none of 'em seems worried about it."

"You're absolutely right," I said, recalling the complacency that the Tillmans and Rosemary Sullins exhibited upon hearing the news. "Except maybe Cassie, or at least her husband. Ilona Weaver, who could tell? But I know I'd be fit to be tied if my personal information was in unknown hands. And I've done nothing to be ashamed of." Seeing his amused glance, I went on. "I'm speaking of legal and/or criminal matters, Mr. Pickens."

Mr. Pickens let that lie for a few minutes as he concentrated on his driving. Then he said, "Interesting, though, don't you think, that the Sullins woman brought up Cassie's husband. We had the same thought, remember?"

"Yes, and he was the only one who showed any anger about it. But I couldn't tell if he was mad at the thief for stealing Cassie's information or at Sam for gathering it or at her for letting Sam have an interview. Or for serving a bad meatloaf."

Mr. Pickens laughed—just a little, but more than he'd been doing. "Ah, well," he said, "at least we've done the footwork. Now I need to do some thinking. And I'm hoping that one of them, after doing some thinking of their own, will give me a call. I left a card with everybody, and of course they all know you and Sam. Any kind of call from one of them might give us a break, so if you get one, be sure and set up a meeting. Anywhere, anytime."

"That reminds me. I should give Cassie a call and invite her to lunch. If she'll come over to the house or if she wants to meet downtown, do you want to be there?"

"Let me think about it. She might open up to you when she wouldn't if I'm there. Just let me know if she agrees, but better not count on her husband letting her do anything."

"Lord, Mr. Pickens, wouldn't you hate to live with a man like that?"

He turned his black eyes on me, laughing again. "I don't believe I'll ever have to make that decision."

"Oh, you. You know what I mean. I just feel for her having to put up with such a domineering and *oppressive* man. That's no way to live in my opinion."

I bit my lip then, thinking that I'd lived

most of my life with a man of similar disposition. Wesley Lloyd Springer, though, had never been rude or disagreeable when there was an audience around, I could give him that. He'd saved his scathing words and marching orders for the times when we were alone.

Deliberately closing my mind to such thoughts, I said, "Well, what do we do next?"

Mr. Pickens cocked an eyebrow at me. "Am I invited to dinner tonight?"

"Of course you are. Lillian's fixing creamed corn, fresh from the field. Or rather from a local produce stand."

"Okay, then why don't we sit around afterward and see if we can figure out where we are and where we go from here?" Before I could answer, he thought of something else. "Unless you think we'd disturb anybody."

"If you mean Hazel Marie, no, we won't. The doctor's letting her get up a little today. But she's not supposed to do anything strenuous, and he specifically told her not to get all upset over anything. Which," I said with a baleful glance at him, "she's been doing a lot of here lately."

After a second of silence, he mumbled, "Maybe I better not come over."

That wasn't the response I wanted, so I had to think fast. "No, you come right on. Doctor Hargrove's known for being overly cautious, and besides, there's no reason you'd upset her, is there? I mean, the two of you have broken up and, as far as I'm concerned, that ought to be that. I'll let her know that you're coming for Sam's sake and not in any way to bother her. Besides that, she wants Latisha to come visit—for the entertainment value, you know. And that child will keep Hazel Marie's mind off any disturbing influence you might have. Not that I think you would," I hurriedly added, "but still."

"Okay," he said, as if he wasn't sure about it, "for Sam's sake, then."

Chapter 30

Mr. Pickens walked in that evening bearing a huge box of Godiva chocolates. He must've driven to Asheville after he dropped me off, for there wasn't a place in Abbotsville that carried such expensive candy. A Whitman's Sampler was about the best the town had to offer.

He handed the fancy box to me, saying, "Hazel Marie might like this. I don't know if she's well enough for candy, but . . ." He shrugged with a deprecating smile as if he knew it wasn't much of an appeasement under the circumstances.

"That's very thoughtful of you, Mr. Pickens," I said. "I'm sure she'll appreciate it."

"Well, if she doesn't," he said, somewhat sadly, I thought, "maybe the rest of you will."

"We all will, I assure you. I would suggest that you take it in to her since she's up for a while, but she's pleasantly occupied right now. I'd hate to stir up anything, which, I'm sorry to say, your appearance might do. Lloyd and Latisha are with her. And Sam, too. They're putting a jigsaw puzzle of the Washington Monument together, and so far it's slow going. I'll tell you, Mr. Pickens, it has stretched my imagination to come up with ideas to entertain her. You'd be amazed at how little there is to do that doesn't involve physical activity or emotional stress."

Sam came out then to welcome him, shaking his hand as if they hadn't spent the last few days together. I left them in the living room and walked back to see how Hazel Marie was getting along. After a moment of indecision, I left the box of chocolates on the chest in the hall. I'd give it to her later when Lloyd wasn't around to witness whatever her response would be. Besides, nobody should be eating candy so close to dinnertime.

Hazel Marie and the two children were sitting around a card table in the bedroom. She was still in her gown and robe, which seemed to imply that she didn't intend to show up in the dining room. Just as well, I thought, for Mr. Pickens needed to keep his mind on Sam's problem tonight. Still, I hated for an opportunity to effect a reconciliation to pass by.

I walked over and stood between Hazel Marie and Lloyd, one hand on each of their shoulders. Looking down at the table where about a thousand pieces of puzzle were spread out, I said, "How is it coming?"

Not well, I could've answered myself, for they had only one corner and part of the top of the puzzle put together.

Hazel Marie looked up and smiled, indicating to me that she was enjoying the children's company and that her stress level was on an even keel.

Lloyd said, "Hey, Miss Julia," then watched Latisha as she tried to force two pieces together. "If they won't go easily, Latisha, then they don't fit."

"Well," Latisha said, discarding one piece and rummaging around for another. "I don't know how them puzzle people 'spect us to put this thing together. They's so much of this blue sky, you can't tell one from another."

"Let's leave it for now," I said. "You need to get your hands washed for dinner."

Latisha, her little head covered in rows of plaits with colored beads on the ends, looked up. "I'm gonna eat in here with Miss Hazel Marie. She said I could, 'cause I never eat in no bedroom before."

"That's fine. You'll be good company for her. Lloyd, do you want to eat in here, too?"

He glanced at his mother, seemed to hesitate, then said, "I guess I'll come to the table. I wouldn't want J.D. to think we don't want to see him. It might hurt his feelings."

I felt Hazel Marie stiffen under my hand, but she gave no other sign of distress. "It's all right, Lloyd," she said. "You run along. We'll work on the puzzle after dinner."

When the children left to wash their hands, I ventured a suggestion. "If you feel well enough, Hazel Marie, there's still time for you to dress and come to the table, too. I mean," I quickly said as she turned away, "you don't have to, just if you feel like it. To be hospitable, if nothing else."

"I don't feel *that* good," she said. "I wish he'd just leave and never come back. When he's in the house, I start feeling all edgy and upset. Quivery, like I'm going to throw up."

"Well, we certainly don't want to start that again. You just stay in here and enjoy your dinner. But I will tell you that we'll be going over the little we have on Sam's problem afterwards, so Mr. Pickens will be staying later than usual. You might want to close your door."

"It gets too hot," she mumbled, and I marveled at the fact that even though she didn't want to see him, she was making sure she could hear him.

I patted her shoulder and turned to leave. "I'll ask Sam to check the vents in here tomorrow."

❈❈

After dinner, Sam, Mr. Pickens, and I adjourned to the living room where both men brought out folders and opened briefcases. I heard Lillian finish up in the kitchen, then walk to Hazel Marie's room to collect Latisha.

Before we could get started, Latisha appeared in the doorway. "Great-Granny say for me to say good night, an' thank you for supper, an' can I come back tomorrow?"

"Why, of course you may," I told her. "And we thank you for being such good company for Hazel Marie. Did she eat a good dinner?"

"No'm, she jus' pick at it a little bit, but Lloyd, he tell her he gonna hand-feed her, she don't do better."

"I'll give her a snack a little later on," I said. "She probably didn't need a heavy meal anyway."

"Well, I tell you what she do need," Latisha said, as firm and confident as a medical practitioner. "She prob'bly need some of that choc'late candy I seen settin' in yonder."

We couldn't help but laugh, knowing who really needed it. Mr. Pickens said, "Latisha, I think you're right. Why don't you take the box and give it to her. Tell her it's for everybody and you need some to take home with you."

Latisha's eyes lit up. Before she left, she

turned back and said, "If you the one that brung it, I sure do thank you. I been cravin' some choc'late candy this whole day."

I followed Latisha out into the hall, watched as she carefully took the box and carried it in to Hazel Marie. Thinking that Hazel Marie would be more receptive of the gift if I wasn't there, I lingered outside the door.

"Look!" I heard Latisha say. "That big, ole black-eyed man brung us all some candy. He say for us to open it right up."

"Law, chile," Lillian said. "That candy's for Miss Hazel Marie. Come on now, we got to get home."

"Oh, wait, Lillian," Hazel Marie said. "Let's all have some. Lloyd, you open it and pass it around."

I breathed a sigh of relief, realizing that I'd been afraid she'd throw it across the room, out the window, or in the trash when she learned who it was from. The children certainly had a calming effect on her, and I determined to have Latisha over again not only tomorrow but for as many more days afterward as possible.

Then Lloyd said, "Mama, there's a card here. From J.D., I guess."

There was silence, while I held my breath. Then Hazel Marie, sounding as if she were gritting her teeth, said, "Put it on the dresser, honey. I'll look at it later."

Going back to the living room, I thought that the gift-giving-and-receiving had gone better than I'd feared. And all because the children had been around. If they hadn't, it wouldn't have surprised me if she'd come flying out and thrown the Godiva box straight at Mr. Pickens. I'd have to tell him that Lloyd and Latisha most likely saved him from suffering great bodily harm.

❧❧

By the time I got to the living room, Mr. Pickens had drawn up a chair to the coffee table where there were papers and notes spread out. Sam was on the sofa jotting down more notes on a yellow legal pad.

Excited at the prospect of uncovering the mystery of the missing files, I took a seat beside Sam, then looked from him to Mr. Pickens. "I can't wait to hear what you've found."

"Not much, I'm afraid," Mr. Pickens said, tapping his paper with a pen. "But let's see where we are. We got nothing from the four people we went to see, less than nothing, in fact, because they closed right down on us. I'm convinced, though, that something has to tie them together."

"I am, too," Sam said. "But I've looked and looked and I can't find a thing. I've checked arrest dates and court dates up one side and down the other, and none of them were ever arrested at the same time or arraigned at the same time. They didn't live near each other, and there's no indication they ran around together. I've about reached a dead end."

Mr. Pickens leaned back in his chair and gazed at the ceiling, moving into his deep thinking mode. "Okay, but we're agreed that something connects them, right?" His black eyes settled back on Sam. "You didn't find anybody else during that time who got the same special treatment as these four? Five, I mean?"

"Not a one," Sam said, shaking his head. "That's what caught my attention in the first place. Everybody else arrested during those years got exactly what you'd expect, given the charges against them. No question about that. These are the only ones who slipped through, time after time."

"Okay, hold onto that for a minute," Mr.

Pickens said, turning his pen around and making a note. "Tell me again about the sheriff and the judge."

"Well, like I said," Sam said, "Al Hamilton was the sheriff back then for twenty years or more, and that covered the time we're interested in. I knew him, and it's hard to believe he'd let these people squeak by, especially since all of them, except the Weaver woman, were repeat offenders. Now, Al wouldn't qualify as the greatest sheriff around, but he was a big law and order man, which is why he kept getting reelected." Sam shook his head, unable to figure out the problem. "I just can't see him flagrantly flaunting the law for people who had no pull that I can see. If anything, putting them away for a stretch would've been to his advantage. Of course," Sam went on, "you never know about people."

"All right," Mr. Pickens said, turning his pen around and making a note. "Let's think about the judge. Tell me about him."

"District Court Judge Robert Eugene Baine," Sam said with a long sigh. "He was a piece of work. Ran his courtroom like it was his own little kingdom. But a lot of judges did that—up until 1968, that is. That year, the legislature set sentencing guidelines that clamped down on the freewheeling judges we had then." Sam smiled, a look of nostalgia crossing his face. "I was just starting out in the early sixties, and I'll tell you, when we walked into a courtroom, we never knew what a judge would do."

"All right," Mr. Pickens said again. "Let me be sure of this. The cases involving these five people, they all happened before 1968? And they were arrested while Sheriff What's-His-Name was in office and they all appeared before Judge Baine?"

Sam nodded. "Sheriff Hamilton, right. And those that got as far as a courtroom, yes, they all appeared before Baine. But, remember, some of the arrests never got to the courtroom. That's why it's hard to pin on one or the other. It would have to've been both of them, and that's hard to imagine, given their personalities. So maybe I'm seeing problems where there aren't any. The cases could just be anomalies, even though there're five of them, and it kept happening over and over." Sam sat back, resting his pad on his knee. He ran his pen down the list. "But something or somebody has to tie them together—

Cassie Wooten, Teddy Tillman, Ilona Weaver, and Rosemary Sullins."

And Rafe Feldman, I thought.

Mr. Pickens leaned back in his chair, stretched out his legs, one foot crossed over the other. "Okay, let me add a kicker, here. I spent some time today going through the Index of Deeds at the courthouse, looking through the entire decade of the sixties. I found one thing of interest—a deed registered in 1969 by which a certain Amelda Capps Tillman sold a small tract of land to Albert H. Hamilton. The survey indicated that it was a little less than an acre, bordering a river. She got three hundred dollars for it, which I guess for the times would've been about right."

"Well, that *is* interesting," Sam said. "Amelda Tillman, that would be Bob and Ted's mother, all right. Where in the county was it?"

"Place called River Bend."

"Huh," Sam said, concentrating hard. "That area was nothing but wilds in sixty-nine, away in the southwest corner of the county and barely accessible except by the river. Too bad she didn't wait a few years. It really built up later on."

I thought back to that time several years into my marriage to Wesley Lloyd Springer and couldn't recall knowing either the sheriff or Amelda Tillman, much less any kind of land deal between them. Still too busy trying to adjust to Wesley Lloyd's requirements, I guess.

"The thing is," Mr. Pickens said, "the timing is suggestive. If the judge, for whatever reason, had been letting Ted slip through the cracks for several years, then lost his discretionary powers, Mrs. Tillman may have had to look elsewhere. What I'm saying is that one thing happened in sixty-eight and the other right soon afterward in sixty-nine. Does that tell us anything?"

Mr. Pickens scratched his head with the blunt end of his pen, and Sam looked lost in thought. Finally, Sam said, "Looks like it tells us that both the judge and the sheriff were involved."

"Maybe," I said, adding my opinion for the first time, "but sometimes a cigar is just a cigar, as somebody said. Because why would the sheriff want a piece of land so far off the beaten track that the only way to get to it was by boat?"

Chapter 31

"Here's what we do, then," Mr. Pickens said, not deigning to answer the question I'd posed. "Let's look at both of them, find out everything we can about the judge and the sheriff, and see what pops up." He stared at Sam for a minute, thinking. Then he went on. "Would the judge have had any influence over the sheriff?"

"Oh, yeah," Sam said, a flash of hope passing across his face. "Politics could've been behind it all. Judge Baine had political ties everywhere. Nobody got elected to anything without his backing. And, believe me, he had his way until people got their fill of it and turned him out of office. But that was way down the line. He was on the bench for close to thirty years."

Mr. Pickens said, "All the more reason to think he's our man. If he could do as he pleased on the bench, plus having some kind of hold over the sheriff, then he was in the catbird seat."

I could keep silent no longer. "But they've both been dead ten years or more. How could either one of them break into Sam's house?"

"Well, that's the question," Sam said, running his hand over his head. "We're still missing something. Maybe we ought to look further into that land deal."

"That's on my list of things to do tomorrow," Mr. Pickens said. "The office closed before I finished, but I think now I'll look through the fifties and the seventies, see if any of these five sold any property to anybody at anytime. But one more time before we wrap this up, is there anything else that could connect those five people to each other? Anything you can think of that they have—or might've had—in common?"

Both Sam and Mr. Pickens leaned back and gazed at nothing, as they thought over all the possibilities. While they were doing that, I gazed at Mr. Pickens, noting for the first time the deep lines on his face and the flecks of gray in his black hair. I wondered how much Hazel Marie had had to do with putting them there. As I looked at his tired face, I felt a tug of pity for him. Poor thing, as much as he was going through now, he had no more idea than the man in the moon what he was in for.

"Sam?" Mr. Pickens said, coming out of his reverie. "You come up with anything?"

Sam shook his head. "No, nothing. Except they were all residents of the county and their crimes were all misdemeanors. Well, except for Ilona Weaver's embezzlement. Other than that, I just don't see a thing."

"Me, either," Mr. Pickens said, turning his gaze to his notebook. "Well, keep thinking about it, and let's move on."

"Good hair," I announced.

Their heads swiveled toward me, both foreheads wrinkled with frowns. "What?"

"Good hair," I said again.

"Julia," Sam said, a smile playing around his mouth, "where in the world did that come from?"

Glancing at Mr. Pickens who was frowning at what he assumed was my trifling with his serious case, I said, "Well, you asked if they have anything in common and that's what they have—at least the ones I've seen. Some are grayer than others, but I couldn't help but notice that every last one has a good, thick head of hair, except Bob Tillman who hardly has any, but he doesn't have an arrest record, either." I set my mouth, preparing to defend myself. "Hair is important, you know, since it tends to get thin with age. Not that either of you need to worry about that." I reached up and touched my hair, so recently styled by Velma. "Or me, either. But not a one of those four people has suffered any thinning or hair loss, and I think it behooves us to check Rafe Feldman's head to determine the state of his scalp."

Sam started it. He looked at Mr. Pickens and began to laugh, then Mr. Pickens cut loose. So there I sat, having offered what I considered a valuable clue, while they leaned back and laughed their heads off.

"Julia," Sam sputtered as he tried to get his breath, "I'm sorry, honey. It just struck me as funny."

"Yeah," Mr. Pickens said, "we don't mean to hurt your feelings. It's just . . ." He had to stop and wipe his eyes. "It's just that I'd've never thought to consider hair."

"Well," I reminded him, "you said anything and that's all I could think of." I laughed along with them, but I didn't think it was all that funny. I was just happy to have given them a moment's release from all the heavy thinking they'd been doing. Besides, what had they come up with?

When breakfast was over the next morning, I walked upstairs to Lloyd's room, where he was gathering his tennis gear for another day on the courts.

"Lloyd?" I said, tapping on his door. "You have a minute?"

"Sure, Miss Julia, come on in." He zipped his racket cover, then picked up a can of balls.

"I know you're ready to go, but I was wondering if you'd have time to go visiting with me this afternoon."

That stopped him. Not wanting to turn me down, he hesitated. Visiting with me was not something he'd ordinarily be eager to do. "Um, well. I guess I could."

"No, that's all right. You probably already have plans."

"Well, yessum, I do. It's the last week of the tennis clinic, and school starts Monday. So we're all planning to have lunch at the Grill, then go to the pool."

"Then you go right ahead," I said, pleased that he was enjoying the summer with friends. He was so inclined to be a loner, you know. "Just be sure and not go in the water right after you eat. I'd just thought that, if you were free, you might want to accompany me. But I can manage alone. In fact, it might be better to do it alone."

I turned to leave, but he said, "Miss Julia? Can I ask you something?"

"Of course."

"Do you know what's going on with Mama and J.D.? They're sure not acting the way they used to."

Oh, my, I thought, looking at the concerned frown on the boy's face. How in the world had we expected him not to notice the definite chill in the air?

"Well, honey," I began, my mind running over all the possible answers I could give. Should I flat out lie? Should I tell him the truth, without telling the whole truth?

Only one thing was for sure: Hazel Marie had to tell him something and not leave it up to me.

"Well, honey," I began again, "it seems they may be going through a cooling-off period. But I think that when she's feeling better, they'll be able to sit down together and smooth away any differences. Right now, though, she's still recovering her health."

"Whew," he said, a smile lighting up his face, "that's what I kinda thought. I expect she didn't want J.D. to catch whatever she had. I mean, we're probably all immune since we've been around her the whole time. But he's been gone a while, so he might could've caught it."

I nodded. "That's probably it. Now, you have a good time today, and I'll see you when you get back."

After he left, I went in to see how Hazel Marie was feeling. I found her up and dressed. Well, halfway dressed, for she was wearing a pink running suit or workout outfit or whatever those athletic things are called.

"Hazel Marie," I said, "I believe you're feeling better."

"I guess I am, physically, anyway. I talked to Dr. Hargrove on the phone this morning, and he said I should begin to be up a little. Just as long as I don't do too much. The only problem is I don't know how much too much is."

"Well," I said, laughing, "I'm sure he doesn't mean for you to go running."

She smiled, then looking down at what she had on, she began to cloud up. "Look at this," she said, as she pulled up the top to reveal the elastic waistband on the bottom part. "It's all I can wear. Everything else is too tight. I can't believe I'm already showing."

"Oh, my," I said. "We're going to have to do something about that." Meaning, of course, shopping for maternity clothes.

But she didn't take it that way.

"I know we are," she said, a stricken look on her face. "But I don't know what! Miss Julia, I've got to get away from here. Somebody's going to find out and then what would I do? Please help me, Miss Julia, and I won't ask you for another thing as long as I live. Help me move away, because I can't stay in this room forever."

She was right, and I'd been putting off

facing the problem long enough. Something had to be done before the whole town began buzzing with news of Hazel Marie's sudden suspicious weight gain. The fact of the matter was that people wouldn't be so much scandalized at the idea of Hazel Marie being pregnant as they would at what she'd been doing to get that way, especially since she'd recently been elected secretary of the Lila Mae Harding Sunday school class. And to my shame, I couldn't help but think of what it would do to my own standing, for it occurred to me that the only disadvantage in being known for the proper forms of conduct and holding one's self above the common fray is that people took such pleasure when you proved to be human. I wondered if it would've been better if I'd had a less spotless reputation.

I had to mentally shake myself. It would be Hazel Marie and Lloyd and those unborn babies who would suffer, and here I was, worrying about myself. What was I doing fretting over what a bunch of old biddies would say or think? Of course, those old biddies were all my contemporaries, which meant that I knew them well. And let me tell you, when I considered them one by one, I could truthfully say that I didn't give a rip what they thought. Let them whisper and gossip and pass along rumors all they wanted to. What I had in this house in the form of Sam and Lloyd and Hazel Marie and Lillian more than canceled out any concern about being the number-one topic over a bridge table. I could hold my head up high, regardless of what Hazel Marie decided to do.

"I will help you, Hazel Marie. I'll do whatever you want. But first, let me talk to Dr. Hargrove. If you don't mind, that is. I'd like to be reassured that you'd suffer no harm from a move, and I'll also ask him to recommend some doctors wherever you decide to go. So, if you can put up with it a few days more, we'll do whatever needs to be done."

"Thank you," she said as she reached for another Kleenex. "Thank you so much. I am such a mess, I can't hardly think of what to do next."

"One thing, Hazel Marie, you must do, and that's to talk to Lloyd. The boy has noticed that things aren't the same with you and Mr. Pickens, and he's asking me what's wrong. I can't keep telling him half-truths and beating around the bush. You have to tell him something."

Well, that about did her in. "I know it," she said, collapsing in a chair as if she'd just lost the strength to stand. "I just . . . Give me a few days more and I will."

"Good," I said, patting her shoulder. "A few days more and things will be a little clearer." And, in a few more days, school would start, making it harder for her to move Lloyd. That thought brought to mind the old dilemma: I didn't want her to take Lloyd with her, yet I didn't want her to be off by herself.

Sighing with frustration, I told her that I had one more errand to do for Sam and would be back soon. I left then, my mind roiling with all I had to do in that tiny breathing space of a few days more that she'd given me.

Chapter 32

I drove to the Morningside Rest Home, parked in the shade of an oak tree, and looked around. From the outside, the long white building with azalea bushes along the foundation looked nice enough. As these things go, that is. But, Lord, I wouldn't want to end up in one. Not to be selfish about it, but that was another reason to keep Hazel Marie with us. Once, in an embarrassing outpouring of gratitude, she had said that she'd take care of me until the day I died. At the time, I hadn't fully appreciated her promise, unwilling to accept that I might be nearing the age of decrepitude. Now, though, with the thought of losing her forever looming in my mind, ending up in the Morningside Rest Home or another of its ilk became a real and disturbing possibility.

But, gathering myself to do this last errand for Sam, I walked inside and told the plump, little woman at the desk that I was there to visit Mr. Rafe Feldman.

"Oh, really?" she said with an inappropriate titter. "Well, that's good, 'cause he doesn't get many visitors. I think he's in the sunroom. Let me call somebody to show you where that is." She swiveled her chair around and yelled toward the hall, "Sally! I need you out here!" Then, turning back to me, she said with another giggle, "That's our temporary in-house phone service."

I nodded, not wanting to comment, and waited until a large, more than plump, woman in a white nylon uniform shuffled into the lobby. "What you want?" she asked the receptionist.

"This lady wants to see Mr. Rafe. Show her where the sunroom is."

The woman—she couldn't be a nurse with those black running shoes on her feet—smiled and motioned me to follow her. As we walked down a long hall, the sharp odor of Pine-Sol became more pronounced. As bad as it was, though, I knew it covered something even worse.

"You know Mr. Rafe?" Sally asked as her heavy body waddled along beside me.

"No, I can't say I do," I said. "I'm just visiting for, well, because it's a nice thing to do." I'd started to say I was making a call for my church, then decided it was better not to involve the church in a deliberate deceit. She didn't need to know my reason, anyway.

"Well," she said, "he's having a pretty good day, but I'll stay close by. In case he starts yellin' at you. There he is, over on the settee."

She pointed to a thin, white-headed man who was sitting stiff and upright on a floral sofa in the sun-filled room. His hands rested in his lap while, in spite of a few other patients watching a television game show, his eyes stared straight in front. A smile flitted off and on around his mouth.

I walked over into the line of his sight, leaned over and said, "Mr. Feldman? I'm Mrs. Sam Murdoch. How're you feeling today?"

It took a second, but finally his eyes came to rest on me as I took a chair beside him. "Fine," he said in a voice that was so soft I could barely make it out. "How're you?"

"I'm fine, too. It's a lovely day, isn't it?"

His eyes searched my face. "You look like somebody I used to know," he said mildly. "Came to town married to ole man Springer, stingiest man around. Handsome young woman, though."

I stiffened. *Handsome?* Even when I was young? Well, some people are never pretty, and I should've been accustomed to it by my present age. Shaking off that half compliment, I was pleased that he seemed alert enough to answer a few questions.

"Mr. Feldman, do you remember talking to Sam Murdoch last year? Well, I'm here to . . ."

"Did somebody go to Walmart?"

"What? Oh, I'm not sure. I'll try to find out for you. But, Mr. Feldman, I wanted to ask if . . ."

He chuckled deep in his throat. "Never did know what that woman saw in him. Money, I guess, since he made it hand over fist. She was a looker back then, but stuck-up? You wouldn't believe how high she'd stick that nose in the air."

I didn't think I could get any stiffer, but I did. "That, Mr. Feldman, is called holding your head up high, which I had every reason to do. But, listen . . ."

He turned his guileless eyes toward me. "Did she go to Walmart?"

"Uh, not yet, I don't believe. Could you just think back to last year and . . ."

"What'd you say your name was?"

"Why, I'm Julia Murdoch, formerly Julia Springer. You said you knew me years ago."

His faded eyes roamed over my face, then he said, "You sure got old in a hurry, didn't you?"

"At about the same rate you did," I said with some asperity. "Now, look here, Mr. Feldman, I didn't come here to be insulted. Put your thinking cap on and tell me . . ."

"Did she go to Walmart yet?"

"I declare, I don't know! Are you talking about Sally? Maybe she went. If you'll just talk to me a minute, I'll get her over here and you can ask her."

Well, I guess that did it, for a low humming noise rose up from his throat and grew in intensity while he sat there, perfectly still, until it became an eerie and frightening scream. I scrambled to my feet and backed away. Sally came to the rescue, thank goodness, and began to croon comforting words to him.

Clutching my pocketbook, I hurriedly turned and left, apologizing for creating a problem as I went.

❦

Lord, I thought as I sat trembling in my car, is that what I have to look forward to? I was sorry that I'd upset him, but he'd done worse to me. Rafe Feldman hadn't known who I was, even though he claimed to have known me in the past, and who was supposed to go to Walmart and what had he wanted from there? Sam had been right, we'd get nothing from him. It had been a wasted trip.

But maybe not so wasted, I thought as I ran back over my unproductive interview. That hair, for one thing, if I could overlook the laughter my clue had elicited from Sam and Mr. Pickens. Rafe Feldman had a thatch of white hair so thick that it had stuck up like tail feathers from the back of his head where he'd rested it against the sofa.

I cranked the car and headed for home, but I couldn't rid myself of the memory of that poor man sitting so still and proper while a scream of epic proportions emanated from his throat. It had terrified me in more ways than one.

"Lillian!" I called as I hurried into the kitchen, intent on making an end run around the possible onset of Rafe Feldman's condition. "Where's the newspaper? You haven't thrown it out, have you?"

"No'm," she said, looking up from the sink. "I don't never th'ow it out till the next one come. It's in there in the livin' room. They's nothin' in it, though."

"Yes, there is," I said as I pushed through the swinging door into the dining room. "I'm looking for the crossword puzzle."

After an hour of fiddling with the crossword puzzle, I put it aside until I had time to use Lloyd's dictionary. There was no use going overboard in pursuing mental acuity, anyway. Besides, the puzzles at the end of the week were always difficult, and I had Hazel Marie to deal with, which was enough excercise for anybody's brain.

I walked out into the kitchen, thinking to discuss matters with Lillian, and the first thing I saw was the box of Godiva chocolates on the counter.

"Lillian, what's this doing here?"

She tore off a paper towel and dried her hands. "Miss Hazel Marie, she say she want it outta her sight. She say for me to eat it up or give it to somebody or th'ow it away, she don't wanta look at it no more."

"Well, my goodness," I said, disappointed that the gift had not softened her heart. "I thought maybe she'd appreciate it, as well as the giver. Did she eat any last night?"

"No'm, not a piece. All us did, though, but she say the thought of it make her stomick turn over."

"Maybe it did. As queasy as she's been, I doubt that chocolate candy would sit very well. Oh, Lillian," I said, sitting down with a sigh that could've easily become a sob, "I don't know what to do. She's bound and determined to have nothing to do with Mr. Pickens, and he, for goodness sakes, won't unbend enough to court her. And that's all it would take, I'm convinced of that. She needs help so bad that I think she'd jump at the chance to marry him, even though she wouldn't touch his candy."

Lillian came over to the table and drew out a chair. "We got to do something, Miss Julia. I don't know if you know this, but she been making lists of what she gonna pack, 'cause she not s'posed to go upstairs yet. An' you might not know this either, but she already showin' an' people gonna know about it pretty soon."

"Oh, I do know it, Lillian, but I'm at my wit's end to know what to do about it." I reached over and took her hand. "Tell me what you think. Should I just confront Mr. Pickens and tell him it's his responsibility to talk her into marrying him? And tell him why? But then, what if Hazel Marie feels I've betrayed her and gets upset enough to go ahead and move off somewhere? And what about Lloyd? He's asking questions I dare not answer because that would be another betrayal. I am just beside myself, trying to figure out the best thing to do."

Lillian patted my hand. "Maybe she have another little spell an' have to go back to bed. Maybe the doctor say she can't go nowhere. I know some ladies have to stay in bed the whole time, else they lose they babies. If I was you, I'd go talk to Dr. Hargrove an' see can he do something."

"That's a good idea, Lillian, and I was thinking of doing that. But even if he says she shouldn't move away, that won't help the bigger problem of making those babies legitimate. Only Mr. Pickens can do that." I took a deep breath to get my voice under control. "Would you believe that he's acting like *his* feelings are hurt? All he does is wander around like a martyr, determined to stay away from her and suffer in silence. I could just wring his stubborn neck."

Chapter 33

Early Friday morning, I called Dr. Hargrove's office and told the receptionist that I needed fifteen minutes of his time to discuss an urgent matter. Of course, she went into a song and dance about his busy day, until I said that the doctor had invited me in anytime I wanted to talk to him and today was when I wanted to. She put me on hold for the longest time, then came back to tell me that he could see me at twelve-thirty.

"During his lunch time," she said with emphasis, just to make me feel bad.

It didn't since it was during mine, too.

Just as I hung up the phone, it rang under my hand. I answered a little snappishly since I had things to do. Emma Sue Ledbetter said, "Why, Julia, you sound upset. Anything wrong?"

A lot was wrong, of course, but nothing I could mention. "I'm sorry, Emma Sue. I wasn't thinking."

"Well, I just wanted to tell you that I'm bringing supper for you tomorrow night, so tell Lillian not to cook. She doesn't come in on Saturdays anyway, does she?"

"As it happens, Lillian does work the occasional Saturday, and tomorrow's one of them. It's awfully nice of you to offer to bring supper, but you don't have to do that."

"Well, I want to," she said, a note of excitement in her voice. "I know Hazel Marie's getting ready to leave and I might not have another chance to do something for her. You'll be home, won't you?"

I assured her we had no other plans, then recalling what I'd intended to ask her, I said, "Emma Sue, while I have you, you know Cassie Wooten, don't you?"

"Why, yes. We're on a committee together. She's so sweet, a little strange in some ways, but very nice. I didn't know you knew her."

"Well, I don't. Not well, anyway. I just wondered what you thought of her."

"Oh, she's a committed Christian, no doubt about that, and I hope you get a chance to know her better. She'd be very good for you, Julia."

I should've known better than to ask Emma Sue. She never had an unkind word to say about anybody—unless they were unchurched. So I let it drop, thanked her for her thoughtfulness and hung up the phone. Then I put Emma Sue aside, gathered my thoughts and prepared to go see the doctor.

෫෫

"Dr. Hargrove," I started, ready to pour out my troubles as I sat across from him with the desk between us. Then, remembering my manners, I began again. "Thank you for seeing me, and I do apologize for delaying your lunch."

"Don't worry about that," he said, with a wave of his hand. "How's Hazel Marie? I've been keeping up with her by phone, but how do you think she's doing?"

"That's exactly why I'm here and, in case you're wondering, she knows I've come to see you and she doesn't mind at all. But first let me thank you for keeping in such close touch with her. Your phone calls have meant the world to her. And to me. I declare, she gave us such a fright when it looked as if she might lose those babies." I paused to rummage in my pocketbook for the monogrammed handkerchief I'd thought to bring, feeling that I might need it any minute. "Of course at the time we didn't know there were two to lose. Now our problems have just multiplied. As you can well imagine."

"Yes, I can. She mentioned to me that she was thinking of moving away, but I'd like her to wait until she's well into her second trimester. But then she shouldn't wait too long. By the third trimester, she'll need to be closely monitored. Not only because of multiple births, but her age is a factor, too."

"Oh, I'm glad to hear it! Have you told her that?"

Dr. Hargrove frowned. "Miss Julia, maybe you don't understand. This is a high-risk pregnancy."

"I *do* understand, and it's just as I

thought. You see," I said, scooting up to the edge of my chair, "I don't want her to move away. None of us do. We want her to stay with us—both her and Lloyd. And what you've just said is all the more reason for her to stay put. Now, of course, I don't want her to have any problems whatsoever, but I don't at all mind her knowing that there's a *possibility* of problems. You might mention that to her, if you would."

He fiddled with the file on his desk for a minute, then looked back at me. "Look, Miss Julia, I can't interfere in a patient's personal situation, unless the patient, herself, asks. So, still speaking in general, why doesn't the daddy step up to the plate?"

"Because the daddy, as you say, is not in the ballpark. She won't tell him, and she won't let me tell him. Why, she hasn't even told Lloyd, and already she can't wear anything but something with an elastic waistband! But," I said, calming myself down, "I'm doing everything I can to get those two back together. So, I need time to work things out, yet time is working against me, too, for those babies are growing apace."

"I see your problem," he said, his mouth

twisting as he recognized the burden I was bearing. "I'm not sure I have any help to offer."

"But you could keep her here. You could tell her the complications she may have to face—I don't mean I want you to overdo it and frighten her unnecessarily. Just make sure she knows the risk she runs by being on her own. I declare," I said, dabbing my eyes, hoping to gain his sympathy, "if you can't help, I don't know who I can turn to."

He sighed and leaned back in his chair. "Consider this, Miss Julia. For what it's worth, it could be better for Hazel Marie if she had those babies somewhere else. You know this town as well as I do, and she'd have a hard time here."

"Oh, I do know it, and that's why I know I'm being selfish in wanting to keep her and Lloyd here. But, on the other hand, it might be worse if she's off by herself somewhere."

Resigned to the fact that he had no answers for me, I folded my handkerchief and prepared to leave. "Well, I'll let you have your lunch now, but could you talk to her? Just, you know, so she'll know what to expect, what could happen and . . ." I stopped, struck with a sudden thought. My eyes dried up and hope bloomed afresh. "It's not Hazel Marie you ought to talk to, it's *him*! That's it, Dr. Hargrove, you should talk to the father and tell him the danger she's in. Don't you do that with your other patients? I mean, don't you talk over any possible problems with the husbands?"

"Yes," he said thoughtfully, "yes, I do. But Hazel Marie doesn't have a husband."

"Well, she would if you'd talk to him!"

"You're sure you know who the father is?"

"Dr. Hargrove! Of course I know and you would, too, if you thought about it."

He smiled then. "I could make a good guess. But, Miss Julia, that'd be pretty close to meddling on my part. I'd have to have her permission."

"But that's exactly where I am! Stymied at every turn, because she won't give it." I stuffed my handkerchief into my pocketbook, preparing to leave. Then I took it back out to keep it handy. "Well, thank you again for seeing me. I'll let you have your lunch now."

Urging me to come back anytime I wanted to talk, he walked me down the hall to the waiting room, then gave me a comforting pat on the shoulder. I left, not feeling comforted at all. No one had any help for me, although it seemed to me that all would be resolved if he'd break just one tiny part of his Hippocratic oath and talk some sense into Mr. Pickens. Which would keep me from having to do it.

⊗·⊗

"Miss Julia," Lillian said as soon as I walked into the kitchen at home, "Miz Allen, she call and say can you come over to her house. She say she have something to tell you, an' she got no mind to tell it on the telephone."

"Well, my goodness, what could be that important?"

"I don't know, but she say to come over soon as you walk in the door, so you better go on."

"Lillian," I said, going over and taking her arm, my heart thudding with anxiety, "do you think she knows? Could the word have gotten out? Oh, my word, what if rumors are running rampant already. Mildred has never called me over like this before.

It's got to be something awful if she can't tell me over the phone."

"Listen here now," Lillian said, "you don't know if she know a thing. Don't be puttin' the cart 'fore the horse, jus' go on over there an' see what she say."

"But what if she comes right out and asks if Hazel Marie is expecting? What will I do?"

"I guess you do the same thing you been doin', makin' up one story after another."

I slumped against the counter. "I don't know if I can. It's awfully hard to tell a story to Mildred. She seems to see right through me. And to tell the truth, I've about run out of stories, especially now that Hazel Marie has practically bloomed overnight." I gripped her arm again. "And that's another thing. Lloyd's going to notice what's happening before too much longer. I declare, Lillian, I don't know how much more I can put up with."

She patted my hand. "You got to leave some things up to the Lord, Miss Julia. Don't be thinkin' you can handle it all. Now, you go on over an' see what Miz Allen want. You might find out you be worryin' for nothin'. It might be 'bout yo' church or something."

&⅌

Well, it almost was.

Mildred and I sat companionably in cushioned wicker chairs on her side porch, welcoming the soft breeze stirred up by the ceiling fan. Clematis vines wound around the Doric columns of the porch, and afternoon shadows stretched out before us on the bright green lawn. A pitcher of iced tea with mint leaves from Mildred's herb garden sat on a table before us. It was a perfectly lovely visit, although I was too much on edge to enjoy it to the fullest extent.

I could stand the suspense no longer. "All right, Mildred, enough about your hemlock fungus and your bad knees, although I commiserate with you about both. But we've talked about everything under the sun except what you called me over to talk about. What in the world is so important that it couldn't be discussed on the phone?"

"Well," she said, "I've just been sitting here wondering if I ought to tell you. I was convinced I should when I called, but now I'm not so sure."

"Oh, no, you don't. Don't tell me there's something I need to know, then say you can't tell me. That won't do, Mildred, and you know it."

She sighed and shifted uncomfortably in her chair, loosening the folds of the caftan she wore. Mildred had a thyroid condition that required loose and voluminous clothing to accommodate her mature figure.

"Well," she said again, "it's just that I don't like surprises, and I know you don't, either. On the other hand, it's hardly fair to the ones planning the surprise to give it away. So if you'll promise to act surprised and not tell them I told you, I'll tell you."

"A surprise!" I said, smiling with what I hoped was delight and not with the relief I felt. Mildred didn't know a thing about Hazel Marie and had not even guessed. This was something entirely different from what I had feared. "What kind of surprise?" I went on. "And who's planning it?"

"Emma Sue, wouldn't you know. And she's so excited she can hardly stand it. She's invited everybody from the garden club, your book club, and, of course, from our Sunday school class. And, Julia," Mildred said, leaning with some difficulty toward me for emphasis, "she's even planning to play *games*. She made me promise not to tell you, but when I heard she was going to have games, I knew you'd want to know."

"My goodness, Mildred, she just called to say she was bringing supper for us tomorrow night. What's she doing having a party, too?"

"Oh, you know Emma Sue. When she decides to do something, she goes all out. Anyway, the party'll be on Monday afternoon at her house. She's planning to get you over there with a made-up excuse—a church problem or something. And if that doesn't work, she's going to have everybody show up at your house." Mildred laughed. "That would really be a surprise party, wouldn't it?"

Well, that certainly set me back. Emma Sue was taking on a lot, what with bringing supper for us on Saturday, and planning a surprise party for me on Monday. I couldn't think of a thing I'd done to warrant such a celebration. It wasn't my birthday, and I'd not had perfect attendance at Sunday school, nor had I recently been elected to anything. The only thing I could think of was the longevity of my church membership, but others much older than I deserved that honor. Not that I considered being the subject of a surprise party much of an honor. On the contrary, I thought such things were slightly tacky and, if you weren't careful, somewhat cruel. A lot of people don't like surprises, however well-meant, and I was one of them.

"Listen, Mildred," I said, "I do thank you for warning me. Now help me think of a way to nip this in the bud. If she's determined to have a party for me—although I can't think why—let's see if we can talk her into a nice reception, maybe in the Fellowship Hall at the church, where games would be most unsuitable."

"Why, Julia," Mildred said, laughing, "the party's not for you. It's for Hazel Marie, of course."

Lord, my heart dropped right down to my feet. A surprise *baby* shower? Was that what Emma Sue was planning? And then, joy bloomed in my soul, and I gave thanks for answered prayers. A baby shower given by Emma Sue Ledbetter, of all people, meant that Hazel Marie would not suffer the scorn I thought would be heaped upon her. Tears welled up in my eyes at the outpouring of love that would be showered on her, along with an abundance of baby things she would need.

"Oh, Mildred, that is the dearest thing. You can't know how much Hazel Marie will appreciate it, or how much I do, either. Emma Sue can have all the games she wants to, and we'll enjoy them. I'll tell you the truth, I have never before realized how deep Emma Sue's Christian commitment is, but this just goes to show, doesn't it?"

Mildred eyed me with a raised eyebrow. "I'm not sure a going-away party indicates any particularly deep spiritual commitment on Emma Sue's part. Of course it's thoughtful of her to want to give Hazel Marie a nice send-off, but she told me it was the perfect way to pay back her social obligations and do a good deed at the same time."

"Oh," I said, taken aback by how my mind had leaped to such an easy but totally improbable outcome for Hazel Marie.

And, even worse, it had been on the tip of my tongue to tell Mildred that all the guests should know, before they purchased their shower gifts, that Hazel Marie would need two of everything.

My breath caught in my throat as I realized how close I had come to making Hazel Marie the talk of the town.

Chapter 34

Walking home from Mildred's house, I hardly noticed the late afternoon heat—except for having to mop my face now and then. My footsteps were dragging, for I found myself dreading to face again the problems that abounded at home. I'd never felt quite so defeated before. Well, yes, I had, right after I learned what Wesley Lloyd Springer had been doing during the last decade of his life. But even so, I had quickly discovered a way to handle it, unorthodox though it might have appeared. And it had worked out brilliantly, I must say.

But this, this with Hazel Marie left me

with no way to turn. Oh, there was an easy solution and its name was Mr. Pickens, but how to tell him? And when to tell him? And what would Hazel Marie do if I did tell him? I fondly pictured her falling into his arms as soon as he fell onto his knees, but what if I were wrong? What if she felt so betrayed by him for getting her in the fix she was in and by me for breaking my promise, that her trusting heart began to break and she ended up a mere fragment of her former self?

It could happen, you know. You could be so hurt by those you've trusted that nothing, including yourself, is ever the same again.

I stopped beside a holly tree on the edge of Mildred's yard, pretending to examine the leaves and berries in case anybody was watching. But all I wanted was to delay taking up my burdens again.

My rows were getting short and, if you don't know what that means, it means that the end was approaching. Time was running out with Hazel Marie getting bigger by the minute, as well as getting well enough to take off on her own. At the same time Mr. Pickens was working as hard as he could on Sam's case, and, if he was right about either the judge or the sheriff, he'd soon come up with an answer, then be off on his own, as well. Something had to give before they flew off in different directions.

I walked past the holly tree and stopped at the graceful limbs of an abelia bush. That was worth a minute or two of study, so that's what I gave it. While I fingered the leaves as if I knew what I was doing, my mind sifted through the options open to me.

First of all, I couldn't let Hazel Marie face the going-away party that Emma Sue was planning. She would never be able to withstand the questions about her new job that didn't exist or the scrutiny of her new waist expansion that would be part and parcel of any social gathering where she'd be the focus of all eyes. I'd have to tell her that according to Mildred, Emma Sue would call us late Monday afternoon to come over for an important discussion about some church problem. And, furthermore, if either Hazel Marie or I declined to come, she would move the whole party, lock, stock, and barrel, to my house. Whatever it took, Emma Sue intended to surprise us with a party that would send Hazel Marie off with the town's best wishes to her new job in Palm Beach.

I shuddered at the thought, knowing what the news of that would do to Hazel Marie. She'd start packing with a vengeance. She might even leave before the weekend was out, and here it was already Friday with me floundering around about what to do. And still, Lloyd knew nothing— no what, why, or when, especially why.

One good thing—Hazel Marie could hardly take him with her if she left in such a hurry. The school year started on Monday, so there was every reason in the world to leave him with us. But, oh, how would I sleep, knowing that Hazel Marie was alone and friendless in the wilds of south Florida?

But then, out of the blue, some of the ideas that had been randomly floating around in my mind began to fall into place. I quickly turned away from Mildred's horticultural display and, with determined strides, headed for home. I'd made up my mind.

I realized that there was a remote possibility that Hazel Marie would refuse Mr. Pickens because of his heretofore mulishness, even if, contrary to his track record, he promised lifelong marital fealty. But I had decided to take that risk. Hazel Marie might never speak to me again for betraying her trust, but I had decided to run that risk, as well.

❦

I stopped midstep as a sudden bright thought zinged into my head. Maybe she wanted me to!

Of course, I thought, that's it! She doesn't want to give in to Mr. Pickens after having turned her back on him and flounced off as if he didn't matter to her. She had her pride, but it had worked her into a corner of her own making, which she couldn't unbend enough to get out of. I could understand that. I'd done it to myself more than once.

But she wanted him back, I was convinced of that. I mean, what woman, facing the arrival of not one but two infants, wouldn't want another pair of helping hands, if nothing else?

❦

"Lillian," I said, quickly closing the door behind me to keep the cool air inside the house, "My mind is made up, and, regardless of the consequences, I know what I have to do."

"Well, 'fore you do anything," Lillian said, dipping green beans from a saucepan into a bowl, "you better get on in yonder, 'cause supper almost ready. An' Mr. Sam an' Mr. Pickens in the livin' room starvin' to death, they been waitin' on you so long."

"Is it that late?" I glanced at my watch and saw that it was. "Is Lloyd home?"

"He settin' in there with 'em, 'bout to cave in he so hungry."

"They'll just have to wait a few minutes more because, Lillian, you won't believe what Mildred told me." I walked over close to her so I could whisper the news. "Emma Sue is planning a going-away party for Hazel Marie! Can you believe that?"

"Why, Miss Julia, that so nice."

"*Nice!* It's terrible. Well, I mean the thought is nice, but if there's anything that'll send Hazel Marie away from here—maybe even tomorrow—it's hearing about a party where everybody'll be looking at her and asking questions."

"Well, yessum, I see what you sayin'. She not up for something like that, the pore little thing."

"The only good thing, it's supposed to be a surprise party, so I'm not obligated to tell her about it. But come Monday, she'll know and so will everybody else. Something's got to give before then, Lillian, and I intend to see that it gets done."

I paced between the stove and the refrigerator, then turned back to her. "Well, I can't do it right now, so go ahead and call the others to the table. I'll just slip through the back hall and speak to her. I've hardly seen her all day. Is Latisha with her?"

"No'm," Lillian said, opening the oven door and turning her head from the blast of heat. "I leave her with the neighbor lady. Miss Hazel Marie, she act too sad today for any kind of play-pretty foolishness." She pulled a pan of yeast rolls from the oven, then looked up at me. "An' she kinda gettin' up on her high horse again, too."

"Oh, my. What's upset her?"

Lillian nodded toward the living room. "I 'spect it 'cause of him settin' in yonder. Soon as she hear him come in talkin', she say she lose her appetite, an' feel like she 'bout to start th'owin' up again."

"Well, that just does it," I said, dismayed that my recently-decided-on plan was coming apart at the seams. I walked over again to Lillian and whispered, "Lillian, I had made up my mind to go ahead and break my promise to her. I was going to get Mr. Pickens off to himself—tonight, if possible—and just flat out tell him what's what. But I need to do it when she's in a good mood, because I know that just as soon as I tell him, he's going to go flying in there. And it would be a disaster if he went in when she'd already worked herself into a state. He wouldn't stand a chance." I grabbed Lillian's arm and held on. "But I am going to do it before the weekend's out, and I don't care what I have to suffer for doing it. It's for Hazel Marie's own good, and his, too."

Lillian sighed and patted my hand. "I been thinkin' an' prayin' 'bout the same thing, wonderin' when you gonna do something. I know you hate to break a promise, but look like when you 'tween a rock an' a hard place, they's nothin' else to do. Jus' look what happened to Jephthah when he make a promise he ought not to make, an' wouldn't go back on it. I can't help but b'lieve the Lord woulda let him off, if he jus' ask right."

I stared at her a minute, trying to remember who Jephthah was and what kind of ill-advised promise he'd made. I didn't have time to look him up, but I could trust Lillian. She knew her Bible, and if she thought he'd have been better off breaking his promise than keeping it, well, that certainly set a precedent, didn't it?

Chapter 35

"Hazel Marie?" I said, as I tapped on her door and walked into the room. At the sight of her blotched face and puffy eyes, I came to an abrupt stop. "Oh, my goodness, are you all right? What's wrong?"

"Everything," she sobbed, sitting there in her pink work-out outfit, dabbing at her eyes. "*He's* here again, and I just can't stand it."

"Well, honey," I said, taking a chair next to her, "he's here only for Sam. He's not going to bother you, and, Hazel Marie, I do think he's trying to make amends. He brought you that lovely box of candy, which shows he's trying to be nice, don't you think?"

"No, ma'am, I don't." She threw down a wet Kleenex and snatched a fresh one from the box. "It just shows how selfish he is. *He's* the one who likes candy so much, not me." She blew her nose, threw down the Kleenex and snatched another one. "I'd like to take that candy and cram every piece of it down his throat!"

"Now, Hazel Marie, you mustn't get so worked up. It's not good for you."

"Well, he ought to know what he's done."

I took her hand and held it a few minutes, trying to comfort her. But in just that instant, my mind lit up like the sun rising in the east. There it was! Exactly as I'd thought.

As Lillian began tinkling the little silver bell, summoning us to the table, I stood up and said, "Hazel Marie, try not to worry. Things are going to work out, I'm convinced of it."

❦

Hurrying through the back hall to the kitchen, I grabbed Lillian's arm as she headed to the dining room, almost tipping over the platter of fried chicken she was carrying.

"Lillian," I whispered, since I could hear

Sam and Mr. Pickens at the table just beyond the door. "Wait a minute. I just got the green light from Hazel Marie. She wants Mr. Pickens to know!"

Lillian set the platter on the kitchen table and looked at me in some disbelief. "What she say?"

"She said, '*He ought to know what he's done.*' That's exactly what she said as sure as I'm standing here. And if that doesn't release me from my promise, I don't know what does."

Lillian studied on it for a minute, repeating my words. "He oughta *know* what he's done, he *oughta* know what he's done. I don't know, Miss Julia, I can see it mean he oughta know 'thout bein' told."

I waved my hand, not wanting to be deterred. "A technicality, Lillian. Let's not get tangled up with alternate meanings. She said it, plain as day. And tomorrow morning Sam's taking Lloyd to buy school supplies, and I'm going to get Mr. Pickens off to himself and lay it on the line." I thought for a minute. "I might need you to help me."

⚮

"He left everything in a trust," Sam said, after we'd finished dinner and Lillian had cleared the table. With Lloyd excused to visit with his mother, Mr. Pickens and I sat listening to Sam's report on Judge Robert Eugene Baine. "A will is open to the public, but a trust is not, so that's a closed door. But I got to talking with a woman there in the records office who knew the family—I think I just missed you, Pickens. Anyway, according to her, the judge's wife died about thirty years ago, and an unmarried daughter stayed on, looking after the house and taking care of him in his old age. Apparently, she's still living on the home place out on Staton Bridge Road."

"When did the judge die?" I asked, as I stirred my coffee. We were lingering around the table trying to decide what our next step should be.

"Sometime in the late nineties," Sam said, consulting his notes. "Anyway, the clerk I was talking to lived fairly close to the Baines, and she told me that he turned into a bitter old man in his last years." Sam looked up and smiled. "Couldn't have been much of a change, though, from what he was on the bench. According to her, everybody felt sorry for the daughter, but she never called on anybody for help—just put up with it, I guess. I'll tell you this, though, I couldn't find a lawyer in town who'd kept up with him after he lost that last election. It was like he dropped out of sight, and everybody breathed a sigh of relief to have him gone."

"My goodness," I said, "it's a shame when old people get so cranky nobody can stand to be around them. And, Mr. Pickens, no need to look at me that way. I wasn't speaking of Sam."

That was worth a laugh from all of us, from me especially since it had gladdened my heart to see Mr. Pickens's teasing smile and cocked eyebrow aimed at me. He had lately been entirely too despondent, and I wanted to reach across the table to comfort him. As the laughter died away, though, the lines on his face reappeared and I had a great urge to just tell him what he needed to know, then and there.

But I had had time to think over my decision, and a cooler head was prevailing. To be on the safe side of keeping my promise to Hazel Marie—in spite of what I'd taken as a clear release from it—I now thought it best to get Sam to tell him, and to tell him right away. I reasoned that Mr.

Pickens would take it better coming from another man—a man whose esteem he valued. Because, see, it had occurred to me while we were eating Lillian's fried chicken that I had been assuming a lot in thinking that Mr. Pickens would immediately do the right thing as soon as he knew. But what if he didn't?

What if, as soon as he heard that twin babies were in the offing, he up and took flight? His moving to Charlotte as soon as things didn't go his way certainly proved his propensity to run from trouble. I was hoping that hearing the news from Sam, rather than from me, would make him think twice before pulling up stakes.

"Well, okay then," the man himself said, turning us back to the case at hand. "I guess the next thing is to go see this daughter." He glanced up at Sam. "She doesn't have a record, does she? I mean, she wasn't involved with the group you interviewed, was she?"

"Nope, and I looked. There's nothing on her. Tell you the truth, though," Sam said, scratching his head, "I never knew he had any children, much less one that took care of him. From what I could gather, she was, and still is, pretty much of a homebody, nobody seems to know much about her."

"What's her name?" I asked.

"Um, let me see." Sam flipped the pages of his notebook. "Here it is. Roberta, according to Lila Boyd, the clerk I talked to."

"I've never heard of her," I said in some surprise, since I thought I knew, or knew of, just about everybody in the county.

"Me either," Sam said, "but I wasn't interested in knowing any more about Judge Baine than I had to. I did get the impression from Lila that she's a little strange. Which might explain why she's stayed home all these years."

Mr. Pickens had been doodling in his notebook, but he looked up and asked, "How old would she be now?"

"I'd guess around sixty or so," Sam said. "Lila's retiring this year, and she went to school with her. Rode the school bus together, anyway. So they'd be about the same age. You think she's worth interviewing?"

Mr. Pickens nodded. "Yeah, I do. But it'll be dicey. If we go in there implying that her daddy was the reason those records and tapes were stolen, we won't get much out of her."

Sam ran his hand down his face. "He's got to be the reason, though—him or the sheriff. There's no way around it, they keep turning up, one way or another, in every case I'm looking at."

"But," I said, "she may know nothing about any of it. If she never left home and never had any social life, how would she know what her father did in the court-room?"

"Yeah, well, still," Mr. Pickens said, "we ought to talk to her. To be thorough, if nothing else. Sam, maybe you should be the one to approach her since you knew the judge." Mr. Pickens leaned back in his chair, thought for a minute, then went on. "You could say you want to interview her about her father for your book, without making any mention of the theft of the records. In other words, don't let her think you're looking at him for any reason other than his prominence in the county."

Sam nodded. "I can do that. And would've done it even if there'd been no theft." He smiled with some chagrin. "And if I'd known there was a daughter to be interviewed."

"Okay," Mr. Pickens said, "put that on hold for a minute and let me add something else to the mix." He pulled some papers covered with jotted notes from his briefcase. "Would it surprise you to know that Judge Baine sold a large tract of land to Sheriff Hamilton in nineteen fifty-nine?"

Well, yes, it would, for Sam had a startled look on his face. "How large? Where was it?"

"Couple of hundred acres in the River Bend area. Bordering as near as I can tell from the survey maps that tiny piece that Amelda Tillman sold to the sheriff ten years later."

Sam and I looked at each other, both of us realizing exactly what that meant. "River Bend," Sam said, leaning back as things began to fall into place. "That, my friend, is where the River Bend Inn and Country Club are. Along with a gated community of single-family homes and condominiums owned mostly by summer residents." Sam rubbed his hand across his face. "I missed that because I was concentrating on the sixties, but, wait. That tract wasn't developed until the late seventies, and I don't remember Al Hamilton having anything to do with it."

"He didn't," Mr. Pickens said, "except for selling it to a development company in seventy-three."

"Well now," Sam said, "his buying a useless piece of land from the Tillman woman makes sense. He was adding to what he'd already gotten ten years before from the judge. Maybe by that time, he saw development on the horizon."

"I expect he did. Interesting thing, though, Judge Baine missed out all the way around. He sold that land to the sheriff for ten dollars and other valuable considerations, and the sheriff sold it to the development company the same way. But that deed had enough document stamps on it to indicate a sizeable amount of money changed hands. No stamps on the first deed."

"So," Sam said, "what that suggests is that the 'other valuable considerations' of the Baine sale could've been for Sheriff Hamilton's silence and/or complicity in the dispositions of these cases."

Mr. Pickens nodded. "That's what it

looks like to me, and eventually it paid off for the sheriff, big time."

Sam twisted his mouth, thinking it all over. "That puts a different light on things, doesn't it? I don't know what, but I'll certainly have a new chapter to write if I ever get back to writing. But to be thorough, as you say, I'd better go ahead and try to interview the Baine woman. Julia," he said, turning to me, "will you go with me? I have to run over to Asheville tomorrow afternoon to see a retired judge who knew Baine, so I'd like to see her in the morning."

Well, there went my plan. How could I get Sam to talk some sense into Mr. Pickens if they were going off in a dozen different directions? But I nodded in answer and said, "She'd probably be more comfortable with both of us instead of a strange man showing up by himself. But wait, Sam, weren't you going to take Lloyd to get his school supplies in the morning?"

Mr. Pickens's head snapped up. "I'll take him. I'd like to, in fact, if it's all right with Hazel Marie."

My heart warmed toward him even more. "Oh, I'm sure it'll be fine. Since she's been under the weather, we don't bother her with little decisions like that. And Lloyd will be thrilled. He's missed you, Mr. Pickens."

He bent his head to shuffle through his notes, mumbling, "I've missed him, too."

"I'll have Lloyd make a list of what he needs so you won't forget anything. Walmart is probably the best place to go and, believe me, I am delighted to let you have it."

With our plans made for the morrow, Mr. Pickens prepared to leave. I drew him aside in the kitchen while Sam was gathering his notes and files.

"Mr. Pickens," I said, "I'll have Lloyd ready to go about nine o'clock, so if you'll just pull up outside I'll send him right out. There's no need for you to come in. That way you'll save some time."

He gave me a sick sort of half-smile. "And that way she won't know I'm taking him, right?"

"Well, the thing of it is, she's supposed to avoid emotional upsets. And in spite of your thoughtfulness in keeping your distance, your presence just seems to set her off. But I assure you, I am not telling her any stories. I'm just not telling her everything. So you go on with that boy and have a good time with him. He needs you, Mr. Pickens."

"If you're sure then."

"I am sure. You don't need to worry about it. People in Hazel Marie's condition are known to be somewhat erratic in their emotions, and we have to make allowances. Hormones, you know."

"Okay," he said, the frown between his brows deepening as his black eyes bored into mine. "But tell me this, Miss Julia. Just what exactly is wrong with her?"

Well, there it was—the perfect opportunity to tell him and be done with it, my decision about Sam doing it notwithstanding. I opened my mouth to do just that when Lloyd walked into the kitchen.

"You leaving, J.D.?"

"Yep, it's been a long day. But I'll be back in the morning. Nine o'clock on the dot, so you be ready."

The boy's eyes lit up. "Where're we going?"

"To Walmart," I intervened. "To get your supplies since Sam has some work to do. Now, Lloyd, let's not bother your mother with our little arrangements of who's going with whom, unless she out and out asks, of course. I wouldn't want you to tell any stories."

"Oh, okay," he said, but his eyes flitted from one to the other of us.

He knew there were problems between his mother and Mr. Pickens, and he probably suspected that there was even more going on than he knew. He was too smart not to have figured that out, and if we let things go along as we were doing he would soon figure out what that *more* was.

All the more reason to clear the air once and for all. Enough of hiding things from those who needed to know. Enough of walking on eggs for fear of upsetting somebody. Enough of being afraid to open my mouth.

And to that end, I opened my mouth and said, "Mr. Pickens, sometime tomorrow afternoon when you're back from Walmart and Sam's gone to Asheville, Lillian wants to talk to you."

Chapter 36

As soon as Lloyd came downstairs the next morning, I had my plans laid out for the day. Pursuant to those plans, I suggested that he go to the pool or find someone to play tennis with after Mr. Pickens brought him home. "I want you to enjoy the last Saturday of summer," I said, for I, myself, had some big fish to fry that afternoon and didn't want him around to witness whatever the outcome might be.

I watched as Lloyd hurriedly ate breakfast, excited about his forthcoming shopping trip with Mr. Pickens. My heart ached at how much the boy cared for him. "Tell

Mr. Pickens," I said, "that he's welcome to have lunch with us, unless the two of you want to eat downtown."

As soon as Mr. Pickens's rumbling car turned in the drive, Lloyd went scurrying out to meet him. I was pleased that Hazel Marie was still sleeping and unaware that her son was consorting with the enemy. If she asked, I told Lillian to just say that Lloyd was getting his school supplies and leave it at that. I don't believe in upsetting anyone unnecessarily.

Having gotten everybody settled to my satisfaction, I slid into Sam's car beside him, fastened my seat belt and took note of my handsome husband in one of his summer suits—seersucker with blue stripes, set off with a handsome tie. Sam always dressed well and to the season, making me proud to be with him. My only request soon after we married was that he forswear bow ties. They had been Wesley Lloyd Springer's trademark adornment, and it would've suited me never to have to look at another one again. Not long after making that request, I noticed that James began sporting bow ties even when he was mowing Sam's lawn.

I made myself comfortable as we started out, anticipating a nice drive with Sam and a pleasant visit with the judge's daughter.

"So," Sam said, as he pulled the car onto Polk Street, "Emma Sue's throwing a surprise going-away party for Hazel Marie."

"Yes, and it's a surprise to me that you remember." I reached over to touch his arm. "You were half asleep last night when I told you about it."

"Oh, you'd be surprised at what all I remember." He smiled and released one hand from the steering wheel to hold mine. "How're you going to handle it?"

I sighed. "It's brought me right down to the wire. What I'm going to do is make sure that Mr. Pickens knows everything there is to know before Monday night and pray that he'll take matters into his own hands. And, to that end, Sam, I want you to be prepared to tell him if something else rears its interfering head and Lillian's not able to."

"Lillian?" Sam's eyebrows went straight up to his hairline. "Why is she telling him?"

"Well," I hedged, "she's better at these things than I am, although not as good as you. See, Sam, I've thought it all out. Hazel Marie let it slip that she really wants him to know, and Lillian and I were going to do it this morning while you and Lloyd went to get his supplies. But then this visit to the judge's daughter interfered. So after thinking about it, I decided it'd be better for all concerned to wait till this afternoon and let you do it. But then your trip to Asheville came up. I kept having to change my plans, because, see, it can't be done when Lloyd's in the house, so I have to work around him. There's no telling what Mr. Pickens's reaction will be, or Hazel Marie's, and I don't want him anywhere around while it's going on. It could be traumatizing."

"Um-hmm, I see." He kept driving, making the turns out of town into the countryside and onto Staton Bridge Road. After a while, he said, "What're you going to do if it doesn't work the way you want it to?"

"Don't say what am *I* going to do, Sam. Ask what *we're* going to do, and the answer is: I don't know. Every time I think about it, which is just about all the time, I get so distraught I can hardly stand it."

"We can count on Pickens, Julia. I'm sure of it."

"Maybe, but can we count on Hazel Marie? I tell you, Sam, half the time she doesn't know what she wants or what she's doing." I took my lip in my teeth, thought for a moment, then said, "How would you feel about moving?"

He gave me a quick glance. "Away from Abbotsville?"

I nodded. "Far away. Where nobody knows us or where those babies came from. We could do it, Sam, and it would keep us all together." I stopped, bit my lip again, and went on. "A new church, new friends, new everything. A lot of people do it when they retire, and we could, too." I took a Kleenex from my pocketbook, feeling a fullness in my eyes. "If it's all the same to you, though, I wouldn't choose Florida."

Sam squeezed my hand. "That boy means a lot to you, doesn't he?"

"More even than I realized," I said, "until the possibility of losing him came up. But, Sam, the only thing that holds me back is you. It's an awful lot to expect you to leave the town where you've lived and worked for so long, and where everybody knows you and respects you. This is your home, and I would hate to ask that of you."

"Julia," he said, "my home is wherever you are. If it comes down to it, we'll do whatever we have to."

"Oh, Sam," I said, glad I had a Kleenex in hand since I was right before about needing it. "You are, without a doubt, the finest man in the world."

"Well, hardly," he said, patting my hand. "But it's not going to come to that. Look ahead five or six years when those babies will be starting school. They'll have been absorbed into the community by that time and nobody'll think a thing about it. Oh, every once in a while, a few busybodies might do a little whispering, but it won't affect them or us. The way things are going these days with all the odd-couple adoptions and test tube babies and surrogate mothers and who-knows-what-all, they'll have more than enough to occupy their minds. At least," Sam said with a smile, "we're getting ours the old-fashioned way."

"Thank goodness for that, I guess. Still," I went on, "it comforts me to know that you'd be willing to move if it comes to that."

Sam glanced at me with a smile. "What about Lillian? How would you get along without her?"

I did need the Kleenex then, and not just one but the rest of them in my pocketbook. Unable to answer, I just sniffed and wiped and blew and cried some more.

"Honey, listen," Sam said, "I think you're jumping the gun. We're not moving anywhere, so you're not going to lose Lillian or your friends or your home. Why, just think, what would you do off somewhere without Pastor Ledbetter and Emma Sue to keep things lively?"

I had to laugh in spite of the flow of tears. "You're just trying to make me feel better."

"Am I succeeding?"

"A little," I conceded. "I know I tend to jump to the worst that could happen, although when you come down to it, maybe the worst has already happened." I dried my face. "Who would've thought just a few weeks ago when everything was going so well that we'd be in this situation today? And Mr. Pickens could fix it all with only a word or two if he'd just do it. That's why he vexes me half to death."

"Hold on, Julia," Sam said as he slowed the car and leaned over the steering wheel to look out the window. "I think we're about there. Help me look for the mailbox."

I not only looked at the names on the widely spaced mailboxes as we passed, I looked at the surroundings as well. It was farm country with small patches of vegetable gardens, lots of open pastureland, and some acres of gnarled and stunted apple trees. The houses that I could see were small and set far off the road, usually hemmed in by large trees and fronted by sweeps of well mown lawns.

"Wait, Sam. I think we just passed it."

He stopped the car, looked in both directions of the empty road and slowly backed up to a black mailbox on a leaning post. The stick-on letters, B A   N E, were on one side with one letter obviously unstuck and gone. The rutted, once-graveled drive on our left had weeds and wild oats growing on the center hump. The fields that stretched on each side of the drive were full of the same wild oats, left to go to seed.

Sam turned in and drove carefully up the drive as the car dipped and swayed, and weeds swished along the sides and bottom of the car. Fully half a mile in, we came to the typical ring of shade trees and shrubs that enclosed a two-story, once-white house and a few ramshackle outbuildings.

When the car stopped in front of the narrow porch, I sat and took in what might have once been the judge's pride and joy. Square posts, imitating columns, held up the two-story roof of the porch. The windows were placed symmetrically on the facade, but they were too small and narrow to carry the attempt at Georgian architecture. And, would you believe, there was an abundance of Victorian gingerbread along the roofline? Whoever had designed the house had certainly not known what he was doing. But that was just my opinion.

"Well," Sam said, turning off the ignition, "let's see if she's home."

"You didn't call her?"

"Unlisted." Sam opened the car door, then hesitated. "I don't see a car."

"How about a dog?"

He grinned. "No dog, either."

I got out and walked with him up three steps onto the concrete floor of the porch. "Somebody needs to get out here with a broom," I whispered, noting the dirt that had been blown up against the house, as well as the twigs and leaves scattered across the porch.

"Nobody's home, Sam. People in the country always come to the door as soon as they hear a car, and nothing's stirring around here."

"Let's knock and see," Sam said and proceeded to do just that, rattling the screen door with his fist.

All was quiet, except for the rustle of a breeze through the surrounding trees. I looked up at the high ceiling of the porch and nudged Sam. "Is that a dirt dauber or a wasp nest up there?"

Sam glanced up. "Dirt dauber, I hope."

We both turned as the front door opened some few inches. It was dark inside compared to the bright sunlight where we were, so it was hard to see the woman peering out at us.

When she didn't speak, Sam in his smooth and easy way took the initiative. "Miss Baine? I'm Sam Murdoch and this is my wife, Julia. I wonder if we could visit with you a few minutes? I'm writing a history of Abbot County, and your father was such an important personage that I'm thinking of devoting an entire chapter to him. I'd like to talk it over with you, get some personal anecdotes, and so on. It's my intent to show every reader just how influential he was in making Abbot County what it is today."

I thought he was laying it on a little thick, but it seemed to work. Miss Baine continued to stare out at us for a minute or two longer, then she opened the door and stepped back. "You can come in," she said.

We walked into a dark hallway, and it took a while for my eyes to adjust. The hall was a room-sized square with wide, uneven pine boards on the floor and a staircase on the right side. One spindly-legged table stood against the left wall with a framed picture of a grim-faced woman above it. An old-fashioned coatrack, complete with a hazy mirror, suffering from dust or old age, was on the other side. It was loaded down with raincoats, men's hats, and umbrellas.

As we followed Miss Baine into a sitting room, or perhaps it was called a parlor, I got my first good look at her. She was a sight. You couldn't miss that hair. It made her look like a wild woman, for the iron-gray strands had no bounds, falling around her face and down her back. It had ripples or crinkles in it, as if it had been plaited and only recently brushed out. The amazing thing about it was that it seemed full of static electricity, and in this humid weather, too. Every time she moved, a fuzz of hair floated up around her head like a halo, or like she was in touch with one of those scientific exhibits in a museum that stands your hair on end. From the intense look in her eyes, it was my guess that she was generating all that electricity herself.

She wore a man's white dress shirt, the sleeves rolled up and the shirttails hanging out. Below that was a black, gauzy skirt that reached her ankles and, below that, bare feet.

The parlor she led us into was filled with ornate Victorian pieces that would've been remarkably improved by some reupholstering. Maroon velvet covered the Duncan Phyfe sofa, every uncomfortable chair in the place, and draped the sides of each of the two windows. A small woodstove rested on a square of tin in front of the fireplace. Above the fireplace in the place of honor, so to speak, a large oval, wooden frame dominated the room. In it was a life-sized photograph, hand-tinted in washed-out colors, of the face of a frowning, hulking man. His eyes peered out from under thick eyebrows, as if to condemn whomever they lit upon. The judge, I judged, and shivered.

"You can set," Miss Baine said abruptly, taking the center of the sofa herself and leaving the stiff chairs to us.

The room was hot, airless, and obviously rarely used. Sam took out his handkerchief and muffled a sneeze before saying, "We appreciate the chance to speak with you. I knew your father, worked with him when I practiced law, but I was never close to him. If you . . ."

"Nobody was close to him but me," Miss Baine interrupted. "He didn't suck up to everybody who come along, wantin' this and wantin' that. He was a great man. A smart man, smarter than all them lawyers and things that drove him out."

Sam was quick. "I think you're probably right. I think . . ."

"They's no probably about it. He was done in by all them folks that don't do nothing but tear down and whip up on and run people off. The judge oughta been governor of the state and he woulda been, but they wouldn't have it, would they? Oh, no, get rid of the judge, they said, and they banded together and run him out."

I was struck dumb by her tirade, which was just as well since I didn't want to tangle with her. All the time she spoke, her angular face betrayed no emotion at all. Her voice did, though, for it was filled with bitterness and pent up resentment. Her brown eyes stared at Sam as if he'd been a ringleader in running her father out of office, when in fact the county voters hadn't needed a ringleader. They'd put up with the judge's arbitrary rulings long enough and had done the job by themselves.

"Well, Miss Baine," Sam said soothingly, "your father served long and well on the bench, and the county owes him a debt of gratitude. I want to see that he is properly recognized, which is why . . ."

"The judge," Miss Baine pronounced, "is right up there in that picture." She waved her hand at the portrait above the fireplace but didn't move her eyes from Sam. "I don't never move it. He watches over this place. He built it, and he takes care of it, like he always done. Can't nobody tear him down no more. They already done all they could do and it didn't 'mount to a hill of beans. They all just jealous."

This woman is crazy, I thought and glanced around to see how far I was from the door.

But Sam, in his mild and comforting way, said, "With your help, Miss Baine, I'd like to set the record straight. If you'll let me, I want to formally interview you for my book. In that way, people can understand the kind of man he was."

I thought Sam might've gotten through to her, for she continued to stare at him. Then I realized that she wasn't looking at him but through him, her eyes and mind fixed on something in the room beyond. I turned to see what was there, but saw only dust motes in the sunlight that streamed through the half-opened curtains.

Then without any notice, the woman suddenly stood up, her lean body engulfed in the outsized clothes she wore. Sam immediately came to his feet, and I followed somewhat stiffly.

"Miss Baine?" he said.

She started for the door, then turned back to look up at the portrait. "Time to go," she said. "The judge needs his dinner."

Disappearing down the hall, she left us to find our way out. We immediately did so, uneasily closing the front door behind us and happily getting into the car.

"Sam," I said, locking the car door, "that woman is crazy."

Sam cranked the car and eased around the bare yard, looking for the opening to the drive. "Seems so, doesn't it?" he said. "Pitiful, though. All alone out here with the memories of her father."

"The judge," I corrected him, smiling. Then with a shiver running down my back, I went on. "You reckon he's really in there with her?"

"In her mind, Julia. Only in her mind."

Chapter 37

I glanced back at the house as Sam carefully maneuvered the car around the bare yard toward the opening to the drive.

"Oh, Sam, she does get out, at least some," I said, craning my neck to see along the side of the house. "An old green pickup's parked back there. Remind me to watch out for it. I wouldn't want to be on the road when she's driving."

"Goes out for groceries, I expect," Sam said, his attention on the rutted lane. "I'm glad she's not a total recluse. Even so, I'm going to ask the patrol deputies to look in on her every now and then. Make sure she's all right."

I smiled to myself, thinking that this was just one more instance of the kind of man I'd married. Thoughtful, he was, and concerned about others, even one as strange and unfriendly as Roberta Baine.

"So," I said, as we bumped our way down the drive toward the highway, "it doesn't look as if you'll get much help from her. Even if she agreed to an interview, how could you trust anything she said?"

"Probably couldn't. Still, it'd be interesting and worth doing if only for my own understanding of the judge." Sam glanced at me and smiled. "Not sure I could use any of it in the book, though."

I was quiet for a few minutes, thinking about the unusual woman we'd just left. The thought of her alone in that big, dilapidated house fixing dinner, as country people called lunch, for her father who'd been dead for ten years made me shudder. What went through her mind when it didn't get eaten? How did she explain that? And, even more intriguing, what had made her the way she was? The judge himself? If he'd been anything like Sam said he was on the bench when he was home, he would've been awful to live with—awful enough, perhaps, to warp an only daughter's mind.

Well, I thought, *parents in general have a lot to answer for, and I was glad I'd been spared.* Which brought me right back to Lloyd, because the way I worried about his welfare made me realize that I'd not been spared at all.

Sam spoke up then, distracting me from my thoughts. "I may try again," he said. "Maybe take her something, like a certificate of honorable service, or some such, for the judge from the county. That should please her if I can get the county to do it."

"That's a good idea. At least, it'd get you in the door again. But, Sam," I said, struck with another idea, "think about this. The judge's name was Robert, and she's Roberta, so he named her for himself. A lot of fathers used to do that. Why, I once knew a woman named Willie, and it wasn't a nickname. It was on her birth certificate. But I guess that's not the same as Roberta, which is a feminine name to start with. Even so, it tied her to him right from the cradle, don't you think?"

"Maybe so," Sam said, "but I wouldn't read too much into that. I'll tell you this, though, after meeting her I can understand why the judge put his estate in a trust. Well," he said with a smile, "besides for the tax benefits. There'll be a trustee who looks after her finances and makes sure she has what she needs. It relieves my mind to know somebody is looking after her."

"Can we find out who the trustee is?"

Sam shook his head. "It's probably a bank."

"Then they're not doing a very good job of it. That place is so run-down, it's a wonder she can live in it. Then again," I went on, "maybe the judge didn't leave much of an estate. Maybe what he left is about to run out. I wish we could find out more about him. And her."

Sam nodded and kept on driving. After a few minutes, I thought of something else. "If we could find out what those 'other valuable considerations' were—the ones the sheriff granted Judge Baine when he bought that land—it might open up everything else."

"Or a whole can of worms," Sam said

with a short laugh. "But that's not so unusual. A lot of people don't want a public
record of the money involved in a land
transaction."

"Well, I'd think Judge Baine would've
had a whole lot of resentment when the
sheriff made a killing on land he'd gotten
for a song. I say, ten dollars for acreage of
that size."

"We don't know, Julia. Each one may've
gotten exactly what he wanted at the time,
both of them figuring they'd made a good
bargain. And, there could've been more
money paid for it or some other consider-
ation, like an exchange of property. I'd say
it's likely, though, that there was some resentment on the judge's part, although
whether it carried over to his daughter, I
don't know. Even if it did, what part would
the other five people play? None of them,
except the Tillman woman, had anything
to do with it."

"Maybe Bob and Teddy? No," I said,
shaking my head, "that's too far-fetched.
They might steal Ted's records, but they'd
have no reason to take the others. What
about the sheriff? Did he have any chil-

dren? They'd be about the same age as the people we're looking at, wouldn't they?"

"He had two sons, but he kept them on a tight rein—no records on them at all. And now that I think about it, Al Hamilton died not long after he sold out to the development company. That was, I don't know, maybe in the early eighties, and his wife soon after that. Those boys would've come into a nice inheritance, but they were gone by then and as far as I know, they've never been back.

"Come Monday morning, though," Sam went on, "I'll get Pickens to help me go through the phone book and the tax rolls. There're a lot of Hamiltons around, and we need to know if any of them are the sheriff's kin. If so, then we'll have a few more suspects, though I can't imagine why those particular files and tapes would be important to them. The only reason I can think of is that they might not want the details of the land deal getting out. Because almost any way you look at it, Sheriff Hamilton was bought off. Except we don't know why."

"And except," I added, "you wouldn't

have known anything about it if those files hadn't been stolen."

"Right. Whoever stole them shot themselves in the foot. Anyway," Sam said, "I'm hoping Judge Anders over in Asheville can shed a little more light on both of them. If he can't, then we've hit another dead end."

"Well," I said, "that'll leave us having to deal with what we have. And I think Roberta Baine could clear up a lot of things if you could catch her in the right frame of mind. That commendation or whatever you spoke about might just do the trick. And something else," I went on after thinking about it a few seconds, "did you notice that she completely ignored any mention you made of your book?"

Sam smiled somewhat ruefully. "I think she completely ignored anything I said. She was off in another world, Julia."

"Yes, well, it just seems to me that as obsessed as she is with the judge, she would've latched onto the idea of somebody publicly praising him in a book. No matter how far off she is, I would think that would've reached her. Unless," I said after a moment's thought, "she wanted to put us off by *acting crazy.*"

"Oh, I don't think so, Julia." Sam slowed at an intersection, then continued on toward town. After a few minutes, he said, "But it's worth considering. You may've picked up something I missed. I'll talk it over with Pickens, see what he says and try to get back in to see her." He reached over and took my hand. "Anyway, I appreciate all your help, taking the time to go around with Pickens and with me. I know you've had other things on your mind."

"I was happy to do it, Sam, and I'll be glad to do anything else you need. I just don't want you to be discouraged."

"Well, it's looking more and more like I'll have to try to reconstruct everything without the records and do the best I can with it." He shrugged his shoulders and smiled. "Maybe instead of a book of facts, I'll be writing a book of fiction."

❧❧

"Miss Julia," Lillian said as soon as Sam and I walked in the kitchen door. "I hope I done the right thing."

"What? Has something happened?" My

mind flew to all the dire possibilities involving Hazel Marie and her condition.

"No'm, nothin's happened, 'cept Lloyd come in here with all his notebooks an' pencils an' papers an' things, then got his bathing suit an' left again."

"That's all right, Lillian. I told him he could go swimming and stay all afternoon if he wanted to."

"Yessum, but did you tell him Mr. Pickens could go, too?"

"Why, no," I said with a sinking feeling, seeing my plans for the afternoon being foiled again. "I didn't think of it."

"Well," Lillian said with some relief, "I hope it was all right, 'cause I don't know if them country club folks let jus' anybody in."

Sam started laughing. "There's some question about Pickens, that's for sure. It's fine, though, Lillian. Lloyd will just sign him in as his guest. I'm glad they're enjoying the day together."

But I wasn't glad. Lloyd was supposed to be at the pool, but Mr. Pickens was supposed to be right by himself at Sam's house where he could be told his duty. I declare, people were just going hither and yon, with nobody where they should've been. What was I supposed to do now?

⊗⊗

Well, there was one thing I could do, and I'd thought of it coming home in the car. It didn't have a thing to do with Mr. Pickens, and if I'd given it more thought I might not have done it at all. As it was, I wanted to help Sam, so I'd come up with an idea that just might shake things up and get all those tight-lipped people talking again.

Telling Sam and Lillian that I needed to freshen up, I took my pocketbook and went upstairs to our temporary pink bedroom, ours only until Hazel Marie could go up and down stairs again. Taking from my pocketbook a list of the interviewees and their phone numbers, I went straight to the telephone and dialed the first one.

"Mr. Tillman? Bob?" I said when he answered. "This is Julia Murdoch and I'm calling to tell you that we may not have to worry any longer about those files and interviews that Sam lost due to the theft at his house. Even though his computer got smashed in, Mr. Pickens—you remember him, don't you? Well, he's an expert in these matters, and he thinks he can recover all the information Sam had in it. And," I went on before he could respond, "as soon as he does, he'll move it from Sam's house to an undisclosed location to prevent a recurrence of the previous mishap. Of course we'd still like to know who ransacked his house, but as far as his book is concerned, Sam thinks he will have exactly what he needs—dates, times, arrest reports, and final disposition of the charges. I do hope you'll buy a copy when the book comes out."

Bob stuttered around a few minutes, then threatened a lawsuit if the book hurt his brother's reputation. Assuring him that Sam would not write anything but the facts, from which his brother had no recourse, lawsuit or no, I wished Bob a good day as pleasantly as I could and proceeded to call the others with slight variations of what I'd told him.

Ilona Weaver hung up on me, but not before she heard the gist of my message. Rosemary Sullins, in between yelling at a child, wanted more details—what exactly did Sam intend to write? Would her name be mentioned? How could he get anything out of a broken computer? I had to pretend ignorance of it all, but since I was already engaged in a great deal of pretense, that wasn't too difficult to do.

When I called Cassie Wooten, I got William instead. I almost hung up, but decided he was the one that needed to hear what I had to say. His response was a long moment of silence, then he came out with a nasty pronouncement that Sam Murdoch wasn't the only man who could write a book so he'd better be sure he had nothing to hide himself.

My hands were shaking when I finished the calls, hoping that I'd implied rather than outright lied. There's a fine line between saying something and letting somebody think you've said it. I hadn't mentioned that the stolen records hadn't been in the computer in the first place. And, in fact, the only blatant lie I'd told concerned Mr. Pickens's electronic expertise. I didn't know whether he had any or not.

Be that as it may, though, my deepest concern was having put Sam's house in jeopardy again if, in fact, any of the four had been the thief. Thank goodness, Sam's house now had both a burglar alarm and Mr. Pickens installed there, so it should be safe enough.

I bypassed Rafe Feldman entirely, since he wouldn't be able to find his own house, much less Sam's. I considered calling Roberta Baine, but decided that she wouldn't know what I was talking about and it was best not to confuse her any more than she already was.

Then I went downstairs, hoping that I hadn't stoked the fires too high. On my way down, I determined I'd just keep my little deceptions to myself and see what, if anything, came from them.

Hazel Marie came to the table in another sweat suit or workout outfit or whatever it was. This one was light blue with a white stripe down each leg. She had lunch with Sam and me but hardly ate a thing. She didn't have much to say either, although Sam tried to draw her out by describing our visit to Roberta Baine.

She didn't express much interest, too wrapped up in her own problems to be concerned about somebody else's, but Lillian did. We were eating at the breakfast table in the kitchen, so Lillian perked up at the first mention of Roberta Baine.

"I hear 'bout that woman," she said, coming around the counter to the table. "Everybody do. They say she not right in the head and best to stay away from her."

"Oh, she seemed all right to me," Sam said. "A little distracted, maybe, but other than that . . ."

"Distracted!" I said. "Why, Sam, she was on another planet, as Lloyd would say. She didn't know who we were and she didn't care."

"Well," Lillian said darkly, "jus' ast James. He see her ever' now an' again, driving that ole pickup of hers right by his house. He say he used to wave at her, but one day she aim that old truck right at him an' he don't wave no more."

"I didn't know James knew her," Sam said.

"He don't," Lillian told him. "She come to town 'long his street, an' he jus' bein' friendly. You know how he always act like he know everybody."

And everything, I thought to myself, and

started to say, but the ringing of the front doorbell interrupted our conversation.

Hazel Marie dropped her fork and pushed back her chair. "I can't see anybody," she said as she got to her feet. "Excuse me, Miss Julia, but I just can't."

"It's all right," I said. "Go through the back hall, and I'll take care of whoever it is."

Sam and I looked at each other as she left the room. He shook his head. "She's having a hard time, isn't she? And you're right, Julia, something's got to give. If you want me to talk to Pickens today, I'll reschedule my visit to Judge Anders."

"No, you run on and see him. There's not much either of us can do with Mr. Pickens over there splashing around in a swimming pool. And afterwards if he comes by here, Lloyd will be in the house." I leaned my head on my hand and sighed. "I declare, we might just have to wait till the middle of the night to catch him alone."

"Miss Julia?" Lillian pushed through the swinging door from the dining room. "Yo' preacher come to see you. I tell him you jus' finishin' lunch, an' he say he wait, so he settin' in there in the livin' room."

"Oh, my," I said in some dismay. "What

can Pastor Ledbetter want on a Saturday afternoon?"

Sam grinned and got up from the table. "You can tell me later. I'm on my way to Asheville."

"Oh, you," I said as Sam leaned over to give me a kiss. I put my napkin beside my plate, took a deep breath and prepared to greet my visitor.

Chapter 38

Since house and hospital calls on church members were made by the visitation committee and not the preacher, I knew I was in for something unpleasant by having him show up for a personal visit. Generally, when he felt the need to consult or counsel with a member of the congregation, he called and set up an appointment in his office. I, myself, had been the recipient of more of those calls than I cared to remember.

"Pastor Ledbetter," I said, walking into the living room with a welcoming smile on my face, "how nice to see you. Do have a seat."

He had stood as I entered, as he should've, so I quickly sat across from the sofa where he immediately sank back down.

"May I offer you something cold to drink?" I asked, trying to appear unruffled by his unexpected drop-in. "It's so warm outside, I'm sure you need something after walking across the street."

"No. No, thank you," he said, bracing his feet firmly on the floor and leaning toward me. "Miss Julia, I am deeply, deeply concerned about Hazel Marie. I'm sure you know that numerous, dire rumors are floating around about her condition, and the Lord has laid her heavy on my heart."

"Oh, I assure you . . ."

He held up his hand to stop me. "I have prayed for her without stint, but seems like every day there's been a new report on her, so that how I prayed the day before has no connection to the current news. It's hard, you know, to lay a burden at the Lord's feet if you don't know what the burden is."

Have I mentioned that Pastor Ledbetter and Emma Sue believed in specifics? They wanted details, specific details, fearing, I suppose, that prayers in generalities would not or could not be heard or answered.

But his words struck fear in my heart. What rumors were now floating around about Hazel Marie? And had any of those rumors lit upon her true condition?

"May I ask what rumors you've heard?" I asked, clenching my hands in my lap.

"I don't normally repeat rumors, but let me just say that they range from a fatal wasting disease to plans to move away to take a job somewhere." He took a white handkerchief from his pocket and mopped his face. He'd had time to cool off after his walk from the church, but his face remained red with what I'd at first thought was exertion. Looking more closely at the peeling across his nose and brow, I realized that he was sunburned.

"Well," I said, laughing a little to divert suspicion, "it's typical of this town to get things wrong. Hazel Marie has been ill, but not with anything either dire or fatal. And she's much improved now, just slowly regaining her strength. She is considering a position that's been offered to her, but, of course, that involves a lot of changes. Right now, I think I can say that nothing definite has been decided."

"That is good news, then," he said and leaned back against the sofa. "I am greatly relieved to hear that she's improving and hope to see her back in church real soon."

Back in church? That was something I didn't want to think about. How welcoming would he be if she presented new growth every Sunday that rolled around?

"But I'll tell you, Miss Julia," he went on, "the last thing I heard, and this was from Emma Sue, who doesn't engage in gossip, is that Hazel Marie is moving away."

"Um, well, actually that is her current plan, but I'm hoping that she'll reconsider. I don't know what I'd do without her, even though, of course I don't want to stand in the way of this new opportunity. It's sort of up in the air, you might say."

"If that's the case," he said, a smile breaking out on his broad, peeling face, "I guess I better warn you. I'm quite good at keeping secrets—all pastors have to be. But perhaps you should know that Emma

Sue is planning a surprise going-away party for Hazel Marie. When I left home this morning, she was already up making plans and cooking and getting ready for it. But if Hazel Marie's not moving—and I hope she's not—I guess it'll be a surprise for everybody. Well," he said, slapping his hands down on his thighs and getting to his feet, "you've relieved my mind, Miss Julia, and, oh, by the way, don't tell Emma Sue I told you about the party."

"I wouldn't dream of it," I said, walking to the door with him. "Thank you for your visit and for your concern. I'll tell Hazel Marie that you're holding her up in prayer."

After seeing him out and closing the door behind him, I leaned against the wall, hoping I'd put any suspicions he might've had to rest.

Then I had to smile to myself. I'd been warned about the party by both Mildred and the pastor, so there was one thing for sure. The next time Emma Sue planned a surprise for anybody she'd better keep it to herself.

❧❦

"Lillian," I said as I went back into the kitchen, "he doesn't suspect a thing. Or if he does, he didn't let on. I think that, as many problems as it might create, Hazel Marie's age is protecting her from any wild guesses. If she were ten years younger, even five, that would be the first thing people would think of."

"I always say," Lillian said, "they's a silver linin' in every cloud."

"Well, right now all I see is a little tarnish on the edge. I declare, something's got to be done to resolve this, and, every time I plan something, it goes awry."

"I don't know 'bout that. But I tell you this," Lillian said, giving the countertop a swipe with a sponge, "Miss Hazel Marie's not lookin' too good today."

"I noticed that, too. And she hardly ate a thing. Of course, Pastor Ledbetter showing up on our doorstep would unsettle anybody." Then with a sudden jolt, I said, "She's not . . ."

"No'm, she all right that way. Jus' her spirits be low, an' that not good for her or them babies."

I put my elbows on the table and my face in my hands, facing at last what I'd been unwilling to acknowledge all along. I didn't want to do it, that's what it came down to. All this putting off or hoping it would resolve itself or expecting Sam or Lillian to take it on or thinking Mr. Pickens would suddenly see the light—all of it was simply because I couldn't bring myself to tell him. In spite of all my big talk about shaking him till his teeth rattled and making him toe the line, all I'd been doing was delaying the final reckoning. And why? Why, because I was mortally afraid that either Hazel Marie or Mr. Pickens—or maybe both of them—wouldn't do the right thing for those babies. As long as I could put off telling Mr. Pickens, the longer I could keep hoping that everything would work out. Once he knew, it would be out of my hands, and, if he didn't respond in the appropriate manner, there'd be no light at the end of the tunnel for any of us.

"Lillian," I said, coming up for air, "where is Latisha?"

"Oh," Lillian said, smiling, "she at the neighbor lady's house, playin' with her grand all day long. They went to a church party this mornin', an' this afternoon they makin' mudpies an' havin' tea parties. She

can come over an' play with Miss Hazel
Marie if you want her to."

"No, I wasn't asking for that. I thought
you might need to go on home. But if
she's all right, I could sure use you for a
while longer." I patted my chest, finding it
hard to breathe. "See, Lillian, it's got to be
done and done now. With Pastor Ledbetter coming around asking questions, and
Emma Sue throwing a surprise party to
celebrate a job that doesn't exist, something has to give. And now is as good a
time as any."

"What you thinkin' 'bout doin'?" Lillian
was looking at me through narrowed
eyes.

"Telling Mr. Pickens, and telling him now.
Well, of course, not now since he's still at
the swimming pool. But as soon as he
brings Lloyd home and goes to Sam's
house, you and I are going over there and
we're going to lay it on the line for him."

"Well, yessum, he sho' do need to know,
but I don't know as I ought to be goin' with
you."

"Oh, Lillian, you have to. I need you. He
thinks so much of you, he'd listen to what

you say. You know he doesn't pay attention to anything I say and, believe me, this will be our only chance to fix things the way they ought to be fixed."

Lillian walked across the kitchen to the refrigerator. She opened the door, looked inside, then closed it again. Then she walked back and leaned on the counter. "I don't know, Miss Julia. What if he get mad at us for meddlin' in his bidness, what we gonna do then?"

"Smack him." I laughed, though it took an effort. "No, I'm teasing. But that's what I'm afraid of. Not of him getting mad at us, but of him getting mad at the situation and deciding it's not his problem. Oh, Lillian, I hate to put it this way, but of all the men in the world, he's the least dependable when it comes to marriage."

"Well, I don't think it up to me to be doin' this," Lillian said with some skepticism, "but I guess you need some kinda help. You gonna tell Miss Hazel Marie we gonna tell him?"

"Lord, no! I wouldn't tell her for the world, even though she as good as said she wants him to know. Even so, there's no telling what she'd do. No, I, I mean, *we're* going to tell him, then stand back and see what he does. And see what she does when he does whatever he'll do, and hope for the best."

Lillian nodded. "Yessum, that seem like what we oughta do. Jus' pass on the word, then get outta they way."

Chapter 39

"There's Lloyd," I said, hearing the rumble of Mr. Pickens's car as it turned into the drive. One car door slammed, so I knew only the boy would be coming in—just the way I wanted it. Lillian and I would hem Mr. Pickens up at Sam's house where he'd be alone and defenseless.

"Hey, Miss Julia," Lloyd said as he came in, looking more burned than tan. His hair had dried in stiff peaks around his head, and a faint odor of chlorine drifted my way. But he was happy and full of his day with Mr. Pickens. "Hey, Lillian. Boy, we had a good time. You oughta see J.D. swim. He's like a fish. And he can dive, too. He tried to teach me how to do a jackknife off the high dive, but I kept doing belly flops. Look how red my stomach is."

"My goodness," I said, noticing not only the redness there, but also on his face and shoulders. His freckles stood out uncommonly large. "I hope you used your sunblock, Lloyd. You'll be hurting if you didn't."

"Oh, I did. J.D. kept reminding me, so I used it. This'll all be tan tomorrow. How's mama? Is she feeling all right?"

"Well, she's a little blue this afternoon and needs some cheering up. Lillian and I are going to take a walk, so I'd like you to keep her company while we're gone."

As Lillian opened the refrigerator and began removing dishes, Lloyd looked at me in wonder. "You're going to take a walk?"

"Now, that's not so unusual," I said. "We need to get out and stretch our limbs a little. Let me have that wet bathing suit. I'll hang it in the bathroom for you."

He handed me the damp rolled-up towel that held his bathing suit, then eyed the snacks that Lillian was putting on a tray.

"You don't need to put much on it, Lillian. Me and J.D. had some hot dogs at the pool. Then I had a Nutty Buddy, so I'm not real hungry."

"Law, boy," she said, "you done ruint yo' supper. Well, I fix this for yo' mama mostly, anyway. See, I got some good, cold fruit punch here and all these little vegetables and some dip to make 'em go down easy. They good for both of you, so maybe you able to nibble on 'em, too."

He picked up the tray, grinned and told her he'd try. Then he headed for the back hall and his mother's room.

"We won't be gone long, Lloyd," I said, motioning to Lillian toward the back door. "Just around a couple of blocks. But you make sure she's all right, then run up and take your shower." Opening the door, I nudged Lillian out and whispered to her. "If our timing's right, he'll be in the shower when Mr. Pickens gets here. *If* he gets here, and if I don't lose my nerve before we get there."

❧❧

The sun was still high in the sky, but the shadows were lengthening as Lillian and I walked along the sidewalk on the shady side of the street. The heat was at its worst since there was no breeze, and both of us were gently perspiring before we'd gone a block toward Sam's house.

"I'm about to melt," I said. "We should've taken the car."

Lillian didn't answer, just shuffled along beside me. I knew her silence indicated a less than eager desire to be a part of this mission. I wasn't feeling so confident myself, but I bolstered my courage by reminding myself that it was something that had to be done.

"Lillian," I began, mostly to keep bolstering, "how do you think we should do this? Should we go in and visit a while, you know, just sit and talk, ask how he's doing and talk about first one thing and another, then maybe ease into the purpose of our visit? If we sort of hint around about it, he might figure it out himself. Except we've already done that a few times, and it hasn't done any good. Or maybe it'd be better to come out with it all of a sudden? I mean, like a special bulletin with no build-up or preparation to protect his sensitivities? Which, of course, he may not have any of, but I would think any man, regardless of how thick he is, would be shocked to hear he's about to be a father. Twice over." I glanced at her as she trudged along, hoping for her guidance or at least an opinion of some kind.

"Miss Julia," she finally said, "I tell you what's a fack, I jus' come along to kinda hol' yo' hand. I don't know what to tell him or how to tell him or when to tell him. All I know is somebody oughta tell him. But if you really want my 'pinion, I think it be better to ease into it. I think you oughta go all the way 'round Robin Hood's barn 'fore you spring something like that on him. He need to be got ready to hear something like that, 'less he have a heart attack when he hear."

"You're right," I agreed, nodding. "You're absolutely right. That's what we'll do. We'll just drop in for a visit and play it by ear. And when we judge he's fully prepared for the news, we'll carefully and gently break it to him."

With that decided, we turned the corner on Sam's block and I could see his lovely old house with its wide porch before us. My breath kept getting shorter and shorter, and I couldn't tell if it was caused by the heat, the exercise, or the anxiety.

As we stepped up on Sam's brick walkway, I grabbed Lillian's arm and held on. "Pray that we'll do it right, Lillian. Everything depends on breaking it to him as kindly as we can. I don't want to do anything that would set him off."

"Yessum," she mumbled. "I jus' hang back an' listen."

So there we were at last, up on Sam's front porch, standing before the door, ready to do what we'd come to do. I reached out and mashed the doorbell. We waited a few minutes, but heard no sound from inside. I pressed the doorbell a second time and kept my finger on it. Hearing no footsteps from inside, I mashed it again and again. He'd have to be deaf not to hear it.

"He's got to be here," I said, my anxiety level steadily rising. "His car's right there in the driveway. Knock on the door, Lillian. The doorbell may be broken."

She reached around me and gave the door a tentative rap. "Harder," I said, and pushed the doorbell again, leaving my finger on it for the longest.

The door sprang open and an angry Mr. Pickens stood there, his hair plastered to his head and water dripping from his face and shoulders to the floor, with not a stitch on to his name—just a skimpy towel wrapped around his middle.

"What in the . . . ?" he demanded, then when he saw us his mouth fell open, and so did mine. I stumbled back against Lillian, while he stood in shock, clutching the towel.

"I'm sorry, so very," I stuttered, mortified by our ill-timed visit and his ill-clothed state.

"I was in the shower," he said, quickly sidestepping behind the door as he began to ease it closed.

"We can come back," I said, still awed and tongue-tied by the eyeful I'd gotten of his almost naked body, browned by the sun and glistening with water. "More convenient, maybe another time. Let's go, Lillian."

But she hadn't moved and wouldn't move. She stood her ground, blocking my retreat while she gazed beyond me at Mr. Pickens although there was nothing to see by now except one eye and a bit of wet hair sticking out from behind the door.

"Mr. Pickens," she sang out, strong and determined as only Lillian could be when she had something to say. "Mr. Pickens, you gonna be a daddy, an' ain't nobody tell you but us, so don't be mad. We jus' bring the message, that's all we have to do with it."

Mr. Pickens's head slid further out from the door. I could see both eyes, part of his nose and mouth, and a shock of wet hair. "What'd you say?"

"She said," I said, encouraged by Lillian's boldness, "that your former sweetheart is expecting and she's sick to death of having to expect by herself."

His black eyes darted from me to Lillian and back again. "She's . . . ?"

"Yes, she is."

The towel fell in a puddle at his feet, and he slammed the door in my face. "Wait," he yelled. "Wait just a damn minute!" We could hear his feet thudding away from us as he ran along the hall.

"Well, Lillian," I said, turning away and heading for one of Sam's rocking chairs, "we certainly eased into that, didn't we?"

Then I stopped, grabbed Lillian's arm with a grip of steel. "Run around back. Quick! He might go out that way. I'll stand guard here."

Lillian gasped. "You think he gonna run out on us?"

"I don't know what he's going to do, but we better be prepared. Now hurry and get back there."

She lumbered down the steps, muttering about not knowing how she'd stop him if he took a mind to leave. I leaned beside the front door, wondering about the same problem if he took a mind to come out the front.

Lord, we had messed this up to a fare-thee-well, I thought. Yet it was done. He now knew where his duty lay, and all we could do was stand aside and see what he'd do about it. Well, guarding the exits wasn't exactly standing aside, was it? Still, he might want to know a few more details unless he'd heard all he wanted to hear and was, even now, preparing to hightail it out of town.

The door beside me was suddenly jerked open and I came to attention.

Mr. Pickens stood there, dressed in jeans, a misbuttoned and partially tucked-in shirt and still no shoes. His hair had been toweled semi-dry and hand-combed, signs of a hurried toilette. "Get in here," he barked.

From the narrow-eyed look on his face, I thought he was going to jerk me inside, so I quickly sidled into the hall and kept my distance.

"Where's Lillian?" he demanded.

"Guarding the back door," I quavered, uncertain as to how to deal with him. I'd never seen him quite this cold and demanding, though I'd been on the receiving end of his quick temper several times before. But now there was a scowl on his face and an iciness to his manner that unsettled me.

Issuing another order, he said, "Sit and wait. I'll get her."

I did as I was told, and soon he appeared with Lillian, who came in wide-eyed and fearful. Ordering her to sit, he stood before us, his fists clenched and his face dark and threatening.

Much to my surprise, the next words out of his mouth were calmly said. "You're talking about Hazel Marie?"

Taken aback, I said, "Why, Mr. Pickens, who else would it be?"

"Lord," he said, falling into a chair as if his legs had given way. He buried his face in his hands, then came up for air. "How long has this been going on?"

I glanced at Lillian, who was studiously avoiding both of us. Gathering my courage, I answered, "I believe since San Francisco, wouldn't you say?"

His head flopped back against the chair, and I could see his manly chest going up and down as he absorbed the information.

"All right," he said, sitting up abruptly, his investigative mind apparently putting the pieces together. "She's pregnant, is that what you're saying?"

I nodded, as Lillian decided to jump in then. "Yessir, jus' as much as she can be, an' then some. An' the daddy need to be helpin' with them babies."

His black eyes darted from one to the other of us. He swallowed hard, started to speak, stopped, then tried again. "Babies?" he croaked. "Did you say babies?"

"Yes," I confirmed. "But don't worry. There's only two of them."

Chapter 40

Mr. Pickens had always been a quick study—he rarely had to be told anything twice. But in this instance, it took the longest time for him to come to grips with the news of the change in his circumstances. I don't know what I expected, but it wasn't the lengthy interrogatory session he put us through.

Well, I did know what I expected. I expected him to either run with open arms to Hazel Marie and put an end to all our worries, or else I expected him to take off for parts unknown and never be heard from again. One or the other, but not these picky, picky questions about every aspect of the past few weeks.

"When did she find out?" he asked, beginning to pepper us with questions. "How long has she kept it from me? Who all knows about it? Why didn't somebody tell me? Why didn't *she* tell me?"

His eyes bored into mine with that last question, so I felt beholden to answer as best as I could. "I can't answer that, Mr. Pickens, because I tried everything I knew to get her to tell you. But she'd have none of it. She even made me promise not to tell you, and, see, here I've just done what I promised not to do although it was really Lillian who finally told you and not me, as you well know. So please don't tell her I told you because she'd know I broke my promise and might never trust me again." I paused to catch my breath. "Anyway, Hazel Marie said it was her problem and she had to deal with it herself. Besides," I went on, deciding that since he'd asked, I might as well tell it all, "knowing how determined you are to shy away from another marriage, she thought you wouldn't care one way or another and would just leave her holding the bag, so to speak, regardless of what you knew. So whether you knew or didn't know, it wouldn't change anything as far as she and those babies were concerned."

With his elbows on his knees, he leaned over and covered his face with his hands. "How could she think that?"

"Easy," I said, emboldened by this unusual display of tractability. "She told you it was over, and you believed her. She said she didn't want to see you again, and you believed her. She said she wanted to be married and make a home with you and Lloyd, but did you believe that? Oh, no, you didn't. And this was all even before she knew what you'd done to her, and, Mr. Pickens, believe this if nothing else: She didn't want to force you into marriage. I'm quite proud of her for that although I'll tell you the truth, there's not a viable alternative, and, believe this, too, we've considered every other option under the sun."

"Yessir," Lillian chimed in, "we have and she have, too. Why, no tellin' how many times she been packin' up to move off somewhere where nobody know her. An' Miss Julia, she been doin' all she know to do to keep her an' Lloyd here, but they hardly any way out 'cept Miss Hazel Marie stay here an' have two little yard chil'ren for everybody to talk about."

He groaned, pulled his hands down his face and stared at the floor between his knees. "I can't believe this."

"Why, Mr. Pickens, every word we've said is the absolute truth."

He glanced at me, then back at the floor. "I don't mean that. I mean I can't believe she'd think I wouldn't care."

"Then you better do something to show her you do because she's serious about leaving town. And she'll be up and gone this weekend if she finds out that Emma Sue Ledbetter's giving her a surprise going-away party Monday night."

He sprang from his chair, walked across the room, turned around and walked back. Then he stood there for a minute like he didn't quite know what to do next. "I'm going over there," he finally said. "She may not want me, but I'm going."

As he headed for the front door, Lillian and I exchanged a triumphant look, then we came to our feet, calling, "Wait! Mr. Pickens, wait."

"What?"

"You need some shoes," I said, pointing to his bare feet.

He looked down and said, "Oh. Well, just hold on a minute." As he started down the hall toward the bedroom he was temporarily occupying, he stopped and came back. "Do not," he said, pointing his finger at me, "leave this room. I don't want you running over there and telling her I'm coming."

"Oh, I wouldn't do that for the world," I said, stepping back to my chair to show I had no intention of ruining his big moment.

Lillian sank down in her chair again, and we sat there gazing first at each other, then toward the hall where we expected to see him return.

"He takin' a long time to put on them shoes," Lillian whispered, a hint of worry creeping into her voice. "You don't reckon he slip out the back, do you?"

"Well, he just better not." But a sense of dread was filling my mind. If he flew the coop after knowing what he needed to know, then he was a lost cause and we were back where we'd started from.

Then, to my great relief, we heard the

sound of well-shod feet striding purposefully down the hall. He appeared in the doorway, dressed in gray slacks and an ecru linen jacket over a white shirt and paisley silk tie. And shoes. His hair was neatly combed and ready for business.

"Why, Mr. Pickens," I said approvingly, "you look so nice. Perfectly appropriate for a late afternoon wedding proposal."

He glared at me, opened the front door, and strode across the porch toward his car.

"Come on, Lillian," I said, jumping up and running after him. "Let's ride with him."

Easier said than done, for Mr. Pickens's car was not made for backseat passengers who were any larger than Lloyd. And both of us were.

Mr. Pickens already had the engine rumbling as I reached the passenger door and opened it. "We'll go with you, if you don't mind. It's awfully hot to be walking."

I stepped back, holding the door wide, and motioned to Lillian to crawl in the back. But seeing the problem after she flipped down the front seat, I said, "Wait, I'll get in the back. You sit up front."

We jostled each other, trying to change places, as Mr. Pickens impatiently revved the motor. "Just get in, one way or the other," he said, his teeth clenched together. "I don't have all day."

"Well," I said right smartly, as I crawled over the front seat, "you've waited this long, you can at least give us time to get in."

I got settled and buckled in with some difficulty, but when Lillian righted the front seat, it smacked my knees straight up into my lap. "Oh, Lord," I moaned. "Hurry, Mr. Pickens, I'm so crimped up back here I can hardly breathe. Lillian, move your seat up a little if you can."

"I can't, Miss Julia," she said. "I already on top of the dashboard."

Mr. Pickens clunked the gearshift into reverse and we spurted out of the drive onto the street. "Will you two just hold on for two minutes?" He slammed the car into gear and off we took, nearly inflicting a whiplash injury as my head was jerked backward. "You could've walked, you know."

I didn't reply, making gracious allowances because Mr. Pickens was under some stress and shouldn't be blamed for injecting a little sarcasm now and then. Poor man, he had a lot on his mind.

But I'd made all the allowances I was willing to make when he suddenly swerved the car to the side of the street and slammed on the brakes. We came to a screeching halt as my head snapped forward from the loss of momentum, and Lillian let out a piercing shriek.

"What! What is it?" I yelled.

"Siren," Mr. Pickens said calmly, as if he hadn't just put me in double jeopardy as far as whiplash was concerned.

I heard it then, coming up fast behind us. Mr. Pickens waited, his thumbs impatiently drumming on the steering wheel, as the car idled on the side of the street. The sirens, for there were more than one, increased in volume as two sheriff's patrol cars, a first responder ambulance truck and a long, heavy fire engine raced past us, one after the other. The car shuddered with the shock waves of their passing.

Mr. Pickens looked over his shoulder to be sure the street was clear, then he eased the car into the lane and drove a little more sedately toward my house and Hazel Ma-

rie. Maybe the sight of the emergency vehicles had calmed him down. What good
would he be to her if he got all banged up
in an accident?

"Wonder where they're going?" I mused
aloud, not expecting an answer.

"Could be anything," Mr. Pickens answered, "from a three-car pile-up to a cat
in a tree. They go all out for every call."

"Might be a fire somewhere," Lillian said.

"Not necessarily," Mr. Pickens said. "The
fire truck rolls, regardless."

He was approaching the last turn before
Polk Street when Lillian said, "I don't hear
them sireens no more. They done stopped
somewhere."

"Hazel Marie!" I shrieked as fear jolted
through me like a streak of lightning. The
same fear must've jolted Mr. Pickens, for
he stomped on the gas, took the turn on
screeching tires and straightened up on
Polk Street.

Then he slammed on the brakes a full
block from my house, and a good thing he
did for the street was crammed full. Cars
were parked along both sides and emergency vehicles with red and blue lights

flashing and white lights strobing blocked the center.

"Let me out, it's our house!" I screamed, unbuckling the seat belt and pushing the back of Lillian's seat. "Hurry, Lillian, something's happened to Hazel Marie!"

As she fumbled to unbuckle herself, Mr. Pickens flung open his door and ran toward the house, his very nice tie streaming over his shoulder. He was running full steam, zigzagging among parked sedans and SUVs and the fire engine until he came to a patrol car that had skewed to a stop sideways in the street. It didn't even slow him down. He took a leap up onto the hood, came down on the other side and made tracks across the yard.

"I can't get outta this thing!" Lillian cried, but by the time she finally did, I'd already flattened Mr. Pickens's seat and crawled out the driver's side.

I wanted to run to the house, but I was too fearful of seeing what I feared to see. Holding onto the car, my limbs quivering, wanting to go and wanting to stay, I could see the heads of a mob of people swarming on the porch and in the yard, giving way only when the paramedics parted the crowd with a loaded stretcher.

"Lillian," I moaned, as she came around and put an arm around my waist. I clutched at her, fear of the worst filling my mind with a white haze. "Don't let it be Hazel Marie. Or Lloyd. Oh, Lord, please, not Lloyd."

Chapter 41

The paramedics slid the stretcher into the back of their vehicle and closed the door with a thunk. In a second or so the truck began to back and fill to untangle itself from the traffic jam, lights flashing and siren working up to a wail as it sped off toward the hospital. Deputies disengaged from the crowd, got into their patrol cars and edged away from the cars parked along the street. Firemen waved at the deputies and headed toward the rumbling fire engine.

"Do you see Mr. Pickens?" I asked, clinging to Lillian's arm. "Did he go with them? Oh, Lord, Lillian, I'm afraid to know which one it was."

"We not gonna know 'less we go see," Lillian said.

So we hurried toward the house, picking up speed as we passed the huge red fire engine hovering over us, my heart thumping with every step.

"Who're all these people? Where'd they come from?" I asked, as we broke into a run.

"Folks always come when something awful happen," Lillian panted, as she trotted along beside me.

When we gained the sidewalk in front of my house, I saw that the mob of people, which turned out to be a fairly small mob, was all women. One or two familiar faces began to emerge out of the haze that filled my head. But I didn't stop, just plowed on up my walkway toward the porch as the crowd parted for us. I heard a low murmur of sympathy and a few moans issuing from both sides—none of which alleviated my anxiety.

As we approached the three steps to my front porch, my breath suddenly caught in my throat and I came to a dead stop, falling back against Lillian. I thought my heart had stopped, too, for there, spread across the steps and onto the walk, was a large, red puddle, still dripping from step to step.

I had never been a fainting kind of woman, but for just a second or two I lost any sense of where I was or what I was doing. "Hazel Marie," I moaned, as visions of the recent disaster flooded my imagination and the irony of the situation nearly did me in. Just when we'd gotten Mr. Pickens of a mind to do the right thing, after all the trouble and worry we'd been through, a fateful occurrence had just released him to go his carefree way.

I could've cried and, in fact, did. If Lillian hadn't been there holding me up, I would've crumpled to the ground.

"Miss Julia, Miss Julia," Lillian said, patting my face. "Get hold of yo'self. It not what you think. Look at it, jus' look. See them little bits an' pieces?" She propped me up, urging me to look more closely. "See, that's jus' some of that Mexicum soup been spilt. Look at them cucumber pieces and there's some little bell pepper chunks all cut up. It's all right now. It's not bad as you think."

Lord, she was right! As my mind and eyes cleared, I could see what she'd pointed out. *Gazpacho*! Swinging around, I looked at one face after another, recognizing Mildred, LuAnne, Helen, and a dozen others from the Sunday school class, the book club, and the garden club, all of them with beautifully wrapped gifts in their hands. Some were holding trays or covered dishes as if they were on their way to a Wednesday night prayer meeting. And there at the top of the steps stood Emma Sue, wringing her hands as tears flowed copiously down her face.

"Oh, Julia," she wailed, "we wanted to have this cleaned up before you got here. I'm so sorry there's such a mess, but you won't believe what happened."

My mouth had fallen open at this unexpected reception, and I couldn't seem to be able to close it. Gazpacho? Why? What were they doing at my house? Where was Hazel Marie? Mr. Pickens? Lloyd?

Emma Sue, smiling bravely through her tears, picked her way down the steps, sidestepping the dripping liquid. "We're all so sorry. We wanted to surprise you and Hazel Marie."

"You have, but where is she?"

"Well, I don't know. We just got here," Emma Sue said, looking around at the women who had closed in on us as if she expected to find Hazel Marie among them. "See, what happened was, I was just about to ring the doorbell when Miss Mattie Freeman came up the steps right behind Clarice Bennett. And she, I mean, Miss Mattie, was carrying a big bowl of her gazpacho—you know how good it is—and she missed a step, or at least we think she did. So she stumbled against Clarice, knocking her down, and then fell right on top of her. Well, that big bowl she was carrying went flying up in the air and gazpacho spilled all over the place. It ruined Clarice's dress, so she's gone home to change, but the bowl didn't even break, and we were afraid Miss Mattie had hurt herself so we called nine-one-one on a portable, and they took her to the emergency room. Just for observation, don't you know. I don't think she got hurt, but you never know. You do have homeowner's, don't you, Julia? Anyway," Emma Sue summed up, looking beseechingly at me, "Surprise!"

I had so many questions I didn't know

which one to ask first. "Mr. Pickens," I said, choosing what I hoped was the safest one. "Did you see him? He came running up here to help as soon as we saw all the commotion."

"Why, yes, he helped them get Miss Mattie on the stretcher." Emma Sue looked around. "But I don't know where he went."

LuAnne pushed her way through the crowd. "I saw him. I think he ran around to the back."

"Well," I said, choosing the question I probably should've asked first, "what're you all doing here?"

"Why, it's obvious, Julia," Emma Sue said with some exasperation. "We're having a surprise going-away party for Hazel Marie, and now it's just ruined."

"Today? I thought you were having it Monday night."

"I knew it!" Emma Sue said, swinging around and searching the crowd. "Mildred told you, didn't she? I knew she would, that's why I told her the wrong day. Mildred Allen, where are you?"

"Miss Julia," Lillian said, "we better get these ladies inside 'fore they melt. We be callin' that ambulance back here, it so hot."

About that time, the front door opened and Lloyd stepped out on the porch. A startled look swept across his face at the sight of so many women. His head switched around from one to the other. "Hey, Mrs. Allen, Mrs. Ledbetter. What's going on?"

Bless his heart, he couldn't believe his eyes at finding a mob of women ebbing and flowing on the porch and in the yard.

"It's all right, Lloyd," I said, finally loosening my grip on Lillian's arm and heading for the door, skirting the spill of gazpacho as I went. "These ladies have come to visit. Come in, everybody. Come in where it's cool." I grabbed Lloyd's arm, swung him around and through the door with me. In a fierce whisper, I said, "Where's your mother? Have you seen Mr. Pickens?"

Unaccustomed to such abrupt treatment, his eyes got big and he whispered back, "I don't know. I just got out of the shower. Is J.D. here?"

"He's supposed to be. Run back to your mother's room and see if he's there. He probably came in the back door. And, Lloyd," I said, pulling him back as he started to dart off, "warn her of what's going on out here."

Women in filmy afternoon dresses bearing gifts and food surged in behind us, talking and laughing in a party mood, now that tragedy had been averted. Lillian began to direct traffic around the dining room table. "You can put that tray right down here, Miz Stroud. I start gettin' out plates an' things."

"Run on, Lloyd," I urged. "Your mother needs to get prepared for this."

"But, Miss Julia," the boy said, frowning, "J.D. couldn't get in the back. I made sure to lock all the doors before I got in the shower because Mama was taking a nap. Where could he be?"

Well, that was the question wasn't it? Where *could* he be? Had he changed his mind and gone back to Sam's house? Was he even now making his escape?

"Julia," LuAnne said, walking up to us, "where's Hazel Marie? I can't wait for her to open my gift."

"Me, too," Maggie Austen said, joining her. "But I just hate to hear that she's moving. She is just the sweetest thing. I'm going to miss her."

There was nothing for it but to leave Mr. Pickens to his own conscience and go drag Hazel Marie out to face her public. How well she'd be able to do it, I didn't know. She didn't enjoy being the center of attention under the best of circumstances, and this circumstance certainly didn't qualify as the best. For one thing, there would be a sea of sharp eyes watching her every move and reaction, and I wasn't sure that a loose-fitting workout outfit would be an adequate disguise. Well, she'd just have to sit in a chair and not get up. I'd keep a present in her lap, one after the other, and maybe if she never presented herself in profile, we could bring it off.

"I'll see what's keeping her," I said. "She was taking a nap, but she'll surely be awake by now. Lloyd, you run help Lillian, if you will."

"I thought you wanted me . . . ?" he said, slightly confused at my telling him one thing, then switching directions.

"No, I better do it. She might need some help dressing, and I need to freshen up a little, myself. LuAnne, would you make sure everybody's food is displayed right?" I tried to laugh a little, just to divert her. "This certainly is the easy way to have a party— having the guests bring all the food."

"It was Emma Sue's idea," LuAnne said with a sniff. "And frankly, I think it's a little tacky, but don't tell her I said so. If it was me having a party, though, I'd provide the food myself."

And frankly, I agreed with her, but I only nodded, then slipped through the crowd to the hall and hurried on to Hazel Marie's room. The door was closed, just as I expected, but still I hesitated to knock. She would've heard all the commotion, so I knew she'd be trembling and cowering from the thought of facing guests. And she didn't even know yet they'd come specifically to honor her.

Well, the sooner the better, I thought, gave the door a sharp rap, opened it, and stepped in. I blinked in surprise and slammed the door behind me.

"Mr. Pickens!" I cried, taken aback at the sight of him, as he was at the sight of me. "How'd you get in here?"

He was in the far corner of the room half-turned in one lap of the pacing he'd obviously been doing. Hazel Marie in another elastic-waistbanded running suit— yellow, this time—huddled, knees up to her chin, on the bed, her face screwed up, looking ready to cry or to throw some-thing.

Mr. Pickens pointed at one of the back windows, the bottom half of which was thrown up, letting out the cool air, and lack-ing a screen. A sprinkle of glass glittered on the carpet. "The doors were locked," he said with just a tinge of frustration. "And she wouldn't let me in. Sorry I had to break a pane to unlock it, but one way or the other, I was coming in." He glared at Hazel Marie, but it was a toss-up as to whether it was a glare of anger or of fondness. Prob-ably a little of both.

"He got stuck crawling in," Hazel Marie said, then leaned her head on her knees. She may've been laughing, I wasn't sure. "Serves him right, too."

"Well, look," I said, feeling a little anger myself at Emma Sue for choosing such an inopportune time to throw a party. If ever Hazel Marie and Mr. Pickens were going to resolve their differences, now was the time. Instead, though, I had to interrupt their ne-gotiations and set Hazel Marie up as the guest of honor. And put Mr. Pickens on hold and under observation until I could get them back together again.

"Well, look," I said again, "Emma Sue's having a going-away party right out there in the living room. She's brought everybody with her, and they've brought gifts and food and everything anybody would want if they'd happened to even think about moving away somewhere. And it's all for you, Hazel Marie."

Her head snapped up off her knees and she looked at me in stark terror. "I can't," she said, breathing fast and stumbling over the words. "I just can't. Oh, please, please, Miss Julia, don't make me go out there."

Mr. Pickens strode over to the bed where she was crouched against the headboard. He held out his hand to her. "You don't have to," he said.

Chapter 42

She lifted her head, looking up at him bleary-eyed and expectant as if he were her last hope—which, in my opinion, he was—then took his hand and buried her face in his stomach. He clasped her with both arms and held on tight.

As tender and heartwarming as the scene was, we didn't have time for it. There was a party waiting to happen, and I needed to know Mr. Pickens's intentions and Hazel Marie's final state—married and respectable or single and out of town.

"Well," I said, doing a little hand-wringing

as the sounds of the party grew louder and more insistent. "This is all very nice and I'm happy to see it, but what am I going to tell all those women out there? They're expecting Hazel Marie to come out and unwrap presents so they can ooh and aah over them. I can't just go out there and announce that she's indisposed, because somebody like Emma Sue is likely to barge in here to pray over her. So what do I tell them?"

"Tell them . . ." Mr. Pickens started and stopped as the door opened and Lloyd flew in.

"Mama," he started and stopped. "J.D.! Where'd you come from?"

"Close the door," I said, then did it myself and stood against it to prevent any further invasion. It'd be just like LuAnne to take it on herself to come see what was holding Hazel Marie up.

Right at this moment, though, it was Mr. Pickens who was holding her up, for she had slid off the bed to her feet and was leaning against him.

"Oh, you know," Mr. Pickens said, his eyes sparkling at Lloyd, "I just pop up where you least expect me."

"I'll say!" Lloyd said. "But, Mama, everybody's asking where you are, and I don't know what to tell them. Are you still sick?"

"I don't think so," Hazel Marie murmured, her head against Mr. Pickens's shoulder, a more decent place than where it had been. Then, apparently reconsidering her actions, she straightened up and tried unsuccessfully to push Mr. Pickens away. She wiped her teary face with the sleeve of her sweat suit, hiccupped, and said, "On second thought, I don't feel all that good."

"Well," the boy said, his eyes narrowing as he gazed at his mother and Mr. Pickens, trying to figure out what was going on. "They're getting pretty restless."

"Why don't . . ." I began, then as a rap sounded on the door behind me, turned, and held it closed. "Who is it?"

"It's me," Sam said. "Is everything all right?"

I opened the door just enough to let him squeeze in and quickly closed it again.

"Well, hey, J.D.," he said with a surprised smile. "Hazel Marie, Lloyd, Julia. I thought the party was in the living room, but looks like there's a better one back here."

"Hardly," I said. "The party's for Hazel

Marie, but she doesn't want to go, and Mr. Pickens says she doesn't have to. And Lloyd doesn't know what to do and neither do I. We're just standing around waiting for somebody to decide something, which I wish they'd do before there's an insurrection out there." Then I added darkly. "You don't know what Emma Sue Ledbetter is capable of."

"Anyway," Sam said, handing Mr. Pickens a set of keys, "I moved your car. I just drove in from Asheville and saw it double-parked in the middle of the street with the keys still in it. I found a parking place around the corner."

Mr. Pickens, looking a little abashed at forgetting his own car, took the keys, then took matters in hand, even though they were both quite full of Hazel Marie at the moment. "You'll have to handle the party, Miss Julia. Hazel Marie and I need to talk, and this is not the place to do it. We're going to Sam's house."

Lloyd flung out his arms in excitement. "How're you gonna get there, J.D.? There's ladies everywhere you look, just everywhere. They're in the living room, in the dining room, in the kitchen, and more're coming in the front door. They catch sight of Mama, you won't ever get past 'em."

"He's right," Sam said. He grinned, enjoying the moment. "I wouldn't recommend trying it."

"Oh, J.D.," Hazel Marie moaned, giving up her independent stance to bury her face on his shoulder. "I just can't face them. They'll ask so many questions, and I'm not dressed or anything."

He leaned down and whispered something to her. She nodded, then looked at us, her face lit up like the dawn. "We're going out the window," she said.

"Oh, no," I said, immediately concerned about her taking such a risk in her condition. "Hazel Marie, you can't. You might hurt yourself."

"No, she won't," Mr. Pickens said. "I moved a bench right under the window and we'll step out on that. Besides, I won't turn her loose."

"Oh, boy," Lloyd said, running to the window. "I can't wait to see this."

"Mr. Pickens, you do know . . ." I started, then cut my eyes at Lloyd who didn't know. "I mean, you better be careful with her. She's not been well."

"I know," he said, leading Hazel Marie to the window. "Sam, give us hand here, if you will."

"How do you want to do this?" Sam asked, sticking his head out the window to check on the bench. "It's not high off the ground, but getting out could be tricky."

"I'll go first," Mr. Pickens said, "then you help Hazel Marie out. I'll be right there to catch her."

"You *better* catch her," I warned, half under my breath.

So he proceeded to exit the window, starting out headfirst, got halfway through, then decided there had to be a better way. He pulled himself back in, gave Hazel Marie a rueful smile, then with surprising agility he turned around and slid his feet backward through the window, ending up folded across the window sill, head and shoulders in the room and feet and bottom hanging outside. Then he slithered himself all the way through until his feet landed on the bench.

"See?" he said, standing on the bench and looking straight through the window. "It's not high. Come on, honey, I'll be right here to catch you."

Hazel Marie needed no prodding. With the sounds of the party drifting in to us, she might've jumped out the window if he'd told her to. But I didn't like the idea of such acrobatics at all, so I was pleased for the delay when Lloyd reminded her that she needed some shoes. He ran to the closet and came back with a pair of sneakers.

While she put them on, I edged over to Sam. "Sam," I whispered, "she can't go out backward. She'll mash those babies if she hangs over the sill the way he did."

Sam's eyebrows shot up, as he realized that another form of egress was called for.

"Okay, Hazel Marie," he said, "why don't you come over here and just sit in the window, facing us. Help steady her, Lloyd. Now, Hazel Marie, pull your legs up real tight and bend your head. Come on, Lloyd, let's turn her around sideways. Easy now. Pickens, see if you can pull her on through."

That sounded like a plan, but it didn't work for she got lodged half in and half out. I probably wasn't much help, since I kept wringing my hands and warning that they had her folded up too tight.

"Oh, my goodness," Hazel Marie said,

her voice muffled from being squeezed up like a pretzel. "I'm going to be stuck here forever."

"It's okay, baby," Mr. Pickens said. "We'll figure it out. Sam, better try something else."

"Okay, let me think a minute," Sam said, wiping his arm across his forehead. "Hazel Marie, we're going to get you back inside. Help me turn her, Lloyd."

They got her out of the window, and let her stand for a minute to straighten out the kinks. Sam stuck his head out just as Mr. Pickens stuck his in, so there was a slight collision to deal with.

Sam pulled back in, rubbing his head. "Let's try this, Hazel Marie. We'll lift you up so you can sit in the window, facing out. Now then, go ahead and stick your feet out the window and Pickens'll steady you. Okay, now I want you to lean back against Lloyd and me. That's it. Now lie back against us and make yourself as stiff as you can from the waist up. Keep your arms by your side, and we'll slide you right through. Julia, come hold her head for us."

I did, but all I could think was, "Be careful.

Be careful." I probably said it a few dozen times, too.

Just as we were all set, Hazel Marie, half in and half out, stopped us. "Wait, wait. Miss Julia, I want you to know I'm just doing this because of that party. It doesn't mean one thing else, in spite of J.D. coming in here, acting all nice and sweet. He's still got a lot to answer for. Don't listen, Lloyd."

"I understand, Hazel Marie," I said, although I didn't. "Just do the best you can with him. Now hold real still."

We lifted her bottom up off the sill and slid her, stiff as a board, right through to Mr. Pickens. As he eased her to her feet on the bench, Lloyd's face lit up with delight. "Cool!" he said. "Just like sliding a letter through a mail slot."

Mr. Pickens helped Hazel Marie off the bench, and the three of us watched as they hurried across the backyard toward Sam's house. Just as they got to the gate that led to the sidewalk, I saw him reach for her. She slapped his hand away, which didn't appear to bode well for whatever outcome he had in mind.

"Well," I said, turning back into the room

as Sam and Lloyd, grinning, high-fived each other. "It's a good thing Hazel Marie's no bigger than she is. If this'd happened a little further along, she'd still be stuck halfway out."

Lloyd frowned at this, and I could've bitten my tongue off. "I mean," I said, "that her appetite is picking up so well, that she'd soon be too big to get through the window."

He let it go—apparently—for he said, "That was slick, Mr. Sam. We did a good job."

"We sure did," Sam said. "A good thing you were here to help. I thought for a minute there we'd have to call on Lillian, too. Now all we have to do is get a new pane and fix this window, and, Julia, all you have to do is explain to your lady friends why the guest of honor's not coming to the party."

Chapter 43

As the magnitude of the task hit me, I sank down in a chair and leaned my head on my hand. Looking piteously at Sam, I asked, "You wouldn't consider telling them Hazel Marie and I are both sick, would you?"

He grinned and shook his head.

"You could say I picked up her ailment, and we're both in bed." I sighed and began to rise from the chair. "Well, I guess not. Lloyd," I went on, aware that the boy was taking all this in, "it's not right to be untruthful, but sometimes you have to weigh telling a harmless, little story against hurting somebody's feelings. And it would certainly hurt Mrs. Ledbetter's feelings, and all the others out there if I told them your mother would rather sneak out a window with Mr. Pickens than come to a party with them."

"Yes, ma'am," he said, "I understand that. But I bet half those ladies would rather do what Mama did than go to a party, too."

Sam laughed. "He's got something there, Julia."

Before I could answer, an insistent rapping started up on the door. "Julia!" Emma Sue called. "Are you in there? We need you and Hazel Marie out here."

"Oh, my," I said, straightening my dress. "Well, I better think of something."

As soon as I opened the door and stepped out into the hall, Emma Sue pounced. "Where is she, Julia? We're all waiting. You won't believe the gifts!"

"Well, Emma Sue, I'm afraid Hazel Marie isn't here." As Emma Sue's mouth dropped open, I closed the door behind me so Lloyd wouldn't hear any more of my storytelling.

Before Emma Sue could respond, I hurriedly said, "She needed a few things from Target. You know, since she's getting ready to move, so she ran over there. She should be back most anytime."

Emma Sue's eyes narrowed. "I thought she was too weak to be driving."

"Well, yes, but Mr. Pickens took her. And," I went on, warming to my subject, "I told him in no uncertain terms that he was not to let her do too much and that he was to make sure she didn't tire herself out. He knows to get her home as soon as he can. Of course," I said, changing my tune since I had no idea when Hazel Marie would be back, "they may stop for something to eat before coming home."

"But, Julia, I *told* you I was bringing supper tonight. I did that so you'd both be home for the party. Didn't she even *want* it?"

"Yes, of course she did. And so did Mr. Pickens, he said he did. I was going to save a plate for them."

"Well," Emma Sue said with a little flounce of disappointment, "I don't know what I'm expected to do now. The party's just ruined."

"No, it isn't, Emma Sue. It's the best idea you've ever had, and that's saying a lot. And just listen. Everybody's having a wonderful time." I paused so she would listen to the din of a couple of dozen women talking over each other, some louder than others and some shrieking with laughter. "It sounds like this is going to be the party of the year."

Emma Sue turned to look toward the living room whence the noise was emanating, then she turned to me with a questioning look. "You think?"

"I certainly do. You've done it, Emma Sue, and I'm honored that you brought it to my house. No one but you would've thought of such a thing. Hazel Marie's going to be sick that she missed it."

"Well, we can't have *that,*" Emma Sue said with a burst of enthusiasm. "But we won't have to. I brought a digital camera to take pictures, so she would have mementos to take to Florida with her. Oh, but," she went on, frowning, "I was going to take pictures of her opening the gifts. And now I can't, so that's ruined, too. We won't even get to watch her open the gifts, much less see her face when she does."

"How about this, Emma Sue," I said with a sudden inspired idea. "Let's let each guest open her own gift and hold it up for everybody to see while you take a picture for Hazel Marie. I think we'd all enjoy that, and Hazel Marie would have a visual record of who gave what, and we wouldn't even have to make a list for thank-you notes."

"That could work, I guess."

"It will, and it'll be so different that nobody'll ever forget this party." I was beginning to relax, believing that I'd adequately explained Hazel Marie's absence and soothed Emma Sue's feelings, when I looked down the hall and saw a familiar, but completely unexpected, face in the living room crowd. "Emma Sue, is that Cassie Wooten?"

"Why, yes, I invited her. I've gotten to know her on the committee I told you about, and the other day when you mentioned that you knew her, I thought it'd be nice to have her—even though she doesn't know Hazel Marie from Adam. But she's a lovely Christian, Julia, and someone you should cultivate. She'd be so helpful to you on your spiritual journey."

I couldn't help it, I rolled my eyes. Emma Sue was always concerned about my spiritual state, intimating that I was too involved in worldly matters and superficial people, some of whom were her friends, too. But frankly, knowing what I knew about Cassie, I just couldn't see putting myself under her guidance, spiritual or otherwise. Oh, I know people can change for the better, and Cassie appeared to have done just that. But since her testimony had to be pulled out of her by her domineering husband, I couldn't help but wonder just how authentic the change had been.

But Emma Sue meant well, even though I try to avoid people who often mean well, but who leave shattered feelings in their wake. They're the ones who tell you the most hurtful things for your own good and expect you to be grateful. I rarely was.

By this time, we'd walked down the hall and entered the living room. Emma Sue immediately took over, clapping her hands to get the crowd's attention and calling, "Ladies, ladies! I want each one of you to get your own gift and take a seat. We're going to start now."

There was a bustle as people looked through the pile of gifts on a side table for the one they'd brought. Then the women scrambled for a seat—every last one of them programmed to obey when Emma Sue issued a command.

"Lillian!" she called, taking over as was her wont, "we need more chairs out here. Tell Lloyd to bring some from the dining room."

When they were all seated, Emma Sue stood before them, her camera in hand, and announced the procedure. "First of all, I have to tell you that the guest of honor isn't here." This announcement produced a buzz of questions and a low rumble of disappointment. "But that's all right. It just means that Hazel Marie is feeling so much better, and we're happy about that, aren't we? Anyway," she went on with a brief glare at me, "despite the fact that she was *supposed* to be here, we're going to do the next best thing." And she proceeded to tell them exactly how and when each guest was to open her gift, hold it up so everybody could see it and smile for the camera. Of course, it took forever for Emma Sue to get the hang of the camera and to take the perfect picture of each one, so I eased into a corner of the dining room, out of Emma Sue's line of sight.

While Emma Sue was organizing everybody, I glanced around until I saw Cassie Wooten, sitting quietly among the guests. She was wearing a navy crepe dress with a lace collar and flat shoes with thick rubber soles. Foot problems, I suspected. Her hair was pinned up on the back of her head, the way it'd been when Mr. Pickens and I had visited, but today it was put up in a looser fashion and was a little more becoming. She wore no makeup, which was probably one reason Emma Sue had taken to her. Two of a kind, don't you know.

I looked away before catching her eye, lest she realize I thought it strange that she'd come to a party for someone she didn't know.

As the ladies got into the swing of gift opening and gift appreciation, laughing and talking and smiling for the camera, I slipped into the kitchen where there was a little peace and quiet. Lillian and Lloyd were there, but Sam wasn't.

"Where's Sam?" I asked.

"He still in Miss Hazel Marie's room," Lillian said. "He say he don't wanta get mixed up with that crew out yonder, so I took him a plate of party food an' he eat in

there. Lloyd been runnin' back an' forth
through the back hall 'cause he don't wanta
get mixed up with 'em, either." She smiled
fondly at Lloyd. "He been tellin' me 'bout
how y'all slip his mama out the window."

"Sh-h-h, Lillian," I said, looking over my
shoulder. "Don't say a word about that to
anybody. Mrs. Ledbetter would never forgive us." I walked over to the sink where
they were leaning against the counter, as
far from the door to the dining room as
they could get. "Lloyd, did you tell her
about Mr. Pickens breaking a window to
get in?"

"Yessum, I did, and now we're wondering if they're making up. I sure hope so,
'cause it was awful how they wouldn't even
speak to each other. I didn't like it."

"None of us did," I said, as Lillian put
her arm around his shoulders and hugged
him. "And I must say that even though Mr.
Pickens has his faults, well, as most of us
do, he is undoubtedly the only man for
her." I'd never spoken truer words, although
the boy didn't know why and I wasn't about
to tell him. "So maybe they're ironing out
their differences as we speak and we'll
hear good news, but not, I hope, before

those women in there leave and go home. Lillian, have you ever heard the like of such a party? Don't ever mention *surprise* to me again. I've had about all the surprises here lately that I can stand."

It was two more long hours before the guests began to leave, and, by that time, Lillian had their Pyrex dishes, Tupperware bowls, china plates, and other odds and ends washed and ready to go home with the ones who had brought them. Emma Sue and I saw the guests out, thanking them for the gifts and receiving thanks for the lovely party.

"Well, Julia," Emma Sue said when the last one left, "let's get this mess cleared up. I have to teach Sunday school in the morning, so I need my rest."

"You run on, Emma Sue. There's no need for you to stay. I'm going to send Lillian home since she's stayed later than usual, but I'll have Sam and Lloyd to help me." I began to gather up wrapping paper and ribbon, bunching them together before throwing them out.

"Oh, Julia," Emma Sue cried, snatching the papers out of my hands. "Be careful with that, you'll ruin it. Here, let me show you how to smooth it out and save it. I always save wrapping paper and the ribbons, too. If you use a cool iron, the ribbon will be as good as new."

I declare, Emma Sue Ledbetter caused my eyes to roll more than any other one person I knew. But it was better to do it the way she wanted than to argue with her, so I smoothed out dozens of sheets of wrapping paper, wondering where I could store it and doubting that I'd ever use it again.

"Julia, look at this," Emma Sue said, holding up a little ceramic gnome, painted in bright red and green. "Isn't it darling? I know Hazel Marie'll love it. And look at this precious little angel. She's going to have so many knickknacks to remind her of home that she'll have her new apartment decorated in no time."

I nodded and pretended to agree, but it'd taken me years to wean Hazel Marie off darling little knickknacks that did nothing but collect dust and ruin one's more elegant decor. Some of the gifts, however, were of a more useful nature, I was happy to note. There were dish towels, a set of napkins, salt and pepper shakers, and some place mats. But others had brought personal items: A nightgown, bedroom shoes, a little travel bag with a toothbrush in it, and one thoughtful person had given a book on how to decorate an apartment. There was also a photograph album, ready and waiting for Emma Sue's pictures, as well as an address book with every guest's address and phone number in it. Someone, and I could guess who, wanted to be sure that Hazel Marie acknowledged each gift with the appropriate note.

I, myself, would've been hard-pressed to come up with a suitable gift for a person who was moving away, considering the fact that few people would want any more items to pack than they already had. But it occurred to me that almost every gift chosen for Hazel Marie could serve equally as well for a bridal shower gift as a going-away one.

And that, of course, brought my thoughts back to what was happening between her and Mr. Pickens. To show how anxious I was, I was even tempted to ask Emma Sue to join me in prayer for the right outcome. I quickly got over it.

When Emma Sue finally left with her

Tupperware bowl, an armful of recycled wrapping paper that I'd insisted she take and my effusive thanks, I went back to Hazel Marie's room, formerly mine and Sam's.

"You can come out now," I said to him.

He looked up from the book he was reading. "They're all gone?"

"Yes, thank goodness. Have you heard from Hazel Marie?"

"Not a word. Or from Pickens, either. I expect they have a lot to talk about."

"They certainly do, and I just hope they cover all the ground that needs to be covered and manage to come to an agreement as to the proper solution."

Sam grinned, closed his book and said, "And what would that be?"

"Oh, you. You know what it would be. But I'm worried, Sam. They could've decided on the right thing in five minutes and it's been hours since they left here. What could they be doing?"

Sam got up and put his arms around me. "I expect you'll figure it out if you think about it."

"Oh," I said. "Well, if that's the case, then maybe the longer they stay away the better. Where's Lloyd? He didn't go over there, did he?"

"No. He was helping Lillian, but he may've gone upstairs by now. That boy's like me—when there're more women around than you can count, we head for the hills."

I started to laugh, but was interrupted by Lillian appearing in the door.

"Miss Julia?" she said.

"Why, Lillian, I thought you'd gone home. I apologize for keeping you so late. Just leave whatever's not done, and we'll get to it later."

"Yessum, I'm about to go, but they's a lady out here want to see you."

I looked at my watch. "Why, it's almost nine o'clock. Who could be visiting this time of night? I didn't even hear the door-bell."

"No'm, she come tappin' at the back do', an' I let her in. She settin' in there in the livin' room waitin' on you."

I looked at Sam and saw his eyebrows go up, as we both wondered who would be dropping by on a Saturday night.

"I'll see who it is," Sam said.

"Well, Mr. Sam," Lillian said. "That lady,

she say she jus' want to see Miss Julia for a few minutes, an' then she be gone."

"Did she give her name?" I asked.

"Yessum, she say to tell you she Miz William Wooten, an' she need to talk to you."

Sam and I looked at each other, and this time it was my eyebrows that went up.

Chapter 44

I walked into the living room where Cassie Wooten sat in one of my Victorian chairs by the magnolia leaf-filled fireplace—my usual decorative touch for the summer months. Her feet in those awful shoes were flat on the floor and close together. Her hands were clasped in her lap. She sat quiet and composed, serenely waiting. Or so it seemed until I noticed that a long, stringy-looking strand of grayish hair had come loose from the French twist she'd attempted for the party.

"Cassie?" I said softly as I approached. She turned with a jerk, startled at first, then smiled briefly. "Oh, Mrs. Murdoch, Julia, I mean. I hope you don't mind me coming back in. I don't want to disrupt your evening."

"You aren't disrupting anything, Cassie. I'm glad to see you."

She nodded and began kneading her hands in her lap. "You must be wondering why I'm here. And the reason is, well, I couldn't go home without explaining some things." She gave a short self-deprecating laugh. "I only came to the party because Mrs. Ledbetter insisted, and because I hoped to get a minute with you. But there were so many people here. I shouldn't have come at all, but it was the only chance I had, since William . . . Anyway," she said, taking a deep breath, "I've been waiting in the car for everybody to leave."

"Why, Cassie, if I'd known you wanted to talk, we could've gone upstairs."

"No, it's all right. I didn't want to put you out. Anyway," she said again, taking another ragged breath before launching into what she'd come to say, "William told me you'd called. So, first, I wanted to tell you that for Mr. Murdoch's sake, I'm glad his computer wasn't ruined." She gazed at the fireplace and murmured, "William says that means the past will all be raked up again."

She looked down at her hands, while I thought to myself that my deceitful phone call had, indeed, stirred things up. Maybe she was here to admit William's guilt and to throw him on our mercy—wouldn't that be something?

Cassie looked up at me and went on. "The thing of it is, well, I guess what I really wanted to say was I know how William comes across sometimes. But, please," she said, giving me a pleading look, "he doesn't know about this. It would really upset him if he knew I was discussing him with you. With anyone, for that matter."

"What husbands don't know won't hurt them," I said, trying to inject a little levity into the conversation. It didn't work.

"Anyway," she repeated herself again, this time with a heavy sigh, "I know how important those papers and things are to Mr. Murdoch and I hate that they got stolen and his house was all torn up. It just made me sick when I heard about it. And when you and that investigator came by, I got so worried that you'd think William did it. Then when you called about maybe finding a copy, I thought I'd be so relieved. But I wasn't, because you and Mr. Murdoch would still believe William had done it, and you'd always hold it against him. So, what I wanted to tell you is that he really didn't."

I blinked, wondering how she'd known my thoughts, much less Mr. Pickens's, on the subject of William Wooten as a suspect. We'd both thought he had it in him to do whatever he wanted, the way he acted and all, not letting Cassie talk, berating her for letting Sam interview her and doing it in front of us and so on. But I said, "Oh, I'm sure nobody ever thought it was him, Cassie."

She looked down at her restless hands again. "I know how he sounds sometimes, but he's not always like that. And he wasn't very courteous to you and that man when you visited, so it'd be easy to think he might've done it. He can get so angry." She sighed, either in resignation or despair, I couldn't tell which. "I was afraid you'd get the wrong idea."

I sat still for a few seconds, wondering if Sam were listening to this and what he would ask at this point when she seemed so amenable to being questioned. She was either protecting her husband or she truly believed he wasn't a thief and a vandal. Or he was actually innocent. I didn't know how to tell which it was, but I was determined to try.

"Well, Cassie, I believe you, although I can't speak for Sam or Mr. Pickens. William's reaction sort of made him stand out from the others. So let me ask you this: If he didn't do it, do you know who did?"

She glanced quickly at me and away again, but not before I saw her eyes widen with alarm. "Oh, no, I couldn't *name* anybody, that wouldn't be right. Besides, I don't know anything about it except that William couldn't have done it. Why, he's a *Christian*."

Well, Lord help us, claiming to be a Christian hadn't stopped any number of crooks, criminals, and con men before, so if that was her husband's only proof of innocence, Cassie was on shaky ground. But far be it from me to judge anyone's spiritual status, not wanting to be judged myself.

Having said what she'd come to say,

Cassie stood and I did, too. I wasn't sure that she felt any better, for her hands smoothed the hair from her forehead, felt the buttons at the neck of her dress, then rubbed along her forearms—nervous gestures that belied the lack of expression on her face.

"I better be going," she said. "William will be worried." She started to leave, then turned back. "You'll tell Mr. Murdoch, won't you? Tell him it wasn't William."

"Yes, of course I will, but if you want to talk to him, he's here."

"Oh, no. That's not necessary. You tell him for me." She walked hurriedly toward the kitchen where she'd come in, and I followed her.

"Wait, Cassie," I said, "let me call Sam to walk you to your car. It's getting dark out there."

She gave me a brief, backward glance as she sailed into the kitchen and headed for the back door. "No, that's all right. My car's not far. I don't want to disturb him."

She didn't want to see him, either, that was clear. When she reached the back door, she paused to thank me again and to assure me, several times, that our search should go in a different direction. It was all I could do to stand there and listen over and over to her defense of her husband—my mind was on something else. As I'd followed her to the door, my eyes had focused on the long, coarse shank of iron-gray hair, shot through with silver streaks, that had come loose and hung down her back.

"Cassie," I said, stopping her as she opened the door, "do you know a woman named Rosemary Sullins? She runs a day care center. Well, it's not so much a *center* as it is her living room, but she takes care of children."

She stood still with her hand on the doorknob, her head down looking at it, not me. For a minute I didn't think she was going to answer. Then pushing the door open and stepping out as if she wanted to be gone, she said, "I've heard of her. Why?"

"Oh, no reason, particularly. It's just that her records were stolen along with yours and a few others. And you reminded me of her, or rather, your hair does. You both have lovely, thick hair that's about the same color and texture."

Her hands flew to her head, felt the

shank of hair and quickly whirled it around and pinned it with a hairpin. "I don't usually wear it this way," she said. "It won't stay up."

"It looks better than Rosemary's," I said. "The time I saw her, she had it up in a ponytail. But before you go, let me ask you this: Do you know Ilona Weaver or Teddy Tillman? Or Rafe Feldman?"

Her eyes darted toward me. She bit her lip, then said, "Not personally. We don't socialize much. I have to be going. It's getting late." She stepped out, still talking. "William'll be worried."

"Wait, Cassie. What about Roberta Baine? Do you know her?"

Cassie shot me a glance filled with shock or fear or maybe both. "No. And I don't want to. I've heard bad things about her. You'd do well to stay away from her, Julia. But," she said, visibly calming herself, "I don't like to speak ill of anyone."

"Well, me, either," I said, "but sometimes that's all that can be spoken. About some people, I mean."

"I have to go," she said, stepping out into the yard. "William'll be worried."

I watched her walk away, thinking that

William wasn't the only one. I closed and locked the door, then went to find Sam to tell him about Cassie Wooten's odd behavior.

☜☞

"Sam," I said, entering the back bedroom where he was still waiting, "that was the strangest visit I've ever had. Cassie wanted me to tell you that her husband couldn't have stolen your files because he's a Christian. I'm sure that reassures you."

Sam smiled. "She's gone?" When I nodded, he rose and said, "Any other stray women around? Can I come out now?"

I had to laugh. "I guess you have been stuck back here for a while. Yes, let's go to the living room and I'll tell you what all she said. But, listen, she knows Rosemary Sullins or rather, knows of her. And she knows the others, too, though she said not personally. I think that means something."

As we took our accustomed places on the sofa, Sam said, "Everybody in the county could say the same thing, Julia. I'm not sure that's indicative of anything."

"Well, I didn't know any of them until all this came up. But something else, Sam, and I know you and Mr. Pickens laughed when I mentioned it before, but Cassie and Rosemary have the exact same kind of hair in color, texture, and the distribution of gray. And both of them would benefit from some conditioner. I wouldn't have noticed it, except part of Cassie's had come loose from her French twist and hung down her back like Rosemary's ponytail."

"What's a French twist?"

"It's when . . ." I started then stopped when I saw the twinkle in his eyes. "Oh, you, stop teasing me. I really think this could mean something. Every last one of those people have unusual hair. Well, an unusual amount of it, anyway. For their age, I mean, and I think it's worth looking into. They could be kin to each other for all we know. Actually, Sam, they could be part of the Hamilton family—I wish I'd thought to ask Cassie about that. But maybe not, since you said the sheriff made a pile of money when he sold out to that development company, then died before he could spend it all. But as far as I can tell, none in that group benefited from any kind of inheritance. Poor as church mice, most of them."

Sam frowned, considering the possibility. "I don't know, Julia. That's a real jump."

"I know it is, but just think about it. If you line them up and compare them, it might tell us something. Ted Tillman's hair is still mostly black with just a few flecks of white in it, but he has a full head of it. He might be the youngest, don't you think? Or maybe he's not bright enough to have any worries. Ilona Weaver, well, we can't tell about her because her hair is dyed as black as shoe polish. It's pitiful that nobody's ever told her that the older you get, the lighter your hair should be. But Rosemary Sullins and Cassie, I declare, Sam, they could be kin." I thought for a minute, picturing the gaunt and skinny Sullins woman and the short and plump Cassie Wooten side by side. "Well, not close kin, since they don't look anything alike. But we're only talking about hair now, and theirs *is* alike. And then there's Rafe Feldman, who I'd say is the oldest."

Sam cocked an eyebrow at me. "When did you see him?"

"Oh, didn't I tell you? I must've forgotten, because you were right, Sam, about the state of his mind. I went to see him in that nursing home, and all he did was insult me and sit there looking as old as

Methuselah. But I noticed his hair, all right, and it was a thick thatch just like Teddy's, parted the same and everything, except for being as white as cotton. And another thing, Sam, that I just thought of. They both have cowlicks."

Sam ran his hand over the top of his head. "So do I."

"Yes, but theirs is on the *wrong* side." I squinched my eyes up, recapturing an image of the heads of the two men. "I'm sure of it. They both part their hair on the right side, while most men part theirs on the left. Right?"

"I haven't given it a lot of thought," Sam said, a note of amusement in his voice.

"Well, think about this: Line them up in your mind, Sam, from the youngest to the oldest, and think *hair.* They go from almost totally black to totally white, with a mixture of white, black, and gray in between. Except, as I said, for Ilona, since she's using a hair product that throws her out of kilter."

"That's a stretch, Julia," Sam said, but I could tell he was beginning to consider it. "I doubt we could establish kinship on the basis of hair color."

"There is a way we could establish something," I said, my mind speeding on. "If we could find some pictures, we could check both heads—the sheriff's and the judge's. I just wish I'd paid more attention to that picture in Roberta's parlor. Although it was so dark, the only hair I could see was bushy eyebrows. But I tell you, Sam, the cowlicks on Teddy and Rafe are *distinctive,* color notwithstanding. All we'd have to do is look for pictures of the judge and the sheriff and see which one has a matching cowlick on the wrong side."

"Well," he said, his mouth twitching just a little, "we'll think about it." He patted my knee, an intimate gesture that was perfectly fine since no one was around to see. "I'll run it by Pickens and see what he says."

"And Hazel Marie, too," I said. "I wish she could see every one of them, because if there's one thing Hazel Marie knows, it's hair."

Chapter 45

"And speaking of Hazel Marie," I went on, "where is she? What in the world could they be doing for so long?"

"I think I've already answered that question," Sam said, smiling as he looked at his watch. "It's not all that late, just a little past ten."

"It seems later than that. Maybe because the day's been so long. Just think of all that's happened. Our visit to Roberta Baines, Emma Sue's party, Hazel Marie's narrow escape, a nine-one-one call to our house, Miss Mattie's trip to the hospital and, oh my goodness, I forgot to ask you.

How did your visit to Judge Anders go? Did you learn anything?"

"Not a whole lot, although it was interesting. He said he'd probably known Baine as well as anybody, but that wasn't saying much. He told me that Baine was an odd duck—his words, and that he'd enjoyed and *used* the authority of the bench more than any judge he'd ever known. According to him, Baine bitterly resented the legislature's interference when they limited a judge's discretionary powers." Sam paused, gathering his thoughts. "Then, cautioning me that it was just his opinion, he said he'd always worried about the judge's daughter. Said, from his viewpoint, Roberta had been too wrapped up in her father, and that her father had encouraged that dependency. She'd been a loner since she was a child, and he thought that Judge Baine and his wife took advantage of her, keeping her home to take care of the mother, who was always sickly, then later to do the same for her father."

"Is he still in touch with Roberta?"

Sam shook his head. "No, and I think he felt bad about that, but he's had some health problems himself and doesn't get out much. Then he said something that's been on my mind ever since. He said that it seemed to him that Judge and Mrs. Baine had produced that one daughter for the sole purpose of having a nurse and housekeeper. Because that's all she'd ever been."

"Why, Sam, that makes me want to cry. Could it be true?"

"I don't know, Julia. It's sad to even think about a little girl growing up in such a household, burdened with responsibilities too heavy for her. No wonder she's the way she is."

"Just think, Sam, if she was born and bred to look after her parents and they're both gone, what's her purpose now? That's the most pitiful and maybe the cruelest thing I've ever heard."

"Yes, it's a shame." Sam slapped his knees and started to rise. "Well, it's been a long day and I'm about ready for bed. How about you?"

"I wanted to wait for Hazel Marie to get in. I'm not sure I can sleep without knowing what they've decided. For all we know, our worries could be over. Or," I said, getting to my feet, "just starting over again, depending on what that undependable Mr. Pickens decides to do."

Sam laughed. "Just give it time, honey. I expect we'll know all we need to know by morning. We'll leave a few lights on, in case they come in, but I wouldn't be surprised if they decide to spend the night at my house."

"You'd think by now they'd have learned what kind of trouble that can get them into. Besides, it's just plain tasteless to spend the night together when they *know* we know what they're doing."

"I expect they're just talking." Sam looked at me, his eyes sparkling. "They do have a lot to talk about, you know, and it could easily take all night. And speaking of such, one other thing Judge Anders told me. He said that at one time there was talk about Judge Baine liking the ladies a bit too much. He wasn't sure he believed it, but he knew Mrs. Baine had been an invalid for twenty or so years before she died, so who knows? There could be something to it."

"I never heard anything like that. Did you?"

"Nope, not a word. All I ever heard was

lawyers moaning about what a tyrant he was." Sam turned off the living room lights and we started up the stairs to bed.

Reaching the second floor, I turned toward Lloyd's room. His door was open and the lights and television were on. I looked in and saw him sitting propped up on the bed, still in his shorts and polo shirt.

"Hey, honey," I said, "you about ready for bed?"

"No'm, not yet. I'm going to stay up till Mama gets home."

"I wouldn't wait up if I were you, she could be late getting in. Can't you just imagine what all they have to talk about? They have weeks to catch up with. Why, I figure Mr. Pickens is over there pleading for his life, while your mother is holding his feet to the fire."

He smiled at the thought, which was better than him thinking about what, in all likelihood, they were really doing. But I quickly put that out of my mind, too.

"Anyway," I went on, "you know Mr. Pickens will look after her."

"Yessum, I know. But I'll probably worry till she gets home."

After giving him a few more assurances,

which probably didn't help, I left to prepare for bed. Thinking I would just catnap until I heard Hazel Marie come in, I fell fast asleep as soon as my head hit the pillow. The day had worn me out, as it had Sam because he was asleep before I crawled in beside him.

My eyes flew open sometime later, but not too much later for I saw by the clock on the nightstand that only a couple of hours had passed. Something had awakened me, a soft thump somewhere in the house. Sam was still breathing steadily in deep sleep beside me, while I lay there picturing Hazel Marie tiptoeing in downstairs. I started to get up, anxious to hear what had passed between her and Mr. Pickens. Then I decided I shouldn't appear too eager, so I settled back down.

It didn't take long to get enough of that. I slipped out of bed, found my robe and did a little tiptoeing myself. I eased down the staircase, trying not to wake Sam or Lloyd, but not wanting to scare Hazel Marie either. With the few lights we'd left on, I had no trouble seeing where I was going, but the hall was filled with shadows and silences. I heard no more thumps, no more footsteps, and by the time I reached the front hall and crept back toward Hazel Marie's room, I was beginning to think that my mind had played a trick on me and nobody was there at all.

And sure enough, when I peeked into her room where a small lamp was on, the bed was still made and there was no sign of her. Well, except for the cardboard patch over the broken window pane, but of course that concerned her exit, not her return.

I padded softly into the back hall, thinking I'd check the kitchen. She might be looking for a midnight snack after her marathon session with Mr. Pickens.

Just as I walked into the kitchen where only the light over the stove was on, I walked right into Lloyd. We both screeched and jumped back. My heart pounded until I realized who he was, while he gasped, "Miss Julia! I thought you were a ghost!"

"You about scared me to death, too." I patted my chest, trying to get my breathing back to normal. "I thought I heard your mother. Has she come in?"

"No'm, and I'm really worried. I tried to call her, but all I got was a busy signal. I asked the operator to break in for me, but she said Mr. Sam's phone is out of order. She wanted me to call an eight hundred number and report it, but that'd take forever, the way they put you on hold. So then I tried J.D.'s cell phone, but it just goes to voice mail." He squared his shoulders and looked me straight in the eye. "Miss Julia, there's only one thing to do. I'm going over there."

Lord, he was growing up. I looked right back at him. "Wait till I get some clothes on. I'm going with you."

I raced upstairs, hurriedly put on a housedress, grabbed some low-heeled shoes, and pulled the door closed behind me. For a second, I considered waking Sam to tell him where we'd be, then thought better of it. Why disturb his sleep when he'd do nothing but worry about us? Or get up and go with us? Neither of which he needed to do.

"Be real quiet," I whispered to Lloyd as I joined him at the back door. "Wait. Let me slip on these shoes. Okay, let's go. You want to walk or take the car?"

"Well, I was gonna run, but let's just walk. If the lights're on and they're just sitting around talking, they won't have to know we're checking on them. But if a car pulls up, they'll know what we're doing." He took my arm as we went down the back steps in the dark. "Watch your step, Miss Julia. Let's go through the back garden. It's nearer that way."

"You lead on. I'm right behind you."

We crossed the lawn, pushed aside some overgrown azalea and forsythia branches until we reached the gate that opened on to the sidewalk. Then we picked up speed as we headed toward Sam's house. The streets were empty of cars, except for a few parked along the sides. Streetlights made the going easy, although I wondered what people would think if they saw us power walking at this time of night. Most of the houses along the way were dark, so hopefully nobody was looking out a window.

When we turned the corner at Sam's street, we both stopped. There were lights on in the house, but not many. One lamp burned in the living room window, and the kitchen was dimly lit. But the carriage lamps on either side of the front door were not on, so the porch was in deep shadow.

"What do you think?" Lloyd said.

"Um, I don't know. I thought there'd be more lights on." Actually, I didn't. In fact, I was sort of surprised that any were on at all. I thought they'd prefer to carry on their negotiations in the dark. "Mr. Pickens's car's there, so they haven't gone anywhere. Maybe we ought to go home, Lloyd. They may be in the kitchen, fixing something to eat. Neither one of them had any supper."

"Yessum, maybe so. I sure don't want to just bust in on 'em, but looks like Mama would've let us know something."

"It surely does, but you know she's had a lot on her mind here lately, being sick and all. And worrying over the situation with Mr. Pickens hasn't helped matters."

But even as we discussed returning home, we'd both eased our way a little closer to the house. For some reason, even with a few lights on, the house felt empty. No one moved in front of the windows. No shades, curtains, or blinds were drawn. No music or television was playing.

Two things came to mind: They'd decided to take a walk or they were in Sam's back bedroom on the far side of the house, the windows of which we couldn't see. If it were the latter, they wouldn't be caring if the lights were on or not. For that reason, I didn't suggest that we go to that side of the house. There were some things that Lloyd didn't need to see or know.

We stopped on the sidewalk at the edge of Sam's front yard, watching closely for any signs of life inside the house. Instinctively we both slid into the shadow of the huge hemlock at the end of the driveway.

"Think we ought to knock on the door?" Lloyd asked.

"Let's wait a few minutes. They wouldn't appreciate us interrupting when they might be at a critical juncture. In their conversation, I mean." Unsure of whether to go or to stay, I bit my lip as we continued to watch the house. "Lloyd," I finally said, "I think they're all right. For a lot of people, this time of night isn't late at all. And, for all we know, they're out for a moonlight stroll. They could even be on their way home, while we're standing here under this tree."

"Well," Lloyd said, "I'd feel a lot better if the phone wasn't out. I just don't like the sound of that. There's not even been a thunderstorm."

The boy was right. Even though I was

beginning to feel just slightly ashamed of myself for essentially spying on Hazel Marie and Mr. Pickens, Sam's out-of-order telephone was worrisome.

Still, we couldn't hang around under a tree all night, so just as I opened my mouth to suggest we go, Lloyd clamped a hand on my arm. *"Miss Julia!"* he hissed. "Somebody's at the window."

"Where?" I whispered, scanning the lit windows. "Nobody's looking out."

"No," he croaked hoarsely, "somebody's looking *in*."

Chapter 46

Just as he said it, I saw the outline of a head rise up between one of Sam's ancient boxwoods and the dimly lit side window of the living room. "Oh," I gasped, "I see him!"

I felt the boy tense beside me, preparing himself to dash toward the house. I grabbed his shoulder and held on. "Stay here. Don't let him see you."

"I'm gonna yell for J.D. That'll scare him off."

"*No,* sh-h-h," I said, holding him close. "It may be a peeping Tom, and I don't want you near him. Let's wait and see if we can tell who it is."

"I think we ought to warn Mama and J.D.," Lloyd whispered hoarsely.

"We don't even know if they're in there. Let's see what he's going to do."

We were both trembling by this time, but actually the more I watched that head, the more I wondered if we were just seeing things. It didn't seem to move, just stayed motionless as if staring intently through the window. What if it were only a shadow from *inside* the room? I blinked several times, trying to clear my vision.

"He's moving!" Lloyd hissed.

My heart started pounding in my ears as, sure enough, the head disappeared from the window and a shadowy figure slipped past the boxwoods toward the porch.

I leaned down to the boy and whispered in his ear. "Run, get Sam. Hurry! Tell him to call the sheriff."

"Let's both go."

"No, I'll stay here and see where he goes. Run, now," I said, giving him a little push. "We don't want him to get away."

Lloyd dashed off, his tennis shoes hardly making a sound as he ran back the way we'd come. I eased closer to the tree trunk, hiding as much as I could in the shadow of its long-needled branches, but keeping my eyes peeled on the house. I had told Lloyd it might be a peeping Tom who was creeping along the foundation plantings, but, given all that had happened, that wasn't likely. It had to be the same breaking-and-entering sorry soul who'd done so much damage before and who'd been stirred up by my phone calls. One of the five, no, four since I hadn't called Rafe Feldman, was even now bent on another criminal invasion of Sam's house.

Except now, *Hazel Marie and Mr. Pickens were in it!* Lord, I had to lean against the tree to keep myself upright. Maybe Lloyd had been right the first time. Maybe we should've both gone screaming bloody murder for Mr. Pickens. Maybe I should do it now.

But what if Hazel Marie and Mr. Pickens weren't in the house? What if they had gone for a walk or gone back home? What if I were here by myself? Alone with that dark figure which—*Lord,* it suddenly sprang up over the banister and blended without even an outline into the deep gloom of the porch. I clutched at the tree until my fingers dug into the bark, trying to stay hidden while peering as hard as I could at the front porch.

The one thing I didn't want to do was lose sight of that figure. He, whoever he was and I had a good idea of who, was up to no good, and the longer I stood there, trying to make him out, the madder I got. William Wooten, in spite of his wife's defense, was going to get his comeuppance, if I had anything to do with it. And I didn't care if his name got splashed all over the *Abbotsville Times* so that everybody in Abbot County would know he was a thief and a vandal and, because of it, his spiritual testimony got ruined forever. I say, *Christian*. William Wooten, I thought, I'm going to see that this little episode stays a blot on your name forever.

If, I reminded myself, that's who it was. But who else could it be? No one else had gotten so exercised at the thought of having the sins of the past published for all to see. No one else had been so belligerent. He was the only one with the nerve and the intensity of purpose, and the agility to leap over banisters, to come after Sam's computer again.

For one frightening second I thought I heard something behind me. I pressed myself against the tree and held my breath. Where was Sam? Where was Lloyd? Anybody? After a minute or so, I peeked out around the tree again. Everything at Sam's house was quiet. Nothing moved. No shadows changed shape on the porch, and with a lurch of my heart I realized I'd lost sight of the creeping figure.

Then, against the ambient light of a street lamp at the end of the block, I saw a dark shape crawl over the far banister and disappear behind the other side of the house. That's where Sam's study was and, behind that, his back bedroom, temporarily occupied by Mr. Pickens and, likely enough, currently occupied by Hazel Marie as well. And that was also the side of the house with the thickest bushes, where somebody could break a pane and open a window with the least fear of being seen.

But Sam had put in a burglar alarm! That gave me an immediate sense of relief. I wouldn't have to do a thing but stand here and wait for help to arrive. Yes, I thought, that would certainly be true if Mr. Pickens had had his mind on anything besides monkey business long enough to turn the thing on.

I glanced over my shoulder to see if Sam and Lloyd were coming, but the sidewalk stretched out behind me empty. Nobody was coming from either direction, so I stood there, trying to decide what to do. Maybe I could slip up onto the porch and squat down in the shadows. I could reach up and keep my finger on the doorbell until Mr. Pickens came thundering to answer it.

If he was there.

Well, one thing was certain. Standing around under a tree while a crime was in progress wouldn't solve anything.

I moved away from the tree and, bending over, scooted as fast as I could to Mr. Pickens's car. Crouching there, wishing he drove a bigger one, I waited to see if my movement had been noticed. Nothing stirred, no shadow flitted from one place to the next and no untoward sounds came from the house.

Practically on my hands and knees and

ignoring the ache in my back, I slid from the safety of the car to the foot of the huge, old boxwoods that lined the porch. I envied Sam those beautiful boxwoods, planted there when his house was built, long before mine had been.

But even though boxwoods were important for curb appeal as well as for hiding among as I was doing in this case, I had to keep my mind on the business at hand until Lloyd could get back with Sam.

Gritting my teeth to work up the courage, I scrambled across the brick walkway that led to the center of the porch to the boxwoods on the other side. Then I had to sit down on the grass for a minute to get my breath back. What in the world was I doing, sneaking around in the dark on the trail of a house breaker?

Slowly I sat up and lifted my head above the bushes so I could scan the porch. As soundless as he was, he could've come back over the banister and be looking down at me. Trembling at the thought, I peered into the shadows and almost fell into the boxwoods.

A tiny light suddenly flared in the window of Sam's study. Not the overhead light, not a lamp, but a flame. Oh, Lord, *fire!* He was in the house, lighting a fire! I turned and scurried toward the far side of the house, intent on running to the back bedroom and getting Hazel Marie and Mr. Pickens out.

Just as I turned the corner of the porch, my feet flew out from under me as something came out of the bushes, scratching my arm, hitting me on the head and putting me flat on the ground. Scrambling to untangle myself, I came as near to consigning James to eternal torment as I'd ever come. He'd left a long-tined rake leaning half-hidden on a boxwood, and I determined then and there to teach him a lesson he wouldn't forget about putting things back where they belonged.

On the other hand, I thought as I pulled myself together, when defenseless, one weapon is as good as another. Snatching up the rake with both hands, I clutched it, tines pointed forward and held high, running now past the porch toward the back bedroom. With fire in the house and in my eyes, I no longer cared about seeing or being seen. I had to get Hazel Marie and Mr. Pickens out of the house and, if it took breaking another window, why, I had just the implement for it.

Just as I came abreast of the second side window of Sam's study, two legs popped over the sill right beside me. Stopped in my tracks, I watched as more of the dark figure slid out of the window until it dangled by its hands from the sill.

I didn't hesitate. I slammed the rake against head, back, legs, whatever I could hit. The figure dropped from the window to the ground and curled up in a ball, trying to fend off the blows.

"Mr. Pickens!" I shrieked, whacking at the scrambling figure as hard as a garden rake would let me. "Hazel Marie! Get up! Get out! Fire! Help! Help!"

Screaming my head off, I aimed the rake at the face and head of the figure as it regained its feet. Using the rake to push and shove it against the house to hold it there until somebody came to help me, I was almost pulled off my feet. The figure had grabbed the handle and was using it to sling me back and forth. I tried to pull my weapon away, but the criminal held on tight, screaming as loud as I was.

With a mighty effort, I whipped my end

of the rake around and toppled the figure to the ground, loosening his grip on it. I pulled on the rake to cock it for another blow, but it wouldn't come. It was stuck in something, and as the figure regained his feet, I frantically jerked and pulled, eliciting unearthly shrieks from my opponent. Then Mr. Pickens flashed by me, coming out of nowhere, and took him down. Then Sam was there, clasping his arms around me and pulling me from the fray. At the same time, headlights rounded the corner and tires squealed as squad cars and a fire engine pulled to the curb. A swarm of deputies spread out across the lawn and headed toward us.

Sam held me back, while Mr. Pickens struggled with the squirming figure on the ground. Lloyd bounced up and down, yelling, "We're here! We're here! Don't worry, Miss Julia, we're here!"

"Julia!" Sam cried. "What in the world?"

"Fire, Sam!" I gasped, holding on to him. "Fire in the house. Get Hazel Marie."

"She's out," Mr. Pickens yelled, as he snatched the dark-clad figure upright, then clasped his arms tightly around him, while ducking under the rake that swung around from the figure's head like it had a life of its own.

Sam pulled me farther back and told me to stay put. Then he ran for the porch, yelling for the firemen as they uncoiled a hose. A deputy offered his arm as I leaned over, trying to stop the trembling that rippled through me from one end to the other. I could hear the firemen dousing the flames inside, as a little whiff of smoke eddied out the open window.

"Miss Julia," Mr. Pickens said, as he pushed the stumbling captive toward the front yard, "I have never in my life seen anybody captured with a leaf rake before. This thing is so tangled up in her hair, we might never get it out."

"Her?"

"Yes, ma'am, it's a her."

Chapter 47

"Do you mean to tell me," I said, as we all sat around the kitchen table a couple of hours later, still up long after our bedtime, "that you weren't even *in* the house?"

"No'm," Hazel Marie said, looking somewhat confused from all that had happened, which she was only just hearing about. "We walked around for a good while, just talking, then J.D. walked me home. We'd just gotten here when Lloyd came running in, all out of breath and yelling about somebody breaking into Sam's house. I didn't know what to think."

Lloyd grinned. "You shoulda seen Mr. Sam come out of that bed when I woke him up. And J.D., why, we couldn't keep up with him."

"What I don't understand," I said, looking from one to the other, "is why didn't we meet you on our way over?"

Mr. Pickens leaned toward Hazel Marie and gave her an intimate smile. "We took the long way."

She flounced her head away from him and stuck her nose up in the air. "Lot of good that did."

"Oh, I think it worked out okay," he said, sliding an arm across the back of her chair. She immediately sat upright so she wouldn't touch him, and my heart sank. What was she thinking? If she was still holding him off, what in the world would it take to bring her to her senses?

I looked from one to the other, trying to determine just what they'd concluded. Mr. Pickens seemed quite pleased with himself, and if he were the only one I had to go on, I'd have rested easy, convinced that all was well between them. Hazel Marie, on the other hand, was still acting standoffish, refusing to meet his eyes or mine, and giving every indication that she was not happy with whatever had been decided. If anything.

"Pickens," Sam said, as he offered the coffeepot, "tell us again what the deputies got out of Roberta Baine. It's still hard to believe."

"Well, as you know," Mr. Pickens started, holding out his cup to Sam, "I went to the station with them. For one thing, to manage the rake that was still tangled in her hair." He laughed. "We almost couldn't get her in the squad car, finally had to roll down the window and let the handle stick out. Anyway," he went on with a disbelieving head shake, "seems that what she was doing was protecting her father. That's about all they could get out of her. Sam, she thinks you're bent on ruining Judge Baine's reputation and good name, and all she had in her head was destroying everything about him in your house and at the courthouse."

We frowned at each other, wondering how she'd come up with such an idea. Anybody who knew Sam would know that he would never knowingly damage anybody.

He'd just let the facts speak for themselves. But maybe that was exactly what Roberta Baine was afraid of.

Lloyd suddenly threw back his head and laughed. "No, J.D. That wasn't all she had in her head. She still had that rake in it."

"Yeah, well, you're right. They finally had to call in a matron to cut it out of her hair."

"She sounds crazy," Hazel Marie said.

"Not too crazy, though, Mama," Lloyd said. "One of the firemen told me that what she'd done was pile Mr. Sam's papers on his desk and light a candle in the middle of them. And she had one of the drapes stuck under the papers so it would catch fire, too. That way, she'd have plenty of time to get away before the candle burned down. I think that shows she was pretty smart."

"Yep," Mr. Pickens agreed. "It does. But the big question is still motivation."

"What's going to become of her?" I asked.

"They have her at the hospital now, up on the psychiatric ward. I expect she'll get a full workup later today. We may learn more by then."

"It's the strangest thing I've ever heard,"

I said, still dissatisfied by what we'd learned so far. "Why would she go to such extremes as breaking into a house, destroying records wherever she went, and then trying to set Sam's house on fire? I don't understand it. What was she trying to keep secret?"

"We may never know, Julia," Sam said, putting his hand on mine.

But we did come to know, for it was Cassie Wooten who came ringing my doorbell later in the morning. Since we'd been up way into the wee hours and our nerves were so frayed by the night's activities, we'd all slept late, and on a Sunday morning, too. But missing church once in a blue moon probably wouldn't be held against us in the circumstances. Besides, I might've slept through the sermon if we'd made the effort. As it was, I hadn't even had a chance to question Hazel Marie about her future since she was still in bed, and now here I was, having to entertain a visitor.

I answered the door, surprised to see a distraught Cassie on my doorstep. "Why, Cassie, do come in."

"I can't," she said, even as she walked in. "I'm sorry to bother you again, but I had to know if it's true what I've heard. Has Roberta Baine been arrested?"

"Yes, she was caught trying to burn down Sam's house last night."

"Oh-h-h," Cassie moaned, wringing her hands. "That's so awful. It's just terrible, and I don't know what to do."

"Why, you don't have to do anything. She's under the care of a psychiatrist even as we speak, and frankly, as far as I'm concerned, that's the best place for her."

"You don't understand," Cassie said, half under her breath, although there was no one else around to hear her. "I have to do something, even though William will have a fit."

I certainly didn't understand, but just then Sam walked out, unaware that we had a guest.

"Why, Mrs. Wooten," he said, welcoming her with a smile. "Nice to see you again. Come in and have a seat."

"Oh, Mr. Murdoch," she said, burying her face in her hands and beginning to sob. "I'm so sorry for everything. So very sorry. I didn't know she'd go this far. Somebody could've been hurt or even killed. It's just awful."

Her shoulders shook as she turned away from us, crying pitiably. Sam tried to comfort her, assuring her that no one had been hurt, that his house was intact, and that he was sure Roberta Baine was now in good hands.

I wasn't quite so sympathetic. As Cassie accepted Sam's proffered handkerchief, I stood back and asked, "Why are you so concerned about her, Cassie?"

She slid the handkerchief down her face, looking up at me with brimming eyes and said, "She's my sister."

Well, in spite of my previous rampant speculations on the subject, that statement shocked the daylights out of me and, from the looks of him, from Sam as well. We got Cassie situated on the sofa, even though she continued to protest that William would be worried. Sam drew up a chair in front of her.

"Now, Cassie," he said in a gentler tone than I would've used, "tell me about your sister. It's going to come out sooner or later anyway, and since I've been on the receiving end of all the damage, I think I deserve to know."

"Are you going to write about it?" she asked in a voice that would've rent a more tender heart than mine.

"It depends," Sam said. "But I won't mislead you, if it's public record, I probably will."

"William won't like it," she said, tears pouring from her eyes. "He really won't."

I could stand it no longer. "What William likes and what he doesn't amounts to about a hill of beans, Cassie. We're talking breaking and entering, theft of public records, attempted arson, and assault and battery on me. If you know anything that will clear this up, now's the time to tell it and let William take care of himself."

Sam put a hand on mine to hush me, but I saw him hide a smile. "We'll do whatever we can to help Roberta and you," he reassured her.

So then it came out. To say that Judge Baine had liked the ladies, as Judge Anders intimated, was putting it mildly. Not only was he Roberta's father, but Ilona Weaver's, Rosemary Sullins's, Teddy

Tillman's and Rafe Felder's. Oh, and Cassie Wooten's, too. The man had plowed fields all over the county because every one of them had different mothers. I couldn't begin to imagine how busy he'd been.

"Roberta," Cassie said, sniffling and gulping, "has always been so protective of him. She was furious when she learned we were included in the trust he set up. He didn't leave us much, but enough to confirm what she didn't want to believe. None of us knew he was our father until then, and it's still hard to take in. He'd never had anything to do with us, and we hardly even know each other."

"What about Sheriff Hamilton?" I asked. "How does he fit in?"

Cassie looked up, frowning. "Who?"

"You know, the judge and the sheriff and a couple hundred acres at River Bend."

"I don't know anything about that," she said, looking confused.

"Never mind," Sam reassured her. "It's not important."

By this time, if Sam's handkerchief had been a Kleenex, it would've been in shreds, the way Cassie was pulling and kneading it. Swiping it again across her face, she went on. "So when you," she glanced at Sam, "came along and interviewed us, well, I hated the thought of all my sins be- ing published. But, see, all I was thinking about was myself. I didn't realize that you might put two and two together and come up with the judge. But William did. He was just beside himself when he found out what you were doing. He, oh, I hate for you to know this, but he told Roberta about your book and how, if you looked closely enough, you'd figure out that it was the judge who kept us out of jail, even though we didn't know it at the time. And, well, Roberta just went crazy. She was still unhappy that her father had acknowledged us, and she was determined to keep us from ruining his name. She threatened us. Told us we'd better not to tell anybody, that she'd deny it to her dying day, and she'd take us to court for defamation and slander and all sorts of things if she had to. She said her father wasn't in his right mind when he set up the trust, and she'd do whatever it took to keep his reputation pure and unstained." Cassie trembled as the words poured out. "I believed her, too. That's why I couldn't let you interview me again. None of us could. We were afraid of her."

Well, Lord, I thought to myself as we finally ushered Cassie on her way, they were right to be afraid. I knew I wouldn't have wanted to tangle with Roberta Baine. Then I had to smile to myself, for I *had* tangled with her. And it wasn't me who was locked up on a psychiatric ward.

Sam, bless his heart, was still offering aid and comfort to Cassie as she started out the door. I shifted from one foot to the other while she lingered.

As soon as the door closed behind Cassie, I had a few questions that wouldn't wait. "I don't understand, Sam. Why would the judge go to such extremes to keep his children from being prosecuted if he didn't care enough to acknowledge them?"

"Maybe that's the reason. He didn't want the relationship to become known, and one or more of the mothers held it over him. Amelda Tillman comes to mind. When I knew her, she was a woman nobody wanted to cross." Sam took my hand as we walked down the hall. "Or, on the other hand, he could've been exercising some paternal oversight, but in secret, so he could enjoy the power of influencing their lives without anybody knowing it."

"Well, I hope he enjoyed something, because that's all he got. Don't you know he could've kicked himself when that developer came along and paid a fortune for what he thought was useless?"

"I expect so," Sam said, nodding. "Sheriff Hamilton sure hit the jackpot then. But he lost out, too, since he didn't live long enough to enjoy it."

"Serves them right—both of them. The idea of manipulating the law for their own ends. Now, though, thanks to you, Sam, their chickens are coming home to roost. But would you have ever figured it out on your own?"

He shook his head. "I doubt it. All I saw was that those five people kept getting free passes, over and over. I was going to point that out in the book, but leave open the question of *why*. The record shows—when you put all the cases side by side—that somebody was manipulating the system, and the only ones who could've done it were the sheriff and the judge. But I couldn't *prove* anything against either one. Still can't, for that matter."

"Well, but you can point out the kinship and the land deal, and let people draw their own conclusions, can't you?"

He nodded and put his arm around my shoulders. "I'll see. A lot of damage has already been done. No need for me to add anymore."

I hugged him, telling him he was the kindest of men, but wondering if I would be so considerate. But then, I wasn't writing a book that could get me sued.

But other things were still hanging fire, so I sent Sam to the kitchen for breakfast and hurried to Hazel Marie's room to wake her. I couldn't wait another minute to know the upshot of her late night tryst.

"Hazel Marie," I said, as she sat up and yawned, "you won't believe what all we just heard about Roberta Baine. Sam is going to have a best seller on his hands. It'll have everything: Mystery, suspense, courtroom drama, and illicit goings-on. But it'll all have to wait, because right now I can't stand it any longer. What happened with Mr. Pickens last night?"

"I guess we're getting married."

Tears of thanksgiving sprang to my eyes as relief flooded my soul. Raising my eyes to heaven, I was moved to overwhelming joy at having been delivered of a great burden. And by Mr. Pickens, of all people. Feeling as weak as water and trembling from one end to the other, I had to grab hold of a chair to steady myself.

"Why, Hazel Marie," I gasped, "that's wonderful! When? What are the plans?" I watched as she slowly pushed back the covers and swung her feet to the floor. "But wait a minute, you don't sound very excited."

"How can I be? He's only doing it because of the mess I got myself in."

"Well, young lady, you keep one thing in mind: You didn't get in it by yourself. Besides, that wasn't the way he was behaving last night. He couldn't keep his eyes off you or, as I happened to notice, his hands, either."

"Yes, and see, he's already going back on his word." She stood up and, my word, she was continuing to blossom. This news hadn't come a minute too soon. "I can't trust him as far as I can throw him."

"You mean he might back out? Hazel Marie, we've got to get you married before he takes off again."

She shook her head. "No, I mean he's pretending to be all worked up and excited, saying he's thrilled about these babies and being married and all. But I know it's just an act. He's just doing it because even he can't get out of it. So all that touching and looking is just put on. But I told him, Miss Julia, I told him that this was going to be a marriage *in name only*. And I mean it."

"Oh, Hazel Marie, you can't mean it. Now listen, I know you've never been married before and don't know what it's like, but, honey, that doesn't sound like much of one to me."

"Well, that's the way it's going to be. He can take it or leave it."

I didn't know what to say, but I was thinking that she'd been free enough outside the marital state, and now she was planning to close up shop when she got *inside*? That didn't make sense.

"I believe I'd rethink that, if I were you. Why, you know that you and Mr. Pickens belong together, even though I admit I've had my doubts about him. But those babies change everything, so his willingness to accept responsibility is the absolute best thing that could've happened. You'll have a husband to go through this with you, those babies will have a father, you won't have to move away, and, think of this, you're going to make your son the happiest boy in the land. So the least you can do is be grateful that he's solving all your problems. And," I went on, "you might also try to call up some of the loving feelings you had for him in the past."

She frowned and twisted her mouth. "I'm not about to jump up and down just because he's been roped into marrying me. I know a shotgun wedding when I see it. We'll get married, all right, but he's going to have to keep his hands to himself. He's marrying me only because of these babies, and I've told him that's the only reason I'm marrying him." She sniffed and grabbed up a robe. "Besides, he needs to suffer a little, too."

"Well, I don't know what to say. It beats all I've ever heard. I thought you'd be walking on air and thrilled to death if he ever wanted to get married."

"That's just it," she said, wrapping the robe around her middle tight enough to give me pause. "He *doesn't* want to, he's being forced to, and as soon as these babies are born, I'm getting rid of him." She snatched up a hairbrush and for a minute I thought she was going to throw it. But we already had one window pane broken, so she just ran it through her hair with a vengeance. "I'm not putting up with somebody who's just putting up with me."

I had to sit down then. Of all the terrible ways to begin a marriage, this took the cake. Who would've thought that it would be Mr. Pickens who was the eager one, while Hazel Marie nursed her grievances to the extent of planning to divorce him as soon as he'd served his purpose? Poor Mr. Pickens, the man was snakebit when it came to keeping wives.

But I couldn't worry about him at the moment. I was heartsick that Hazel Marie wouldn't be a happy bride. After all she'd been through in her life, after all her starry-eyed plans and hopes of someday having a dream wedding, complete with bridesmaids and groomsmen and veils and flowers like the ones in her magazines, to end up like this was the most pitiful outcome I could imagine.

"Well, Hazel Marie," I said, hoping but not saying that she'd change her tune once Mr. Pickens was securely locked in, "sufficient unto the day and so forth, I guess. I'm sorry to hear that you feel this way. I hate to see you marry with a heavy heart, especially since you've waited so long for it. Is there anything I can do to help you?"

She was on her way to the closet to select another of those workout outfits that was all she could wear, but stopped when a commotion started up in the kitchen.

Mr. Pickens's voice, coming nearer, reached us both. "Hazel Marie! Where are you? Your honey's here, needing some lovin'. Come on out here, little girl. We've got plans to make, 'cause I'm gonna marry you in the morning."

Lillian shrieked, "Glory! Glory!" and Lloyd yelled out in surprise and joy. A chair fell over somewhere, and something or somebody tumbled down the stairs.

Hazel Marie stopped and turned to me, her face suddenly alight with a rush of color. Her mouth dropped open and her eyes sparkled with anticipation. I could almost feel the waves of excitement rippling off her. The whole room seemed to vibrate as she trembled at the sound of his voice.

In name only? I thought with a wry, but greatly relieved, smile. A likely story that would be. Why, just the thought of her long-held dream becoming reality had created a shimmering and magical field around her.

I stood there marveling at the transformation she'd undergone. And then, as all her angry independence fell away, my starry-eyed, naive, and artless Hazel Marie reasserted herself.

"Miss Julia," she said, almost gasping for breath, "there's one thing you can help me with. Would it be all right for me to wear white at my wedding?"

"Hazel Marie," I said, as I surveyed her burgeoning figure and thanked the Lord that I wasn't having to contend with her over a big church wedding. That being the case, I could afford to give a little. "Honey, we don't have time to look for a maternity wedding dress, if there is such a thing. But if you have another one of those sweat suits in white, there's not a reason in the world you can't wear it."